I0748565

The Sibyl and the Thief

Cordelia Kelly

THE SIBYL AND THE THIEF

A Brown Cat Press novel

browncatpress.com

Book design by GetCovers.

For Zach
I wouldn't be the person I am today without you
All my love

Contents

Illyamor

Tuneric Mountains

Royal Scoria Mines

Malgris Lake

APOROS

Dikisi Forest

Alioch

Oracle Grove

cordelia kelly

The Sibyl And The Thief

Cordelia Kelly

The Faerie of the Wilt

As Sabine Gillesella descended the market road, her cardinal rule was always at the forefront of her mind: never, *ever* touch anyone. She twisted through the bustling crowd, a dance she had perfected over the past months: a sway of the hip here, a trip of the foot there.

Sabine had learned this rule the hard way. In a world where people blessed with magical abilities were viewed with suspicion and fear, she knew to not bring attention to herself. A ghostly brush on somebody's arm was not greeted gently but rather with the swipe of a knife. A disembodied voice calling for help was met with cries of alarm.

Being cursed with invisibility was hardly a blessing.

Passing unseen offered some rewards, though. Sabine stood at the edge of the market, watching the Halwardian baker puffing as he worked. A group of Awhye children begged at his feet.

Sabine flinched as the baker pulled out an iron poker and whipped it at the wide-eyed beggars. His aim was poor, and the children scurried away, giving her an opportunity. When the portly baker turned his back, muttering about Awhye scum, Sabine darted to his market stand. From the display she grabbed a large bag of morasu, grain used for good-quality bread. With practiced ease, she stowed it in her leather satchel, smiling as it disappeared from view. On the counter sat a bag of wild mushroom pasties, and she swiped it as well.

Her heart beating rabbit-fast, she barely missed knocking over the baker as he turned back to his goods. He paused as though he had felt her passing breath before his gaze fell on the empty holes in his display.

His eyes bulged from his head. “Damn Awhye brats. Guards! I’ve been robbed.”

The children were far away at this point; Sabine had made sure of that. She backed up until she hit the sun-warmed stones of the building behind her. Nobody seemed to notice the ghostly rustle of her skirts.

The baker gesticulated in the face of the bored Halwardian guard. “Something must be done about these thieves. How are good, hard-working people to make a living?”

Sabine bit into one of the stolen pasties, knowing what all Awhye learned at a young age: Thieves didn’t starve. The pasty was nowhere near as good as her mother’s, but she hadn’t eaten yet today. Besides, the baker was a bully. She’d seen him refuse to sell his old bread to an Awhye mother. He dumped the stale baking into a pile of animal dung, stomping on it until the lot was a filthy mess. He laughed, watching if she would stoop to digging out the food in desperation. Her children went hungry that day.

Sabine took another bite. She’d sleep just fine tonight.

She inched along the wall to get away from the fuss, and her foot disturbed something on the ground. With a quick glance to ensure no guards approached, she scooped up the object and stuffed it under her cloak, then ducked into the less-crowded alleyway.

Out of the crowd, she examined her find, a doll that had been sitting in the street for some time. Likely forgotten by a child who had more than one. She blew dust from it and tucked it into her pocket. Perhaps she could find someone who would better care for it.

The alley opened onto another unevenly paved street, much quieter than the market. From her vantage point near the top of the fortified hill, she overlooked the city sprawl of Aporos, the capital city of the kingdom of Illyamor.

Excitement caught in her throat when she saw the North Gate open, and a long queue of wagons pulled by oxen waiting to enter. The miners were home after a three-week shift in the Royal Scoria Mines.

Her brother, Rafi, was scheduled to return today, and she had time to spare. She tripped down the cobblestones toward the gate.

In the upper streets of Aporos, lanterns hung on posts every few paces, burning chunks of scoria rock, an innovation in the city. The black rocks, known as slag, produced light, energy and heat, but they also created foul fumes that settled along the ground and discolored people's clothing. Citizens coughed as they waded through the ashy fog.

Sabine descended a rickety flight of stairs, down to where the Awhye were forced to live. Lanterns didn't burn here in the lower streets, but the black fog still drifted downward, and she had to take care to avoid putting her foot in a squelching mess left by a passing animal.

By the time she'd entered the slum called the Wilt, she could no longer see daylight through the haze. She had grown up here. Though the Awhye people did their best to brighten the streets with flowers, life struggled to grow. Sunlight didn't reach this far through the inexorable fog.

Sabine displaced the mist as she walked, wafts of air giving the impression of a ghost pacing the streets. Or an invisible woman.

The streets grew busier as Sabine approached the North Gate, hoping she hadn't missed Rafi's entrance into the city. The way was lit by metal barrels burning wood. It wasn't the height of technology, but the wood smelled clean and burned brighter than what slag lanterns could produce.

Carts clattered through the open gates, bearing full loads of scoria. The men on their off shift perched on top, filthy from the long journey from the Tuneric Mountains.

The oxen pulling the carts seemed aware of her presence, moving out of her way automatically. Sabine pressed through the crowd, careful to keep to the edges as she searched for Rafi. One man was telling another about an accident in the mine, relishing in the garish details; several men had died badly. Sabine spun, desperate to hear more, but the men had already passed by, and she couldn't follow them into the crowd.

She pressed a hand to the back of her neck to calm herself down. It couldn't be like Papa. She couldn't lose Rafi to the mines as well.

Finally, the crowd shifted, and she caught a glimpse of his dark curls. She let out a slow breath, inspecting him for injury from afar. Seventeen now, Rafi was no longer the little brother she remembered. The mining labor had hardened his body, but he still held himself tall where others had cracked under the drudgery.

He'd worked at the Royal Mines since he was sixteen, the age of majority. It broke her heart each time she watched him disappear with the Awhye men as they departed to toil in the dark.

His hair was pulled back in the style of their people, the sides above the ears shaved. The bonfire caught the proud line of his profile. The men he stood with laughed at a joke, relieved to be back in the city for a week. Rafi accepted a light from one of his companions, blowing smoke into the air.

Approaching Rafi was a problem. Her "little condition," as he called it, made things awkward. He was one of only two people who knew of her invisibility. She waited for an opening and darted closer.

As she neared, a group of older men passed, and one of them caught Rafi's eye. Her brother gave a sharp nod. Throwing his smoke into the dirt, he jerked his head at his companions, giving them a sign to follow. Sabine's heart thudded. What was her brother getting himself into?

The miners made their way up the street toward an Awhye tavern, The Oasis. As the men filed in and found tables, Sabine settled in a corner behind a potted palm, where few people would be likely to bump into her. It reeked of stale ale and tobacco juice, and Sabine wrinkled her nose at the state of the floor.

The barman sent rounds of watered-down draft to the miners, who accepted it with shouts of thanks. One of the men stood and clapped his hands to get their attention. Boldo Carew. He'd worked in the mine alongside her father and helped support their family after Papa's death as her mother struggled to hold them together.

Boldo's eyes burned in anger as he spoke; no sign of the kindly father figure tonight.

"For too long, we've slaved for the Halwardians, for barely enough to put food in our mouths and clothes on our backs. They don't care about us. Just this past week, three men were lost in the bowels of their blazin' mines. They kill our women when they practice the Old Ways; they get rich while our children starve. We must end this cycle of suffering. It's time to do something!"

His voice roared over the crowd, his call to action answered by cheers. Sabine's gaze flicked over the crowd, her hands twisting in front of her. The miners weren't even trying to hide. Anybody could be a spy. Even her.

"What can we do about it?" someone called.

"We hit them where it hurts—the mines! Without those riches flowing in, they'll have to listen to us."

"We should burn the mines right down to hell." The speaker sat at Rafi's table. "Make sure the overseers are inside. That will take care of the whole lot."

Sabine did a double take. The bloodthirsty speaker was Jaime, a childhood friend of Rafi's. He used to follow her around like a puppy, reciting terrible poetry about her eternal beauty. Now, murder lit his eyes. The mines had changed him, like so many others.

"Violence isn't going to solve anything," Rafi called out over the agitation. The men stopped to listen, and Sabine's throat tightened. Already, he was a man worth listening to. Already, he was making himself a target. "If we use violence, it will be answered by more violence against us and our loved ones. If reducing their riches hurts them the most, then I say we simply stop working. We strike until they're willing to listen to us. If we are all in this together, they will have no choice."

He sounds just like Papa, Sabine thought with a shiver of fear. A decade ago, their father had tried to organize a strike. The next time he was in the mines, there had been an explosion, her father one of the nine men who perished.

Talk of striking stopped after that, for a few years.

The discussion spiraled into shouts, angry debates about whether killing Halwardians would have a greater effect.

She'd heard enough. Sabine sidled through the crowd, coming up at Rafi's elbow. His brows were pinched; talk of violence had that effect on him.

She squeezed his arm, and he startled, tensing when he saw no one. "It's me." Sabine raised her voice to be heard over the din.

Rafi relaxed and nodded.

"Meet me outside, around the corner."

She released him and made her way through the crowd. The men were riled, and it was a relief to get outside, though the smoke-filled air was hardly fresh.

A few moments later, Rafi pushed out of the crowd, joking with some of the men. He received some good-natured teasing about going to meet a girl. Sabine smiled at the thought of her little brother with a sweetheart.

"Are you with me?" he asked, his voice lowered.

"I'm here," Sabine said. He strode away from the crowd, out of sight where they could speak without raising eyebrows. She noticed for the first time that he clutched something in his fist, a bunch of yellowing weeds like a bouquet. "What's this? A posy for me?"

He glanced at the weeds with a brief smile. "Olini bitters. They grow in the foothills of the mountains. They taste like slag but are full of nutrients. We chew them while we work, and I gathered some for Mama on my way home. I thought she could use them in her pasties."

Sabine shifted so the firelight fell full on Rafi as she inspected him. "Are you well? How are they treating you?"

He shrugged, his eyes puzzling over the empty space in front of him. "As well as anyone. They cut back rations again due to food shortages."

"Blazing hell. How are you surviving?"

"We all suffer together. Well, most of us do." The censure was evident in his tone.

She ignored his barb; she'd made her choice, and there was no going back. She thrust the stolen bag of morasu grain into his hands. "This will help. Give it to Mama."

He fumbled in surprise at the weight. "I couldn't afford this on a miner's salary. Where did you get it?"

"Never you mind that." Defensiveness edged her voice. Every one of her conversations with her brother eventually led to this. "You just make sure Mama gets it. If it keeps the bakery open for another month, then all the better. Just don't tell her it's from me."

"I can't keep on lying to her. She deserves to know what's happening to you."

"She deserves to know her daughter is dying?"

Rafi's face went ashen. "No. Not yet."

Remorse flooded her; she had caused that grief on his face. "But I haven't given up. As long as I have two feet under me, I will not stop trying to find a cure. But take the grain anyway. In case..."

The silence lingered between them. In case one day she stopped bringing them stolen gifts, and he'd know she hadn't been able to beat back the inevitable.

His shoulders slumped. "I wish you would come back home. You should be with us."

Sabine swallowed hard. She wanted nothing more than to be with her family. But it would be admitting defeat. He wanted her to be with them when she died, but she wasn't ready to die yet.

"You know that's not possible."

"It is. Perhaps the *Vadovis* could do something for you."

"Like all the other magelings cursed with magic? Each and every one died on her watch."

"Maybe you're different. Your magic didn't come until later. Maybe there's something..."

"If there was something to be done, it would have been done already. I studied as an apprentice healer at her side for years. The only person who has been able to keep the curse at bay is Duke Aurich and his school for magelings."

"The duke." Rafi's tone was scathing, and he crossed his arms over his chest. "What's he done for you?"

"He's trying. But I'm far too old to learn to control my magic, no matter how hard I try. The young children brought in for training have a real chance. But he's attempting experiments to keep me here. He'll help me as long as I—"

"As long as you spy for him."

"I make myself useful." She cleared her throat.

"And do you spy on me?"

"Never, Rafi. Listen, the duke wishes me to spy, so I tell him things. He doesn't have to know the things I tell him about the Awhye are not exactly true."

"You give him false information." A brief smile lit his face. "Still watching over us, after everything. It's you, leaving your little presents for the children, isn't it? They call you the Faerie of the Wilt." His gaze turned down. "There are other rumors too. I don't know if you heard." The words spilled out in a quick burst. "About you and the duke, how you..."

"That we're lovers?" Sabine finished when her brother was unable to. "That his head was turned by my *exotic* beauty, and he whisked me off to his tower and showered me with jewels? I've heard them all." She sniffed. "People have a right to believe what they want, but it doesn't change the truth. I work for the duke because he can help me. Once I'm cured, I'll come home. Until then, I'll do what I must."

Rafi nodded, jaw clenched.

"One warning, though." Sabine's voice was low and intense. "What you're doing with these insurrectionists is dangerous. Even whispers of strike can lead to a backlash."

"If we all stand together, we can make a change."

"Not if you're dead." She wrapped her arms around herself at the thought. "Anyone can hear what you're planning, see who's involved. There are spies everywhere, trust me. If you insist on being involved with this folly, at least move around. Don't gather in the same place twice. Tell your friends to get out of The Oasis and scatter. Now."

Rafi squinted as if he would argue but finally nodded. His face changed then, brightening at a thought. "Everyone will be heading out soon anyway. The *Toamna* festival is tonight, remember? We're lucky to be home for it. Will you join us?"

Toamna, the Awhye autumn feast day, when the harvest was brought in, and everyone shared a meal. Her people danced to uplifting songs played on strings: it was a beautiful ceremony.

But dancing in the streets with her friends and neighbors belonged to a different life, a different Sabine. "Perhaps." She turned to go, but Rafi reached into the emptiness and found her hand, giving her a gentle squeeze.

"Don't give up hope, Sab. You're strong; you can get through this. Maybe one day you'll be a leader here like the *Vadovis* wants."

Sabine snorted and patted Rafi's cheek. He flinched at the

unexpected touch. "I just want to survive. I won't keep you from plotting any longer. Be safe, Rafi."

The bells of the Ofhellen rang out, calling the midday hour. It was later than she'd thought, and she had matters to attend to. "I have to go."

"Until the next time, Sab...take care of yourself."

"Be seeing you, though you won't see me," she said, a teasing edge to her voice. A frown tugged the corners of her brother's mouth down as he sought her out in vain.

Sabine left the miners behind, making her way through the neighborhood where she grew up. The ramshackle homes had become even more decrepit, or perhaps she had become used to life in the Keep.

She snorted at her arrogance to think she could outgrow this place. Every corner held a memory. She had wanted so much more than what was offered, for all the good that leaving had done her.

A wooden shack leaned against the side of the stone building. The meager stoop was scrubbed spotless, with neat rows of flowers planted out front. A small stool sat next to the door, and on it slumped a doll, a tatter of cloth tied around straw. Well-loved, certainly, despite her humble looks.

Sabine knew the little girl who lived here. She'd been present at her birth, helping Gregoria, the *Vadovis,* with the midwife duties. She had been fourteen then; Pippa was nearly four now.

Pippa had been the first baby Sabine helped deliver, cuddling her afterward, warm and covered in birth pulp. Sabine had marveled at the fists windmilling the air and her piping cry, a child's fury at the indignity of entering the world.

She brought out the stolen toy from the bakery. This doll had a painted face and wore a gown of light green, like a springtime faerie. Sabine settled the new doll on the stool and arranged the faded one in her arms as though cradling a baby. She kissed her fingers, then brushed them over the top of the faded doll's head, blinking back unexpected tears.

Pressing the heels of her palms under her eyes firmly, Sabine told herself not to wallow. No point fussing over the things she couldn't change. She'd focus on that which was still within her power and left a mushroom pasty on the windowsill for Pippa in hopes it would fill her belly.

Her reflection flickered in the window, and Sabine halted, transfixed. She had not seen herself since she had disappeared from sight months ago. But as she stared at the warped glass, she realized it was Pippa gazing out the window on the other side. Sabine drew close and pressed her hand to the glass as if she could touch the child. Aching sadness wrenched her heart.

Then Pippa drew forward and placed her hand against Sabine's on the other side, smiling. Sabine jerked back. Could she see her? Then she saw the handprint she'd left on the window. That was what Pippa saw, an otherworldly greeting. Shaken, Sabine left the little shack.

The Faerie of the Wilt, indeed. If only her people could see how far she'd fallen. Still, other children lived on the street, so she placed a pasty on each windowsill as she went. She continued until the bag was empty. She had already eaten; some of these children would go days without.

She turned toward the stairs that would take her to the places her people weren't supposed to be seen, and began the long trudge upward into the sunshine.

The Blind Seer

With imposing gray stones and jagged peaked roofs, the Ofhellen sprawled on the crest like a thunderhead. The seat of the Order of Fire loomed over nearly all other buildings in the city. Only Asael Keep, where the Halwardian nobles resided, reached further into the sky.

The Ofhellen was led by an army of Helms, women devoted to the gods of fire. They dressed in swaths of red fabric, and each sported a pinched, dour expression.

According to the myths, the Halwardian fire gods resided in the wheeling sun and the underworld realms, where fiery liquid bubbled and stewed. In some places, such as in Lunengren, the northern island where Duke Aurich hailed from, fire spurted from the ground.

The duke was a fire mage, his power strengthened by these gods, and when it came to their religion, Aurich was genuinely devout.

Taking in the vast building, Sabine hesitated, her blood beating fast in her ears. These grounds were forbidden to her, and yet she couldn't refuse the duke's command.

Since she'd begun working for Aurich, she'd broken into the

homes of the most powerful Halwardians in the kingdom. She'd gone through their personal documents, and she'd stood to the side of their dining rooms as they supped with their families, thinking it was safe to vent their real opinions. She'd even overheard the whispered pillow talk between lords and their mistresses.

She had come to know the political landscape of the Illyamor upper class very well. She was also a deft hand at pilfering coins and items, small things she could bring to the Wilt to help her people.

The information she gained was valuable, but lately, the duke had been seeking objects of magical power. His theory was that with enough accumulated power, he could reverse the effects of the magical blight that cursed Illyamor.

For many years, the land had been drying up, unable to produce the rich harvests once plentiful. The blight also affected the natural magic that appeared in some Awhye children. Those magelings born with magic were consumed by their own wild power; magic was a death sentence.

This morning, Aurich had informed her there had been a disturbance in the fire magic surrounding the Ofhellen, an unprecedented event. An object with that magnitude of power could be the tipping point, allowing him to heal the land. So, she was to investigate its source.

The duke himself could not enter the institute of the Order of Fire and accuse the Helms of withholding enchanted objects from him, so she would be his eyes and his sticky fingers on the inside.

Sabine had never stepped foot inside the space. It was illegal for Awhye to enter the Ofhellen grounds unless they relinquished their own beliefs first, and Sabine would never do that. She'd foregone much, but she wasn't willing to forget the worship of her people.

The whole place made her skin itch. She centered herself before jimmying open a side door with a blade she kept for that purpose. A damp chill blanketed her as though the heat of the day couldn't penetrate the walls.

Sabine got her bearings in the labyrinthine structure, one corridor twisting into the next. She wasn't entirely sure what she was looking for. Something strange, something worthy of a duke's attention. Something with power to break a curse.

Like a ghost, she traveled down the dank hallways. She ignored the main hall of worship. Treasures of gold and jewels were displayed there, but the duke knew of these. What Sabine sought would be hidden away, where things of great power are always kept.

Few Helms or their novices roamed the halls, and she didn't observe any security in the form of guards. She barely needed to be invisible to sneak around the Ofhellen. Perhaps they believed the fury of the fire gods enough to discourage trespassing.

A faint clatter sounded from the other end of a deserted hallway. Increasingly spooked by the empty corridors, Sabine approached on cat-like footsteps. As she neared, a sweet voice began to sing. Though Sabine didn't understand the language, she understood the song was one of unknowable sorrow and swayed under the power of it.

At the end of the hall, she stopped, transfixed. Through a narrow window, a thin stream of sunshine illuminated a girl at a loom. As she sang, her hands moved fluidly over the strings, weaving a tapestry. Her looks were familiar, somehow. The girl's hair tangled in coppery curls down her back; pale skin marked her as Halwardian.

Her collarbone peeked out sharply from her drab robe, off-white and much too short for her, exposing her bare, filthy feet.

Her eyes were closed even as she wove. Curious, Sabine crept closer to see the tapestry, and the singing stopped abruptly. "Who's there?" the girl called out, her voice without fear.

Sabine froze. Could she see her, somehow? Then the girl opened her eyes, milky white. Sabine let out a silent breath, understanding. A blind girl may be able to hear things with acuity, even a thief used to stealth.

Still, the girl followed her movements with unseeing eyes. It was unnerving. Since nothing precious hid in this cobwebbed corner, Sabine backtracked, shaking off the dread that settled over her.

"Wait." The girl lifted a slim hand. "Please, stay awhile. It's so rare someone visits my little nook." She tilted her head. "You've never been here before."

Sabine shuddered as milky eyes inspected her. "How do you know?" Her voice was a rusty whisper, creaking with tension.

"Some things I know. My name is Anora."

Sabine stared until Anora lifted a coppery brow. "It's typical to respond with an introduction of one's own, is it not? People don't normally speak to me, but I know that much, at least."

Sabine was caught off guard by this pitiful creature. "How do you weave when you cannot see?"

"The string calls to me, and I listen. Please stay. Nobody ever wanders by."

Although the girl must be close to Sabine's age, she sounded young in her pleading. Sabine hesitated, then shifted her hips as she leaned against the wall, really taking in the girl. "I'm nobody interesting."

Anora tsked. "It's beneath you to lie. I've been waiting for you."

"For me?"

"You will help me, won't you?"

Sabine remained silent. It seemed unlikely she could help a blind girl when she could barely care for herself.

"Besides," Anora continued as though Sabine had agreed. Her blind gaze locked onto Sabine's. "It's not every day a blind girl meets an invisible girl."

Sabine's pulse thundered through her veins.

"But how do you...?" Her throat closed over. Who was this girl?

As though pulled by a string held in Anora's hands, Sabine

faltered one step then another, not entirely of her own volition. Something inside her clamored to see what the girl wove. Moving as though through sand, Sabine rounded the frame.

The colors were vibrant jewel tones, the embroidered tapestry of a woman so real Sabine thought it might jump to life.

"H-how is this possible?"

The weaving was of Sabine in a tattered gown. The same gown she wore, though invisible now. Her face, perfectly rendered, looked to the viewer with heavy-lidded eyes.

Anora watched her. "Inside the darkness, there is knowledge, and I know you, Sabine."

With a hesitant hand, Sabine brushed the threads that made up her face. "How do you know my name? What is this magic?" She tried to sound commanding, but her voice cracked.

"I see things and I am compelled to weave them."

"You are a seer?" The girl was a mageling. Impossible that she hadn't been discovered before now.

Anora shook her head. "I see the truth." A frown creased her brow. "It gets all jumbled inside my head. But when I weave, it clears up and doesn't trouble me so." She gave an unexpected smile. "Over the past few weeks, your face is all I've seen in my dreams. I enjoy weaving you, Sabine. You feel strong. And you are very beautiful."

"How can you know that?" A deep longing rose in Sabine's chest, to be seen once again. Then she noticed something odd about the tapestry. "What's this?"

At the base of the weaving, black thread crawled up the portrait girl's feet like spidery veins. The magical blight, blotting her from existence. "Is this what will happen to me?"

Anora stared, unblinking. "It shows what will be. Your essence is being consumed by the magic. If nothing is done to prevent it, you will be lost."

Even as Sabine took a trembling step back, she knew the truth of the weaver's words. The invisibility was devouring her. Soon, she would be gone. For real.

"How long?" she asked.

Anora looked down, sorrow lining her face. "The thread connecting you to this world is very fine now. A fortnight, maybe."

Her whisper was a death sentence. *Two weeks.* That was no time at all. Everything Sabine never had a chance to do flickered through her mind like a dying candle. To see a sliver of this world outside of Aporos; to see Rafi settled down with children of his own. To see the light come back to her mother's face.

Sabine had only lived a short bleak existence, toiling as a maid and then a thief. None of her dreams had ever been met; she'd never even had a chance to fall in love.

Her chin trembled. "I was trying to find a cure."

An icy hand touched Sabine's, and she gasped, coming back to herself. She hadn't found what she came for, but she had to get away from there. She pushed off the wall and made to flee down the corridor.

"Wait. There is a way. I know a place where you can be healed."

The futility of it caught up to her, and Sabine wanted to simply sink into the earth. The laugh that came out of her was bitter and broken. "I've heard that before."

"Sabine, you cannot trust him. He has no interest in helping you."

"Wh-what?"

"You know what I mean."

"I have to go." The words came out more like a plea.

"Wait; take this." Anora gestured to the embroidery. "I made it for you."

Though she wanted to flee, Sabine's fingers moved without thought toward her portrait. It felt as though it belonged to her, that her heart would break if she had to leave it behind. She brushed against the threads and felt them humming under her fingertips as though alive with magic.

She hesitated. "It's not finished."

"Neither are you. Take it; it belongs to no other."

Sabine struggled to rip the tapestry from the loom. Fumbling, she groped for her knife and slashed through the strings. Anora let out a breathy gasp as though she could feel the slice of the blade, but her face was alight with excitement. Sabine dropped the frame of the loom, one of the edges cracking on the stone ground.

"Sabine, you must come back. We won't survive without each other." Anora's warning echoed down the shadowy hall as Sabine fled.

She lost her way in the gloomy Ofhellen, taking one wrong turn and then another. She stopped to catch her breath and looked back, shaking. There was no sign of the haunting girl with copper hair and milky eyes.

Sabine inspected her woven portrait and whimpered. It was a true likeness, down to her clothes clinging to her curves and her hair flowing loose to her waist. Sabine stroked the face, then folded the cloth into a square. When she tucked the embroidery into the folds of her gown, it vanished from sight.

She tore through the empty corridors, not stopping until she found an unguarded door. Yanking it open, she fell into the streets, panting in the chill air.

When a scream ripped through the air, she pressed herself back against the wall, forgetting she was invisible.

A group of soldiers marched up the cobblestone street. One of them struggled to hold a moving bundle, as a woman dragged at his arms. "No!" she screamed over and over. "Not my boy, not him. Please, have mercy. Give him back!"

The bundle was a child, no older than three, his brown eyes wide with terror. He wailed as he stretched out a thin arm for his mother. Sabine made to run after the child, but after a moment's reflection, slumped back. What could be done?

One of the soldiers barred the woman's way. "Return to your home and stop making a scene. There have been reports of objects moving in your son's presence. It is for his own sake and the sake of the community that he is removed to a safe environment."

The woman shook her head, tears dripping down her cheeks. "They were wrong. That never happened. My son would never hurt anyone."

"Mama! Mama!" the toddler shrieked. The mother fought with the strength of desperation until the soldier lost his patience. He struck a baton against her temple, and she fell heavily to the cold stones.

Sabine did run now, to protect the unconscious woman from further beatings, but the soldiers left her in the streets, bearing her son away from her.

Sabine crouched over the woman's body, ensuring she was alive, as she watched the soldiers' grim procession up the streets toward Asael Keep. From there, magelings met with the duke and were shipped out to the school to the north. Their families would never see them again.

It used to be that attendance at the school for magelings was voluntary. It was the only way to break the mageling's curse. Families could choose to let their loved one go and perhaps survive or stay within their community until the magical blight killed them.

The choice had been removed since the fire seven years ago, which had destroyed part of the Wilt and threatened to consume the neighborhoods higher up. Sabine had been there where it started, at the schoolhouse when an older girl began to shriek as though being tortured. She'd thrust her arms into the air as bolts of lightning erupted from her over and over. She screamed and flailed for far longer than her horror-struck classmates could have imagined, until the thatched roof of the school caught fire. They fled the schoolhouse, only to find the flames spreading like a wave along the rooflines.

Dozens of lives were lost that day, including the mageling girl's. Since then, any children showing signs of magical abilities were taken away.

The screams of the boy mingled with the screams in Sabine's memories. She huddled next to the fallen mother feeling as insignificant as a mouse, stroking the woman's cheek where she had been struck and wishing there was any comfort to offer her. She hated that it was necessary to take children from their homes. But if it gave that tiny boy a chance, how could she argue?

Sabine glanced behind her. A man ran up the street, followed by others. Sabine waited long enough to confirm they were Awhye before leaving the woman to them.

The deep tolling of bells called the time, and she realized she was late to report to Aurich. He had wanted her results of the search at the Ofhellen before the mid-afternoon bells. She would never make it to his chambers in time, and it would not do to displease the most powerful man in the kingdom.

Asael Keep

"Blazes!" Sabine dashed up the royal road, which wound between the Ofhellen and Asael Keep.

She passed within a step of the Royal Guard, standing to attention in his shining green and black armor. The sun rode high in the sky, meaning she was impossibly late. She entered the Keep unchallenged, unseen.

Once past the guards, she tore across the Keep's courtyard to the duke's tower. Halfway there, she remembered the duke would be attending the Halwardian council meeting. It could take hours, and Sabine would have nothing to do but wait and worry.

She halted in indecision. She often sat in on the council meetings when Aurich couldn't make it, so he had eyes and ears everywhere. But he disliked her presence when he attended. He'd turned her into a spy but hated being spied upon himself.

Despite this, Sabine turned toward the Great Hall of the Keep, fists clenched in determination. She needed to know how much the Halwardians knew about the miner's insurrection and her brother's involvement, and this meeting provided the perfect opportunity.

Twisting her way through the Keep, she passed through the

crush of Halwardian nobles, all gathered in Aporos for the autumn court season. By habit she avoided hems of gowns as the women preened past. Even before she was cursed with the blight, Sabine worked as a maid in the Keep. It had been good practice for being invisible.

Most of the courtiers were assembled in the Keep to ensure their best interests were met, even as the kingdom suffered under famine and drought. Gilded vipers, everyone.

Sabine paused. One of the more uppity noblewomen she'd served swanned across the hall, leaving a sumptuous fur stole hanging over the back of a chair. Aware of the oncoming chilly weather, Sabine changed directions and plucked up the fur as she passed. It disappeared as she wrapped it around her shoulders, giving her delicious comfort both in its warmth, and from taking something away from the spoiled woman who had been cruel with her words and her slaps.

Inside the Great Hall was the enormous throne room, where the monarchs would meet visiting dignitaries. This room remained locked since old King Johann died several years earlier of a wasting fever, leaving behind his four-year-old son, Leopold, and his young wife, Queen Liesl of Lunengren.

Facing the throne room was the council room, no less extravagant. Here, the Halwardian council met to make decisions about Illyamor, and the king's justice was meted out.

Sabine passed the guards at the door, following an elderly Halwardian council member. The nobleman gave a perfunctory bow to the queen, already seated at the head of the table. Queen Liesl didn't seem to notice.

Duke Aurich was last to enter, sweeping in with an order to shut the doors behind him. He wore the finest fabrics, black cloth embroidered with metallic thread. Rubies wound around his throat, lined the cuff of each ear, and studded his nose.

His copper hair and unlined face gave the impression of a young man barely older than Sabine herself, though she logically knew that couldn't be true. She wondered at the secret to his agelessness; he seemed to exist outside of time.

She wasn't the only one who noticed. With his strong jaw and fashionably tousled hair, Aurich had always been eye-catching. As the most powerful person in the land, with a face like his, many Halwardian noblewomen would give up much to find their way onto his arm. Or into his bed, for that matter.

During her work as a maid, his every move was noteworthy. The Halwardians were utterly fascinated by the Royal House of Lunengren and their unprecedented takeover of the kingdom.

Sabine circled the table, keeping space between her and the duke, never taking her eyes off him.

Aurich first approached the council members. "My Lord Pieterson," he said, reaching out a hand to one with a pleasant smile. "I was impressed with your latest report on the financial forecast of the Royal Mines."

"It was your project." Lord Pieterson, Head of Finances, was gray and flabby, and puffed up even more under Duke Aurich's praise. "An astute investment that has done well."

"And my Lord Boehm," Aurich said, turning to a man equally gray but whipcord thin. "How are things proceeding with your mountain villa? Last I heard, things were moving along smoothly despite the concerns of intemperate weather."

Sabine narrowed her eyes at the councilor he spoke to. Lord Boehm, Head of Order in Illyamor. Responsible for the Wilt's latest raid, where guardsmen slaughtered two women for possessing illegal herbs in their homes. If anyone was going to act against the miners as they organized a strike, it would be at his command.

The duke sat on the other side of the queen with a warm smile. "And how are you, my dear sister?"

Sabine could see every muscle of Queen Liesl's body tense. The air around her charged as she stared at the table as though to burn a hole through it.

"Well, my brother," she said, her voice a whisper.

"And my nephew? How is the little man faring?"

Liesl twined her hands together and faced her brother. Queen Regent Liesl had been an oddity since she arrived more than fifteen years ago with her brother, and her refusal to play Illyamor's nasty court games was no small part of it. Although the youngest princess from a poor northern island, her fiery beauty had captured the heart of old King Johann, and he made her his queen. It was the scandal of a generation, and some were still bitter over it.

Now, though, Liesl's fair skin appeared dull and her copper curls tarnished. Her lips pulled in a grim line as she met her brother's gaze.

"The king is fine," she said. She hesitated, then curled her hands into fists. "He would like to go outside for some air. It is not good for a child to be cooped up. I would like to arrange for him to visit the stables, perhaps even find a small pony he may ride."

Aurich reached out to pat her hand, and she flinched. "The world is a dangerous place. I'm sure you understand. With his delicate constitution, I worry how the young king would react to the rougher world outside. We do, of course, want to make sure he remains safe. It is our utmost priority."

The queen's knuckles showed white and bloodless. "There is little I won't do to keep my son safe."

"Your goodness is an example to us all. We must ensure that you both are well cared for." Aurich leaned in so as not to be overheard. Sabine crept forward to catch his lowered voice. "Are you certain you're feeling well? You look tired. Perhaps you would prefer to rest than be here during these deadly boring discussions."

The queen glanced up to meet his gaze. "I am fine, brother."

"Good." The duke swiveled to the other council members. "This kingdom needs its ruler, after all." The nobles chuckled on cue. "Now, to business. I have a few administrative issues..."

The duke flipped through the papers in front of him, servants passing them to the council members before they ended at the queen. She signed each without reading them.

Though Aurich did not hold an actual position on the council, he led the meeting as though he did, and the rest followed without question. He came to a long scroll and stood.

"Now, this is a fascinating project. I have been experimenting with scoria in the production of energy, as seen with the lanterns throughout the city. I propose we use scoria to power farms and factories in the countryside. This is the future." He set the document in front of the council members, who murmured in agreement as they read it.

When the document rested in front of the queen, however, she paused, her quill hovering over the page.

"Is the burning of slag not dangerous?" she asked. "I have heard the smoke it produces is making people sick. There are children in the city with enduring coughs. Should we not consider the health implications of having so many people working near the fumes?"

The duke stood, a frown furling over his brow. "Health implications? I do not believe so. I've had the finest royal physicians inspect the effects of the fumes, and they have returned to me with their approval. The burning of scoria is safe and productive and has not been shown to be deleterious to health. But perhaps you have other information? Who can we speak to about this? I want to be absolutely sure our citizens are healthy."

Liesl paused for a long time, her quill hovering over the paper. Twice she seemed about to say something, then finally let out a long breath. "It's just a rumor I overheard." She bit her lip before signing off on the document.

Sabine watched the queen, fascinated. Why was she trembling? Rumors of the queen being mad had long floated through the Keep's halls.

"Now, Lord Boehm, where do we stand with these rebel miners who have been giving us trouble?"

Sabine straightened, forgetting the queen in an instant.

"No more than a minor inconvenience, Your Grace," he said. "Groups like this pop up every few years or so and are easily dismantled. We weed out the instigators and make an example of them, then offer a temporary bonus to the miners who remain loyal to the royal company. It works every time."

Sabine stiffened as he spoke of examples. She would never forget the day her father's broken body was brought home, tossed casually over a cart of the rocks he had died for. The explosion had burned off most of his skin and he was unrecognizable but for the wedding band on his finger.

An example had been made; one Sabine would never forget. She would also never forget how her mother's screams rang through the streets that day.

Now, her gaze skewered Lord Boehm as he peered at the papers in front of him.

"Just this afternoon, we had reports of insurrectionist activity with the latest mining changeover. My men raided a drinking establishment deep in one of the Awhye slums."

Sabine's heart pounded so hard she couldn't believe the others didn't hear. She stared at Lord Boehm, willing him to continue as he perused the document.

"No sign of rebel activity. We rounded up a couple of slum rats, but there was no indication of organization." Lord Boehm looked up. "Everything is under control."

Sabine couldn't help it; she let out a sigh of relief. The sound carried, and the duke paused, frowning. She froze as he scanned the room.

The silence stretched, then Lord Boehm leaned forward, confused by the duke's reaction. "Your Grace, was there something else?"

Aurich turned back to the council, smiling as though nothing unusual had occurred. "Good work, Lord Boehm. Keep up the pressure on these upstarts."

He glanced at the paper left in front of him. "One last thing. Here is the report on the health and safety of the magelings living in the School for Blighted Children. Two noblemen have inspected and reviewed their situation, along with a royal physician and Helmine Marthe of the Ofhellen of Aporos. Our work to keep their powers under control continues to produce good results."

The lords nodded as they reviewed the document.

When it arrived at the queen, her eyes roved over the list of children living at the school. "No one ever sees them again," she said, almost to herself.

"It's best for them." Aurich approached his sister, a consoling look on his face. "You know the dangers they face if not kept in a controlled environment."

This time she did not back down. She stood, leaning on the table to face him. "But where do the magelings end up, Aurich? They leave for the school, but then no one gets word of them again. Just a list of names." She gestured at the paper. "No wonder mothers hide their children."

"It pains me to admit that not all magelings survive their curse, though the greatest efforts are made to help control their magic. But yes, of course, there are grown mages living among the students. They teach the others in continued safety, for the benefit of all."

His eyebrows turned up in a look of compassion as he addressed the nobles in the room. "My sister's compassion is great. No doubt it is her empathy as a mother that causes her to think so long on the cause of the blighted Awhye children. The love of her own child has transferred over to all the children in her kingdom, which is only right for a queen. But we are not able to work miracles."

The queen's flushed face drained to white as Aurich spoke. A very long pause ensued as Aurich watched her with a gentle furrow of his eyebrows. When she made no move to sign the report, his frown deepened. "Your Majesty, would it be best to relieve you of some of your duties? If your workload is too taxing, I'm sure we could find a solution. Perhaps you would like to spend more time with your son?"

With a look of utter loathing, Liesl snatched up her quill and signed the report with a scrawl. Her head bowed as Aurich came to delicately remove the paper. "You did the right thing, Liesl," he whispered.

The other council members gathered their papers and bustled out of the chamber. Duke Aurich gave Liesl's arm a squeeze, then turned to leave with the rest of the crowd. Before he exited, he gave one last glance over his shoulder, his gaze flickering over the emptiness where Sabine stood. Her belly tightened, but still she hesitated.

The smart thing would be to hurry across the courtyard to arrive at the duke's tower before him. But she was mesmerized by the queen.

Her hands flat on the wooden table, the queen breathed harder and harder until she was hyperventilating. Then she jolted upright. Glancing at the table, she let out a terrified sob.

She spun and strode out of the room, her head held high as she reached the door. "The table needs to be sanded and polished," she called to a servant. "At once."

"Yes, Your Highness."

Sabine approached where Liesl had sat and drew back with a gasp. Two perfect handprints were scorched into the wood.

The Queen

Sabine sprinted through the halls of Asael Keep, not to catch up with the duke but rather with his sister. He might fume, but she needed to see the queen. Nobody knew Liesl had powers; of that, Sabine was sure. She had heard all the whispers: They said she was mad, but never that she was a mage like her brother. How could she have kept such a secret from the duke? And better yet, why?

Sabine slowed as she caught up with the queen outside her chambers. Liesl nodded to the guards at the door. They both wore the green and black insignia of the Royal Halwardian House, and both were quite young. Sabine slipped in behind the queen.

Liesl stopped in her receiving room and took several steadying breaths. Sabine had been within these walls several times, both as a maid and as a spy. She admired a tapestry hanging on the wall, woven with a skilled hand, of a knight standing in front of his lady. Both in profile, the lady looked at their entwined hands as the knight gazed at her in sorrow. There was a sense of a heartbreaking farewell, evoking a romantic faerie tale of a tragic princess.

Another guard came into the room. "Your Highness?" He gave

a low bow. "Your meal is ready. The king is in his room and asks for you."

"Of course, Erik." The queen's smile came easy for him. "I'll be there in one moment."

When she thought she was alone in the room, she went to her desk. Sabine rarely spied on the queen, thinking she was boring, but she'd been neglectful. Queen Liesl hid much of herself away. It was something Sabine could relate to.

Liesl took out a document, holding it in shaking hands. Sabine crept next to her to read over her shoulder. It was a report as to the health implications of scoria fumes. From what Sabine could see, it was damning.

"Blazes." The queen's fingers tightened around the paper. She had clearly made her own inquiries into the fumes and yet hadn't brought her proof with her to the council meeting. Why? Sabine's curiosity about the woman deepened.

"Mama!" came the cry from the inner room. The queen shoved the report back into the desk. Sabine hovered for a moment, wondering if she should see if there were other illuminating documents, but decided to follow the queen as she made her way to her son.

Liesl's demeanor changed as she shook off her anger. When the little king rushed into her arms, her face softened and she twirled him around, laughing.

"Hello, my love. Have you been playing with your soldiers today?" Ranks of wooden men were set out on the floor. Her private salon had been transformed into a playroom, which caused no end of sneering among the courtiers of Illyamor. It was common for noble children to be raised by nursemaids, then sent away to school. Liesl's refusal to follow protocol was another reason to treat her like some uncouth country maid.

She didn't act like a powerful monarch as she giggled and tickled her son. He pressed his face into her neck, and Sabine turned away from their private moment. The shame of her work as a spy pressed heavier on her.

"I hear a meal is waiting for us," Liesl said, setting the boy down and leading him to a simple dinner of soup and meat and bread.

"Your Highness, kindly wait," the guard said. He brought out a set of cutlery and tasted each dish. He took a sip from the goblet set for the king, wiping it carefully with a cloth when he was done. "You may proceed."

The queen nodded. "Thank you."

He gave a low bow, his face clear at setting the queen's mind at ease. Sabine tilted her head, noting the devotion Liesl inspired. Did she handpick her guards, surrounding herself with men she trusted? Sabine hadn't expected that of her, assuming she was little more than a mouse who married well.

As the monarchs dined, Sabine inspected their chambers. The queen slept in the same room as her child, something else that was common knowledge and thoroughly mocked.

"Mama," the boy's sweet voice piped as he sipped his soup. "You told me you used to live in the forest? And you played outside?"

"Yes, my love. It was a beautiful place."

"Can we go outside?"

Liesl gave the windows a fearful look. "Not today."

King Leopold's shoulders slumped, but he didn't whine. Sabine felt a wave of sympathy for the young monarch.

"Want to play our new game?" The queen's eyes took on a glint.

"Yay!" The king raised his hands in a cheer. "The game!"

The queen fetched two unlit candles, setting one in front of her and one in front of the king.

"Now, like we practiced. Remember the spark that tickles inside of you?"

"Tickles in my tummy?"

"That's the one. Now, close your eyes. Hold on to the wick and let the spark flow into it."

Liesl pinched her fingertips over the wick, and a flame appeared.

"Yay, Mama!" Leopold cheered.

"Now you." The king scrunched his eyes shut, the tip of his tongue peeping out the side of his mouth. "Do you feel the tickle?"

"Yup." Leopold's whole face furrowed in concentration, then he pinched the wick on his candle. When he opened his fingers, a flame flickered, then held.

Sabine slapped both hands over her mouth to keep from crying out.

"I did it!"

"You did." Liesl scooped the king up as he ran to her in triumph, pressing him close. "Now remember, this is our secret." Her eyes flicked to the guard standing at attention, watching from the doorway.

Heart beating fast, Sabine slipped away, her head full of what she had seen. The queen kept secrets from her brother, and both she and the king were endowed with magical powers. The king was a mageling. Duke Aurich wouldn't be able to remain angry at her failure in the Ofhellen if Sabine shared this information.

The Pyre

The courtyard had been lit with torches by the time Sabine scrambled across. She nearly knocked into a slow-moving servant and slowed, shaking her head. She was getting sloppy and needed to find control immediately. But her mind kept flipping over the implications of all she'd learned.

Unlike his mother and uncle, who were born on the fiery island of Lunengren, the little king had been born with magic in Illyamor. Did that mean he was blighted by the cursed magic of the land, like the Awhye children? If the king was going to be consumed by his magic, surely he should be at the duke's School for Blighted Children.

Was that why Queen Liesl was so interested in what happened to the magelings? Because her son would be taken away from her?

Sabine's footsteps dragged further. If the king died young or was shut away for good with cursed children, there was no clear successor to the crown of Illyamor. Some distant cousins of the old king might try to step in, but in an already unstable land, the very news of the king's condition could set off a civil war. In truth, only one man held enough power to take control, but of course he was a foreigner.

Her gaze drifted up to Duke Aurich's tower, the Pyre. It was rumored to spout bursts of flames from the upper windows, although Sabine had never seen it. It was a known fact that when the duke had first taken residence in the tower, the original wooden roof caught fire and burned away entirely.

The Pyre guards wore the red and gold of the Lunengren crest instead of the royal family's black and green. These were the duke's men and loyal to him alone.

Unlike the regular Royal Guards, these men were not easily distracted. Trained and honed as weapons, their sharp gazes dared anyone to approach. It was enough to send both servant and courtier alike skittering away.

The man guarding the entrance, Captain Kosoch, had a heavy blond mustache and an oily smile that didn't match the hardness in his eyes.

Sabine crouched and twisted to avoid contact with him. It was a deadly game she played. Kosoch would not hesitate to skewer her with the unforgiving scimitars he held in each hand. Silent as a spider, she held her breath and her skirts as she passed.

At times, she wished she could simply state her intentions, but that was a quick way to being gutted. Nobody knew she lived. At the time of her disappearance, there had been some speculation on whether the duke, who had taken such an interest in the pretty Awhye maid, had been involved. But it was gossip spent within the week. Nobody cared about a slum rat upstart who dared to live among them. Most figured she'd gotten what she deserved.

Sabine drew her dark thoughts around her like a thunderstorm and slipped past the guard. The enormous man shuddered as though a cold breeze had passed, but he did not turn.

More men perched along the winding stairwell overlooking the courtyard. They were easier to pass, their attention focused outward. Still, she only relaxed when, at last, she arrived at the duke's chambers.

She tapped at the door and waited a long moment, but there

was no answer from inside. Was he there? Was he angry with her for being so late? Steeling herself, she pushed the door aside and entered Duke Aurich's quarters.

The first floor was an impersonal space, with chairs and tables set up to allow him to take meetings, as well as his desk where Sabine often found him working, laboring over reams of paper. But the duke was not there. She circled the stone room, calling out with uncertainty, "Your Grace?"

A curved staircase led to the next level. Here were the duke's personal chambers, a place Sabine was reluctant to enter. But she could see the glow and hear the crackle of a fire and knew she'd find him there. Swallowing, she climbed the stairs.

"Your Grace?" Her voice was little more than a whisper when she peeked beyond the doors. Duke Aurich had never insisted on formality between them. Their relationship was not defined by the rules of society, and she knew more about him than most of the Halwardian courtiers.

But he did not approve of her spying on him, so when she saw him seated on a cushion on the floor in front of a crackling brazier, she cleared her throat. "Your Grace," she said louder. "I apologize for my lateness. I..." She trailed away. Though Aurich's eyes were open, they were blank and staring, reflecting the fire. His hands were shoved into the flames, and he was unnaturally still. Gemstones were arranged around him in an intricate pattern.

"Aurich?" She crept close enough to ascertain he was breathing, but his muscles were tight and straining, as though he was fighting something. The skin of his hands was blackened.

She grasped him by the shoulders, tugging him back. With a choking gasp, Duke Aurich came back to himself. He dropped onto his back, arms spread wide and stiff as if in agony. After several moments of choking, he let out a low, guttural moan. Acrid smoke curled from his lips.

"Your Grace?" Sabine hovered over him, horrified.

"My bag," he croaked. One of his charred hands gestured toward a leather satchel on the ground. "Green."

Sabine dug through it, bringing out healing supplies until she reached a jar containing a green salve. It smelled sharply of herbs and earth. She spread the salve over the open wounds on the duke's hands and forearms. As she did so, he hissed, then let out a long sigh of relief.

"Thank you, Sabine." His eyes searched for her, even as she sat next to him. "I don't know where I'd be without you."

"Were you trying to burn yourself alive?" Fear made her more familiar with him. But even as she watched, the wounds healed, closing as the skin returned to its normal fair color.

"I was trying to travel through the fire." Sweat still stood out along his brow, but Aurich's face had relaxed from the screaming tension of moments before. He tapped the textbook that lay open next to him. "Firewalking. The ability to transfer my spirit into the flame. I can appear in other places, other fires far from here. I thought I could control it, but I hadn't anchored myself sufficiently." He frowned at the heavy book. "I might have been consumed by the fire here and now. Good thing you stopped by to help me out." He gave her a boyish grin.

"You play rather carelessly with your life, Your Grace." She spoke through gritted teeth. "If I had been a moment too late, would I enter your Pyre to discover your charred carcass?"

He caught her hands. "Thank you, truly, Sabine. I'd certainly not survive if you weren't here to care for me." He held on far longer than appropriate, the bonfire heat from his hands warming hers. Then Aurich gave a lazy smile and his grip tightened, reeling her toward him invisible as she was. Off balance, Sabine fell into his arms.

He seemed entirely recovered from his brush with the flame. Sabine gasped as heat flashed up her body and, for a moment, allowed herself to be held against him. It would be so easy to allow herself to give in to his wishes. Surely, he would save her if she allowed him everything he desired? For a moment, she softened.

Then she saw the triumph in his look, and she yanked out of his grasp. She would not be the plaything of a handsome duke.

"If you need me to ensure you don't turn into a human torch, I'll remind you that I won't be around much longer if nothing is done about my condition. Try not to kill yourself until you've saved me. What possessed you to attempt firewalking by yourself?"

"I was looking for you." The duke's face was open, penitent. "I was worried when you didn't show up."

"You were worried about me?"

"Of course. I wish you'd reconsider my offer. I would be less anxious knowing you had a safe place to return to. If you would only consent to stay in my quarters with me, I could take such good care of you." His eyes flickered over the empty air, seeking the beauty he'd once believed in his grasp.

Sabine retreated to the furthest reaches of the room. "I'm rather more concerned with securing a cure for my curse."

His hands clenched into fists at being denied, but Sabine was better at evading him now that she was invisible. "You are such an unusual case. I remember discovering your secret."

Sabine remembered the moment as well, in the glittery halls of the Keep. After being mocked by a group of Halwardian ladies for her Awhye looks, Sabine stopped in front of a mirror, staring at her face. For a moment, she hated everything about herself. Her reflection flickered, then disappeared. It was the first time it had happened. She had gasped and reappeared in an instant, but the damage had been done. Behind her in the reflection, the duke had been watching.

"I thought you would send me away," Sabine said. "Or that you were going to eat me up and spit me back out."

The duke's smile became wolfish. "Maybe that's what I wanted to do. I had never seen a young woman of such ravishing beauty.

And magical to the core. Can you blame me for wishing to keep you?" He reached out as though she might come to him.

"It wouldn't be appropriate." She was thankful she didn't have to hide her face from him. His interest in her had been flattering at first, but it was a relationship where he held all the power. She didn't ask to be his object of lust. She did her best to keep Aurich at a distance; she did not wish to be his dirty little secret. "I'm just a slum rat, remember? Even if no one can see me."

"Don't ever say that." Duke Aurich's voice was sharp. He reached into his satchel to pull out a miniature of her face. She had sat for a painter before she had disappeared. "You were designed to drive me insane. Sometimes, I believe you've made yourself invisible only to deny me your beauty."

"I am dying, Aurich." Sabine tried to keep the snarl from her voice. "I have maybe weeks left, and you believe I do this as a petty vendetta against you?"

He turned to her voice and let the miniature drop; his face furled in concern. "So little time. Is it that soon, sweetness?"

Sabine thought about the blind girl. Anora's Sight could see what she could not, and she had given her the damning sentence. "The darkness is wrapping itself around me. I feel as though my essence itself is disappearing."

What would death feel like? She was losing substance every day; soon she'd be little more than air. Would everything that made Sabine *her* simply blow away in the breeze? Would she be aware of it happening—would she notice she was gone?

Aurich knelt in front of her. "I will do everything in my power to keep you here with me. What about the Ofhellen? How did you come to be so late?"

Sabine licked her lips. With her fear of the duke burning up, she had forgotten. She gazed at his face, the hint of boyish charm creasing his eyes. It was a look that made her want to tell him everything. She hadn't found an object of magical power in the Ofhellen, but she had found a mageling seer.

But the seer had said she couldn't trust him. And after all these months, Aurich had done nothing to help her beyond his pretty words. She hesitated. The blind girl had been strange, but she said she could save her. She needed to speak with her again.

"I searched for hours but was unable to find anything," she said. She watched Duke Aurich's response carefully.

Flickers of flame flashed through his eyes. Whatever he sought, he wanted it badly. "I thought I could trust you with this. The protective magic placed around the Ofhellen has been disturbed. There must be an object of great power within."

Again, Sabine thought of the seer, and she wondered if *she* was the power Aurich sought. "Maybe it isn't an object at all," she said, testing him. "Maybe it's a person."

"A mageling? There are no magelings in the Ofhellen. The Helms would never keep them from me."

Sabine was silent long enough that he frowned. "Do you know something?"

"No, Your Grace. It was just an idle thought. Perhaps one of the Helms?"

Aurich's lip curled. "The Helms are Halwardian. They bear no magic in their veins. And the Ofhellen is designed to dampen the effects of magic, so this disturbance is strange." His eyes gleamed. "I'm desperate in my search for a way to control your magic before it consumes you. I had put rather a lot of trust into this power source you have failed to find. If nothing comes of it, have you other recourses? Perhaps you could return to your own people."

It was as if he'd knocked the breath out of her. If she didn't find this power source, he would leave her to fend for herself? "Nobody can help me there. You know that."

He tilted his head, a half-smile playing over his lips, as though he knew exactly the position he held her in. "Your people have a sorceress. Why not go to her?"

Sabine shook her head. "Gregoria is no sorceress. The *Vadovis* is a spiritual leader and helps deliver children. She has some knowledge of herblore but not of spells or enchantments. I worked under her for years, so I know there is nothing she can do for magelings."

"Still, the *Vadovis* is an averred position in your community, is it not? Why leave that position to work as a maid?" Aurich always wanted to break her choices apart, as though she was a puzzle he could put back together to better understand.

Sabine held her breath, frustrated. *Because it was boring* was hardly the insightful answer he sought. Because she wanted to see more of the world than a slice of the Wilt. Because Gregoria was poor and smelled funny, and if Sabine became the next *Vadovis*, she would be poor and smell funny too.

Or maybe it was because every Awhye who put themselves forward as leader ended up dying. Often terribly.

"It doesn't matter anymore."

"I understand more than you think," he said. "I was the fourth son of an impoverished royal house. I was overlooked, though I was the sole child of my family to inherit the power of fire."

Sabine stilled. Not the only child.

"I had so many ideas, so many ways I wanted to change the world for the better. But I was always told to stay in my place. I didn't listen. I studied at every university, with every great scholar in my land, then went further afield seeking more. I wasn't content to know my place, either. And I arrived here, in Illyamor, once a powerful kingdom but now obviously dying. And I wanted to make it better. I want to help all the people here, and especially the magelings who bear the blight of the land so horrifically. I can make a difference. But I need more power."

He paused, gazing into space, then let out a defeated sigh. "Is there anything you can tell me? How fares my sister?"

"The queen?" Sabine's heart raced. If she were to denounce Liesl, she may gain favor with the secrets she harbored. But her words could send their kingdom into a collision course with civil war. Not to mention condemning a child. Sabine fumbled. She needed more time, more information.

"She *is* my only sister," the duke prompted.

Sabine swallowed, wondering at her own loyalties as, once again, she lied to her benefactor. "Nothing, my duke. She spends most of her time with the king. They are dull creatures."

He turned to her voice and snatched at the empty air, seizing her upper arm. His voice didn't seem angry but rather perplexed. "You work for me as a spy, and yet I get very little useful information from you. You wouldn't hold anything back from me?"

"I would never."

"Only yourself, it seems." A blaze grew in his eyes, a reflection of the fire that came so close to consuming him. The grip around her arm grew warmer, then heated like an iron in the fire.

She screamed at the scorching pain. White-hot fury bolted through her as she ripped out of his grasp, her arm exploding with agony.

Duke Aurich stepped backward and ran his hands through his hair. "Sabine, I... did I hurt you? I don't know what happened."

He crowded into her space and tried to embrace her. Sabine twisted away, biting back a scream. She circled away from him, wary. "Is that everything, Your Grace?" She bit the words off.

Aurich's face was white as ash. "I'm sorry. I'm so sorry." She fled, his words following her down the stone stairs.

The Ofhellen

Sabine paced the streets, her every step counting down the time she had left, quickening as it neared the end. She had laid out the tapestry weaving from Anora in an empty room before she had left the Keep. When she released the fabric, it became visible in a ripple of color.

There she was, aloof and beautiful and alone. Sabine lingered over the details, a part of her marveling at the skill of the blind girl; she was obviously a mageling, but how had the Helms allowed her to stay? They made it their duty to weed out magical children from the population.

Peering closer at the portrait of herself with the black veins winding up her feet, a stab of fear passed through Sabine, and she reached out to touch it. The tapestry disappeared.

Sabine needed to speak to Anora. The blind girl knew more than she had said, and Sabine was running out of good options. Duke Aurich was full of promises, but he had done little of substance for her. His fire was unstable, and she didn't have time to keep faith in him. She might burn up under his touch before he ever found a cure for her.

She entered the stone halls while the Helms gathered at the fire altar, preparing to sing the light away for the day. As the sun touched the horizon, the chanting began, and Sabine forced a door open with her knife. The wound on her arm pulled, and she stifled a whimper. She had tended to it as best she could, stealing ointment and clean linens at the Keep. The skin had blistered, and the wound was weeping; it would take weeks to heal completely.

As she padded the empty halls, the chanting rose in intensity, echoing down the corridor, evoking fire and angry gods. Windows set high in the walls were designed to capture the light of the sunset, which bounced off the cool stone like living fire.

Around a corner, faint light spilled from an open door. Sabine peeked in. The sighs of young girls rose; a gentle snore. One girl wept, the sound smothered by her pillow. This was the dormitory of the Awhye children, taken in by the generosity of the Helms. Sabine shuddered at the thought of being trapped inside these barren gray walls with nothing but penance as comfort. She searched for a head of coppery curls, but there was no sign of Anora with the Awhye girls.

The novices were taken in as charity, those who were orphaned or starving. Some of her friends from the Wilt had ended up here.

They were forced to forget the Old Ways of their people, never allowed to leave the premises of the Ofhellen. They worked for the glory of the gods of fire and for the Helms who oversaw them. Their long black hair was shorn and sold for a profit. Sabine burned as she listened to their crying, wondering what could be done for them. If she could only hide all of them under her skirts and whisk them away.

But life outside was uncertain as well; at least inside, they would not starve. She bowed her head as she passed.

She found her way to the weaver's cobwebbed corner, finding Anora there. Her loom had been removed, and she seemed very small without it. She clutched a tattered bag on her lap with both hands. When Sabine turned the corner, Anora looked up as if she could see her clearly.

Her fair face broke into a glowing smile. "I knew you would come back."

"Why aren't you with the others?" Sabine asked.

"I don't consort with them," she explained. "Helmine Marthe forbids it. She believes my time is better spent at the loom."

"Helmine Marthe?" The name sounded familiar to Sabine.

"She leads the Ofhellen. She controls the novices, what we do and the privileges we receive."

Anora's shift barely covered her knees, and Sabine suspected the eerie girl was given very few privileges. She pulled the tapestry from her pocket, the fabric warm and softened. She thrust the square at Anora, who took it without faltering.

As the fabric left Sabine's hand, the gorgeous colors shaped the portrait. "That's magic." She stabbed her finger at the portrait. "Are you a mageling? Do you know what magelings are?"

Anora considered the question. "The children who are taken away because they are magical and the blood in their veins is cursed by the blight on the land." Her white eyes squeezed shut. "I do not see the children once they are taken away behind stone walls. But my magic is not the same as theirs; it comes from a different place. I may very well be cursed, but not like you."

"You said you could help me." Sabine felt the unexpected desire to weep.

"I know where to find your cure." Anora stood and brushed out her skirt. She was taller than Sabine, all skinny arms and legs like a colt. "With apologies, though, I must ask you to help me first. I must leave the Ofhellen tonight. As soon as possible, really. But I need a guide."

"I thought you could see without seeing, or whatever."

Anora gave a gentle smile. "I may know your heart, Sabine, but I'm still blind. I've never stepped foot outside the Ofhellen. I suspect it is a cruel world for a girl in my situation. Please." Anora sighed, and it was the closest she had looked to being anxious.

"The Helms were unhappy about the state of my tapestry, and I believe they mean to put me out."

Sabine bit her lip. "It's my fault," she said. "I took your work."

"Don't fret, my friend. I gave it to you. This is the beginning of a marvelous adventure. I can take you where you need to go. The Dikisi Forest."

Sabine grabbed Anora's arm with bruising force. "The Dikisi Forest? People don't survive going there. It's full of ghosts and deadly creatures."

"There are ways to pass, and I know them all."

Sabine's heart sank. The girl must be mad. The Dikisi Forest was a good place to die, little else. "Why go to the forest at all? What could we possibly find there?"

Anora's face glowed. "Salvation. A place that lies hidden deep in the woods, a sacred place. You will be cured there." She brushed delicate fingertips over her temple. "I have seen it."

Still, Sabine hesitated. The duke had also promised to help her, and she had given up nearly everything to follow him. Could she really turn her back on that now?

The burn on her arm throbbed. Where had his promises gotten her?

Anora held out the tapestry. "The time has come to make a choice. Follow your destiny or fade away. Only you can change the course of your future."

The woven image had changed. Her self-portrait stared straight at her, arm outstretched, as if pleading for help.

She hadn't told Aurich about Anora because she wasn't sure if she could trust him, especially with her life. For better or worse, she needed to put her faith in something else.

Sabine accepted the tapestry. She had no intention of fading away. Even if it meant following a mad girl into a haunted forest.

"All right, then. No need to get melodramatic." Sabine took Anora's outstretched hand and led her out of the corner. The girl's footsteps were light as an imp's, her hand nothing more than calluses and bones. Her shift hung off her shoulders. Sabine was unsure the frail girl would make it five steps out of the city, let alone safely through the Dikisi Forest. Did she eat anything at all?

Anora's smile slipped and she answered Sabine's unspoken thought. "I eat what they leave for me. There simply isn't very much for a poor blind girl. But I am stronger than I look, and I will do my best to guide you safely through the forest if you guide me through the city."

"They starve you, you mean." Outrage at the girl's treatment brought a growl to Sabine's voice. "We'll find you something to eat."

Sabine led Anora along the passageway, thankful for the darkness. Anora appeared to be pulled by an invisible force, a marionette without its strings.

When the girl's eyes widened in alarm, it took Sabine a heartbeat to realize what had happened. The chanting had stopped earlier than it should have.

"What is it?"

Footsteps clattered down the hall and Anora's face blanched. "He's come for me." Her whisper bounced off the stone walls.

"Blazing hell." Sabine whipped around, trying to figure out an escape. They couldn't make it out of the corridor before being overtaken. Behind them was only the quiet spider's corner where a girl used to weave.

Next to them, the archway of the hall formed a small alcove. It was hardly a hiding place. Anyone turning their head as they passed would see Anora cowering there. Still, Sabine pressed her back against the wall, spreading the skirts of her invisible gown as though to shield her.

Armed men rattled toward them. Sabine imagined drawing the shadows around her until there was nothing to see but forgotten space.

The men came into view, and Sabine held back her gasp: four guards wearing the duke's red and gold, blades bristling. Aurich hadn't believed her when she said there was nothing in the Ofhellen. Or had he done his own digging to discover there was a blind seer housed within the walls? It was clear that Anora was their target.

The men bore an awful lot of weaponry for one starved blind girl. As they approached the alcove, Sabine's determination to hide Anora sharpened. Whether by luck or magic, no one looked to the girl in the alcove.

A formidable figure followed the men. The woman was tall and portly, icy eyes crowded over a long nose. Her robes dripped with jewels, as did her elaborate headdress.

Sabine recognized her now, Helmine Marthe. She prayed over the Awhye children once a year, as prescribed by the Ofhellen's charitable rules. As a young girl, Sabine connected this hag with misery as she lectured over them with condescending righteousness that they would burn in hellfire for eternity. Sabine prayed all the harder that Anora would remain unseen.

Her focus shattered at the sound of the voice behind the Helmine. Duke Aurich strode down the hall behind his men. His charming façade had slipped away. There was no evidence of mischief or sympathy here. The controlled fury in his look caused her to huddle further back, her arm stinging where he'd burned her. What would he do to her if he found her trying to conceal the very prize he'd come to claim?

"You should have informed me beforehand," the duke said in clipped tones. "You were concealing a mageling right under my very nose. This is unacceptable."

"You know that at any sign of the *unnatural*, I immediately send the orphans your way." Helmine Marthe's voice was loud and nasal. "I have no desire to harbor an unstable mageling within our walls. This one was always a handful but did not seem magical. She suffered from nightmares when she was young and screamed up an unholy fuss. Unmanageable. But she hid her condition. She was a shifty child."

Anora whimpered. Gripping her lip between her teeth until she tasted blood, Sabine reached out to give her hand a squeeze.

"*Any* child showing powers should be brought to me." Aurich's voice was rich with menace.

Helmine Marthe halted, taking her time to face the duke. "That is the arrangement. For the paltry sum you provide to support these insufferable brats, you come and take those of your choosing. And what happens to those children, *Your Grace?*" The weight of generations of Halwardian blue blood added to her heft. "The uncanny children seem to disappear from the very earth. I'd hate to think we need to look further into this situation."

The duke, political upstart that he was, had long ago learned to navigate the upper classes' pretensions. The air crackled, smelling of sulfur. He towered over the Helmine, who finally had the good sense to look apprehensive.

His voice lowered so only the Helmine could hear him. And the two women eavesdropping next to them.

"Indeed, we have an arrangement. I line the pockets of this godsforsaken Ofhellen, and you provide me with uncanny children. What's more, you sign a document every year, signing off on the safety of the magelings. Let's not forget no one here is innocent, and your complicity in this matter is complete. If you value your neck, you'll keep your mouth shut and do your part. We do this to bring peace and prosperity to the land. Now is not the time to lose faith." He opened his palm, and a plume of fire shot to the ceiling.

Helmine Marthe swallowed, her face lit by the burning red flames. "Of course, Your Grace. We do what we must for the good of the kingdom."

Duke Aurich emitted waves of heat as he assessed the woman. "You say she's a weaver of some skill, and blind. An interesting detail, would you not say?"

The Helmine scratched underneath the edge of her headdress. "We always encourage our young ones to learn skills."

"And profit off the results, no doubt." Helmine Marthe looked away, and the duke smirked. "Very well. Let us find this weaver then."

Sabine stared at Aurich, the man she'd shared far too many secrets with. She'd assumed his substantial donations to the Ofhellen were due to his devout worship of the fire gods, but she had been misled as to what drove him. He was buying off the Helms' compliance and silence. But what was happening to the magelings?

He swept past them, the Helmine scurrying to keep up. Miraculously, neither of them looked their way during their heated exchange.

Tense as a bowstring ready to snap, Anora's normally peaceful expression was twisted in horror. "He's a monster," she whispered, frantic. "He devours children."

"He does no such thing," Sabine said, although the arrangement he had spoken of shook her to the core.

Exclamations rang out as they discovered Anora was not where she was supposed to be.

"Well, I never!" the Helmine's voice bellowed. "The girl is behaving so strangely. First, she cuts away that beautiful tapestry and breaks her loom. Now, she runs away!"

"What embroidery?" The duke sounded preoccupied.

"An Awhye girl. Some enjoy that kind of thing." Marthe sniffed.

"Awhye girl?" Sabine's heart beat faster as the duke's voice sharpened. "Anything particular about her?"

"They all look the same to me. I suppose you could say she was somewhat attractive."

Sabine grabbed Anora. "We need to get out of here. Run down the hall as fast as you can. I've got you."

Anora clutched her bag to her chest. "Of course you do. I know you won't let me falter." Together they dashed down the hallway. Sabine turned back with every step, waiting for the alarm to sound.

She let out a breath as they rounded a corner, seeing their reprieve. "Up ahead; there's a door."

It was barred by a heavy iron lock. "Blazing hell," Sabine hissed. "Back up and let me figure this out." She brought out her knife, using it to force open the rusty metal lock. "Blaze, blaze, blaze." Every second was a moment closer to being grabbed. She banged the door with her hip, and it finally shifted.

A cry sounded as one of the duke's men sprinted around the corner, spotting them. Anora moaned, but Sabine shoved her through the door.

"Run, Anora. As fast as you can."

"Where do I go?" The girl panted. "Sabine, I can't..."

Sabine twined her fingers through Anora's. "You can, and you will. One foot in front of the other. We'll lose them in the streets."

Toamna

They burst into the fresh night air. Anora dashed at full speed despite her blindness, Sabine holding on tight.

Men bellowed behind them, and Sabine's heart slammed in her chest. She looked to Anora, and the girl flickered from view, as invisible as Sabine.

"She disappeared," a guardsman shouted.

Sabine whipped around to see Duke Aurich breach the door, his copper hair tumbling over his forehead. "Sabine!" There was a time when she would have turned back to him, but not anymore.

They cleared the courtyard, whipping through the winding alleys surrounding the Ofhellen. Anora, barefoot, stumbled and cried out, slowing to a limp as she became visible again.

Sabine sought a hiding place, finally settling on a half-opened cellar door, tugging Anora in that direction. They plunged into the cellar, Sabine guiding Anora. Once she pulled the doors closed, they were enveloped in darkness.

"It's okay now," she whispered. "We're hidden. They won't find us."

"They're coming." Anora's tense whisper floated out of the darkness. Her frail hand found Sabine's. They held each other in silence as boots pounded overhead. Sabine scrunched her eyes shut like a child.

"I've lost her," a guardsman in red and gold said. "How could she just disappear?"

"Are you sure what you saw?" A rough voice answered. "A girl in a tattered white dress who vanished from view? Perhaps you saw a shade."

"No such thing as shades." The first man's voice was harsh with contempt. "I saw a girl."

"A girl with white staring eyes."

"She's blind, is all." The voice became more cautious.

"I've heard stories of this place, that the Ofhellen is haunted. You've been led away by a spirit."

"You talk of children's stories," the first guardsmen scoffed and then paused. "I don't know what I saw. Anyway, there's nothing here, so let's return. His Grace will not be pleased to find us missing."

"Hopefully, he found his mageling and we can forget this night."

They shuffled away. In the cellar, shapes took form as moonlight crept in through the cracks. Anora huddled on the cellar steps, clutching herself with bony fingers.

"Here." Sabine removed the fur from her shoulders, wrapping it around the girl's thin frame. Anora's pale face was luminous in the dim light.

"Thank you, my sweet protector. You saved me from a fate worse than death."

"Listen, the duke doesn't eat children or whatever stories you've heard. I work for him. He's trying to find a solution to the blight on the land."

"He's come before, although never for me. Those that go with him do not return."

"They're taken to a school. The duke teaches those with powers to control them, so they don't harm themselves or others."

"You've seen this?"

"Not personally." Sabine frowned.

"You say you work for him, yet you fled. You could have handed me to him, but you did not. Why?"

Anora's questions were making her head hurt. Sabine rubbed the space over her eyebrows. "Everything just happened so quickly."

"You trusted your instincts."

"I did what anyone else would have done."

"Stop underestimating yourself; you know that's not true. There is much I do not see, Sabine, but your soul shines brightly in front of me. You are a guardian, a protector of the light."

"Okay, I'm a protector of the light," Sabine said to pacify Anora as she became impassioned. "But guardian or not, we have to get out of here."

"Yes, to the Dikisi Forest."

"Anora, you have no shoes. How can you make it through a forest you've never visited?"

"It calls to me. I know the path ahead of us as though I've traced it a thousand times before."

"It's dangerous."

"No more dangerous than here."

Sabine couldn't argue with that. By whisking Anora away from under his nose, she had infuriated the most powerful man in the kingdom. It would be best to get out of the city. "And you say I can be cured of the blight?"

"Without a doubt. But you must trust me."

Sabine eyed the earnest girl. "We're going to need provisions. And you need shoes."

"I'll put my trust in you as well. We'll be sisters of the spirit."

Her words rippled over Sabine's skin, sounding a chord deep within her. She shook off the unsettling feeling. "I think they're gone."

She opened the cellar door inch by tantalizing inch so the

hinges wouldn't creak. "All clear." She reached for Anora's hand. "Follow me."

The two stole through the winding alleys, heading deeper into the black fog toward the Wilt. Anora stepped carefully now, feeling out each footstep. Sabine carried her bag, heartbreakingly light.

"Where do we go?" Anora asked.

"My people gather tonight. I'll find help there."

"Why do they gather?"

"It's the *Toamna* festival," Sabine explained. "A harvest celebration."

"Ah, yes. Also the transition from life to death."

"How do you know?"

Anora held up a palm. "As winter follows summer, so too does death follow life. Your people are wise. You understand the cycle."

"Blazes," Sabine muttered as she followed a steep road down into the heart of the Wilt, where the hovels led to a central square.

Usually, this space was packed with merchants' tents. But tonight, the Awhye were here to have fun. Lanterns were lit and faces were painted with colorful grease. In times of plenty, cakes of nuts and honey were passed out to children.

Even in their hardships, the Awhye people knew how to celebrate. Pride stirred in Sabine's chest at their grace in the face of injustice. The art they created was far more beautiful than anything the Halwardians could make. Their music was better, their food more delicious, and nothing their oppressors could do would change that.

She followed the flickering lights and sound of stringed instruments to the hub of the gathering. Anora gasped when they entered the square. Sabine wondered what she experienced as delight spread over Anora's face. "Oh, Sabine, it's wonderful!"

Sabine nodded at the *Toamna* celebration, now in full swing. "It is. But I need to find my brother in this crush."

Anora pulled back. "Will he help me? A blind orphan?"

"Rafi will help anyone. Besides, he knows I'm invisible."

"You must trust him a great deal." Anora's shoulders relaxed as Sabine's deft hand guided her. Sabine darted nervous glances at the crowd, aware of the odd looks Anora was drawing. And Rafi would be in the middle of the crowd, as usual.

Finally, she spotted the top of his head, laughing within a knot of men. The group sipped cider at ease, tapping out the beat of the music. Several of the men had been at The Oasis, and her stomach twisted at the thought of them ending up in shackles. They had no idea how closely the trap had been set about them.

Leading Anora, Sabine cursed as people bounded in front of them. She had to twist every step to avoid a collision. Finally, they were within calling distance of Rafi. Sabine hollered his name, but in the din, he couldn't hear. Gritting her teeth, she dragged Anora forward.

"My brother is ahead of us, and I need you to get his attention. Tell him his sister sent you."

"I'm afraid." Anora's steps faltered. "What if he laughs at me?"

"Rafi would never." Sabine pulled her with a firm hand.

As Anora made a tentative approach, the group of men noticed her, sharing doubtful looks. Her milk-pale skin and fur stole screamed *outsider*.

"I...sir," Anora's voice shook. "Rafi..." She trailed off, but Rafi caught his name. He glanced at his companions, confused, but stepped forward.

"My good lady. Have we met?"

Anora's gaze drifted over his shoulder, and Rafi noticed her white eyes. His face furrowed in concern. "Do you need help?"

"Yes." Her voice was breathy, as though she was about to faint. "Your sister sent me."

"Sab?" Surprised, Rafi stepped backward and crunched Sabine's foot.

"Ouch! I'm right here, you oaf."

"Sorry, I..." Rafi glanced back at his smirking companions. He waved and took Anora's arm, leading her through the crowd into an alley.

He cursed under his breath. "Do you know what this looks like?" he whispered furiously.

"I'm sorry, sir," Anora said, chastened.

His face softened. "Not you. I can't imagine this was your idea. It's my blazing sister. Where are you?"

Sabine tweaked his nose hard. "Right here."

"Ow! What was that for?"

"What was that for? You and your stupid need to get involved. You were almost caught this afternoon, Rafi! They know all about you. Do you know what they would do to you at the Keep?"

Rafi rubbed his nose, grinning in Sabine's direction. "Good thing you got us out of there in time. I went back and told everyone we should get gone."

"You got lucky, that's what happened."

"Are you here to give me more tips?" Rafi inclined his head to Anora, as though just remembering her. "Forgive me, likely not. What's going on?"

There was a very long pause before Sabine cleared her throat. "I need help."

His eyebrows shot up. "I thought you were going to take care of everything on your own."

Sabine stifled an impatient groan. "Circumstances have changed. Yes, Rafi, I need your help. Are you satisfied?"

He crossed his arms over his chest, smirking. "Somewhat. And what about your precious duke?"

"He's a monster who consumes souls," Anora said. "He came for mine tonight."

"I...see." Rafi peered at her—probably to determine if she was mad. "What can I do for you, then?"

"We need to leave the city. The duke's men are hunting Anora, and I have to get her away."

"This is the duke who would make the world a better place?"

"Rafi." Her voice held a warning, that of a big sister not against using underhanded tricks to bring her brother into line. "I need to figure this out. I need a place I can think."

"Let's go to Mama's. We can discuss this without drawing attention to ourselves."

Sabine wasn't sure if she would be welcome at Hesta's Hearth, but they had nowhere else to go. She hissed out a breath. "All right, we'll go there. Help Anora, Rafi. She can't see."

It took Rafi a moment to realize she meant the girl standing in front of him. He reached out to take her arm, and Anora started.

"Good lady, I apologize for the intimacy, but we need to get away from this crowd. You may not be aware of it, but you're attracting a great deal of attention. Allow me to guide you."

Anora reached out and he gently placed her hand on his arm.

They skirted the crowd. At the center were the musicians, their song spinning high into the sky. Around them, fires glowed inside metal bins, a nod to the bonfires lit by their ancestors. They worshipped the Old Ones, the spirits of nature; it had always been this way.

Next to the musicians was Gregoria, the *Vadovis*, her face painted in a skull mask to represent the god of death. Arms raised to the starlit heavens, she wailed. The eerie melody sent shivers over Sabine's skin. The song was ancient. It spoke of generations and death and life that passed by and the thread connecting them all. Gregoria spun, chanting words all Awhye knew.

"*Our blood is our own, stronger than chains.*"

As the people in the square heard, they took up the chant. The fiddlers caught time, playing a desperate reel that ripped through the air. The square was alive with the beat, and people twirled and spun. Gregoria let out a whooping cry, the sound thrilling inside Sabine.

Next to her, Anora's breath caught. "What does it mean?"

"That no matter how we are oppressed, our spirit is free," Rafi said, firelight reflecting in the tears in his eyes.

Sabine grabbed his arm. "Rafi, we don't have time. The duke's men are after us. The fastest way through the crowd is to dance through it."

Rafi blinked. "What?"

"We have to get to the other side of the crowd." He still looked confused, and she hissed, "Dance Anora to the other side."

"Oh." Anora's pale cheeks stained pink.

Completely unlike himself, Rafi's color also deepened. "I couldn't..."

"Now," Sabine ordered, shoving him toward Anora. Rafi's arms automatically went around her waist.

"Forgive me the liberties, good lady," he shouted as he swept her into his arms. With her bare feet swinging above the stones, he danced her with grace. Anora's sweet face lit up, and she laughed, her copper hair spinning out behind her as Rafi's strong arms carried her with ease.

Sabine entered the dance. The beat pulsed in her veins, and she moved in time to the rhythm as it called to her. She had no control over it; the song demanded she move. She answered, connected to the music and with every soul who danced alongside her.

She closed her eyes and felt Gregoria chanting nearby, and Rafi as he danced, and thousands of others. A thread of light inside her chest spooled toward them. She lifted her arms, the starlight twining over her skin in shimmering waves, decorating her with light.

People spun her way with cries of wonder. "A goddess!"

"The Old Ones walk with us tonight!"

More and more people moved toward her.

"Sabine, what in the blazes are you doing?" Rafi said next to her. His body curved over Anora's to protect her from the growing crowd. "I can see you."

Sabine didn't know how it was possible, but she wanted to explode from the exhilaration.

Other cries went up in the crowd, but these were different,

more urgent. Fearful. In a rush of red and gold, the duke's men entered the courtyard. They grabbed Awhye revelers, searching their faces before letting them go.

The Awhye men fought back, and a skirmish broke out. The fiddlers broke off on a dissonant squeal as one of the bonfires was kicked over, sending up a spray of flame and burning ash. People called out for their loved ones, hurrying away from the guards.

"We're looking for a girl with red hair," a guard cried. "Give her to us and you'll be left in peace."

The hum of energy left her with a snap, leaving Sabine invisible once more. Someone near her let out a shriek of terror, pointing at the fallen bonfire, where crackling embers had spread out along the paving stones. From the cinders, a figure stirred and arose, shaped of flame. Though he guttered in and out of view, Sabine made out the form of Duke Aurich.

"Firewalking." Sabine let out a low breath. He could appear in any flame; he could be anywhere. And right now, his fire spirit looked straight at her.

"Sabine." The flames spoke, deep and wispy like smoke. "Sabine, I see you."

"Blazing hell, Rafi, we have to get out of here." Sabine whirled to find her brother, grabbing his arm and sprinting away from the duke's fire soul.

"Forgive me the liberties," Rafi cried again as he scooped Anora into his arms and barreled through the riot.

Sabine stumbled on the uneven ground. In the flickering light, she saw a huddled child crying. "Mama? Papa?" The child let out a sob of terror.

Pippa. Sabine recognized her little neighbor. She careened to a stop, searching the chaos for her parents as Pippa mewled, terrified.

Sabine sprinted back to the girl, slamming into a fleeing celebrator, who cried out in fear at the unseen obstacle. Sabine dodged the fist that flew at her and made it to Pippa's side.

A guardsman bore down on the girl, sword out.

"Don't be afraid," Sabine whispered as she lifted Pippa into her arms. "I will keep you safe." Then Pippa became invisible.

"What in blazes?" a guardsman shouted, staring at where Pippa had been.

Sabine would have laughed if she wasn't so scared. "I've got you," she said in the girl's ear.

The whispered voice sizzled behind her like steam. "You can run, Sabine, but you'll never hide from me."

Doubling her speed, Sabine flew down the battered streets. She followed Rafi as they fled with their charges.

Aurich was a monster; she was sure of it now. Sabine had no idea why he wanted Anora so badly, but when she thought of his firelit form, like a demon from the stories, she could believe he devoured the souls of children.

Hesta's Hearth

The crowd thinned the further they ran from the square but screams still echoed in the distance. Rafi made for the bakery, but Sabine paused to lower Pippa to the ground in front of her house, pressing a kiss to her head. Pippa reappeared, rumpled but safe. Her parents were running down the street, screaming her name.

"Pippa!" Her mother dashed to her and snatched her into a tight embrace. "I lost you in the crowd."

"I was fine." The girl's face broke into an impish grin. "The faerie saved me!"

"Sabine." Rafi held the door of the bakery open for her. Sabine stole into her mother's shop, Hesta's Hearth.

The sign above the door was faded, the paint barely visible and the wood splintering in some places, but still legible. It could use some love and attention, but that was true of most things in the Wilt.

The iron oven, her mother's pride, brought a swell of memories. It was a blessing on winter days, heating their home against the biting winter chill. People dropped in during the day to purchase a pasty and warm their toes. Children came to play in the back room with Sabine and Rafi. It had been a gathering place, the oven at the center of it.

Their family had once slept in the back room, all four of them. Now it was just her mother; Sabine hadn't stepped foot in the place since her mother had thrown her out for choosing to work for the Halwardians.

Rafi lit a candle but Sabine hissed. "No flames." The thought of the duke entering their home to spy on them made her shudder.

"Right." He blew it out and paced the room. "Will someone please tell me what's going on?"

Anora sat to tend to a cut on her foot. Despite everything, her smile was wide and free. "You saved my life."

"This is crazy." Rafi collapsed in a chair. "Sab, I saw you. You were glowing in silver. You looked like a ghost." Grief flickered over his face.

"I'm not a ghost." She pinched him, and he yelped. "I'm right here. And I'm going to get my whole self back."

"And how are you going to do that?" Rafi's voice was low with disbelief.

"The Lady of the Forest," Anora broke in.

Both siblings spun toward her. "The Lady of the Forest is a child's story," Rafi said.

"One that is true. We'll go to her, and she'll make things right."

"Sab, what is this?" Rafi's eyes flickered over the empty space where she stood. "You bring this girl and you're chasing after a myth? Is this just you, running away once again?"

Sabine didn't know how to answer him. A day ago, she would have scoffed at the girl's claims, and yet here she was, considering following her. The Lady of the Forest was a goddess, one who had great healing powers. According to the old legends, the sick and dying would make pilgrimage to her. But she had disappeared centuries ago, if she ever existed.

"I'm no good to anyone dead, Rafi. We live in strange times, maybe we have to trust in strange things. Rafi Gillesella, this is

Anora. She is an orphan and up until tonight lived her entire life in the Ofhellen, forced to weave for the Helms."

"A blind weaver?"

"She's special." Sabine pulled out the weaving from the folds of her dress, unfurling it on the table in front of him.

Her portrait reappeared. In it, her legs were entirely wrapped up in black thread, her hips and torso emerging as though from a cocoon. Behind her, a shadow hovered. Her face glowed from the surrounding darkness, the expression one of great sorrow. "I believe her when she says she knows things we don't."

Rafi picked up the fabric carefully. "Why did the Helms keep her, then? Uncanny children are taken away."

"They sold my tapestries." Anora wiped mud off her foot with the hem of her threadbare dress. She seemed used to people speaking about her as though she wasn't there. "I made them a lot of money. They're really very good, you know."

Rafi smiled, charmed by the guileless boast. "What changed? Why is the duke after you now?"

"There was a disturbance in the magic around the Ofhellen," Sabine said. "He thought he was looking for a magical object, but now I think he believes it's Anora." Shame flooded her. "I was helping him."

Anora's smile was warm. "But you decided to help me instead. You're beginning to trust your own power."

Rafi stared at the picture of his sister. "You looked like a spirit tonight." He pointed at the tapestry. "Does this mean the blight has nearly consumed you? You'll be gone for good?"

"What's for good?" came a sharp voice. Sabine gasped as her mother entered the shop. Hesta Gillesella stalked into the room, ceremonial coins and beads dangling from her gray-streaked hair. Her thin face was painted in woad-blue lines, her dark eyes burning behind the paint.

Sabine's heart ached at seeing her mother again. It had been long months since she'd laid eyes on her, and so many terrible things had happened in the meantime.

"Have you any idea what's going on out there?" Hesta asked. "There's talk of faeries dancing in the crowds, and the duke's men stormed in."

Hesta stopped in front of Anora. Her bonfire hair was distinctly non-Awhye, and Hesta Gillesella had no time for outsiders. "Who's this hussy?"

Anora beamed at Hesta. "Well met, good lady. I thank you for your kindness and the kindness shown to me by your children."

Rafi, obviously bemused by Anora's composure in the face of his mother's temper, glanced between the two women. Few could meet Hesta's gaze when she was in a temper, her children included. Anora, blind as she was, seemed up to the task. "Mama, this is Anora. She requires aid."

"Aid. I'm sure." Hesta squinted at her son. "Have you gotten yourself entangled with some Halwardian strumpet?"

"I'm not Halwardian." Anora gave a winning smile. "I'm a foundling. Nobody knows where I come from."

"Of course you are." Hesta snorted. "Is she with child?"

Rafi's face sagged. "Blazing hell, Mama, I just met her."

Hesta spun to Anora. "Wait. You said children."

"I did."

"My *children* showed you kindness." Hesta clutched at her chest. "Have you seen my daughter? Is she well? Sabine–"

Sabine swallowed hard. "I'm here."

Hesta's face drained of color under the greasepaint. "Sabine? Where are you?"

"Here, Mama." Sabine grazed her hand along her mother's. Hesta snatched it back as though it burned.

"Are you dead?" Her voice was a whisper in the dark.

"I'm not a ghost. I'm invisible."

Hesta stared, bitterness creeping back into her eyes.

"You became invisible." She released a slow breath. "You could have risen to help us all. Instead, you turned your back on your community. And look where that got you." She gestured into empty air. "Did the duke do this to you?"

"No, Mama. I'm cursed with the blight. I'm a mageling."

Hesta held very still. "No, that's not possible. You're too old. You were safe."

"We were wrong. I started to become invisible a few months ago. The duke has been trying to help me, but..." Sabine's voice choked off.

Tears sprang to Hesta's black-rimmed eyes, and she held out her hand as though to touch Sabine, though she couldn't see her. "You should have stayed with us. Maybe we could have done something for you. But no, you had to go chasing after something better than what we had to offer, didn't you? Now we'll never know." She let out a heart-rending sigh and swiped at her eyes with her knuckles. "What a disappointment."

The words were spoken with such finality that Sabine's breath left her.

"Excuse me." Anora rose. "You cannot speak to Sabine like that. She is brave and kind and needs our help."

Hesta spun. "What foolishness is this?" In the creases of her face, Sabine could count every struggle, every suffering she endured. She had not always been like this. Before Papa died, she had laughed and loved—the baker who handed out treats to children on festival days. When her husband was killed, her joy and faith vanished.

Anora tugged the weaving from Rafi's hands. The darkness behind Sabine had spread. "The blight is well on its way to consuming her. We must move quickly to save her life."

Hesta lifted a shaky hand to touch the tapestry but let it fall. "Why are you here?" Her voice was a rasp.

"We need provisions," Sabine said. She cleared her throat, knowing how ridiculous it sounded. "We seek aid in the Dikisi Forest."

"You'll lead a blind girl through the haunted forest?"

"No," Anora said. "I will lead her."

"You're all raving mad." Hesta's gaze fell on Rafi. "And you?"

Rafi rose. "I'm going with them. They need protection. Whether or not this is utter madness, I'm with Sab."

"You'll be imprisoned if you're not back for your shift at the mine," Hesta said, eyes narrowed.

"I've six days before my shift. Many things can happen in that time."

Sabine cleared her throat. "We'll leave at once."

Hesta looked affronted. "You'll do no such thing. You'll rest your bones and fill your bellies before I let you out of this house." She pointed a finger toward Sabine's voice. "And don't you think to argue with me, young miss. Even if you get through me, you'll have the duke's men to account for on the streets, so you best do as I say. Perhaps in the morning, you'll have all regained your senses."

"Yes, Mama," Sabine said meekly.

Hesta stomped to her kitchen, banging ingredients on the countertop, muttering about the blind leading the blazin' idiots.

Sabine sat next to Anora. "How do you know about The Lady?"

Anora's impish grin returned. "The Lady of the Forest is my mother."

A pot crashed in the kitchen. Hesta stomped into the room, her mouth gaping.

A baffled look spread over Rafi's face. "Pardon, but did you say The Lady of the Forest is your mother? The Green Goddess? The Emerald Lady?"

"Yes."

Sabine cursed for having put her faith in a mad girl. They should call off this insanity at once.

Anora turned to Sabine with her uncanny eyes. "I said I could help you and I will."

Sabine let out a quick breath. "Do you read thoughts?"

Anora shook her head. "Not exactly. But I know more than others think possible. I am the daughter of a goddess, after all."

Rafi smiled. "That makes you a faerie princess or something."

Hesta smacked him upside the head. "That's enough of that. There's no such thing as The Lady of the Forest. These are faerie stories you speak of. Tales to make children feel safe before they realize how brutal life really is."

"They're not just faerie stories," Anora said, eyes wide and earnest. "The Lady lives, evergreen and undying, in the forest among the Old Ones. She has great powers. She can cure you, Sabine."

"This talk makes my bones hurt. Best to keep your head down and work hard instead of getting lost in these fables." Hesta's eyes flickered over the emptiness, seeking her daughter. "On the promise of a little girl, you'll enter the forest and be killed?"

"I'm not so little," Anora said, a frown marring her face. "I was sixteen in the summer. That makes me of age now."

Sabine bit her lip. She hadn't realized Anora was so grown, thin as she was.

Hesta must have had the same thought because she inspected Anora critically. "Needs to put some flesh on her bones to look a proper woman."

"They were starving her," Sabine said.

Rafi flew to his feet. "I would never expect such cruelty from the Helms."

"I would. You should have seen Helmine Marthe; she looks like she enjoys starving orphans. What are you doing?"

Her brother crashed about the kitchen, his face darkened with fury. "Getting her something to eat."

"Sit down," Hesta said, redirecting Rafi out of her cupboards. "You'll just make a mess." She fetched some smoked meat pasties and slammed them on the table.

"You used to tell us stories of The Lady," Sabine said.

"That was before *I* learned how brutal life was." Hesta wiped her mouth and sat back, watching Anora. "They say The Lady of the Forest has lived forever. Her power is held within a great gemstone. The Chalice of Life."

"Are there tales of her having children?" Sabine asked.

"Yes, she's known as The Great Mother. Her children were fair of face and commanded great powers."

"Like the ability to see the future?"

"The future is best left to the Oracles. If this girly is the daughter of a goddess, why is she a starved foundling?"

Men ran by the bakery, boots stomping the cobblestones. The group inside flinched. After a long silence, Hesta let out a sigh.

"You'll trust a blind girl with your life?"

"A blind woman," Sabine said. Anora smiled and straightened. "And I must do something. All this time, the duke promised he would help me, but I don't trust that he meant it." Now she knew he was lying about the magelings. "I made a mistake. But I'm going to die if I don't do anything, Mama." She held up her hand, looking right through it. "I will brave the forest if I must. It's my only chance."

"There's all manner of beasties that would eat you." Hesta's eyes burned. "You'd leave me alone."

"You told me to leave."

Hesta's lips pursed. "I suppose that gives you the right to leave me again." She got up and headed to the kitchen. "There're fresh pallets in the back. You'll need a good rest if you're to survive the forest. Go on, eat up and sleep. I'll keep watch."

Sabine picked up a pasty and took a big bite. Her mother's pies were always the best.

The Dikisi Forest

After too few hours of sleep, Sabine woke to the smell of early morning bread and a familiar clatter in the kitchen. She smiled and stretched, for a short moment forgetting all that had passed. Then reality came tumbling back, and the joyous sense of returning to her childhood evaporated.

Anora sat in the corner, plaiting her wild hair away from her face. Rafi slept, one arm thrown over his face, snoring with abandon.

The blind girl swiveled at the sound of Sabine's movements. "You're awake. I wanted to thank you with all my heart for saving me. You are generous to bring me to the bosom of your loving family."

"You're welcome to them," Sabine said as Rafi snorted and stretched.

She laid the tapestry on the floor. It had become a compulsion to see what her portrait was doing, wondering if it did portend what was coming. The shadow now wrapped like a shawl around her shoulders. Sabine didn't know what it meant, but didn't think suffocating shadows foretold anything good.

Her mother came in from outside. Though Hesta had

removed the greasepaint and the decorations from her hair, she was no less fearsome. "I've made you something to eat. You must keep up your strength." She prodded Rafi with a toe and he woke with a snort.

A feast was laid out on the table: pasties, morasu cakes, and fresh bread. Sabine wondered if Hesta had slept at all the night before. As they ate, Rafi was attentive to Anora, placing the largest piece of cake on her plate, guiding her hand when she needed aid.

One of the benefits of being invisible was that Sabine could stare without being impertinent, so she drank up her mother. Hesta's face was weary, her fingers scarred from her work. Sabine wanted to hold her hand but didn't know if it was allowed. So she clenched her fist and finished her meal.

"I've packed some extra provisions for you," Hesta said when they were done. "I hope this will be enough." She held out a leather sack filled with food and looked away as it vanished from sight.

"Thank you, Mama." Sabine arranged the sack over her shoulders. Rafi and Anora geared themselves similarly. Anora wore an old dress of Sabine's, which was too full for her frame but sturdier than the rag she had worn before. On her feet were a pair of leather slippers, Hesta's own.

When they were ready, Hesta stood at the doorway to see them off. "You're all a bunch of fools," she said, voice gruff. "Come back to me."

This last was no more than a husky whisper, and Sabine gave in to her impulse, taking her mother's hand as she passed. Instead of jerking away, Hesta gave her a squeeze before releasing her, blinking hard. The bakery door shut, and Sabine was left staring at the wood.

"Sabine?" Anora called. "Are you with us? We must go to the South Gate."

"The sun will rise soon, and the hakas seekers will be on their way into the forest as well," Rafi said. "We'll be less conspicuous if we join them."

"Hakas seekers?" Anora asked. She stumbled over a cobblestone, and Rafi placed her hand on his arm so he could guide her.

"Hakas truffles are valuable," Rafi explained. "Halwardians love them, and our people believe they have healing properties. But venturing into the forest is considered madness. Hakas seekers are the bravest among us."

"Or the most desperate," Sabine said, whispering so as not to bring attention to herself. "Hakas bring a fortune—if you survive."

"Have no fear," Anora said. "I will keep you safe from the forest. We will all find our fortunes there."

They rounded the corner and spied the South Gate. The gates had been carved out of scoria decades ago. The oily black stone was carved with figures twined around each other. Sabine stared at the carving of a woman twisted in pain and shuddered. The gate made her feel weak and cold, and she wrapped her arms around herself. She had never stepped foot beyond the walls of Aporos.

"Wait," she said. "Guards will be looking for a blind girl with red hair. Anora, put your hood up."

Rafi helped her hide her hair, taking extra care to ensure all was covered. Sabine concentrated on Anora—if only they had had time to dye her hair. Under the hood, though, it seemed to be a shade of muddy brown, instead of red.

"It would be best if we tried not to bring any attention to ourselves. Try not to speak until we're past the gates." Rafi and Anora nodded; heads bowed.

A group of shoddily dressed townspeople, mainly Awhye, gathered at the gate. Some muttered under their breath or stared blankly. Others laughed and told jokes, the loudest ones probably the most anxious.

"Beware the blood boar. They say his eyes glow red with hellfire; his tusks sharpened to swords." The man spoke with a boastful voice, as though blood boars could be scared away by bravado alone. "They eat human flesh, you know."

"No, it's the vengeance wolves to watch out for," another said, fingering an amulet. "They slink through the trees behind you, calling out your name. When you turn, they rip out your throat."

"Nonsense." Anora's voice rang sweet and clear over all the grumbled warnings. "Keep to the path, and you won't lose your way."

"The hakas aren't found on the path," one man said. "No point going in if you're not coming out with your fortune."

"Then leave a personal effect on the path," Anora said, as though this made all the sense in the world. "That way, you may return to it."

Several men scoffed, but she continued. "Besides, you needn't look too far for your treasures. Stay close to the edge of the forest, where you can still see the sky. Under a bush with yellow leaves, you'll find what you're looking for."

The blind girl was inspected by the group. "Are you much of a hakas seeker, miss?"

"Never seen one in my life." Anora graced them with a wide smile.

The gates creaked open. Sabine shifted to avoid bumping into the disgruntled men Anora left in her wake. They were wound up enough that she suspected a ghostly brush on the arm would get her stabbed. She muttered a silent prayer that they would go unnoticed, that the guards would overlook them.

As she passed the gate, she ensured her skin did not graze the black stone. It hummed a weird vibration that set her teeth on edge.

By the time she made it out, Rafi and Anora were strolling toward the forest as though out for a picnic.

"What was that?" Sabine asked when she caught up. "We were trying *not* to bring attention to ourselves."

"I'm sorry, it's only they were so scared. I wanted to help them."

"All that stuff you said about the path and the yellow bushes, is it true?"

"Of course." Anora lifted her chin. "Now that we're here, it's my turn to lead. Follow me and do as I say."

"How does one find a myth?" Sabine muttered, feeling peevish.

"She follows the myth's daughter," Anora said. "I was born here. The forest is in my very soul."

They reached the edge of the Dikisi, a sharp line of menacing trees. This late in the season, the only leaves left were tatters of yellow and brown. Wind blew with a desolate howl, rattling the emptying branches.

The hakas seekers spread out along the tree line, likely hoping to stumble over their fortune so they could hurry home to safety. Mutterings about the crazy girl followed them, but Sabine would wager they'd keep a sharp eye for yellow bushes today.

Anora released Rafi's arm and took sure steps into the dreary woods. A narrow path twisted through the trees. Three paces in, she was swallowed by the drifting mists. Rafi and Sabine lunged after her, darkness encompassing them. Vines and branches snarled on all sides, making the way nearly impassable. A screech echoed through the gloom.

"How far is it?" Sabine asked.

"A day and a night and a day. But we mustn't deviate from the path."

"A night out here? Where will we sleep?"

Anora's brow creased. "It won't be as comfortable as your mother's hearth. She's kind, though she thinks she's forgotten how." Then she turned and skipped down the path like a forest sprite, avoiding tangles of roots on instinct.

Anora seemed more comfortable in the forest than in the city streets. Her hood fell back, the copper of her hair bright in the darkness like a torch. Rafi followed her closely.

Sabine trailed behind, glancing over her shoulders. The forest seemed sentient, aware of their every movement, and waiting, though she didn't know for what. She hurried to catch up, shaking off the chill that descended from the creaking branches.

"Sing for us, Sabine," Anora said. "I would like to hear the songs of your people."

Sabine shook her head, unsure if she could. The fog of the forest settled heavily on her, so she was straining for every breath. She didn't have the energy to sing. It was as though she could feel the blight engulfing her, weighing her down.

"Come on, Sab, the spooky one. The one where the wild magic is unleashed and storms through the air and giant wolves ravage the land." Rafi's face held a look of boyish hope, and Sabine took in a deep breath. For that very look, she would sing.

"You always loved that one." Her voice no more than a hoarse whisper, Sabine sang the song Rafi requested. Its melody was haunting and spoke of the wild magic of the earth that traveled freely over the lands, bringing both death and life.

Her voice freed up and she kept on going. There were many to choose from, songs that were silly or uplifting. Papa had taught her them all. If they had lived different lives, he would have been a bard; he had the knack of capturing an audience with his tales.

When Sabine's voice faded with exhaustion, Anora sang. Her songs were in another language, sibilant and strange. Her voice, clear and sweet, rang in the boughs, blanketing them in comfort. Here, the forest did not seem so menacing.

After many hours of this, Anora halted. She stood in a clearing edged by large stones.

"This will do to rest. It's a sanctuary. None who means harm may enter here. We'll gather fallen branches to make a fire."

Sabine thought of Aurich crawling out of the embers and

recoiled. "Wait. The duke can walk through fire. He could find us here."

"No fire?" Rafi's face fell.

Anora knelt on the ground and placed her hands on the earth. Her lips moved as she spoke under her breath. "If he intends us harm, his fire spirit would not be able to enter the sanctuary either. Does he intend harm?"

Sabine remembered his last words to her: *You'll never hide from me.* "Yes," she replied at the same time as Rafi.

"Then we will be safe from him." Anora's blinding smile showed utter faith in the rules of this magical forest. Sabine shrugged at Rafi, and they did as directed, building a large bonfire. Sabine spotted some sunny leaves at the clearing's edge and smiled. She shifted the heavy branches aside to discover a large cluster of hakas truffles nestled underneath.

"We're rich," she whispered as she collected them, letting her hands sink into the loam. She brought her treasures back to the clearing, and Rafi stared at them with wonder, then over at Anora.

"Should we save them?"

Sabine shrugged, brushing the dirt off. "I say we enjoy them." She opened her pack, bringing out the bread made by her mother that morning and a lump of cheese for them to share. Everything tasted better with the truffles.

Anora took a bite of bread and let out a sigh of happiness. "Your mother loves you very much. She baked it right into her bread."

Sabine snorted. "She has a funny way of showing it."

"Everyone has a different way of showing their love. Taste it." Anora held out a piece for Sabine, who chewed it carefully. It was soft and somehow still warm, salty and delicious. She stared at it.

Rafi stood and hefted his knife.

"What are you doing?" Sabine asked.

"I saw a branch over there I want to cut," Rafi said and made to leave the circle.

"No!" Anora held out a hand in alarm. "None who intend harm may enter this circle. If you cut up a tree, you won't be able to find your way back."

Rafi put the knife down. "I'd only thought to cut a walking stick for Sab. It would help us see her."

Anora relaxed. "Your intentions are kind. But could you find a suitable branch already fallen?"

Rafi rummaged the forest floor, passing beyond their circle of light. Sabine was going to call him back when they heard his triumphant, "Found one."

He brought back a gnarled branch, sturdy and long enough that Sabine could use it over the rough terrain.

"Would you like one as well, Anora?"

"Thank you, but it's not necessary."

"I was going to carve away the roughness." Rafi picked up his knife and paused. "Is that okay?"

She tilted her head as though listening to something neither Sabine nor Rafi could hear. "That would be fine."

As Rafi peeled away the bark, he took the time to carve grooves and patterns along the branch, simple designs. He followed the grain of the wood at the head of the staff, where three points reached toward the sky.

"You're good at that," Sabine said, admiring his work. The fire and the bread made her sleepy, and she laid her head on her sack. "I forgot how good you were. Thank you for thinking of me."

"Not a day went by that I didn't think of you, Sab." Rafi's voice was far away.

Eerie

Sabine woke with a start, heart pounding, sweat trickling down her neck. The bonfire had burned down, but the embers still radiated heat. She stared at the flickering coals, certain they would stir and Aurich's red-gold face would appear before her. The surrounding darkness seemed to solidify until it was a lurking creature.

After several moments of panic, Sabine released a breath. Perhaps Anora had been right, and the duke would not be able to reach them in the sanctuary.

Rafi and Anora were asleep, hands stretched toward one another. After shaking the two of them awake, Sabine tidied the clearing, feeling a desperate urge to keep on moving away from the city. The darkness was total, and she suspected it was deep in the night. "We should continue on." Neither of them questioned her, so perhaps they felt the same impulse to move.

Rafi paused before they left. "We're going to need a light."

"What about Aurich?"

"We can't trip along the path without being able to see, Sab. Well, not all of us." Rafi nudged Anora.

"Even if he did firewalk to our torch, what would he learn?" the blind girl asked.

"He'll see that we're in the forest."

"He's probably already guessed we left the city. And he would not know our direction."

"It's true," Rafi said. "The Dikisi Forest is enormous. And deadly. He'll probably assume we'll die out here."

"Why is that far from comforting?" Sabine said, but agreed to it.

After lighting a torch from the embers, they continued along the path. Rafi took the lead, thrusting the flames one way and then another as if to conquer the darkness.

Sabine's new staff was the perfect height, with a pleasing weight and shaped for her hand. She was thinking about how much she liked it when Rafi turned back and came to a jarring halt. Anora bumped right into him and tumbled into the forest with a shout.

"Sorry, Anora." Rafi helped her back on the path, started to brush her off and then stopped, reddening, as his hand came close to her backside.

"What is it?" Sabine asked, half-amused by her brother's antics, half-fearful of his astonishment.

"The staff is gone."

"No, it's right here. Oh no."

It had become invisible. Sabine laid the stick on the ground, where it reappeared. Rafi held out the torch to see better and yelped.

The carvings had changed. Instead of crude markings, they portrayed life-like vines woven one over the other. Sabine spotted animals and birds peeking out behind twisting leaves. Near the head of the staff, now shaped distinctly like a three-pronged perch, were perfectly rendered depictions of her face and Rafi's and Anora's.

Rafi twisted the staff in his hand. "Incredible. It's how I

pictured it if I would have had time to really work at it. How is this possible?"

Anora's wide-eyed look was haunted. "There is only one explanation: magic is stirring in the forest. I fear creatures will follow. We must continue away from here."

As they moved on, Sabine peeked over her shoulder. Whether it was Anora's fear or something darker, the feeling of being watched was more present than ever. Vines grazed her face, leaving wet traces behind. She batted them away, stumbling over roots, moving through the vegetation with frustrating slowness.

Her long hair was invisible, but the branches didn't care. She became snarled in the thorny twigs. Her head yanked back, and she paused with a huff to untangle herself.

"Hang on, I'm stuck," Sabine said, trying to release her hair, which was hopelessly trapped.

Rafi and Anora were getting farther ahead of her and harder to see, as though they moved behind a veil of mist. Sabine hurried to catch up, but it was like wading through water. Pressure built around her rib cage, and more vines snaked out from the forest floor, wrapping around her ankles. Soon the gleam of torchlight would be gone.

"Please wait." Her voice was muffled as though she yelled into cotton wadding. Panic surged, and she tried to run, but the vines held her like inhuman fingers. They wound stickily along her skin, suctioning her scalp.

"Let go!"

She ripped at the vines, and they threw her to the ground. She tumbled off the path into the awaiting branches, huddled in a quivering heap.

The mist curled around her like a blanket of damp misery; the engulfing heaviness made it difficult to breathe.

Poor little wretch, a sinuous voice hissed. It came from the vines and from inside of her. *No one will ever find you now. Better let them go. They're better off without you.*

Sabine tried to scream, but the vines tightened around her throat. Her heart slowed until she fought for every beat.

Struggling was exhausting. Perhaps it would be better to let Rafi and Anora go without her.

You are nothing, a worthless slum rat. No one will miss you. Nobody even realized you were gone. You're halfway to the grave, so better give up now.

Sabine stopped fighting against the mist. It was almost pleasant to let go, like floating down a cold, dark river. Why was she struggling? There was no point in living; she was invisible trash, and no one would mourn her.

"Sab, where are you?"

She raised her head, trembling. The vines wrapped through her hair like ribbons, anchoring her in place.

Nobody wants you; they threw you away like you were garbage.

She could just put her head down and stop fighting.

"Make some noise. You have to fight back." Anora's voice drifted as if from the top of a well. "Rafi, an Eerie has her. It's feeding on her despair. Remind her of good memories. She has to remember what she fights for."

"Sab, remember when Papa would come home from the mines? And he would lift us on his shoulders, and Mama would make those honey tarts you love."

Sabine remembered and shifted, but the vines pulled her close. *Your Papa is dead. You will never have that innocence again.*

"Remember the nights of the festivals when we would dance." Rafi's voice was hoarse. "We would spin in the firelight all night long until our feet ached, and we would tumble home laughing."

Sabine remembered this as well, what it felt like to join the spirit of her people. For a moment, a flicker of warmth licked over her skin.

Leaves wrapped around her, smothering the glow.

They left you to fade away forever.

"Sabine!" Anora's voice rang full of authority. "You're trapped by a soul sucker. It's making you relive your worst moments. You need to fight back."

"But why?" Her rasp was barely more than a breath.

Anora paused, and footsteps rustled toward her. "Because you matter. If you find your fight, you can take on the worst evils of our world. Don't let despair take that away from you."

Left your people, ignorant social climber. Don't know your place. Nothing more than a scrap of mud.

"The children call you the Faerie of the Wilt," Rafi said. "You think no one notices when you bring them food and gifts, but they do. They think you're a spirit come to help them."

Like Pippa. Maybe if those children thought she was worth something, Sabine could grow to fill that hope.

The vines tightened around her, cutting into her skin. The mist smothered her. *You'll be dead in days anyway.*

"No." She gasped for breath. "I'm here." She thrashed against the tangle of branches. The more she struggled, the more she wanted to fight, as though shaking off inertia.

She screamed and raged against the tight hold. Anora thrust the torch against the vines around her legs and they squealed and writhed, retreating from the heat as they dropped Sabine.

Sabine fell back, sucking in air as the encroaching helplessness retreated, as a surge of defiance flooded through her. She would *not* fade away.

Anora knelt, her hand stretched out unerringly for her. "Dear heart, your darkest memories are behind you because you are willing to fight for yourself. Your path is not an easy one, but you will always find the courage to continue."

Sabine let Anora help her up, scrubbing at her face. Rafi nearly bowled right into her, but Anora put out her arm to stop him. "Do not trod on our brave Sabine."

"How do you know she's there?"

"To me, she shines as clearly as the stars. Just now, the Eerie tried to put out her light." Anora thrust the torch toward the vines again, an angry hissing rising from the bushes.

"What in blazing hell gods is an Eerie?"

"They are despicable creatures that make their victims feel hopeless, feeding off their despair." Anora gave a ferocious look at the trees. "It pains me to discover so many have encroached into the forest."

"But you're okay now, right, Sab?" Rafi bent to pick up her staff, which had fallen to the side. "Blazes, you gave me a fright. Don't do that again."

"Don't plan to." Her throat hurt, but she could speak again. She took the outstretched staff, which felt right in her hand.

"Are you okay?"

"Yes, I— actually I feel much better. It's as if I've been unbound."

A wildness thrilled through her veins, all the way to her fingertips. The defiance in her chest bloomed and expanded, like when she danced during the festival, as though energy was breaking through all her broken places.

Anora spun. "Sabine!"

A swell of emotion flooded through Sabine, bursting through her skin. Her desire to keep on fighting grew until she was overcome by the feeling. She let out a crow of laughter, a cry against all that was evil in the world.

A cloud of smoke formed at her chest, building in size and growing darker into inky blackness.

"What's going on?" Rafi rushed toward her, but Anora barred his way.

"An act of creation."

The cloud moved, hovering over her staff. Thick black tentacles boiled as a shape formed out of the amorphous fog. In a flash of violet light, the feeling reached a crescendo inside Sabine.

She screamed into the forest, and her voice rang for miles. An answering shriek went up from the shape.

The outline of the creature sharpened into a winged lizard the size of the cat, clinging to the perch of her staff.

Sabine let out a strangled breath. The creature's iridescent scales shone in the torchlight like an oil spill. Bat-like wings folded around its body, and a pointed tail curled around the invisible staff. Its head was crowned with midnight black horns, and its eyes glowed with purple fire over a sharply curved beak.

"I know you," Sabine whispered.

The creature opened its beak and made a string of clicking, chirping noises. It arched its back and hissed, swinging its head.

"What in blazes is that?"

"It's okay," Sabine said to it. "We're not going to hurt you."

"We're not?" Rafi stared at the shadow thing in dismay. His hand inched to his knife.

"No, you can't, Rafi." Anora put her hand on his arm to stop him, her touch lingering on the muscles of his upper arm.

"Anora, can you...sense this creature?" Sabine asked. "I don't know what it is, but it's connected to me."

Anora closed her milky eyes as she reached for the creature. "This is a surprise. I never thought I might..." Her voice faded away to a reverent hush as her fingers neared its head. Sabine worried the cruel beak would nip at Anora's fingertips. Instead, it let out another string of chirps.

"Oh, yes," Anora said as she stroked the beak. The thing's eyes shut in pleasure. "Well met, indeed."

"You don't think this thing will harm us?" Rafi sounded skeptical.

"Certainly not. This, my dear Rafi, is an Ielzrie. I do not believe one has appeared in centuries."

"An Ielzrie?" Sabine's mouth fell open. "But they are only myth."

"Just like the goddess." Anora let out a musical laugh. The Ielzrie chirruped a melody, copying her.

"Yels-ree?" Rafi asked. "What is it?"

"Papa used to tell tales of them. Flying creatures of great intelligence."

"Dragons, you mean."

"A special type of dragon," Anora said. "Ielzries are born of hope. From out of the most hateful times springs a belief that things can be different. It comes from an act of defiance to persecution, resistance against oppression. Ielzries are the embodiment of rebellion."

"But the Awhye people have rebelled many times against their oppressors," Rafi said. "We're slaughtered in the streets, and still, we fight on. We've never gotten dragons."

"Magic is smothered in the city; nothing can be created there. But here, it's another story. Midnight in an enchanted forest, a girl stood up to her own despair and believed things could be better. A part of your will and a part of your soul have joined in magic to create something new."

"Hello, you." Sabine stretched out a hand to the Ielzrie, hesitant to touch it. The Ielzrie clicked and chirruped.

"What are they good for?" Rafi asked, still suspicious of the creature, who regarded him with one glowing eye, then another.

Anora smiled. "I suspect it will be very helpful. Ielzries keep ancient knowledge and are excellent messengers. But what it needs for the moment is rest. Being created is exhausting work. Luckily, Rafi created the perfect place for it to recuperate."

Rafi narrowed his eyes at where the staff he carved must be.

"There is magic at work tonight," Anora said. "The forces may not be finished with us yet. We must trust in the path we follow."

The Ielzrie had fallen asleep, cooing like a pigeon as it breathed steadily. "I trust in this," Sabine said.

Rafi pointed to the creature suspended in midair. "At least I can tell where you are now."

Spooklights

The night deepened and Sabine missed her fur stole. The misty air permeated her skirts until they were heavy with damp. The smell of the forest changed, murky. It clung to her clothes and hair.

Next to the path, the torchlight reflected off water. Sabine straightened in alarm.

"Are we in a bog?" she asked Anora. The bogs of the Dikisi Forest came with their own warnings to travelers. Maze-like paths led travelers far from their goal, or people entered only to stumble out years later, unaware of how long they had been gone.

Anora sniffed the air. "You're right. We must cross the bog if we wish to find The Lady. Only beware. The bogs can be very dangerous. Step off the path and your life is forfeit."

"The bog is even *more* dangerous than the rest of the forest?" Rafi asked.

"Yes." Anora's white eyes were huge. "We must not stumble here. Otherwise, all is lost."

"That's just great." Sabine let out a puff of air. "I didn't think our journey had quite enough peril."

"I think things are going well."

"Really? I almost got eaten by a misery monster."

"But you didn't, and you overcame dark memories, sparking your rebellion in the process. Now you have a companion."

Sabine glanced at the Ielzrie. It hadn't stirred since falling asleep, lulled by the movement of her staff. She had worried its weight would tire her, yet the creature seemed to weigh nothing, as though truly made of shadows.

"We are together and alive, so everything is as it should be," Anora continued. "We'll let our feet carry us to the end of our journey."

"Okay, crazy," Sabine muttered, but in truth, Anora's sublime faith was soothing. "Rafi, you still good to lead us?"

Rafi gazed at Anora, his face open with admiration. Sabine cleared her throat.

"What? Yes, I'm good."

As they proceeded, Sabine peeked at the murk next to the path and shivered. The stories about the bog were not comforting. A good place to commit murder, the land was haunted by the souls of the drowned.

The air was hushed and tense, no sound beyond the brush of clothing over the undergrowth. Sabine's nerves frayed until she might burst when something flickered ahead of her.

An ethereal light sparkled blue off the heavy waters of the bog. Sabine caught her breath as the faint whimper of a child echoed over the water. "Help me," a small voice cried. "Please, I can't find my way."

A child would drown out there. Sabine stepped to the edge of the path. The Ielzrie cracked open a fiery violet eye and croaked.

Anora spun. "Sabine, stop!"

"Help me, please." The voice echoed from a distance.

"Come this way," Sabine called out.

Rafi swung back in alarm. "Sab, what are you doing?" He grasped at the air, searching for her.

"A child needs our help." Sabine pushed him away. "We have to find her."

"I'm scared," the voice sobbed. It sounded like Pippa.

Anora's searching hands found Sabine's waist and clung to her grimly. "Whatever you're hearing, it's no child."

Rafi peered at the lights dancing over the bog. "Spooklights," he whispered. "They'll make you hallucinate. Don't listen, Sab."

The voice giggled. "Come play with me." Sabine's skin crawled and she came back to herself. She was leaning far over the fetid swamp waters. Only frail Anora anchored her to the path.

Rafi still frowned at the bog, searching the deathly still waters. The only illumination came from the bluish-white spooklights.

His eyes flickered the same blue sheen, and then a smile played over his lips.

"We could play," he whispered. "It would be fun." Before Sabine or Anora could react, he blundered forward headfirst into the bog. The torch went out as it was submerged, leaving them in darkness but for the flickering spooklights.

Anora screamed.

Rafi thrashed, struggling to lift his head. He emerged for a second and took a deep gasp of air. Sticky fingers clutched his hair, pulling him under.

"Play with me," a voice croaked.

"Rafi!" Sabine screamed, but Anora held her back.

"You'll both be lost. No one can best a puka in its domain." She dragged her fingers through her hair, frantic. "Once they have you, they don't let go."

"I'm not going to let him drown. Rafi, take this!" Sabine screamed, thrusting the end of her staff into the water, trying to catch his flailing hands.

The movement upended the Ielzrie, who unfurled its wings with a cry before disappearing into a cloud of smoke.

Rafi grabbed the staff, nearly jerking Sabine off her feet, but she held steady. The muscles in her arms burned, but she dug in her heels. She wouldn't let go, puka be damned.

The flickering lights picked up an iridescent purple sheen on the water. The bog began to boil around Rafi, and he went still. A hideous wailing echoed through the amphitheater of the woods, and his head whipped up, gasping for air.

"Rafi, hellgods!" Sabine trembled as she hauled him to solid ground. He rolled over, choking, and vomited dark water onto the path. "Are you okay?"

"Still alive." Rafi lifted his fist in the air, managing a weak smile.

"You're not hurt?" Anora asked him, placing her hands on his chest, feeling his neck and face, checking his pulse. "We were fortunate the Ielzrie was with us."

"Ielzrie?" From the place where Rafi had nearly drowned, black smoke hovered, then formed into the Ielzrie. It flew to its perch, shaking water droplets like a small dog.

"It battled the puka for Rafi's life," Anora said.

Sabine reached out, hesitated, then gently stroked its neck. It nuzzled into her palm, vibrated with a deep purr. "Thank you, my friend."

"The puka's very angry." Anora sounded frightened, which frightened Sabine in turn, as nothing had shaken her yet. "They don't have much power outside their bogs, but here they are masters, and we are trespassing. I fear they won't allow us to leave without taking a soul."

"We could play."

Sabine whirled around to see the blue light flame in Rafi's eyes again. She thrust out her staff to stop him from diving into the water.

"He's spirit-took," Anora said. "They've tasted a piece of him. They won't be content until they have the rest."

"No." Sabine stepped in front of him, barring his path. Rafi laughed, elbowing her out of the way. When she refused to budge, his face turned hard, and he towered over her.

He shoved at her, and she pushed back. "Stop it, Rafi!"

His face twisted and he snarled, lunging. Sabine fought back as Anora wrapped her arms around Rafi's midsection, struggling with something as she muttered words Sabine didn't understand. After a moment, Rafi collapsed.

"Rafi, no!" Sabine screamed as his weight dropped on her. They fell to the ground, and she rolled to the edge of the bog.

But her brother's hands caught at her and pulled her invisible form back onto the path.

"I'm so sorry, Sab." He hugged her. "Are you okay?"

Sabine wrapped her arms around him, patting his head like she did when he was young. "It's okay. Are you back? It's you?"

"I'm here. But this is a cursed place." Rafi stared into the bog. No sign of spooklights burned in his dark eyes.

"What did you do to him?" Sabine asked Anora.

"I tied protective knots around him, against enchantment," Anora said, pointing to the yarn circling his waist in intricate patterns.

Sabine dragged her fallen staff toward her and searched for her Ielzrie. A chirrup above made her look to the trees, where the creature was perched on a branch. It cocked its head, one slitted purple eye training on her as though it could see her. "Are you coming?" she called, and it dove onto its invisible post.

Anora tied more knots and held out a woven rope for Sabine. "This will offer some protection. But the lights may still lure you into the bog. You need to cover your eyes."

"How will we stay on the path?"

Anora gave a puckish smile. "I will guide you. I'm quite practiced at this. It's easier to avoid illusions without sight. Come, I'll anchor you to me."

She took the length of yarn and tied it to Sabine's belt, then around Rafi's, then looped it around her own waist. Sabine tore strips of cloth from the hem of her gown, entirely ruined at this point. She used them to bind Rafi's eyes, then her own.

Without the spooklights to distract her, the bog transformed. The menacing chitter of the pukas sounded near her feet. She gasped and kicked out.

"Don't pay attention to anything you hear." Anora's calm had returned.

The rope tugged at Sabine's waist, and she took a tentative step forward. Her staff kept her upright on more than a few occasions as they stumbled along. There was a special terror in not knowing what was underfoot. Sabine had renewed admiration of Anora, who traveled through life like this.

The atmosphere of the forest thickened. The mist weighed them down, and the creeping presence of the pukas stalked just under their toes.

The Ielzrie took flight from her staff, then a gentle weight settled around Sabine's shoulders, wrapping her like a shawl. It purred, casting vibrating warmth through her entire body.

"Thank you," she murmured.

The creature made a series of clicks, which sounded like speech. *You seemed to need it.*

Sabine stilled in surprise and was tugged forward by the cord. "I didn't realize you could speak."

I didn't realize you would understand.

Sabine smiled. "A night for realizations." She paused. "Do you have a name?"

The creature was silent for a long moment. Then it chirped, *I am Novi.*

"Well met, Novi. I am Sabine." Novi bumped its face into Sabine's neck.

As they marched through the bog, the light behind her blindfold brightened.

"Can we remove our blindfolds yet?" Sabine called.

"Not yet," Anora answered. "The pukas are still very near. Can you not feel their presence?"

"I can." Rafi's teeth chattered.

"I can't." Sabine spoke to her Ielzrie. "Not since you joined me."

I am deflecting the malevolent magic.

"Could you do this for my brother? He needs it more than I do."

The weight lifted from her shoulders, and a moment later, Rafi let out a startled cry.

"It's only Novi," Sabine called.

"The dragon?" Rafi sounded panicked as Novi trilled.

"The Ielzrie. Its name is Novi."

"If you say so." Already, his voice no longer trembled.

For the rest of the morning, they navigated the bog, Novi traveling from one to another, sharing its warmth. Anora sang again, and when she became hoarse, Sabine picked up. Even Rafi shared some of the raunchy miner's songs he had learned on-site. He was halfway through *Happy Nancy* when Anora called out.

"Stop!"

They staggered to a halt. "You can take off your blindfolds."

Sabine slipped the cloth from her eyes, blinking in the light.

They clustered at the edge of a sunlit clearing. Encircling them was a group of warriors, each with an armed bow aimed at their hearts.

The Lady of the Forest

More than a dozen archers surrounded them. Rafi dove in front of Anora, who stood straight in the face of the attackers.

"We mean no harm." Her clear voice rang through the air. The warriors shuffled at her words. "I come in search of The Lady of the Forest. I offer my lifeblood as the price for the honor."

Anora took a metal pin from her pocket. With solemnity, she pricked her finger, where a ruby of blood swelled. A single drop fell to the ground.

The archers lowered their bows, and one of them gestured the group forward.

"You know our ways. Enter if you come in peace."

Novi cawed and flapped from Rafi to land on Sabine's shoulders, curling around her neck.

The warrior next to her startled although Sabine wasn't sure if it was the Ielzrie or because it appeared to sway in midair.

She spoke slowly so as not to cause alarm. "I am a traveler as well, but invisible."

The guards bowed to her.

Though muscular, none of the warriors were as tall as Sabine.

They wore sleeveless tunics and leather leggings, rugged clothing in shades of the forest. Their hair was the brown of glossy chestnuts, their skin a light grey-brown, though dappled with white and green patches like tree bark.

As they left the twisted woods and entered the clearing, sunlight poured over them. Sabine raised her face to the warmth.

She had been born and raised in the narrow alleys of the Wilt. Even when she was in the Keep, she had been hemmed in by stone walls. Never had she been in a place with so much space, more lush and plentiful than the oppressive forest behind them. The air was soft and sweetened with autumn flowers.

Anora lifted her face to the sun as well, tears streaming down her cheeks.

They followed well-tended paths through plots of land, worked by people like the archers who led them. Many examined them curiously, with no sense of fear. Next to each garden was a large, squat tree crowned with a thick layer of leaves in sunshine colors. People entered them through holes in the trunks.

From an upper opening, a child peeked his head out to spy on the intruders. His skin was dappled like the warriors. He giggled and waved before popping back in.

Deeper in the glade, the unusual trees grew enormous, like towering buildings. They came to a circular garden, where a wheel of plants surrounded an ornate well at the hub. There stood a tall woman.

The warriors led them through the gardens toward her, gesturing them forward before falling back and bowing deeply.

Sabine's shoes crushed flower petals underfoot as she approached the woman, who raised her head, watching them with detached interest from under heavy lashes. Up close, her beauty was so great that Sabine gasped.

Golden-brown hair flowed loose down her back. Although her face was unlined, she gave a sense of extraordinary substance, as though she had lived many years. Her loose shift was made of flower petals, and an enormous emerald pendant dangled at her breastbone.

The Chalice of Life. This gemstone came with legends of its own, said to be the source of The Lady of the Forest's power.

Her face was forbidding, carved from stone. "I am the Green Goddess. This is Alioch, my blessed sanctuary. Who dares intrude?"

Her voice resonated straight through Sabine's bones like deep bells chiming. An immense wave of power pulsed over her, and she fell to her knees. Next to her, so did Rafi.

Tears spilled over Sabine's cheeks. She had made it. She wasn't going to fade into nothingness. She was going to be saved.

Only Anora remained upright. The Lady of the Forest assessed her for a timeless moment.

With a gracious bow of the head, Anora curtseyed. "Mother."

A shocked murmur went up from the crowd. Humanity swirled over the impossible beauty of the goddess's face. The Lady's rose lips quivered.

"Can it be?" she whispered. Like a grieving mother. "My daughter? Lost to me all these years?"

Anora trembled as though fighting for composure. "Yes."

The Lady opened her arms. "Come to me, my child."

Anora's mouth twisted as her tears spilled over, and she stumbled into her mother's arms. She rested her head on her chest, burrowing in as tightly as she could. The Lady appeared stunned, then tear-lined eyes shut as she folded her daughter into her.

"I searched for you for so long," The Lady whispered. "You were stolen from my arms when only a baby." Wrath crept over her features, making her seem more demon than creature of light. But she softened as she took in her daughter. "Through these long years, I never gave up hope that I would find you again."

Anora shook with sobs. "I was so alone." All her prepossession melted away, leaving behind a lonely blind orphan.

The Lady straightened and took in a deep breath, her jewel-bright eyes searching her daughter's milky ones. "All is well now, for we have found each other. Let me look at you."

Anora sniffed and wiped at her cheeks as she composed herself. She gave her mother a tremulous smile.

"So lovely." Anora's eyes closed as her mother ran a finger over her cheek, tracing the spill of tears stroked her cheek. "And gifted with the Sight." She placed a feather-light touch on each of her eyelids. "Connected to the world, even while hidden away from me. I sensed you when you were lost to visions. I tried to send you comfort."

"I knew it." Anora's face was brighter than a sunbeam. "I have dreamed of this place all my life. It was you guiding me back here."

The goddess was silent for a long time before nodding. "Yes. I wanted nothing more than to see you again. Where had you been hidden?"

Anora crumpled. "Behind dark stone walls, where all was cold and hopeless. Please don't send me back there, Mother. I will do anything. Let me stay."

At her crying, Rafi struggled to his feet to stand at Anora's side. He reached out to take her hand. "You'll never go back, Anora. I promise."

The Lady frowned at the interloper. "Who have you brought?"

Anora sniffled and straightened. "This is Rafi Gillesella, one of my rescuers. He guided me from the city." She rested her hand on Rafi's arm.

The goddess raised an eyebrow and paced toward him. "Then you shall be rewarded." He seemed to strain to match her gaze but was forced to bow his head as he was assessed. "I thank you for delivering my daughter to me safely. Braving the dangers of the forest has shown you in your truest light: a guardian."

"Thank you, Great Lady." Rafi bowed and stepped back.

"And Sabine Gillesella," Anora introduced Sabine, who crouched invisibly on the ground. "It was she who breached the walls of my prison and brought me into the light. She shared her home and her family with me."

"You have come seeking my healing powers." The Lady's voice was formidable again. Sabine cringed and struggled to her feet, using her staff to help support her weight.

Novi screeched. At the sound, confidence flooded through her, and Sabine straightened.

"My lady." Sabine was unsure how to address her. "I have been cursed with blighted magic that has rendered me invisible. Soon I will be consumed by it. Anora led me to believe, that is, I thought...you would be able to cure me of this curse before it overtakes me."

The Lady's eyes were the most extraordinary shade of green. They reflected the light, like facets on her emerald.

She placed a hand on Sabine's invisible cheek. Her eyes closed, and her lips parted. "There was a time when magic was a blessing, not a curse, but the magic of the land itself has become corrupted. You carry that chaos inside of you, and if not controlled, it will consume you."

"Can you save me?"

"This magic is a part of your soul, and I cannot remove it. However, I can offer a stay of execution. You must drink the spirit water."

The crowd stirred, turning to the well behind The Lady. Eyebrows raised and pointed glances were shared, and Sabine wondered what it meant to be invited to drink the elixir. One woman, stooped and gnarled like a tree stump, limped forward, her arms thrust out as if to shield the well, glowering.

"No outsider may taste of our water," she said, her voice little more than a rasp. Two fierce-looking warriors stood at either side of her, a man and a woman, short swords brandished. Sabine shied away from their hostility.

The Lady stood unmoved by the old woman's ire. "What is this, Idona? Have we not yet learned to share?"

"She is not one of us. What can she know of our ways, of our mysteries?"

The goddess tilted her chin up and seemed to be fighting a smirk. "She brought me my daughter. I would say she has earned every last drop of her remedy."

Idona glared from beneath her brows, one bulging eye larger than the other. Finally, she swept away with a disgusted snort, her guards following her with mistrustful looks at the crowd.

"Come." The Lady ushered Sabine forward. "Ignore the old crone. She's our apothecary, but she's spent too long distilling her own potions." She brought Sabine to the edge of the well. A clear liquid bubbled below the rim as though it had a life of its own. It smelled of spring.

"The spirit water connects us with life's magics. It will act as an antidote to the blighted magic that runs through your veins. To drink is to know life and to share in the strength of it."

The Lady dipped a wooden cup into the liquid. The water cast its own shimmering light. "This will reverse the damage to your body and spirit, but it is not a cure. In time, the power will fade and the blight will return. But for the moment, the curse will be held at bay."

The fragrant scent of flowers and spices wafted from the cup, as well as something darker, earthy. The liquid was warm, and as it touched her tongue, Sabine's eyes drifted shut. It tasted of pure life. She was filled with more joy than she believed possible, her connection with the world undiluted. Energy zapped to the tips of her fingers, and her aches and pains fell away.

Warmth flowed over Sabine's skin. It felt as when the Ielzrie came to life, filling her to the breaking point. The others gasped.

Color spread over her, bringing her into vibrant visibility again. She traced her hands over herself, hardly believing she was there. Her tears flowed harder than ever as she looked at her hands, her arms. Mud-spattered though she was, she had never felt more beautiful.

"Sabine." Rafi grabbed her arms. His gaze roved over her face, the first time he had seen her in many months. "You look a mess." Sabine laughed, knowing that must be true. "It's good to see you," her brother said, swallowing hard.

"It's good to be seen." Novi let out a low croak. Sabine rubbed the Ielzrie's jaw, and it trilled in pleasure.

"And so, you live to fight another day," the goddess said.

Sabine's knees were weak with relief, so she let them collapse, genuflecting to the goddess. "Thank you," she said, trying not to sob.

The Lady's voice pealed with power. "I am The Lady of the Forest, and this glade, Alioch, is my home. My daughter and her companions are welcomed guests." She held out her hands to Anora. "Blessed daughter, the kingdoms rejoice that we have found each other. Your hardships are over. I beg you, stay with me, that we might make up for lost time."

Tears flowed down Anora's cheeks. "Thank you, Mother, for your generous welcome."

The Lady glanced away from her daughter, as though she was overcome by the sight of her. After taking several deep breaths, she addressed Rafi.

"Rafi Gillesella, I would see you become a knight of Alioch, for you have the heart of a warrior."

Rafi stared at The Lady's perfect bare feet. "I thank you, my lady, for your welcome, but I must return to protect my own people."

The Lady's face darkened. "You refuse my hospitality? Very well. I request that you stay for three days, to make it up to me. On the eve of the third day, we will celebrate our feast of the dead. I insist you are present."

Rafi considered the goddess warily, then nodded. "I agree."

"And you, Sabine Gillesella, you are also welcome to stay," she said. "You would never need fear losing yourself to the blight while protected within the enclave of Alioch."

"That is kind," Sabine said. She knew she must decline, as her brother readily did, but found the words sticking in her throat. Rafi shot her a look, and she lowered her gaze, avoiding him.

Novi cawed from Sabine's shoulder. A few droplets clung to the cup she had drank from, so she brought it to the Ielzrie's beak, and it sipped the liquid. Its whole body shook, and screeching, it sprung into the air. The magical creature looped in an ecstatic dance, embodying the joy Sabine felt.

The people around them knelt as they watched Novi and the crazy curlicues it made in the heavens. Sabine let out a low laugh, her head spinning from the magic coursing through her.

The Lady smiled, watching Sabine from the corner of her eye. Though her lips did not move, she spoke in Sabine's mind.

It takes a great act of bravery to call an Ielzrie from the ether. I expect we haven't seen the end of your power yet.

The Lady held up her hand and spoke out loud to the crowd. "Let us feast and celebrate this joyous occasion."

Brannon

Sabine hesitated. "Could we freshen up first?" Both she and Rafi were filthy and crusted with mud. Her hair was a snarl of knots and bits of forest as if she was a bog creature.

The Lady looked her up and down. "This isn't the Halwardian court, Sabine. We don't place importance on the shallow exterior as they do in Aporos."

Still, Sabine would have been more comfortable if she could wash, but The Lady turned from her with a tight smile. "Kerrick. Feamair."

The two warriors who flanked the glowering apothecary Idona exchanged glances. They had similar features—perhaps brother and sister. "You will attend me," The Lady commanded, and they fell in behind her. The crone's sour expression deepened.

The Lady took Anora's hand. "Come, my daughter. For now that we are together, I will see to your every comfort. I will ensure that life is perfect." Anora glowed as if lit by an inner candle, but sorrow haunted The Lady's eyes as she gazed at her frail daughter.

Sabine bit back her sigh of exhaustion and turned to the female guard, Feamair, with a smile. "Well met. I'm Sabine."

The guard only glared.

The Lady laughed with an airy wave of the hand. "Don't bother with them. Kerrick and Feamair were afflicted with muteness many years ago. Nothing I try has been able to unknot their tongues."

"I'm sorry to hear that." Sabine was unsettled by their bristling silence.

"The people who live here in Alioch are of the Eyanrac," The Lady said.

"The Eyanrac?" Sabine repeated, stunned. "They're from ancient history. They died out thousands of years ago." Novi cawed and clacked its beak, and Sabine swallowed. "I suppose nothing should surprise me anymore."

"Forgive my ignorance, people of the woods," Anora said in her sweet voice. "My education was sadly lacking. I do not know the story of the Eyanrac. Could somebody enlighten me?"

"The Eyanrac were the original people of this land," Rafi said with an uneasy look at the guards. "They lived as one with nature. But their territory was taken millennia ago by the Amaranthians, who settled Illyamor into the kingdom it is today. They laid out the roads, the gridwork of farms across the land, connecting the valley to the rest of the world. Aporos became a great trading capital. But all of this came at the cost of the Eyanrac and their lifestyle."

"It's true," The Lady said. "The Amaranthians enslaved them, using them for labor to build the great cities of the kingdom and worked them to death. What was done to the Eyanrac was nothing less than genocide."

"But there is a story that some escaped into the Dikisi Forest, never to be seen again." Feamair gave Rafi a ferocious look, and he swallowed. "But I guess you guys are doing okay. Good for you."

"They made their home in the forest, using the nature magic imbued in the land to shape a life that suited them." The Lady gestured to the unusual trees towering above them. "These are Rukhas, sacred to Alioch. The first grew when the surviving

Eyanrac fled into the forest, created from their will and desperation. They respond to the needs of the people: sustenance, shelter and clothing. As more are needed, more grow. There are chambers here where you will be comfortable. But first, we will feast."

The goddess led them to a clearing between the Rukhas, where carved tables and benches were lined in rows. Torches set along aisles perfumed the air with smoke, casting a golden glow. Sabine gave these an uneasy look. She didn't want Aurich to discover them in this enchanted glade.

Novi landed on Sabine's staff and let out a low caw. Several of the Eyanrac near her halted and bowed low. Sabine hesitated.

"It's the Ielzrie," a voice boomed behind her. "They are sacred to the Eyanrac."

She turned to the man who had spoken with a question, but when she laid eyes on him, Sabine forgot what she was going to say.

A head taller than she, he was not Eyanrac. He was as well-built as a man could come, and his leather leggings did much to enhance this fact. Knives were tied at his waist, wrists and calves. His skin was warm amber, and his hair a dizzying tapestry of blond and brown and flaming red. Dark chestnut eyes focused entirely on her.

Under his scrutiny, heat rushed to her face. It was rare for a man to stir her interest so immediately. When she was younger, men had been a game to her, one she always won and never took seriously. But since becoming entangled with Duke Aurich, that had all changed. She did not wish to be interested in another man, ever. She didn't even trust her own desires anymore.

And now here she stood in front of a man who made her feel a warmth that rivaled the spirit waters, and she was coated in mud. She closed her eyes briefly, knowing it shouldn't matter in the least.

The man held out his hand. When she reached for him, he gripped her forearm, an ancient greeting. His skin was warm, like he had been laying in sunshine.

"Well met, great lady."

"Well met." Sabine removed herself from his hold. The play of his skin over hers created a furious longing to press herself closer. This lust was not welcome, not when she had just escaped the duke's sway. She needed to find herself again.

She cast about for something to say. "You know of the Ielzrie?"

"They are mysterious creatures, born of defiance and loyal only to their creators."

Novi cawed. *He makes us sound like servants.*

The man bowed low. "Forgive me, young one. I misspoke. I meant only to say there is a bond. You are, of course, your own creature and free at that."

Novi tilted its head as its eyes flashed with purple fire, then gave a dignified bow. *Forgiven, man of earth.*

"You understand it?" Curiosity overcame her hesitancy.

"Most humans likely will not, but I can."

"Are you not human?" He let out a belly laugh, and Sabine blushed.

"I am Brannon, although I have gone by many names through the years. I run deeper than the skin you see." He held out his arm. "Please, allow me to escort you to your table."

Rafi and the others had left her behind. She glanced at Novi for guidance. *In his heart is much joy and laughter,* the Ielzrie chirruped and gave Sabine a big wink, which surprised a laugh out of her.

"Very well, then, Brannon. I am Sabine."

"Already your reputation precedes you, Lady Sabine. Forger of dragons."

Brannon turned as someone called to him. Sabine took advantage and inspected his profile, the strong bones of his cheek and jaw. Under that strength, his features were finely drawn, his eyes rimmed with charcoal black lashes.

A smile played over his lips, and she suspected he knew he was being assessed. Sabine glanced away. She knew men like him, those who knew how desirable they were. She also knew their expectations and wasn't interested. *Truly*.

"Come, let us sit. The food is calling to me."

Sabine agreed, weak with hunger, as the platters were laid out. Herbed-crusted cheeses, grilled vegetables dripping with honey sauce, and roasted meats sent heavenly aromas spiraling into the air. Rounds of crusty bread were distributed. Despite the crowd, there was enough for everyone.

Hundreds of Eyanrac spread out along long tables. Brannon ushered Sabine to the head table, where The Lady waited. High-backed chairs carved from stumps were set in place. Anora was at The Lady's right hand, Rafi next to her. Other Eyanrac at the table nodded in acknowledgment. The withered old woman sat near the end, glaring, flanked by the two mute guards. Next to the Eyanrac, Brannon appeared ever larger, brimming with life. He settled himself at Sabine's side.

The Lady raised her cup in the air, and the buzz of movement faded instantly.

"Welcome all." Her voice reached every corner of the gathering. "For those of you who were not witnesses, three voyagers emerged from the forest today." She paused, and the silence was all-encompassing. "Among them was my daughter, who I believed lost to me forever. Please welcome Anora."

The Eyanrac banged their cups on the tables and whistled through their teeth. Anora stood with a bashful smile, the firelight catching her copper hair.

"Her companions risked great perils to bring her here, and for that, they are welcome among us. Sabine and Rafi Gillesella." Sabine glowed at the attention, letting it shower over her.

Novi let out a screech from its perch, and many startled.

"No, I would not forget you," The Lady said with a gracious smile. "A grand and momentous occasion took place in the wild night hours when an Ielzrie was called from the ether. This has not happened in living human memory, and we must take a moment to acknowledge our blessing to be in the presence of such a legendary creature."

The applause was thunderous. Eyanrac children stood on the benches to catch a glimpse of the fabled creature.

"You like the limelight more than I do." Sabine tickled the Ielzrie under its chin as it preened.

We are made of the same stuff; you and I. Novi spread its wings and leaped into the sky, swooping over the crowds. Eyes flashing with violet fire, it let out a mighty caw as the Eyanrac gasped and pointed.

When the applause died down, The Lady stretched out her arms and sat. The gathering settled together, and all shared in the feast.

Sabine had spent her life hungry. Living in the bakery, she was well-fed by Awhye standards, but there was never enough in the Wilt, even in the best of times. While working at the Keep, she would make do with what she could beg from the kitchens or finish the plates of the ladies-in-waiting when no one was looking. Her life had been spent scraping for every meal. So much food spread out in front of her, free for the taking, was an uncommon delight.

Brannon picked up on her obvious pleasure and made a point of seeking out the choicest foods for her. She tried to dismiss him and failed. Brannon was impossible to ignore, with his rumbling laugh that he shared with everyone. He sent Sabine knowing smiles whenever he caught her eye.

His interest was intoxicating. Brannon was a man who knew every inch of himself, who was exactly sure of his mettle, and it was deeply attractive. Sabine would not be swayed by it.

Just then, he caught her gaze and held it a moment too long, and she looked away, blushing.

What had gotten into her? She used to be the one to make people blush, not the other way around.

A group of Eyanrac children approached him, pulling at his

sleeves and whispering in his ear. He roared with laughter. "You want to hear the tale of my brother?" The children clapped their hands and eagerly settled cross-legged in front of him. This appeared to be a common entertainment, for some parents came over, indulgent smiles on their faces, lingering to listen.

People at their table shifted, too. Rafi perked up at the movement; the Awhye knew storytellers, and Brannon was clearly a good one. Rafi moved to take the chair next to Sabine's, guiding Anora to a seat next to him. Their hands lingered together, and a wistful smile spread over her fair face.

Brannon settled forward, his burnished skin glowing like bronze in the firelight. He looked just like a woodland god. At that thought, Sabine could have sworn he looked her way and winked, but it may just have been the flickering bonfire. Gooseflesh rippled up her arm as Brannon began his tale, his deep voice rumbling across the clearing.

"Which brother of mine would you like to hear of? Yumil, is it? He is a great brother to have. Well, once, many moons ago, a group of Sabagh became trapped during a flood."

Brannon held sway over all of them with his story. Men and women, old and young, all responded to his vibrant energy. Sabine wondered who he was to them.

At the end of the story, a small figure made her way to Brannon. Sabine's eyes followed her, as her skin gleamed the gold of old coins. A real Sabagh, a creature she thought existed only in faerie-tale books. She had stopped questioning what she knew to be true or not; clearly, a world of magical creatures harbored in this forest. The Sabagh stepped forward and shyly handed Brannon something. He held up an orange fruit.

"I thank you, my dear," he said. "This is a rare treat. It was a pleasure to help such kindly creatures."

"Did your brother make you pay for it, Brannon?" asked the Sabagh. Her voice rasped like dried leaves over bark. She spoke like she'd heard the story before and knew where things were going.

"Did I not pay for it for months afterward? It was near winter before my power returned, for all the good it did me then. My brothers are always happy to share in their strength," he confided in Sabine and Rafi, who listened as avidly as the others. "But there is always a price to pay."

"And what was the payment?" Rafi leaned forward like an Eyanrac child.

"My life force. My brothers put a great deal of importance on power, you see. I suspect they've always been jealous of my freedom."

Sabine, not understanding, shook her head. "Was it worth it?"

"Of course it was. I saved three souls that day." There was no boast in Brannon's tone.

She smiled then; he brightened and returned the look. A flash of heat sparked between them, and Sabine looked away, spooked. She wouldn't put her trust in another man.

Rafi and Anora were deep in conversation. Rafi was explaining something about where they grew up. He had taken Anora's hand, drawing on her palm with his finger. She giggled and pushed back her hair. She didn't see the way Rafi looked at her, entranced.

The Lady did, though, with pursed lips that soured her look. Sabine blinked and the goddess's graceful beauty had returned. Sabine peered into her glass, wondering if the drink was more potent than she realized.

Plates of honeyed fruit were passed around, but Sabine waved them off. Her sides squeaked in discomfort with the amount she had eaten.

"Here, drink this." Brannon was at her side with a goblet of clear liquid.

"I can't," Sabine said. "I've had far more than I should tonight."

"It won't muddy your senses. It will make you more comfortable."

Sabine sipped at the liquid. It tasted of herbs. As it slid into her stuffed belly, her discomfort eased.

"That's incredible. I shouldn't have overdone, but I've never..." she trailed off, not wanting to share she'd lived off food scraps her whole life.

"There are times when it is right to have a little too much." His eyes were kind. "What would life be if we couldn't indulge?"

The Lady overheard him. "You know all about indulging, don't you, Brannon?" Her voice took on a sharp edge.

Brannon raised his cup to the goddess, arching an eyebrow. "When there is bounty, I shall take my fill." He swung toward the gathering, toasting them. "So let us eat, drink and make merry, for tomorrow there may be none."

Brannon's declaration, followed by his draining the entire goblet down his throat, was met by raucous claps and whistles. His skin shone like sunlit bark, and his muscles bulged under their leather trappings. Never had Sabine seen anyone look the embodiment of hale and hearty.

More drink was being passed around, and Eyanrac men and women gave Brannon silent nods of appraisal. Brannon greeted a few of these with a wink.

Sabine's smile slipped. Tired of feasting and game-playing, she wanted nothing more than to lay her head down on the table. Unsure how to proceed, she settled on formality.

Standing, she bowed to the goddess, who was tearing into a honeyed shank of meat with her perfect white teeth.

"My lady," she said. "I would ask your leave to make my way to my chambers. Our journey was long and harrowing, and I find myself in need of rest."

The Lady dabbed her lips with a leaf. "Your manners are very pretty, Sabine, as is the rest of you. I can see how you made your way through the Halwardian court."

Sabine paused at the edge in the goddess's tone.

"She's better than the entire lot combined," Rafi said, his voice a growl.

"In every respect." The Lady's voice was all kindness. Had Sabine imagined the barb hidden in her comment? "Of course, you must rest, my dear. You will need help finding your way."

Brannon rose. "I shall escort Lady Sabine."

"Are you sure that's wise, my Green Knight?" No mistaking the archness in her tone now.

Sabine wobbled like a newborn calf. Brannon reached out to keep her steady. "The Lady Sabine is exhausted, and as I do not wish for her to tumble off a tree branch, I deem it extremely wise."

Brannon led her from the table, and Sabine couldn't think of an excuse to dissuade him. Especially not since he was supporting a good half of her weight. Her limbs were heavy, leaden things that didn't want to move.

Novi came to settle on her shoulders, curling around her like an embrace.

"Are you here to protect my virtue?" Sabine whispered to the Ielzrie.

You are more than capable of protecting your own virtue as you see fit, it chirped, and energy trickled into Sabine, who lifted her head. "Thank you," she whispered and turned to Brannon, who graciously pretended he heard nothing of the conversation. "I'm not really a lady, you know."

"I've not met a lady of your caliber in many years."

"I mean, I'm a slum rat. I worked as a servant, then a spy. I steal to eat. I'm no one."

"You have overcome many hardships and delivered the goddess's child to her. You forged an Ielzrie from your own will. You may stand tall among any company you choose, Lady Sabine."

Sabine found herself unable to respond: Brannon made her feel like her worth was unconnected to her looks or her background. They reached the entrance of a great Rukha, and he ushered her inside.

The tree was hollow, with boughs vaulted overhead like a cathedral. Inside was colossal, much larger than it appeared on the outside. Vaster even than the Great Hall of Asael Keep. A hovel in the Wilt could easily fit in a corner.

Evening light filtered through cracks between branches, colored by the bright autumn leaves. The ground level was wide and spacious, a communal space. Living branches wound together to allow places to sit or work. From below them came clattering, like a workshop or kitchen was built into the roots.

Brannon guided her to the wall of the trunk, where oversized knots jutted from the bark and formed a winding staircase upward. Vines draped along the side and were easily grasped as they ascended into the boughs. Brannon carried her staff, allowing Sabine to steady herself on the vines.

The walls above were less solid, flexible branches woven together. Brannon pulled back a heavy curtain of leaves. "These will be your chambers."

Sabine tensed. It was easier to avoid men and their wandering hands when she was invisible. If she had been with Aurich, she would have never allowed herself to consume spirits that made her complaisant. At this moment, weak and vulnerable, she was at Brannon's mercy. Fear trickled through her, clearing her head, and her shoulders tensed.

Brannon noticed the change. He took a step back, brows furling. "What is it?"

"I don't want..." She hesitated, not wanting to offend him. "I mean to say, I hoped I could settle in. Alone. I don't mean to upset you."

His face cleared, but his eyes darkened and he held up a hand. "My lady Sabine, if you mean to say you do not wish my attentions tonight, please know that I would never overstep your boundaries. I had only thought to escort you safely to your rooms and would never press an advantage. I suspect there is a man who lies behind your worry, and to tell you honestly, I wish I could break his kneecaps."

Sabine shivered, whether with the tension of the moment or the pleasure of the thought of this mighty man taking on Aurich for her. He continued. "You do not ever need to scrape or plead to make your wishes known and have them respected. Not ever again. Do you understand?"

Not trusting herself to speak, Sabine gave a shaky nod.

Brannon bowed to her, low and formal. "Lady Sabine, it was a rare pleasure meeting you tonight. I would ask the privilege of showing you Alioch tomorrow if you wish it."

"I...yes, I do."

"Then until tomorrow, may you find your rest deep and fulfilling." Something in his smile made her question what he meant by "fulfilling." Before she could reply, he placed something in her palm and released her, and she entered her chambers alone.

She paused inside the doorway. He had given her the orange fruit. She inhaled its sweet scent as the full impact of his words hit her. To never again have to hide to avoid a man's desire. She straightened her spine as power buzzed through her.

She watched Brannon's silhouette through the leaves as he left, no doubt to partake in more of the festivities. He did not seem like a man ready to turn in, alone, anyway.

Novi cawed.

"Very attractive," Sabine agreed, then yawned. She wouldn't bother where Brannon spent the night, or with whom, because all she wanted was a bed.

A large fluffy mattress of moss dominated the room. She peeled off her filthy gown. As she removed the boned corset, her lungs expanded fully for the first time in days. She reveled in it, strumming her fingers over her bare ribs. She traced higher, lingering over her arms. She no longer felt pain where the duke had burned her; the wound was no more than a faded scar, an effect of the spirit water.

The spirit water healed the body, as well as the symptoms of corrupted magic. That meant that any blighted child might be healed.

Or all of them.

She barely had time to complete that thought before collapsing on the bed. A blanket made of dandelion fluff was folded at the foot of her bed. She pulled it around her, warm and soft like a cloud. She fell asleep wondering if it might be woven from dreams.

Alioch

Sunlight trickled through amber leaves, washing everything with golden light.

Sabine bolted upright. She upended Novi, curled on the bed next to her. The Ielzrie gave a squawk and puffed into smoke, reappearing near the rafters. Tendrils of shadows curled from the creature's body.

Sabine remembered then, she was safe and not about to be consumed by the blight. She rolled the thought around in her head, holding her arms out to the Ielzrie. "I'm sorry, Novi, please don't be angry. I forgot where I was and that this was real."

After a show of preening its wings, the dragonlet swooped and cuddled into Sabine's arms. She inspected Novi, the iridescent scales, the tough skin of its leathery wings, the horns arching over its head. Novi purred from the attention.

This world is very new to me, as well.

"So many changes," Sabine said and spotted her tapestry portrait, having spilled to the ground when she shed her gown. She reached out and unfolded the material.

There she was, all of her, facing forward. Her legs and feet were no longer bound, no hint of creeping black threads, and the shadow hovering at her shoulders had resolved itself into Novi.

Novi let out a twitter. *We look good.*

Sabine's fingers played over her image. Her portrait looked fierce, confident. And she was brimming over with excitement as she remembered the plan she had started to develop late last night.

"I have an idea, and I need to talk it over with my brother," she told Novi. "Could you find Rafi?"

I will find your brother and something to eat. With a cry, Novi disappeared in a puff of black smoke.

Sabine rose and poked around her tree room. Hidden behind a flap of bark was a closet full of functional clothing in forest colors. The leggings and boots were of leather; the tunic woven from tough, flexible leaves, slit along the sides to allow movement. Sabine twisted and lunged to prove she could and laughed out loud with the freedom.

A twig comb sat on a nearby leaf, and she worked it through her snarled and knotted hair. Scraping out the bog mud took time, but she luxuriated in the gentle tug at her scalp. When she was done, her black hair fell in waves to her waist.

A chirruping from the edge of the branches caught her attention. In a hole between the boughs, Novi peeked in and whistled. *He's waiting for you. Down the stairs and outside, I will meet you.*

Sabine contemplated the treacherous stairs outside her room, grabbing her courage to step onto the rough knotted wood. Step by tentative step, she would her way downwards, clinging to the vines. At least she wasn't tangling her legs in her skirts anymore. Her face felt flushed when she reached the solid forest floor, and she was happy to plant her boots there.

A flow of chattering Eyanrac left the Rukha, headed into the sunshine, and she followed. Sabine took a deep breath, taking pleasure in the softness of the air. Dew clung to the life around her, and the world shimmered.

With a screech, Novi swooped and landed on her shoulder. *Took you long enough.*

Sabine reached up to stroke its neck. “Some of us don’t have wings.”

More’s the pity for you. Novi bumped its face into her cheek, turning her to the left. *This way.*

Sabine followed Novi’s directions through the glade until she came to the clearing where they had feasted the night before. The tables were set with wooden bowls of food and drink, and everyone helped themselves. Some gave her assessing stares, and a few smiled, but they seemed reticent to speak with her.

Rafi stood at the edge of the clearing, holding a bowl. His smile was genuine, and the dark shadows under his eyes had faded. “Sab, it’s good to see you. Like, really see you. You look... different.”

“No longer covered in mud and brambles, wearing a dress that is slightly more than a tatter?”

“Not sure it’s that. Although you certainly look like you smell better.”

“Ha, same to you.” Sabine gestured at the glade around them. “Isn’t this incredible?”

Rafi swallowed a giant mouthful before responding. “I have never slept better in my entire life. And you need to try this.” He pointed to a bowl of humble gruel. It was full of nuts and spices, sweetened with honey. Sabine found she was famished despite how much she had eaten the night before.

“Delicious,” she said around her mouthful.

“I haven’t gotten the nerve to try this yet.” Rafi pointed to a cup of green, syrupy liquid.

Sabine eyed it uncertainly until Novi chirruped. *It is the sap from these great trees, very nourishing.*

“Novi says it’s safe.”

Rafi nearly spit out his gruel. “Beg pardon, *Novi* says it’s safe? It talks now?”

Sabine tickled under Novi's beak. "Something like that." She raised a glass of sap to Rafi. He took one and drank, ever trusting. As she emptied her own cup, her mind cleared. The sap smelled of green living things and tasted sweet.

"Where's Anora?" she asked.

Rafi's ears reddened. "Hmm? I don't know. Why would I?"

"Only because you've spent every waking moment with her since you met, and you might be on the verge of proposing."

Though Sabine had been teasing, Rafi's face went serious. "Anora is the daughter of The Lady of the Forest. What could I possibly give her?"

Something in his look stilled her; it was as though his heart had already been broken. "Rafi, I don't think that stuff matters here. This isn't Aporos."

"Thank blazing hell."

"Listen, I wanted to talk to you about something, and tell me if I'm crazy." She pulled him to the side and lowered her voice. "The spirit water reversed the effects of my blighted magic. If it worked on me, it would work on anyone. Why not bring some back with me to Aporos? I could give it to the children with blighted magic. It could save them."

The idea had been percolating in her brain all night, but the more she thought of it, the more she was sure. Hope stirred inside her. Spirit water must be the magical remedy they'd been waiting for.

Rafi, though, didn't seem as excited. "I don't know, Sabine. It's not a cure, right? Even the goddess said the blight would come back."

Sabine waved a hand in the air as if to shoo away the difficulties. "Yes, but if there is a constant supply coming into the city, then it shouldn't be a problem. Magical children could take a spoonful every year or something." She gasped. "They wouldn't have to be sent away from their parents." Her heart squeezed at discovering such a perfect solution.

Rafi pondered it over his glass of sap. "I don't see why it couldn't work."

Novi chittered overhead. *He has come for you.*

Sabine spun, hand going to her throat. "Aurich?" she whispered. Novi disappeared in a puff of smoke, then reappeared at her shoulder, nuzzling her.

No, the merry man. Brannon.

Relief rushed through Sabine as she remembered his promise to show her Alioch. That he had told her she'd never have to fear another man, including himself, and then proved it to her. The world glowed a little brighter around her.

"Right, the merry man. Who is he really, Novi? Not a person like I am?"

Novi tilted her head. *He is and he isn't.*

Before Sabine could respond to that utter nonsense, she noticed Brannon at the edge of the clearing and nearly spilled her juice down her front. His bronze skin, his autumn-colored hair, his clothing like that of the Eyanrac, conspired to keep him hidden, camouflaged in this forest kingdom. But now that Sabine had seen him, she couldn't look away.

He wore a sleeveless tunic, baring his arms to the sunshine, and his riotous hair was pulled back with a leather tie. He lifted a hand in greeting. As he sauntered toward them, a slow smile pulled at his lips, which in turn pulled at something deep in her belly.

She surreptitiously wiped her lip for remnants of green sap, while Rafi snorted next to her. "Show off," he muttered, watching Brannon approach. "Does he need to display his entire chest like that?"

Sabine glanced at Rafi and choked in laughter. "Rafi, you're wearing the exact same thing. Just because he fills it out better than you doesn't mean you have to be hostile."

Mischief flashed in his eyes. "It's like that, is it? Somebody has a crush on the giant woodland faerie man?"

Sabine opened her eyes wide and mouthed "Anora" as Brannon joined them. Rafi shut his mouth, trying not to laugh.

Ignoring him, Sabine turned to Brannon. "Good morning, it's nice to see you. I mean, we were meant to see each other, so that's nice." She stopped, shutting her eyes against her clumsy tongue. Never had a man caused her to stumble. For the first time in a long time, she cared about making a good impression.

He greeted them with an open smile. "Sabine Gillesella, the pleasure is all mine. And Rafi Gillesella." Brannon held out his hand to grip Rafi's. "I did not get a chance to speak with you last night."

"No, you were quite busy attending my sister." Rafi's words were pointed.

His eyes narrowed a fraction, then Brannon laughed as Rafi released him. "I hope this didn't offend you."

"I don't think it offended her."

Sabine aimed a kick at her brother's ankle and turned a beaming smile on Brannon. "You mentioned showing me around Alioch?"

"Yes, if you've both finished, you can come with me."

"Is this the official guided tour?" Rafi asked, surprised to be invited as well.

Brannon looked back as if to size him up. "I could show you the glade, but other things may interest you more."

"Like what?"

"The Eyanrac are a military people. All of them train, men and women, in the art of war when they are old enough. I could show you the training grounds."

The amusement slid from Rafi's face. "Yes. Show me."

Trotting to keep up with his long strides, Sabine asked, "Do they do much actual fighting? This place seems secluded and protected."

Brannon raised an eyebrow. "You're observant. Alioch is peaceful, but they must still hunt for food, and the forest is full of danger. And remember, the Eyanrac were nearly wiped out by invaders. Though that was many centuries ago, they still understand the importance of defending themselves."

Rafi's hands curled into fists. "What I wouldn't give to have that chance. Awhye aren't allowed to train or arm themselves. We're imprisoned or worse if we do."

"You won't be imprisoned here."

Rafi's eyes went from cynical to enthusiastic in a beat. "I could train with them?" He sounded like the little boy Sabine missed.

"See for yourself." They made their way around several large Rukhas, where a clearing opened before them. Dozens of soldiers spread out in straight lines, fluidly moving as one. It was martial and beautiful, and Sabine marveled at their precision.

Brannon gestured for Rafi to follow him onto the field. They approached the man leading the exercises. The man stopped to listen, looking Rafi over. Although Rafi towered over him, he seemed young and vulnerable. When the man nodded, her brother did a small hop before jogging over to join the ranks.

"That was kind," Sabine said to Brannon when he returned.

He shook his head. "Kindness has nothing to do with it. Your brother wants to learn to fight, and that shouldn't be denied. Your overlords in Aporos are foolish to try to oppress men like him. Or women like you," he added.

"I'm no warrior," Sabine said. She enjoyed moving without the constraint of the corset and stays but couldn't imagine actually fighting someone.

"There are different ways to fight."

Something in his look unarmed her, even as it made her believe she might be the powerful woman he claimed she was. "Where shall we go, then?"

"I can show you everything. As long as you don't mind that we are alone together?"

Novi cried from above before swooping down. It landed on

Sabine's shoulder, chattering fiercely. Brannon chucked the dragonlet under the chin.

"I realize she's never alone. I only meant I did not wish to make her uncomfortable."

"You don't make me uncomfortable," Sabine said, even as Novi gave a chirrup and took off into the clear sky.

Brannon held out his arm for her. Sabine took it, feeling the smooth, hard muscles under her palm. He smelled of woodsmoke and spices, and she forced herself not to lean into the warmth that radiated from him. If she hadn't sworn off all men forever, she might find herself unable to resist his appeal. Luckily, she could trust one of them to behave.

He guided her past the fields where people worked crops nearly ready to harvest. Others gathered around a cluster of Rukhas, busy with their work.

"What are they making?" Sabine asked.

"All kinds of things: clothing, footwear, weaponry. The community is entirely self-sufficient."

At the edge of the glade, the line of the Dikisi Forest stood as a solemn sentinel, darkness compared to the light of Alioch.

"I never imagined a place like this could exist," Sabine said, gazing over the peaceful meadows protected by the forest. "Where is Anora? Has she discovered all this?" After all the time they had spent together, it seemed odd not to have the enchanted girl nearby.

"I suspect she is with her mother, who will be reluctant to let her go again. I remember when Anora was stolen from the glade. It seems like such a short time ago; to see her grown is unsettling."

Sabine looked at the sorrow stretched over his face. "You were here?"

"I was journeying to Alioch to pay my compliments to the goddess's child, and I arrived to discover the tragedy. The Lady was possessed with grief, laying blame on anyone near her. It was not a happy time." He shook his head sadly. "And to think that child was raised in a cruel place, without love or warmth. I often wondered, if I had only arrived sooner, how things might have been different."

"You don't live here?"

He shifted toward her, and as he did so, autumn leaves seemed to rustle in his hair. "Not always. In my heart, I am a restless wanderer." His smile was wistful. "There was a time when I traveled to the farthest corners of the world."

"No longer?" Sabine assessed him, trying to figure him out.

Before he could answer, a disturbance caught his eye, near the edge of the forest. "What's this?"

A shape flitted from the foliage into Brannon's outstretched hand. A creature, human-like with grayish skin, collapsed in his palm. Brannon's brow furrowed. "This is not good." His rumbly voice softened to not disturb the feeble creature.

"What is it?" Sabine whispered.

"A forest imp. But grievously ill." The creature raised its head, peeping at Brannon. His face darkened like a thunderstorm. "It's those damned mines. Some of the forest creatures get too close and are poisoned."

"The slag mines? Rafi works there." At Brannon's savage look, she took a step back. "Not because he wants to. The Awhye men are forced to labor there."

His shoulders slumped. "The consequences of this greed will be seen for generations."

"Is it going to be okay?" Sabine nodded her head at the forest imp.

"I have power enough for this." Brannon closed his eyes. Golden light shone from his cupped hands and seeped into the tiny body. The gray tone of its skin brightened to a fiery red orange. Its eyes opened, face breaking into a relieved smile. Popping to its feet, its dragonfly wings sparkled as it fluttered to Brannon's face and kissed his nose.

He laughed. "Be on your way, little one. Tell the others to avoid the mines."

The imp flew away, and Brannon turned to Sabine. Only then did she realize how close she was, her hand on his arm. He held her gaze and made no move away from her, his eyes darkening.

"Oh, I..." Sabine stumbled back like a graceless foal. "Are you a mage? A healer?"

Brannon contemplated her a moment more before answering. "Not in the way you think. But I do have certain powers for magical creatures."

Despite his warrior build, Brannon seemed to genuinely care about the tiny woodland imp. "Speaking of healing," she said, carefully, hoping she wasn't treading on shaky territory. "What of the spirit water? Its effects on the blight were close to miraculous. Is it used as a medicine?"

"The water has profound, life-giving powers, as it is tapped into the source of living magic in the world. There are some salves and some potions, I believe, that use the substance, but sparingly."

"Why only sparingly?"

"The well is running dry." Brannon gave a quick glance over his shoulder. "Many of those who live here now wouldn't know any better, but I have been around for a long time. When the magical forces of this land were in balance, the well was a magnificent fountain. Year by year, I see the waterline sinking lower and lower."

"The goddess must be aware of this."

"Certainly, but The Lady of the Forest keeps her own counsel."

"What caused the magic to go off balance?"

He shrugged a massive shoulder. "That's the question we've been asking for some time. I wish I could enlighten you. The land is dying. Wild magic has long disappeared, and without its renewing power, it seems as though all magic, of life or death, will disappear after it."

"Wild magic?" Sabine licked her lips. "I've only heard of it in stories. It was a destructive force, wasn't it?"

"Yes, but everything needs to be destroyed to be rebuilt. Without it, everything stagnates." He nodded his head to the forest, where twisting branches enclosed the grove. "In the forest, you'll still find pockets of wild magic, biding their time, hoping the land itself does not die entirely. But I'm not sure what it will take to create that regeneration. And I fear for all of us when the well runs dry."

Sabine studied his profile. "Are you a part of this wild magic?"

Brannon turned to her; eyes unreadable in the shadows of the trees. A thin smile pulled at his lips. "You don't miss much, Lady Sabine."

Before she could answer, he nodded into the shadowy mists of the forest. "If you're interested in salves and potions, better ask Idona, the apothecary. There's her workshop." He pointed to a squat Rukha growing beyond the tree line, camouflaged by creeping ivy.

"Why inside the woods?"

"Idona uses many herbs and plants from the forest for her potions, so it suits her to be there. And it suits The Lady that she is not in Alioch proper."

"Why?"

"The two do not see eye to eye."

Sabine thought of the withered old lady who argued against her taking the spirit water when they arrived. "I don't think she would be interested in speaking to me. She is the older woman, the one with two guards who don't speak."

"Yes, Kerrick and Feamair. They are her children. They haven't spoken in many years."

"Why is that?"

"It is a mystery I suspect only they know. And they are not telling."

Sabine glanced up, and his lips twitched. He strolled back into the warmth of the glade.

"Have you considered the goddess's offer to stay in Alioch? You would never have to bear the blight again. You could find a place here, learn the ways of the forest. I would enjoy your company."

The life she could have stretched out in front of her, full of magic and safety. Such a contradiction from the uncertainty and pain where she came from. And the man standing beside her with such strength and carefulness was so different from all she had known before. Despite everything she had been taught about men, she wondered if there might be reason to hope. She bit her lip.

"Growing up in the slums, I could have never imagined a life like this. It's too amazing to even contemplate." She turned her eyes to his. Up close, she saw shimmers of gold within the dark brown. "But..." She pressed her lips together, knowing what the answer would have to be and not wanting to say it out loud. There were blighted children she could help; she couldn't turn her back on them.

"Sabine." A clear voice piped up across the glade. Anora stood along the path, beaming at her. Sabine waved before remembering Anora couldn't see.

Brannon reached out to take her hand as they started toward the flame-haired girl, stopping her. "You did a great service to Alioch, returning the stolen child. You are owed a boon, I believe."

The heat of his hand on hers sent delicious waves of want rippling over her. Sabine wondered at his power as she stared at where their skin met. "What kind of boon would you give me?" she asked.

Brannon responded with a delighted grin. "We'll have to see where our time leads us." The cock of his eyebrow sent Sabine's imagination running in places it had shied away from for a long time, and despite everything, a slow smile spread over her face.

Anora waited for them, seemingly aware of her surroundings.

Dressed today as the honored daughter of the goddess, she was breathtaking. A crown of golden flowers rested on her head, her copper curls tumbling over her shoulders. She wore leggings with a tunic made of diaphanous webbing that caught the light. It fit her frail body, showing off the delicate line of her collarbone.

Sabine lifted the hem of the tunic, which flowed to Anora's knees. "Anora, is this...spider silk?"

"Yes, the dears worked all night to create this for me. Isn't it lovely? I imagine it is. I've been told they captured the morning dew so it shimmers."

On closer inspection at what she thought were pearls, she saw Anora was right: tiny dewdrops enveloped in spider silk so they would not break. "Incredible."

"You sound so happy, my spirit sister. What has given you such pleasure?"

Sabine shot a look back at Brannon but replied, "It must be this place. Alioch is perfect."

Anora's face rivaled the sunlight. "They are serving the midday meal. Did you even know so much food existed?" She took Sabine's hand, and they traipsed off to the clearing. Brannon stayed at the edge of the crowd, watching them. Something in his troubled look caused Sabine to pause, even as she filled her plate. Alioch did seem idyllic, but could she trust something so perfect?

Novi appeared, butting against Sabine's hand. She looked down, surprised, as it stole a piece of honeyed fruit from her fingers. *The goddess wishes to speak with you.*

Anora glowed at the mention of her mother. Like Brannon, she had no problem understanding Novi's chirruping speech. "May I come too?"

She wishes to speak with Sabine alone. She's waiting at the well.

Anora slumped, and Novi hopped over to her lap, snapping for more pieces of honeyed fruit, distracting the girl from her disappointment as Sabine left them behind.

She hesitated as she approached the well, where The Lady

watched her with her profound emerald gaze. Now would be the time to ask about using the water as an antidote for the blighted children. The goddess seemed more open than the apothecary to sharing the magic solution.

"My lady." Sabine bobbed into a low curtsey as she would at court. The gesture lost something without full skirts, and she stumbled.

The Lady smiled and shook her head. "There's no need for that between us. Please, sit with me."

Sabine perched on the edge of the well, watching the goddess out of the corner of her eye. Being close to The Lady made her feel unstable, like the ground might fall out beneath her feet.

"Something on your mind?" the goddess asked.

"Nothing," she answered immediately.

"Sabine, your thoughts are so loud I can very nearly hear them. What vexes you?"

Uneasy at the thought of demanding the spirit water, she cast about for something else to say. "I was wondering how a person, goddess or not, can live for so long. Doesn't it become unbearable?" She caught her lip in her teeth at her impertinence.

"Do you think me very old?" Her green gaze burrowed into Sabine.

"You must be. But you barely look older than me. It seems all that living must leave a mark, somewhere."

The goddess's smile thinned. "Because I am so ancient, I must appear so?"

"I'm sorry." Sabine stared at her hands. This wasn't going well.

"No need to be sorry. You ask of the burden of immortality, and it is a fair question. The life I live does leave a mark; only it is etched on my soul, not my body."

"I don't understand."

"It is not easy to understand. In truth, I was once as human as you. Certainly more powerful, the greatest mage the land had ever seen." The Lady sighed, staring into the well at the depleted spirit water. "I gained enough power to leave mortality behind."

Sabine stared. "That isn't possible. No mortal can become a god."

The goddess's look was bland, not giving anything away. "And yet, here I am."

"But that means that anyone could be a god."

The Lady waved the thought away with a breezy hand. "Not anyone. It takes a great amount of power to transition to immortality. Very few people could ever gather that much magic in their lifetime."

Sabine stilled. She could think of exactly one person alive who had that much power, or was aiming for it. She wanted to ask more about the making of an immortal, but The Lady tugged gently on one of the locks of hair falling loose down Sabine's back. "You must tell me." The Lady shifted closer, whispering as though they were good friends sharing secrets. "What are your thoughts on our resident warrior?"

"Warrior?" Sabine puzzled over the changing topic, unable to keep up with the goddess's shifting mood.

"Brannon is not shy about his feelings for you."

"Oh." Sabine shook her head. "I do not seek his attention."

"Beautiful women do not need to seek." The goddess's smile was worldly. "A word of advice. Do not cut yourself off from the joy in life just because you have found others to be unworthy."

"I don't think that's at issue at all."

"Think it over," the goddess said, standing. "If there's nothing else you have on your mind—"

"Wait!" Sabine held out her hand to stop her, cringing at her lack of grace. "I had a thought. The spirit water is very powerful, and I thought it could be used to help others as it helped me." She said this all very fast; it was nearly incoherent.

The Lady's gaze darkened. "You wish to make everything better with a magical cure?"

"No," Sabine quickly backtracked. "Not everything, but magic-based problems demand magic-based solutions." Aurich had told her this enough times.

The goddess's sigh was heavy. "I should have known you'd ask for more after I was so generous with you. I cannot hand out the life-giving forces of the well to everyone because there isn't enough. One person's need might be met, but the needs of a kingdom? Impossible. The strength of the magic is flagging, as it is everywhere in the land. I've been putting my own magic into the glade for some time to shore up the defenses, but I worry it won't be enough." Her voice faded to a whisper, and for the briefest moment, she was an ancient crone, stooped and wrinkled from the hardships of the world.

Sabine swallowed hard but needed to push. "But surely if only a little bit was taken, it would be all right. There are so many doomed children in Aporos."

Sabine blinked, and The Lady was back, her smile fixed in place. "This is tiresome. You ask for much and what could you possibly give me in return?"

A flash of blinding green light burst from The Lady. When Sabine could see again, she found she was alone at the well. Her limbs were shaking after facing the disapproval of the goddess. She would not find an ally there in her goal to bring the water back to Aporos.

Her disappointment was crushing, but that wasn't what had Sabine on edge.

The goddess had once been human. Humans could become gods.

Sabine's chest constricted at the thought. Aurich's obsession with growing his power, his ageless face finally made perfect sense. This was what he sought.

He was going to make himself a god.

Hope Springs Eternal

"What are we doing here, Sab?"

Sabine sat next to her brother on the fence that surrounded the training grounds, Rafi still sweating from his last combat session. She turned to him reluctantly. She knew this argument was coming; he was more and more restless in Alioch as each day passed. Novi cawed, then reached over to nuzzle him.

"You've been learning what you can about defense and tactics for the Awhye."

He shook his head. "And I wish I could learn more, but I have to get back. We both do."

"Tonight is their festival of the dead, and we'll celebrate with the Eyanrac, like the goddess wanted." She heaved a loaded sigh.

Rafi groaned. "We can't stay in magical faerie-land forever."

Sabine knew he was right, but a treacherous part of her heart told a different story. In Alioch, every one of her dreams had been answered. It would be easy to ignore the suffering in the outside world. "If I leave, the blight will eventually consume me. And the duke is after me. He won't let me go without a fight."

"You can hide in the Wilt."

She fought back tears. Somehow, she had always known that would be her fate, but it seemed crueler now that she'd experienced life outside their slum. "I can't hide from him forever." Her voice was hoarse.

"Your people need your help. The *Vadovis* chose you for a reason."

Sabine picked at the hem of her tunic. "I didn't ask for it."

Rafi's face flooded with color. "This is so like you. Everything you do is to shirk your responsibilities. First, you fled to the Keep as a maid, then you became an invisible spy, and now you wish to live inside a tree."

"I *never* got a say in it, Rafi." A few heads glanced her way, and she lowered her voice. "I never wanted to become the stalwart champion of an oppressed people. The *Vadovis* chose me, and there were Mama's expectations and your disapproval of me being anything other than a perfect Awhye rebel. It's too much."

"Don't you understand what you mean to your people? To them, you're the Faerie of the Wilt. Children make up rhymes about the lady who passes at night and leaves gifts and food for the starving. And you'd happily forget that to play forest wife to your wildling prince."

Sabine flushed. Brannon had done no more than graze her hand with his, but those brief touches left Sabine struggling to fight her attraction. "That's not fair," she whispered furiously. "I've never encouraged him."

"Oh, I've seen the way you look at him. It's encouragement enough."

She glared. "What about Anora?"

His anger faded to bleakness. "Anora is the daughter of a goddess. She has found her home here, and I am happy to have helped." His face said otherwise. "I understand why you want to stay, Sab. I know it won't be an easy life for you back in Aporos. But a part of me wonders..."

"What?"

He glanced over his shoulder. "Do you get the sense there's something strange about Alioch? As though something is just out of place."

She chewed her lip, struggling to find the words because she had the same uneasy sense as her brother. "I can't put my finger on it, but I know what you mean. Maybe it's because we grew up in a slag-pile slum and have never known contentment."

Rafi paused. "It's not that, although we certainly grew up in a slag-pile slum. There's more to it; things that are left unsaid." He was quiet for a moment. "I've considered asking if Anora would return to Aporos with us." He let out a breath. "It's so stupid."

"It's not stupid to want to keep her with us." Sabine wanted the same thing. "But The Lady would murder you if you tried to take Anora away."

Rafi's eyes rounded, spooked. "That's part of the problem, isn't it? The way the goddess is around her. Like she's a possession that belongs to her only. And she won't even look at me, like I'm beneath her notice."

Sabine twisted her hands in her lap. After the unsettling encounter at the well when she refused to supply her with the spirit water for the blighted children, the goddess avoided her too. Perhaps they were both reaching too high.

Novi crooned a soothing note on her shoulder. "I suppose we don't have a right to it. Nor to Anora, though I wish she could join us."

"That would be asking far too much, two slum rats like us." Rafi elbowed her. "At least we got each other."

Sabine cleared her throat. "Rafi, I know I shouldn't have run away."

Rafi placed his hand over hers. "None of this is fair. I know how much pressure has always been placed on you. But will you truly be satisfied until you step up and take your rightful place with the Awhye?"

"Maybe not." She picked at her fingernail and didn't meet his eyes. "But there's one thing I can do for them. I'm going to steal some of the water."

"What?"

"Keep your voice down," she said, glancing over her shoulder to ensure they weren't overheard. "I'm just going to take a little. I'll bring it to Gregoria. Maybe she can find a way to make it last. I'll sneak away during the festival of the dead tonight. Everyone else will be focused on that."

"What happens if you're caught?" Rafi said.

"I've been thieving for months now."

"You were invisible," he said through gritted teeth. "I would consider that an advantage. Things are different now."

"I have to do something."

"You can't just always take what you want."

"We can't help our people while also abiding by everyone else's rules." Sabine's face blazed with rebellion. "You can't have it both ways. And I won't let those children die. Not if there's something I can do about it."

"You won't be able to come back. Not if they find out."

The risk of what she could lose was all she thought of. Not just access to the life-saving water, but the glade itself, and all the people found here. She'd floated through these past few days in Alioch as if in a dream, eating to her satisfaction, laughing with Anora, and exploring with Brannon. All would be gone if she was caught stealing the spirit water.

She gazed over the training grounds and lost her train of thought. The martial exercises broke up; a space cleared in the middle and Brannon stepped into the circle, no weapons on him, wearing only leather breeches so his powerful muscles were on display. The broad swath of his bare chest gleamed bronze in the light.

She forced herself to close her mouth. No matter how she tried to tell herself she didn't want him, her body betrayed her every time.

Four Eyanrac men went up against Brannon in hand-to-hand combat; he was massive next to them. The sparring began slow, but soon they were a blur of fists and kicks. Brannon had the clear advantage one-on-one, but the Eyanrac warriors worked in tandem, communicating with gestures to work against him. Brannon held his own, pulling back only if a strike might injure.

At one point, Sabine believed he might win against all four when he glanced over and caught sight of her. Her hand flew to her throat at the intensity of his gaze. He paused long enough to allow the Eyanrac to regroup and get his feet out from under him. He fell with a crash on his back and let out a belly laugh.

"I give. It was a fair win." As he stood, dusting off his breeches, he glanced back up at Sabine. "Although when an enchantress appears in our midst, I'm not sure how fair it actually is."

The look he threw her simmered before he was harried by the laughing Eyanrac. One of them slapped him in the shoulder. "All of us have eyes but only one of us ended on his ass." Brannon roared with laughter and winked at her, causing a curl of lust to unspool in her belly. She smiled before she caught herself.

Rafi shook his head. "You're absolutely hopeless."

"Listen, of course I'll return to Aporos. Just let me have one more day of make-believe."

She slipped off the fence as Brannon approached, glistening with sweat. "An astonishing defeat," she said. "I thought you had them."

"They're wily, the Eyanrac, and I'm not as strong as I once was. I hope I didn't shame you. I perform better when not distracted. Perhaps I can show you sometime."

Sabine felt herself flush, and a smile curled over his lips.

"I had hoped you would be here," Brannon said. "Would you walk with me, Lady Sabine?"

"With pleasure."

Rafi snorted behind her, and Sabine made a rude gesture over her shoulder. She would leave tomorrow, but today she would forget everything awaiting her in the slums.

Brannon's hand brushed against hers, his smile open and honest. "Have you given any thought to staying?"

Sabine grimaced. "It's all I think about. If it were just me, then truly I would. But..."

"There are others in your life."

"People I walked away from before. I need to make things right."

"Without the spirit water, your magic will consume you again."

"Yes." She stopped and faced him. Her heart ached because she had already made the decision. "But I don't know if I'll ever feel complete if I forget about where I come from. Does that make sense?"

Brannon stopped, his gaze puzzling over her face. "I am constantly fascinated by humans, the choices they make and how each is so different. How some can be so selfish, while others are so wholly generous. I am unworthy of you, Sabine."

Guilt squirmed inside of her. If he only knew of the theft she was planning. "That's not true."

"When I first saw you, your beauty took my breath away. But it's the beauty in your soul that brings me to my knees."

"If you knew me, you'd know I'm not so good. I am selfish and cowardly." He reached for her, his warm palms on her hips tugging her forward. In a crash of lust, Sabine let him pull her into the circle of his arms. She looked into his fathomless eyes, barely able to put up a protest. "I'm vain as well," she whispered.

"Sabine?" he whispered back.

"Yes?"

"I would like to know you." His lips were only a breath away, and there he waited. The choice was hers.

It would make leaving tomorrow infinitely harder. Sabine hesitated, his sweet breath on her cheek, then closed the space between them.

She chose the faerie tale, if only for one day. Perhaps she would never again feel the way she did about Brannon, and she could not let the opportunity pass her by.

His lips were soft and warm and moved with certainty over hers. His arms tightened around her, groaning as he gathered her close. Her breasts pressed against his muscle-bound chest as she deepened their kiss, opening her mouth for him. The brush of lips became rough and urgent as they wrapped themselves around each other.

Brannon tasted of woodsmoke and honey and the sweat that had dripped down his skin while he fought. His hand ran up her spine to take her neck, holding her in place, and Sabine's knees nearly gave out. She could dissolve right into him, lost in the pleasure of his strong arms holding her upright.

"I wish we had more time," he said into her hair before nipping at her ear lobe.

Sabine stifled a gasp and buried her fingers into his unbound hair as he trailed kisses down her neck. "Could you come to Aporos?"

At her words, he stilled. Sabine whimpered as he lifted his head away from hers. Sorrow lined his face. "Ah, my lovely, I wish it were possible. But there are limits to where I may go, and there are places I cannot step foot."

"You can't enter the city?"

"No." He bowed his head. "For all that I am, there is so much I am not, and I must remain in the wild places. What I wouldn't give to be your man, standing at your right hand as you lead your people to a better life. But I would not be able to protect you, not in Aporos."

"If I have to return to Aporos, and you can never go there, then what does that make us?"

"Cursed." The harsh voice interrupted them, and Sabine flew out of Brannon's arm with a gasp.

Idona, the apothecary, stood watching them, arms crossed. Her crinkled face puckered with disapproval. "Brannon. Always trying to be something you're not."

Brannon's face darkened. "Wise woman, I have great respect for you, but I will not be told how to live my life."

"You still think of yourself as living after all this time? Hope springs eternal, I suppose. A curse in itself, hope."

He glowered as though he would argue with her.

"Don't you have somewhere to be?" the woman snapped. "It's nearly sunset."

Brannon looked to the sky. "Blazes. Sabine, I have to go. There's so much I wish I could tell you, but..."

"Let the poor girl be and prepare yourself."

He ignored the woman and lowered his mouth to Sabine's ear, speaking low and fast. "I feel as though everything has changed, but I suppose nothing has. Please remember, despite what you see tonight, I have meant every word I said. I've often wished that things could be different, that *I* could be different, but never more than now. You may feel differently after."

"But wait..." Sabine tried to pull him back. "I don't understand. Isn't there a way we could meet in the middle?"

He gave a swift grin, and his lips grazed over hers, sharp and fleeting. "Hope springs eternal," he whispered, and then he was gone, already heading toward the glade.

"You're a fool," the apothecary said to her. It was the first time Sabine had seen the woman without her guards, her mute children.

"And you are cruel." Sabine whirled on the old woman, determined not to be cowed.

"Life is cruel," she said. "Come, I wish to speak with you."

Sabine had half a mind to refuse, but the old lady was heading to her Rukha apothecary workshop, and curiosity won out.

She stepped into the Dikisi Forest and shivered against the chill that met her there. Idona ducked under a crack in the bark of the Rukha, and Sabine followed, finding herself in a mage's lair. The walls were thick with roots and vines, and from these dangled pots, dried herbs and vegetables. Branches were lined with glass flasks and vials filled with rainbow-colored liquids. Sheaves of thin bark were strewn across a table, covered with markings. Near the back wall, a fire crackled within a stone circle, a copper cauldron simmering on top. The air was thick with smoke and magic.

"This is incredible," she whispered.

The apothecary let out a raspy chuckle. "I still practice the Old Ways here."

"I see that." Sabine ran an idle finger along a cluttered countertop. "Do you use spirit water in any of these potions?"

Idona gave her a sly look. "Interested in herbalism?"

"A little. I used to train under the *Vadovis* in Aporos."

Idona snorted but reached into a cupboard to pull out a jar of green ointment. She opened it for Sabine to inspect. "This salve contains some of the water. It is useful on the battlefield; it heals wounds with great speed."

As the sharp, earthy smell hit her senses, Sabine recognized it immediately. She had used it to heal Aurich's burns. "I know this."

"Unlikely. I make this salve myself, and the ingredients can only be found in Alioch."

Sabine's thoughts raced. "Are we the first outsiders to come to the glade?"

Idona's gaze turned sharp. "It is a rarity, as Alioch bears strong protections. You must know what you are looking for to find it. But every so often, an outsider finds their way here." Her expression darkened. "Taking our riches as though they belonged to them."

Sabine pressed her lips shut. She would receive no support from the cantankerous apothecary in securing the healing water.

"Come now, let me look at you. Let's see how that curse is

faring in your veins." Idona hobbled over to her, arms lifted, and after an uncertain moment, Sabine crouched for her to place her withered hands on either side of her face. "Hmm, yes. The blight has been pushed back, for the time being. But the so-called goddess does not help you further. She could, you know. She could teach you how to control your magic, letting it out slowly to ensure you would never be consumed. Why do you think she does not?"

"Who am I to ask for a goddess's help?"

"Why not you? You were the savior of her daughter. Unless, of course, the goddess does not wish for you to be saved. Perhaps you are inconvenient."

Outside, Novi cried in the forest, a warning. Sabine's heart sped up. Idona glanced up at the sound, and her crafty look shifted to something like worry. "The goddess has not shown you all of her faces. You cannot trust her." Her voice dropped to a whisper. "Keep your eyes open from here on out. I cannot see what the coming days will bring."

Sabine took a stumbling step away from the apothecary, then another, fleeing the magic of the workshop.

The Festival of the Dead

Sabine tried to shake off the dread that followed her since her conversation with Idona. Who could she trust?

She dressed carefully for the festival of the dead in a clean tunic and leggings. Novi curled around her shoulder, the only ornament she needed.

Rafi waited for her outside. He had shaved the side of his head and braided his hair back. Sabine caught her breath, distracted from her worry.

"Rafi, you look just like a warrior from the old stories."

Rafi blushed, bringing out his boyishness. "I wanted to look nice. You know. To say goodbye."

Sabine swallowed hard. "Let's make this a night to remember."

The sun had set as they walked into the darkness, following others to the gathering place. A tense silence filled the air, the heaviness of great ritual. Anticipation hummed over her skin, the buzz before the rush to come. The sun had fallen beyond the line of darkened trees.

"Remind me what this feast is for?" Rafi whispered.

Anora had explained the ancient celebration to her. "To honor the transition from living to dead. I believe there's a ceremony symbolizing the passing of those who died the year before, and the god of death presides."

"I'm hoping that's symbolic as well?"

Novi squawked, cuddling closer to Sabine. Sabine brushed a soothing hand over the Ielzrie's neck. It could feel her nerves, the anticipation and dread that grew inside Sabine.

A crowd gathered in the central clearing. Above the heads of the revelers hung glowing balls of silver witch light, warming the chilly autumn evening. They floated like captured starlight. Sabine stopped short of the pool of light they created.

"I'll meet you soon," she said to Rafi.

He rubbed the back of his neck, forehead wrinkling. "Are you sure about this?"

"Cover for me. It will only take a moment."

Clenching his jaw, he nodded, and Sabine fell behind. Moving serenely to not raise suspicions, she left the crowd for the darkened gardens that surrounded the well.

Rafi was right; thievery was more difficult when people could see you. She was alone, but it felt as though eyes followed her as she crouched at the lip of the well. The water shone with its own shimmering light.

"Am I doing the right thing?"

Only you can answer that. Novi curled closer around her like a hug. Sabine nodded, decided, and dipped a hollow gourd she'd brought into the water.

When she withdrew, the reflections in the water rippled, forming itself into the glowering face of The Lady.

Gasping, Sabine stumbled back, away from the accusing stare. She sprawled over the cobblestones, panting. She should've known she couldn't steal from a goddess.

It was Novi's cry that got her moving again. *You can't stay here.*

Sabine scrambled to her feet and rushed away, putting as much distance between herself and the well as she could. As she rejoined the last of the stragglers entering the clearing, she tucked the gourd into her pocket. If she was going to be kicked out of Alioch in disgrace tonight, she might as well keep what she had risked everything for.

Sabine rejoined Rafi, nodding at his questioning gaze. Her stomach plummeted when she spied The Lady standing at the front of the crowd with a group of black-robed Eyanrac. Would she call her out right here?

Tonight, the goddess appeared as a crone. She clung to a walking stick with gnarled hands, her back twisted and warped, her hair tattered and gray. Only her eyes remained the same in her wrinkled face, clear and shining green, matched by the Chalice of Life emerald that sparkled at her sunken chest.

One by one, the Eyanrac approached, bowing to her. It would be too conspicuous to avoid it, so Sabine filed into line, determined to brazen it out. She wasn't going to hide.

As she reached the front, Sabine bowed low to the goddess. The crone bowed in return, but she never broke eye contact. Her smile seemed mocking, and Sabine sweated, waiting to be denounced. Instead, The Lady turned to the next worshipper in the solemn line.

On the other side of the clearing, watching them avidly, stood Idona, also wearing long black robes. Kerrick and Feamair stood behind her, eyes darting over the crowds as they guarded her.

The old lady warns you not to turn your back on The Lady, Novi chittered.

"You can hear her thoughts?"

As though she is speaking them plainly. Sabine gave a shiver that had nothing to do with the cold. Idona had warned her she had not seen all of the goddess's faces.

"Sabine!" Anora's voice rang across the clearing, and her friend came tripping over the grass. She looked every inch a goddess in her own right. The spiders had outdone themselves, and she wore a full gown of sparkling silver that floated in the slightest breeze. Her copper hair was woven with silvered flowers.

"Anora, you look incredible. How did you know we were here?"

"Sister, I always know where you are." Anora kissed her cheek.

Rafi had been rendered speechless, and Sabine nudged him with her elbow. "Say hello."

"Anora," Rafi finally managed, taking her hand. She squeezed his back.

"I suspect you are very handsome tonight. Come, let us find a good place to watch. The ceremony of the dead is about to begin." Her voice dropped to a whisper as an expectant hush fell over the crowd. People gathered in the clearing, leaving a wide aisle.

Determined to brazen things out as much as she could, Sabine followed Anora to the center of the grove, where a large bonfire was prepared but not lit. She craned her neck, searching for Brannon.

"You won't find him here," Anora whispered. "He'll be along later."

"How do you know everything?"

Anora laughed, and a few people glanced at her in reproach. The proceedings were about to commence.

The Lady brought her hands up in supplication and the bonfire flared to life. The nearby crowd retreated from the searing heat.

The goddess began to sing, her croaky voice suited to the occasion. The Eyanrac chanted alongside her, a groaning sound ripped from their throats. It was chilling, a prayer and an invocation of something all-encompassing.

The voices rose to a crescendo and a disturbance in the air formed at the far side of the clearing, like dark sparks moving in an intricate pattern. The Eyanrac bowed to the movement.

That's when he appeared, lit by the flickering bonfire. She had never seen Brannon like this. His skin was coated with silver paint. He wore black around his eyes and cheeks, and antlers in his hair, which was now raven black.

A steady drumbeat sounded from beyond the crowd. It pounded in Sabine's pulse. Power emanated from Brannon, passing over them in waves. Some of the Eyanrac knelt as he brought his hands up and joined in the chant. His voice was inhumanly low. The light flickered, and he changed, expanding, becoming the embodiment of death.

Sabine fell to her knees as well. A wind howled through the clearing, sending a shower of bonfire sparks into the air. On that wind were voices, whispers and pleas and laughter, and her skin rippled. She bowed her head as the voices passed, sending out a prayer of goodwill to them.

The passing of the living to the dead was not symbolic but very real. The souls of the dead paraded past them tonight, led by Brannon—who was not Brannon. The laden wind twirled around his raised arms, before soaring toward the starlit heavens.

Drums began to beat, their rhythm complementing the chant, then stringed instruments played. The music rose and leaped as the voices died away and the wind swept into the ether. The heaviness lifted, and Sabine was filled with jubilation. The air was imbued with magic, and she floated to her feet.

Others moved to the beat of the drum, and Sabine needed no further invitation. She felt as she had at *Toamna*, as if all the light and magic that existed were found underneath her breastbone.

Rafi spun Anora into his arms, and they whirled in time to the beat. Anora leaned in and pressed her lips to his. Rafi stopped so abruptly she spun away, and he had to scramble to pull her back to his chest, laughing.

"Keeping yourself busy tonight?" a creaky voice said behind her. Sabine twisted to face the goddess-crone. Though her instincts told her to flee, Sabine continued to dance, even as she swept a bow to her.

"Another one of your faces, my lady?"

The Lady let out a bark of laughter. "I suppose I have many. As do you, it seems." Her seamed face gave an exaggerated wink.

Chilled, Sabine watched her move away through the crowd, wondering what she had planned.

But a lick of heat at the edge of her senses caught her attention. Without thinking, Sabine spun toward it to see Brannon stalking through the crowd. The Eyanrac bowed their heads as he passed and murmured words of prayer as he held a hand over them. His eyes caught hers, and they were black as onyx. They gleamed in a way that sent a heavy shudder of anticipation through her limbs. She wet her lips, but he still did not come to her.

The music spun sharply upward into a reeling song that would not be denied. Sabine stopped thinking and allowed the rhythm to take over.

She raised her arms to the stars as she danced, and they responded. A cape of glimmering light settled over her shoulders, stars nestling in her black hair, as though she was the night sky itself.

People cried out in awe as silvered light streamed from her, bursting into the sky. The whole forest was lit with the glow of magic. Sabine let out a wild cry of joy.

Then Brannon stood in front of her as if witnessing her power and held out his hands. Slowly, provocatively, she took the invitation, and he swept her into his arms, taking up the dance.

One strong arm gripped her waist as they spun and spun again. She couldn't look away from his face, his glittering coal-black eyes. A garland of holly was woven around his antlers. A wind whipped around the two of them, pressing them tightly together.

Helpless to their dance, it whirled her away in a crash of heat. She didn't know how this would work or even what Brannon was. But as she spiraled through a veil of stars, she knew with absolute certainty that he was what she wanted. She didn't pause to think.

Lifting her face, she ran her hand down his neck, pulling him to her. Desire threatened to consume her. Their lips met as they claimed each other. He held her fast as his mouth moved over hers, warm and firm. She wrapped around him, wanting to feel every inch of him against her. More. She needed more. She could explode from the heat that erupted between them.

The wind changed, and the world shifted again. For one last moment, Sabine and Brannon were spellbound in each other. Then someone screamed.

Fire Storm

The wizened Lady pointed to the sky with a gnarled finger, her eyes bulging. "It cannot be."

A hot gust of air blasted through the glade, and Novi came screeching into Sabine's arms.

Fire. It's coming.

Sabine looked to Brannon in panic, and he released her as they turned to the crowd.

"Take cover," Sabine cried.

People bawled in terror as the sky exploded. Ember-orange clouds formed, bubbling like a cauldron brew. A churning ball of fire whipped into a cyclone above them, forming a funnel that descended toward the glade.

A pleading voice cried out. Sabine's hair lashed into her face; it was nearly impossible to see. She stumbled into the stinging wind toward the sound.

It was Anora, arms flung out, eyes wide open. Hot ash blew into her face, and she shrieked.

Rafi was there first, folding her into his arms, his words lost in the roar of the wind. Anora curled her face into his shoulder, shaking.

The funnel touched the ground, and the fire roared in earnest. All around her, people were caught in the spiral of flames, wailing in the scorching currents of air.

The heat was unbearable. Sweat dripped down Sabine's face. She was paralyzed by the destruction.

Novi bit her neck. *Do something.*

Her feet moved again at her Ielzrie's command. Two Sabaghs fled on short legs, and she ran over to pick them up. They were heavy like boulders, but she crashed forward, getting them to the relative safety of the Rukhas.

The goddess rushed into the gardens. She reached her hands up, and a plume of water lifted out of the well, answering her call. It spread out like a glittering cage, holding back the fire. Cool mist drifted over them, and Sabine could see across the clearing.

Idona was at the center of the destruction, directing others to gather the injured under the shelter of a Rukha. Rows of people stretched out, groaning in pain. Sabine rushed forward to help an elderly Eyanrac whose skin boiled from a burn.

Returning to the battlefield, Sabine let out a horrified gasp. The water cage had contracted until the cooling sparkles were just over their heads. Beyond it, the fire boiled and raged. The goddess was pale, waning, her effort to keep the water shield intact fading.

Then she heard it: a chuckle sounded from the center of the fire. She would know it anywhere.

"Aurich," she whispered.

The Lady screamed in fury. She thrust her hands upward, and for a moment, the water cage expanded and pushed the fire back.

Then it tore like a net stretched too thin and collapsed. The blaze whirled over them, comets of flame crashing into the ground. One fireball hurtled directly for her.

"Sabine!" a booming voice called out. She turned to see Brannon racing the comet toward her.

He grabbed her, throwing her to the side at the last instant. She landed hard on the ground, winded by the impact. Time stood still as the fireball careened through the sky and hit Brannon straight in the back.

The blast of the explosion threw across the clearing, her head striking a stone. She couldn't move, dazed by the impact. She stared up into the clouds of fire above her. From through the curls of licking flames, Aurich's form took shape, gloating above her.

"You cannot hide from me. I will always find you."

She shut her eyes, shuddering, blocking the nightmare fire creature reaching for her. She would burn; this was the end. Novi butted its head against hers, pleading for her to get up. Sabine cuddled the Ielzrie to her chest, protecting it with her body. There was no shelter from this storm.

Then, in a breath, it was over. The fire clouds bubbled away, and the whirling wind stopped as suddenly as it started. Silence descended over the glade; only the crackling of burning trees broke the thick silence.

Sabine battled to sit up, running her hands over Novi to ensure the Ielzrie had not been injured. Tears streamed down her face as she dragged herself toward the smoldering crater where Brannon had saved her.

He sprawled on the baked ground, his body charred and blackened. His eyes stared into the sky, and he panted as though he couldn't get enough air. He was still dressed as a god, black hair and antlers, all the more horrifying as his skin was burned away.

"No," Sabine whispered, crawling to him.

Someone howled. Her thoughts disjointed; Sabine glanced over to see The Lady of the Forest lying crumpled on the ground.

Two Eyanrac warriors hurtled over to retrieve The Lady. She stirred. "The water," she said through parched lips. "It will heal much of what has been harmed."

The water. Sabine rose, fueled by desperation, limping toward the well. But a wail went up from where she approached, and she didn't get far before she could see the true catastrophe for what it was.

The well was empty; the spirit water gone. The Eyanrac knelt around the edge of the barren hole, keening.

But there was still the water she had stolen. Sabine stumbled back to Brannon's side. She found him sitting up, coughs ripping through him.

"What are you doing?" Sabine guided him back down with gentle hands. His muscles tensed, but then he relaxed and allowed himself to lay back.

"Lady Sabine. Have you come to tend to me?" He gave a weak smile.

"I don't understand. This was much worse." Her hands ran over the smooth, undamaged skin of his chest. "You were burned." Sabine started sobbing.

He caught her hands. "Sabine, I'm okay."

"I thought you were going to die." Her voice caught in her throat as he wound his arms around her, pulling her close. "Do you know how terrifying you looked? Your skin was gone. Here, drink this." She thrust the gourd of stolen water at him.

"I don't need it."

Her eyes flashed as she forced the cup into his hands. "I risked everything for this, so drink."

"Share some with me," he said, obediently taking a sip, then handing it to her.

She allowed herself only a drop. As the soothing liquid trickled down her throat, her sobs subsided. The magic spread through her again, though it didn't fill her with joy as before. There was too much chaos and grief; it was too much to take it. She wished she could block it out.

"Are you steady?" Brannon asked. A gentle hand ran down her cheek.

She hiccupped. "I thought I was done. You saved me." She met his eyes. They were still black as night.

He brushed her hair over her shoulder, his hand lingering on her skin. "I would do anything for you."

Sabine reached for his face, trembling with relief. She tugged strands of prickly holly from his hair. She reached for the antlers and felt where they grew from his head, very real. She pulled away.

"You have antlers."

His black eyes met hers. "Sometimes," he said solemnly.

She brushed her hand against his skin. The glowing silver didn't rub off because it wasn't paint. "You're a..." She trailed off as the enormity of it hit her. Not symbolic at all. "The actual god of death?"

"Is it too much?"

She let out a disbelieving huff. "If you are *death*, then we... nothing between us could be real."

His hands tightened on her arms. "It is real. All of it."

His eyes were impenetrable. Hesitant, Sabine leaned forward, pressing her lips against his, tasting him again. He was woodsmoke and honey, but now also something darker, earth and overripe fruit. But the want, the pull between them, was as strong as ever. It took all her strength to push herself back.

"Sabine..." His voice cracked.

"I must go. I can help." At his questioning look, she gave a helpless shrug. "Give me some time."

He helped her to her feet. "I meant what I said. I would do anything for you."

Sabine could only nod. On unsteady feet, she hurried to the center of the clearing, taking in her surroundings. The Lady of the Forest had been moved into her Rukha, but so many others lay in rows, exposed to the night air.

Novi swooped down to join her. *Are you okay?*

"No. I can't think straight."

Sabine tried to imagine the *Vadovis's* counsel. The wise woman would direct her to those worst wounded. Others were tending to the injured with the healing green salve. So many hurt, and there was so little spirit water. She shook her head sadly at the Awhye children she would not be able to save, but one by one, she attended those on the brink of death, allowing no more than a few drops. The effects of the water were immediate. For those who were unconscious, she spread the liquid along their lips until they stirred and breathed easier.

But nothing brought back the dead. Dozens of Eyanrac and Sabagh had succumbed to their injuries.

As she worked, Sabine kept an eye out for Rafi or Anora. They were not in the line of wounded nor the line of the dead, but she hadn't seen either of them since Rafi fled the clearing with Anora in his arms. As every minute passed, her anxiety rose.

When those around her were stable and the last of the magical water had been spent, Sabine stood on shaking legs, determined to find them, when a heartbroken moan sounded over the crying of the others. Sabine sprinted toward the sound near the apothecary.

Feamair was on her knees, wailing up to the sky.

The sound coming from Feamair's throat was raw and impossible; it hurt to hear it. Even before she arrived, Sabine knew who she would find broken on the ground.

Idona had been hit directly by a fireball. Feamair was half-collapsed over her body as though to shield it. Sabine bowed her head, turning away.

She heard her brother's voice calling for her in the glade and she ran toward his voice, frantic to lay eyes on him.

"Rafi?" she answered. "Anora?"

They were both there in the clearing, whole but despondent, their arms around each other. Anora reached out at the sound of Sabine's voice, finding her outstretched arms and embracing her.

"I am happy you are alive, sister," she whispered. "I do not know what we would have done without you."

Rafi joined them, embracing them at the same time.

"I was so worried I'd lost you both," Sabine said.

"I ran into the forest, and kept on running," Rafi said. "I'd probably still be running if Anora hadn't ordered me to come back."

"I had a vision and couldn't escape it." Anora's white eyes were wide, the skin around them strained and darkened with shadows. "It wasn't until we were deep inside the Dikisi Forest I could come back to myself."

"What did you see?" But the girl only shook her head, visibly trembling, and pressed her lips together until they were bloodless.

Kerrick sprinted past them, to find his sister grieving at their mother's side. Sabine's heart cracked for the open pain carved into his face. He knelt next to Feamair, and together they broke down.

"Come away," Anora said, pulling Rafi and Sabine toward the edge of the glade. There, they found Brannon shoveling as though his life depended on it.

His antlers were gone, his skin no longer black and silver. Instead, he was Brannon, with flaming hair and bronze skin and chestnut eyes glittering with rage.

Sabine halted as she realized he was digging graves. "So much death," she whispered. "How will they rebuild?"

"More importantly, who did it?" Rafi asked, fiery heat in his voice.

Brannon climbed out of the hole he dug when he spotted Sabine. "I would also like to know who dared send cursed fire here."

"Duke Aurich." Sabine's voice was flat, numb.

Rafi spun. "Why? I'd believe it of him, but what does he get out of destroying the glade?"

Guilt crushed Sabine's chest. Had he done this to get at her?

Anora must have thought along similar lines. "What if he was still trying to find me?"

"This isn't your fault," Brannon said, placing his large hand over her delicate shoulder. "The fault lies entirely at the feet of the man who attacked, this Duke Aurich. I will hunt him down and kill him."

"Not if I kill him first," Sabine said. The thought sparkled in front of her, hard and shimmery. Something profound rose inside of her as she realized she wanted to be the one to track him down. To be free of him; to ensure he couldn't hurt anyone else.

Brannon's death magic hovered near. As their gazes met, his eyes flickered black again, and he nodded, approving.

An Eyanrac warrior approached. "The Lady of the Forest wishes to see you," he said to Anora, then nodded to Sabine and Rafi. "As well as the Gillesellas."

"Is my mother well?"

The warrior didn't answer the question. "She has requested your presence."

The Quest

Sabine hesitated, then held out a hand to Brannon. "Come with me?"

His furious look broke apart, leaving behind a vulnerability as he took her hand. He felt human under her palm as they were led to the goddess's Rukha, and gave her a reassuring squeeze. Novi nuzzled close under her hair, vibrating comfort.

Despite her injuries, The Lady of the Forest sat on a root throne in her crone guise. Her exposed skin was charred and seeping.

"What do you know?" she asked without preamble. Even in her injured state, her voice rumbled with power.

Sabine's knees threatened to collapse. Instead, she stepped forward, bowing her head. "I am certain this attack was by Duke Aurich. He is a powerful fire mage."

"Did you call him? The attack occurred after you sent great lights up into the air. A beacon?"

Alarm flooded through her. "I would never. The lights were unconnected." Her heart sank. Had she signaled Aurich without knowing? "But he seeks me."

"Why would such a man seek you?"

"I worked for him." Sabine's voice was tiny as The Lady's piercing eyes pinned her in place. "I belong to him; that's how he views it. He's not the kind of man you walk away from."

"This isn't Sabine's fault," Anora said. "The duke murders children and consumes their power. She saved me from a fate worse than death at his hands. I don't know how the duke found us, but it wasn't her."

Horror crashed over Sabine as she stared at Anora's bone-white face and finally believed her: Duke Aurich was entirely capable of murdering the magelings of Aporos, taking their power in his bid to become immortal. Is that what he was doing with the children?

A long moment stretched between them. Finally, The Lady gave a sharp nod. "I know of this fire mage. He passed through the glade when he was a young man. He was bringing his sister to be presented at the Illyamor court."

"Queen Liesl."

"She was a slip of a girl when she arrived, no more than a lamb."

Sabine thought of the queen's fire. "Perhaps the lamb grew up to have some teeth."

The Lady raised an eyebrow and coughed. "Perhaps. Most lambs are led to slaughter. Better to be a wolf, I say. Of her brother, I was aware of his ascension in power, but I never believed he would dare attack me in my sanctuary."

Her head lolled to the side. "Many things are converging." The goddess's breath rattled in her chest. "Every year, there is less magic, and the natural world bears less power. And now the spirit water has dried up. I fear this spells the end of everything."

"How can this be?"

"Magic has fallen out of balance. The land is barren, the water is poisoned, and the trees are dying."

"There must be something we can do." Sabine glanced at her companions. "This cannot be the end."

"I fear it is." Anora's sweet voice was dark with sorrow. "This night I have seen visions that portend...horror."

Her mother's sigh was heavy with centuries of care. "We need guidance. I cannot leave Alioch, weakened as I am. My daughter will go in my place. She must confer with the Oracles."

"The Oracles?" Sabine had not been expecting that. The Oracles were three girls who lived in the woods next to a divine pool. They ate mushrooms and danced in the moonlight and told prophetic riddles to passersby. Men sought them out to find their fortunes. More often than not, the men didn't return, victims of the Dikisi Forest.

Those who did return, though, were shaken by what they heard.

A strange wind howled through the Rukha. Outside, it rattled the branches, dried leaves flying away in a flurry of color.

"Yes, I will go in your place, Mother," Anora said.

"Are you sure you can handle the journey?" Rafi moved forward to take Anora's arm.

"Did I not lead you through the forest safely?" Her delicate brows furrowed. "I saved you from hideous death. You both would have been lost without me. I am not so frail as I seem." Anora sniffed.

"I didn't mean to offend you." Rafi bowed his head. "I'll follow you if you have to go."

"I must." Anora's face clouded. "Mother is right; the Oracles may clarify matters."

The goddess sank further into her throne. "They will show you the way. They will help us in our fight against the fire mage." Her eyes were hollow and staring. She raised a shaky finger to Sabine.

"Follow my daughter. Seek these answers, little thief, and you may find everything you have ever sought."

Sabine raised her chin. "When do we leave?"

Brannon released Sabine's hand and knelt at The Lady's feet.

"My lady, I'll lend these humans my strength, for their journey is long and perilous."

Despite her injuries, The Lady looked amused, pursing her withered lips. "Really, my Green Knight? It's been a long time since you've meddled in human affairs."

"The cause is worthy, my lady. It's been many centuries since a divine child has roamed the forest."

The goddess's crystal green eyes flicked to Sabine. "And the rewards are worthwhile, are they not?"

Brannon tensed but did not respond.

"You are not mine to command. But the winter solstice approaches."

"Aye, my lady." His tone was clipped. "There is no need to remind me of what I know in my bones."

"Do as you must, then," she said. "Now, I wish to speak to Sabine alone."

Sabine watched the others go, stroking Novi's neck. When she turned back to the goddess, she gasped. In those seconds, she had diminished even more; her wrinkled skin collapsed around her shriveled body.

"Lady," Sabine whispered.

"I am still here, for now," The Lady said, eyes flicking open.

"You never denounced me, for taking the water."

The Lady struggled to sit up. "What you did earlier this evening bears no consequence on what must happen now. It doesn't matter; the spirit water is gone. I know you have good intentions, girl. I'm the last person to be—" She choked on her words. Her skeletal hand reached out and Sabine took it; the goddess pulled her forward with surprising strength.

"There is something important I must tell you." Her voice was low and hoarse from the smoke. "You must listen, though I know you do not trust me. It's about the duke. I wanted someone to know in case I..." The Lady wheezed, her face creased with pain, then cleared her throat and braced herself.

"Powerful forces are at work. The duke stayed at Alioch for a season, learning of our magic. In the end, the subtle energies of the earth did not hold his attention for long. But he knows of this place.

"He was young and powerful and hungry for knowledge. I understood his longing because I was that way once. He was full of ideas of how the world could be shaped by his hand. He longed to prove himself; however, the only task he was given was to deliver his pretty little sister to a faraway court. He made the most of it, though, didn't he?" She jerked her ancient head. "I fear his power strengthens every day as mine weakens. You must...fight. No matter what happens."

"I will."

The Lady shook her head, convulsing. "There is so much you don't understand. You no longer have the crutch of the spirit water. You must learn to control your magic. Listen to Anora; her wisdom is as deep as the earth itself; she can teach you all you need to know. But in the end, it will be you." Her gnarled finger lifted and rested on Sabine's chest. "Trust your instincts, child. You must stand when all others have fallen."

Her eyes fluttered closed. The guards nearby rushed forward to tend to her.

Sabine backed away from the goddess's still form.

Brannon waited for her outside the Rukha. Her heart leaped when she saw him. The knowledge of what he was, a god, was too large for her to deal with right now, so she didn't. Instead, she stepped into his outstretched arms, allowing him to pull her in close as she pretended he was a man.

"What did the goddess have to say?" His eyes were stormy, flickering between forest chestnut and deathly onyx.

"I must learn my powers," Sabine said. "I need to be able to stand up to Aurich." For a moment, the idea overwhelmed her, and she buried her face in the fabric at his shoulder.

"Then I will be with you, shoulder to shoulder," he said into her hair.

Sabine smiled up into his beautiful face. But there was a shadow of doubt in her heart. The Lady had said all others would fall. But surely the god of death could not fall? "It won't be safe," she said.

His arms tightened around her. "I'll be next to you, no matter what." She allowed his warmth to seep into her, lending her strength.

"I'm going to tend the wounded," Sabine said. "Without their healer, they'll need more hands."

"Sabine, don't wear yourself out. We'll need your strength for the journey."

"I'm strong enough for this." She reached up to graze a kiss over his cheek before marching across the smoldering glade to the apothecary, determined to do something good.

This quest they had been sent on did not sit right with her, although it seemed to give her everything she wanted. She had been given a stay from returning to the slums and Brannon would be at her side. The goddess told her she could learn to control her powers, and together, they could help save the dying magical world.

But she didn't trust The Lady, something the goddess herself had acknowledged. Uncertainty prickled at her as though there was something else at play she had overlooked.

Soon, though, there was no time to think. There was no more miraculous water, but many burns to treat. The following hours passed in a blur, spreading salves over wounds, wrapping spider silk around limbs, administering Rukha sap to those able to drink. Sabine toiled at the Eyanracs' sides as they grieved.

Feamair, Idona's daughter, joined her. Her eyes were red-rimmed, and she stared hard ahead when Sabine offered her condolences. So, instead, Sabine handed her some bandages.

They worked through the night, Sabine occasionally sipping

on Rukha sap to wet her parched throat. When the sunlight peeked over the edge of the forest, she wondered when she'd last eaten but was quickly distracted by a crying child. As she took the Eyanrac boy in her arms, Novi took off from her shoulders.

She tended the little one, who cried when the salve spread over his burn, then gave a coo of satisfaction at the cooling sensation.

Sabine sat back on her heels, wiping sweat from her forehead. The sky was buzzing. She searched the air for insects, seeing only sparkling lights.

Only it wasn't the sky; the buzzing was in her head. The earth swooped up toward her as she collapsed.

A strong arm was there to catch her before she hit the ground.

Brannon scooped her against his chest as though she weighed nothing at all, face creased with worry. He faded in and out of view.

Novi settled on his shoulder, peering at Sabine. *You were overdoing it.*

"I told you not to wear yourself out." Brannon's voice was gentle.

"They suffer." Her voice was a rasp.

"You'll help no one in a heap on the ground."

"But who will care for them?"

"I will. I promise to watch over them if you promise to rest."

Sabine nodded, her stomach bottoming out as she did so. "Oh" was all she could say as Brannon carried her across the ruined glade.

All around her was devastation, burned-out gardens and groaning victims. The Rukhas closest to the clearing had been incinerated. Brannon brought her away from the devastation, into the great Rukha, where beds of moss now covered the ground for burn victims. He laid her down with gentle hands.

This was the god of death tending to her with such tenderness, though he felt like a man. She reached into the pocket of her tunic, where she kept her tapestry. It had become her comfort, and she sought that security in her confusion.

When her hand came up empty, she let out a cry of disappointment.

"What is it?" Brannon asked, kneeling at her side.

"My weaving. It's gone." After the whole horrible night, it was that which caused Sabine to crumble. She blinked back tears because the weaving had felt like a piece of herself.

"This weaving was precious to you?"

"When I was invisible, it was a reminder that I was still here. It showed me what would come, what to do. Without it..."

"Whether or not you see this tapestry, you are still here. A person in her own right, able to make her own choices."

Sabine's snort was bitter. "I make terrible choices, Brannon. I shouldn't be allowed."

"Don't be ridiculous." He pressed his lips to her forehead. A swirl of warmth spread from his kiss. "People make choices in their lives. We may not understand the consequences until later, but that doesn't mean we stop choosing." He paused. "You truly believe binding yourself to a fortune-telling piece of fabric will help you be a better person?"

Sabine was silent for a long time. "Yes?"

Brannon chuckled. "It's difficult to determine the outcome of your actions. Life is more complicated than that. You did not attack Alioch; that was the fire mage. Your choice is to fight back." He leaned over and pressed a kiss to each eyebrow, feather soft.

"Yes." Sabine's eyelids were very heavy.

"Your defiance is more powerful than you can imagine. Nothing in life is certain. No one can tell the future."

"Anora can."

Brannon shook his head. "She sees visions. But visions are never set in stone. All action results from the choices we make."

"Do we not go to seek our fortune?" Her eyes shut of their own accord.

"We seek guidance. But we'll choose what we do from there. It will be our resolve to stand up to evil that matters in the end."

"Are you real?" she whispered. His lips brushed hers before she drifted off.

"Rest, so tomorrow you can change your destiny."

Vargas

Sabine blinked, stretching in the comfortable moss. People flitted near the foot of her cot, and through half-opened eyes, she made out Rafi and Anora, both gilded by the sunshine. Despite everything that had happened, she sent up a prayer of thanks they were safe.

Curled up against Sabine's side, Novi crept to press its face against hers as her eyelids fluttered open. *You slept a long time, but you feel stronger now.*

Sabine stroked Novi's head. "Thank you for taking care of me."

Anora approached her bedside. "How do you feel?"

"Better," Sabine said, and coughed, her throat dry as ash.

"Please, may we have some sap?" Anora called, and an Eyanrac guard came forward.

Sabine struggled upright, her body peppered with aches and pains. At her greedy sip of the green liquid, energy flowed through her, and she could move with more ease. She took a deep breath and tried speaking again.

"How long have I been sleeping?"

"Through the day and night. The sun has only just risen. You needed the rest."

"And Brannon? He said he would watch over the wounded, but did he rest as well?"

"Brannon does not need rest as we do. Thanks to him, much of the rubble has been removed from Alioch. It will help with the rebuilding." Anora's voice lowered. "We're lucky he decided to join us."

"He told me he'll keep up my training on the way," Rafi said. "That will at least make up for the fact that I'm going to lose my job."

Sabine stared at her brother. "I hadn't thought of that. The guards will be after you when you return to the city. Nobody walks away from the mines. You'll have to hide with me."

He snorted. "We'll be two renegade Awhye in Aporos. Besides, if I never see those hellgod mines again, it would be too soon." He looked her over, holding up a pack. "Are you up to this?"

"I've never been more ready." Sabine groaned as she tried to rise from the mattress, finally thrusting out a hand for her brother to help her. Tentative steps worked out the stiffness in her limbs. Anora came to her, holding out a cloak that settled over her shoulders. Novi cawed and perched on her shoulder.

Outside, the air was fresh, and sunlight sparkled on the dew that coated the burned-out husks of trees. Faces were downcast and their movements were slow, but the Eyanrac were already rebuilding.

Many dug through the gardens, recovering as much of the harvest as they could. Men and women trundled by with wheelbarrows, and children dashed along the paths bringing supplies.

As Anora had said, much of the debris had been cleared. Sabine shielded her face from the sun as she sought the man responsible. Brannon waited for her near the edge of the forest, dressed for travel.

"You've been working hard," Sabine said as she joined him.

"I do what I can." He pulled her in by the edges of her cloak. "I like seeing you standing on your own two feet."

Sabine blushed at the warmth in his tone. "Are we ready?" She tried to keep her trepidation out of her voice.

Anora held out Sabine's staff for her, and Novi jumped onto the solid perch. "We're ready."

As they passed into the Dikisi Forest, the Eyanrac paused in their work to lift a hand to them. Losing sight of Alioch, Sabine hesitated. What if the blight swirled up to consume her before she could complete this quest?

Unerring, Anora held out her hand. "I am with you, Sabine. I will not let you disappear."

The goddess had told Sabine to trust Anora. But she had also been warned not to trust the goddess. Sabine closed her eyes and listened to what she felt was right.

And she reached for Anora's hand; her spirit sister had never let her down. Anora beamed as though she could read Sabine's thoughts and led them into the woods.

Around the bend in the path, a group of golden Sabagh waited for them.

"A blessing for the Green Knight, to help you on your voyage." The Sabagh spoke in a scratchy voice.

Brannon knelt to them. They placed a crown of autumn leaves on his bowed head.

"You are kind to lend me your protection." He stood, and the leaves blended with his hair. The air around him warped for a moment as though he had come through time and space.

"Keep safe and return to us," the Sabagh said. "We'll wait for you at the solstice."

Their words caught on the wind and blew out over the forest. Sabine shivered and wrapped her cloak tightly to her.

Anora and Rafi moved forward, leaving her behind with Brannon.

"What's the Green Knight?" Sabine asked.

Brannon rubbed his jaw. "It is a name I go by, at certain times and in certain places."

"Can you tell me about it?"

"I don't wish to scare you." His voice was tinged with wistfulness.

Sabine swallowed, thinking of the power rolling off him during the ritual of the dead. If they could be anything to each other, she needed honesty.

"There was another man in my life, before. He, too, was very powerful, and he set the rules as to what was between us. I went along with what he wanted because I didn't think I had a choice."

"You speak of the man who caused you such fear. It is Duke Aurich?" His eyes flickered black again.

She licked her lips and nodded. "Yes, he promised he would help me, and I believed him. He asked much of me, at times more than I was willing to give." Brannon growled, but she held up her hand. "I do not think you are the same man as him. I realize you are not a man at all. But there is clearly something between us, and I want to know more."

"There are deep secrets about me; some lie buried in the ground like graves. I cannot share all of myself with you."

"Then share what you can." Her lips curved because she wanted Brannon to be the merry man again. "You don't look green."

He gave a rueful grin, and she felt a surge of triumph. "There are days I am quite green. But not today." He shrugged his massive shoulders. "I am from the Earth; she is my mother. My brothers are the elements; my sisters are the winds. Our strength rises and wanes with the changing of the world, but we have always been."

Sabine watched, fascinated, as Brannon changed. He was no longer bronze or silver but burnished in golden light. Behind him was a swirling shadow of deepest night. He must always keep a part of himself from her.

She forced herself to remain standing as she faced his shining silhouette.

"A god of nature," she murmured. "But also of death."

"They are one and the same." She glimpsed darkness behind his golden eyes, which spoke of hallowed, ancient places. "You know the Old Ways."

"I studied with the *Vadovis*; she told me of a god who bears holly on the night of the dead, who passes spirits into the next world. I believed you to be a legend, not a flesh-and-blood warrior."

"I am not always like this. But I admit, I enjoy the pleasures of the flesh."

He glowed until he was too bright to behold, before dampening his power. A faint glow remained, and he emitted warming heat.

"I do not wish to interrupt," Anora said, backtracking to the two of them. She clasped Rafi's arm to guide her. "But for now, we must remain in the present. Fearsome creatures are ahead. We should stay together."

"Fearsome creatures?" Sabine asked.

Brannon looked up sharply, scenting the wind. "*Vargas.*"

The name hissed inside Sabine, though she'd never heard the word before, stirring up a well of dread.

Anora nodded. "I sense them as well."

"What are Vargas?" Sabine whispered.

"The Vargas are monsters of old," Brannon said. "I haven't seen one for tens of centuries. It bodes ill they move now, of all times."

"How old are you?" Rafi asked.

Brannon flashed Sabine a bittersweet smile. "Very."

"They are made of vengeance," Anora answered Sabine's question.

"Made *of* vengeance?"

"Magical creatures are created from intent. Your Ielzrie was created from rebellion. Vargas come to being from righteous fury. They seek revenge for the mistreated. They come before the Hunt, the embodiment of wild magic. They are harbingers of destruction."

"Wait, like in that song?" Rafi's eyes were popping from his head, and he spun around. "Giant wolves that ravage the land, unleashing justice and death?"

Correct. The whisper bounced off the trees, coming from everywhere. *Though we really do prefer death.*

The wind whipped furiously. Brannon unsheathed his longest knife, and Rafi followed his lead, though his hands shook. Sabine lifted her staff, determined to protect Anora.

However, Anora was the only one who didn't seem in the least worried. She strode forward.

"Come, Vargas, that we might greet you and give you due deference."

An oversized gray wolf slunk from behind the trees. *Pretty words from a pretty girl.* The wolf's voice slithered into Sabine's head, dark and deep and female. *I wonder if you would be so pretty after the worms have had those eyes.*

Anora raised her palms. "Perhaps they would find more use for them than I. We are simple travelers. We ask leave for safe passage."

The she-wolf approached Anora, who stood perfectly at ease as the rest of them coiled to lunge at any second. The Vargas circled Anora, sniffing, and sneezed.

There is nothing simple about you. You are a paradox. You smell of greenery and greed, of life water and death fire. You should not be.

Sabine stepped forward. "Back off."

The Vargas spun on Sabine. The impenetrable darkness of her eyes was a void of lost things. These creatures had come from a long-forgotten abyss.

Your sins bleed off you, human child; you are drenched in them. The Vargas growled.

A screech filled the air, and Novi swept out of the air to land on Sabine's staff. The Ielzrie drew itself up to full height, wings outstretched. *There are more of them, approaching from all sides.*

"We're surrounded!" Sabine cried. Shadows of wolves swayed in and out of the trees, their growls growing to a frenzy of barking. The sound was maddening. Sabine resisted the urge to cover her ears like a child.

The chief Vargas paced back and forth in front of them. *For too long, we've been chained. But things are shifting, deep within the land. We were raised to take vengeance against the excesses of humans. Two of you are born of men. You must pay.*

Rafi bristled. "The Awhye don't deal in excess."

The Vargas closest to him sniffed. *This one smells of rock and darkness. He rips the heart out of the earth.*

Rafi threw his hands up as the Vargas pounced. Novi's screech rolled through the air, echoing Sabine's helpless terror.

Teeth a hairsbreadth from Rafi's throat, the giant wolf bounced off an invisible barrier.

The other Vargas attacked. They snapped and snarled but were unable to make contact.

Brannon and Rafi spun, weapons up.

"Who's doing this?" Sabine gasped. "Novi?"

It is the divine child, Novi answered.

A wide smile spread over Anora's face. She held a length of golden string, which she looped over and under her fingers, working them like a loom to create a lacy web.

"I was thinking about magic and the power of intention," she said as she worked. "And I thought, magic runs through my veins, and I am a weaver. If I intend to weave a protective shield, who's to say I cannot?" The cord glimmered like sunlight running through her hands.

When Sabine tilted her head, she could see a glimpse of golden sparkles hovering above them.

"I've never seen magic like this." Brannon reached out as if to catch a magical thread.

"String magic is ancient, practiced at the hearth of many goodwives over the centuries," Anora said, chiding. "It might not be flashy, but it is handy."

"I meant no offense." He bowed his head. "It is with great relief I learn of such things."

"Did you know you could do this?" Sabine's voice was sharp because she was still picturing the wolf's jaws around her brother's throat.

"Not exactly. But I knew what I wanted, and the weaving responded. Magic is an interesting thing." With a mild look, she faced the she-wolf.

"I do not wish anyone harmed. We will continue on our journey and take no more than we need. All I ask is that you allow us to pass."

The Vargas snapped at the invisible barrier. When they moved to block Anora, she stepped forward, and they were nudged out of her way. With string looping through her fingers, she passed unharmed through the teeth of her enemies. Anora's casting brought out the flush in her cheeks; she sparkled with her magic.

This is not over. The Vargas bounded away. Their furious howling set gooseflesh crawling over Sabine's skin.

Brannon stared into the forest where they disappeared, then up at the golden net protecting them.

"The creation of magic," he said. "There are powerful forces at work here. I fear we come to a convergence soon, a crossroads between the Old Ways and the new."

ILLUSIONIST

No matter the time of day, the Dikisi Forest was dusky with nightshade. Mist tumbled over their feet, and the wind blew incessantly, rattling the twigs around them.

Though they met no one, Sabine could not shake the feeling something followed them. Novi would often stretch its neck and croak, staring into the gloom.

"What is it?" Sabine asked Novi. She scratched behind its horns, something that caused the Ielzrie to vibrate with pleasure.

I cannot detect the presence of another living creature. It shook its head. *Maybe that's what bothers.*

A few paces ahead, Anora slowed. "This feels like a good place." She had stopped in the center of a clearing.

"Then we'll make camp here," Brannon said.

Rafi set down his pack with a groan. "Thank blazes, I'm exhausted. I'll fall asleep anywhere. That log." He pointed to a gnarled, twisted thing. "That'll do."

"Better than logs, use these Eyanrac sacks." Anora brought out rolls of soft fabric from her bag, like the blankets in the Rukha. She unrolled one, and it puffed up into a giant cushion.

"Should we start a fire?" Rafi asked longingly.

"No." Sabine nearly choked on her fear. "Aurich could find us."

"All right, freezing cold nights it is." Rafi rubbed his hands together, trying to look optimistic.

"Will you do us the honor of dinner?" Anora asked Brannon.

Sabine perked up at the thought of eating.

"With pleasure," the god said, pulling out a silky black sack that appeared empty. But he reached in and brought out a large, crusty loaf of bread. He did so again and pulled out a bunch of shiny purple grapes. Slowly, a feast appeared. Nuts and dried fruits. A large wheel of cheese. Apples. Pastries made from morasu grain, just like her mother's.

She accepted a mushroom pasty, sniffing. The spices were just right. "This is magic."

"Yes." Brannon gave a rumbling laugh at her suspicion. "During the autumn season, I can create food from the ether. For the time being, we will continue to share in the harvest bounty."

"You're handy to have around," Rafi said. His mouth was stuffed with bread as he arranged Anora's sleeping sack close to his. "I thought we'd freeze and starve before arriving."

Brannon smiled at Sabine. "Never when I'm here." She felt a warmth that had nothing to do with the fact that he glowed like the sun. They enjoyed a companionable dinner, full bellies making up for the tense hike through the woods.

Brannon sat near Sabine, offering her choice items of food from his magic sack. She couldn't forget what he was, a force of nature, yet a crash of wanting to be near him made her shiver.

"You are cold. Come, let me share my warmth with you." A hint of teasing flashed through his eyes, telling her exactly what he was offering as he held out his palm. The thought of his touch led to an answering pulse low in her belly.

She hesitated, glancing over her shoulder toward Rafi and Anora, who were already snuggled in their sacks on the other side of the clearing. In the dim light, she could barely make out their forms, but neither of them moved. Novi cooed in sleep, hanging in a tree branch.

"It's just you and I."

Sabine took his outstretched hand. He brought her to him so carefully, like she was spun glass. His hands grazed up her body, coming to the clasp of her cloak.

"May I?"

She nodded, unable to speak in her desire.

The momentary chill as the cloak slipped off her shoulders was quickly replaced as Brannon tugged her into his sleep sack. She pressed her cold face to the heat of his neck, and he let out a whispered laugh. "You are cold as the north wind, beloved. I would warm every inch of you."

She brought her face to his, looking into the eyes that now sparkled gold. He was a man, or very like one. Perhaps there were men worth trusting.

"You have my leave," she whispered and pressed her lips to the corner of his jaw.

Brannon sucked in his breath. Cradling her head in one of his big hands, he shifted so they lay alongside each other, his body partially covering hers. He radiated heat, warming her as promised. His hand ran down the length of her thigh; her leggings were remarkably thin, as she felt every stroke as if against her skin.

She groaned and rolled her hips against him, wanting to get closer. Brannon responded, sliding his tongue along the edge of her bottom lip, then kissing her deeply. His hands tangled in her hair, holding her in place as he ravaged her mouth. When she moaned, he lifted his head, tracing a line along her jaw. His lips trailed lower, and she gasped as he licked the hollow of her throat.

His other hand came up to skim over her breast, his thumb stroking featherlight along the underside.

Held down as she was, Sabine couldn't move, could only whimper against the waves of pleasure that rippled over her.

"Brannon," she whispered, and he groaned against her.

"Enchantress. You tempt the gods with your beauty." His mouth traveled lower, over the fabric of her tunic, pressing his mouth at the crest of her breast. His hand came down to the curve of her bottom, pulling her tight against him.

She felt the length of his hardness against her, proving Brannon truly was a man in all ways. Even as a thrill of want coursed through her, she tensed.

Brannon stilled. "Is this too much?"

"I..." She licked her lips. She wasn't sure what she wanted; she was afraid of what she wanted. "I don't know."

Brannon released her, bracing himself above her on one arm. "I forget myself and move too fast."

"It's not that I don't want this." Sabine turned her face and kissed him. He trailed his lips across her cheek. "I want you very much. But"—she took a deep breath—"there were men at the Halwardian court who tried things with me." Her eyes closed against the memory, of pinching hands, of being trapped in a closed space with a courtier who thought she would be easy pickings.

Brannon growled. "Tell me these men and I will rip their limbs off."

His eyes glittered black and she believed him. "I thought finding favor with Duke Aurich would protect me. But I was so wrong. He was worse than all the others."

"This man you sought protection from hurt you?"

Slowly, Sabine nodded, tears pricking at the memory. "He wished to keep me as a plaything." She brought in a shuddering breath. "That's when I turned invisible for good. I sure showed him, didn't I?"

"You got away from him. That is what matters."

"Only I didn't, not really. He said he could find a cure to the blight that cursed me. He dangled it in front of me, and even though I knew what he was capable of and what he wanted from me, I stayed."

"You were scared, Sabine, and he used that to his advantage. You have no shame in this matter; that lies entirely with him." She could barely see him in the darkness, but the softness in his voice loosened something in her chest.

She pressed against him, and he drew her in, achingly tender.

"Could I stay with you tonight?" she asked.

He wrapped her up in his arms and pressed a gentle kiss to her forehead. "Always, Sabine. I will keep you safe."

She drifted to sleep, more peaceful than she had been in years despite the dangers that surrounded them.

Sabine woke before the morning sun lightened the clearing. Brannon lay next to her, arm draped over her waist. She looked up toward the fading stars and smiled.

She found herself thinking about the pretty globes of witch light during the festival. She imagined them hovering over their heads like stars.

On the other side of the clearing, Rafi bolted upright. "Who's doing that?"

Sabine gasped, and the lights burst like bubbles of molten starlight. They had really been there.

"It was me. I was thinking about them."

"You thought something, and it appeared?" Rafi sounded skeptical.

"I don't know. I didn't mean to."

"You created light," Brannon said, peeping an eye open next to her.

"I didn't know I could make things appear."

"Not things. Light."

Anora woke as well. "What's going on?" Her voice was scratchy from sleep, and for once, she didn't sound like an ethereal faerie.

"Sabine can make light appear," Rafi said, watching her with tenderness as she stretched.

Anora dropped her hands. "Really?" Her white eyes opened wide.

"I'm still not sure I understand the importance," Sabine said.

Brannon found her cloak and draped it over her shoulders. "I've been thinking about your power. All visible things are so because of light and invisible without it. I think you have the power to bend light to your will. You are an illusionist," Brannon concluded with satisfaction.

"Oh." Anora nodded. "Brannon, I suspect you are right."

"What's an illusionist?"

"You can control what people see around them. Or don't see."

"I create light," she said wonderingly. "So, could I use light to make it appear like we are in a stone chamber right now instead of a forest? Could I make it seem like full daylight?"

Brannon paused. "I believe with practice, you could."

"This makes a great deal of sense." Anora's face was lit with excitement.

"Perhaps you could explain it to me." Seeing the silver lights appear and disappear had shaken her.

"For one, why your magic came to you so late...or appeared to."

"You mean I was doing magic before? When I was a child?"

"It's possible you've been influencing your environment with illusions without knowing it. Did things ever become extra lovely when you were around?"

Sabine's hands flew to her face.

A slow grin of mischief spread over Rafi's face. "Are you not as pretty as everyone thinks?"

"Blazing hell, I have no idea." Sabine let her hands fall. She supposed it didn't really matter, thought it was disconcerting to think she'd placed an illusion over herself her entire life.

"But it's not real," Rafi said. "She may be invisible, but she is still there. She could give someone a flower, but there would be no flower."

"But while Sabine is with them, they would think they have a flower," Anora said. "In a way, you can control people's minds."

Sabine shivered. "But that means nothing is real, then."

"The world is as we choose to see it. In that way, it is very real."

Unsettled, Sabine reached out for Novi, who was waking above them. She craved the comfort of the Ielzrie as she puzzled over this. It curled around her neck, cooing.

Anora's voice broke through her disturbing thoughts. "The lights you made were lovely."

"Could you see them?"

"No, Sabine, I'm still blind. But I could *feel* them. They felt like hope."

As they prepared to set out again, Sabine feared that Anora's hope might only be another illusion.

The Oracles

Days later, they approached the Oracle grove. Brannon could tell because the trees were beginning to thin out. Sabine eyed the same somber trunks she'd been staring at hour after hour, not noticing a difference. She was sweaty under her cloak, and her neck itched, and she wanted this journey to be done.

A girl giggled at her shoulder. She spun, seeing nothing. Nerves fraying, she called out, "Who's there?"

"The Oracles," Anora said. "They can sense us. It won't be long now."

An air kiss smacked near her ear and Sabine swatted at it like a fly. "I wish they'd stop."

Another lingering kiss sounded behind them. Sabine spun to see Brannon's face break into a wide grin. She glared and he put his hands up in innocence, trying not to laugh.

"They're harmless," Anora said.

"You speak as though you know them."

"We've never met face to face, obviously. But I sometimes see them in my visions. They, too, are connected to deeper knowledge.

I have woven them many times." Anora smiled fondly. "They are sweet girls, these three, each of them farmers' daughters."

"Do they stay for their whole lives?" Sabine asked, horrified at the thought of being trapped in this gloomy forest forever.

"No, only while they are young women. Most Oracles stay until they are old enough to work or marry, then they are replaced. The people in the south of the kingdom still practice the Old Ways and consider it a great honor to be chosen as an Oracle. They believe they're handmaidens to my mother."

"So, three girls live in a pool of water and can see the future?" Rafi asked.

"Maben, Morag and Poe. Poe is the youngest. She is ever so delightful." Another kiss smacked near Anora. "They don't live in the pool, but they submerge themselves in the water when they wish to bear witness to what will be."

Sabine was brought up short as the trees opened to an airy clearing out of place with the time and seasons. Here, the trees bloomed, heavy with the scent of flowers; warm as a summer's eve, the glow of the setting sun casting everything in amber. A creek trickled through a flower-strewn meadow, tumbling over marble rocks into a clear pool. Next to the waterfall was a cave, out of which tripped three girls.

They each had the looks of the Awhye people. One had black hair, one brown, and the littlest's was streaked with gold. Robes of woven flower petals swirled around them as they danced and spun, laughing merrily as they rushed up to the travelers.

The golden-haired child took Sabine's hands, although up close, it was evident she was closer to her age than she thought. Their dancing made them seem childish. The girl dimpled as though hearing Sabine's thoughts and led her into the grove.

Then the Oracles danced away and entered the pool. Taking each other's hands, they fell into a hushed silence. Even the water made no sound.

"*You seek deeper knowledge*," the Oracles said together. Their voices formed an odd cadence, a song and a hiss at the same time.

Anora stepped forward. "We seek guidance in the name of The Lady of the Forest. The spirit water has run dry, and the land is dying. How can we overcome this catastrophe?"

The Oracles swayed. A thick buzzing filled the air, vibrating over Sabine's skin. The three stopped at the same time, their eyes snapping open as one. Darkness swallowed their eyes. Sabine stepped back, and Rafi flinched next to her.

"*An interesting group*," they said in their slippery melody. "*One whose heart remains forever unrequited. One who is trapped in time. One who is the sibyl. One who is a thief.*

"*Go to the place inside the earth where the mother's soul is being broken, where the Hunt has been caged. Through slag and terrible blooding, all will be restored.*"

The humming returned, more terrible than before. Sabine wanted to collapse, to scream until it stopped. Before her rose a vision of a black stone cliff, broken down the center with a cleft of total darkness. Everything about the place seemed wrong, horrible. Sabine closed her eyes but could still see it, as though the cliff had burrowed in her mind.

"*The goddess child knows where it will end. Follow her to the mines. There, she will do what she must.*"

Anora let out a sobbing gasp. Her shoulders sank, bowing against the horrible buzzing as though a swarm of hornets surrounded them. The words whispered around them: *do what she must.*

Novi cocked its head this way and that, snapping at the air as it sparked. *This magic tastes funny.*

The Oracles stopped abruptly. The three burst out laughing, their eyes brown again. They splashed each other, shrieking, laughter looping higher and higher until Sabine's teeth were on edge.

"It is the water," Brannon said. "In it runs a great connection to life magic. It makes them euphoric. Let's set up camp on the other side of the grove. We do not want to be drawn in and forget our quest."

Anora's fists were clenched, her mouth set in a grim line.

"Did you see it?" Sabine asked. "The cliff?"

"I saw it," Rafi said grimly.

Anora's voice was little more than a whisper. "I have seen the cliff many times throughout my life. It has haunted my nightmares since I was very young. Now is the time I must come face to face with my worst fears."

Sabine's chest ached to see her friend's distress. "Let's go rest."

Anora brushed a tear away and nodded. "Yes. The girls wish to cavort, and I am uninterested."

The brunette Oracle sidled to the edge of the pool, her robe clinging tight to her body. "Great beauty, I am Morag," she said to Sabine. "Won't you come play with me?"

Her wink was so obvious Sabine couldn't help but smile. "I thank you, but I do not wish to play."

Morag moved on to Rafi. "How about you, handsome?"

But Rafi didn't answer, fixated on getting Anora away from the pool.

Morag pouted. "Will nobody play?"

"We must entertain ourselves," Maben said.

The youngest Oracle, the golden-haired Poe, was not paying them attention. Her body trembled and then convulsed in a violent seizure, her body thrashing in the water. Her hand darted out and grabbed Sabine, nearly yanking her into the pool. Her head whipped toward her as if possessed, her eyes glittering black.

"*You cannot save them all,*" she croaked in a harsh, creaky voice.

This prophecy came from a different place, something fathomless. It promised to take someone she loved.

Sabine stared back at the fae eyes, lips curling in a snarl. "Blaze that."

She wrenched away from the girl, who fell forward into the pool. When she emerged, sputtering, her eyes had returned to their usual brown.

Poe glared at Sabine. "Why'd you do that?" Her sisters came to her sides. As one, their heads whipped up, and they glowered under their brows at Sabine. An unseen force pushed her back.

She staggered away, shaken.

The others were already on the other side of the grove; by the time she joined them, the Oracles were back to splashing and giggling.

Rafi paced. "What does it mean? All this talk of ones trapped in time and unrequited hearts. It doesn't make any sense."

"The Oracles were naming us as they saw us." Anora's knees were tucked up to her chin, arms wrapped around them. Sabine's heart ached for her, and Novi swooped to settle in Anora's lap, and she stroked the creature's warm side.

"Thank you, my friend. But our names are not what matters. It's the second part, the part that tells us how we must continue this quest."

"*The place inside the earth where the mother's soul is being broken.*" Sabine grimaced. "It sounds like we have to descend into hellfire."

"You saw it. The scoria mines. A place of slag and terrible blooding." Rafi stared at his hands. "Only it wasn't any mine I've worked in before. I don't know the way."

"I do," Anora said. "I can guide you, if you would follow."

"That's where all is restored? The *mines*?" Sabine shook her head at the downcast group. "What kind of ridiculous prophecy is this?" She let out a huff.

Anora stared into the forest, not sharing what she knew.

Rafi watched her. "Well, we have to trust in The Lady, don't we? She asked us to seek guidance from the Oracles, and they guided us."

"Stupidly. Into a horrible mine."

"Yes, but we will trust in her, nevertheless." Anora sounded resigned.

"You're just going to blindly follow?"

Anora lifted her milky gaze. "What other choice do I have, Sabine?"

Sabine's breath left her. "Anora, I'm sorry."

"It's okay to not understand, sister. It will all come together...if you decide to come."

"Of course I'll stay with you," Sabine whispered. "We'll figure it out together."

A growl sounded from the edge of the woods. Brannon, silent since the prophecy, glanced over his shoulder. "I believe the Vargas have returned," he said in a low voice. "The grove is a sacred place where no blood may be shed. But it wouldn't hurt to place an extra ring of protection. Anora, can we count on your string magic to aid us?"

Anora brightened. "Of course." As she thread the string through her fingers, the creases erased from her face as she did something useful. Sabine shot a thankful look at Brannon, and he nodded with a smile just for her.

Already, Anora seemed calmer. "Tell me a story, Brannon. Tell me about the emerald my mother wears."

Brannon built up a pile of wood at the center of their camp. "The emerald? That stone was unearthed thousands of years ago. The Chalice of Life. The Lady has worn it for millennia."

"It enhances her powers?" Sabine asked.

Brannon shrugged. "I don't study the theory of magic. I can only tell you what I've seen. The Lady ascended to her power with the stone around her neck."

Sabine cleared her throat. "The duke wishes to have the stone, or one like it. I believe he intends to become immortal as well. We can't let that happen." She hesitated but couldn't bring herself to tell them of the other prophecy she'd heard. The one that meant one of them would die. Brannon told her no vision was set in stone; this was one she intended to shatter.

"Blazing hell, the duke of fire with the power of a god." Rafi whistled. "I don't want to see that."

The Vargas beyond their haven howled as if in response.

"All will be restored," Anora said. She stood and paced a circle, letting the woven thread fall behind her, humming gently under her breath. The worry and anger that bubbled inside of Sabine eased, and she wondered whether Anora wove spells of peace into her chain. She lay her head down, overwhelmed.

"So, we travel to the mines." Brannon settled his mat next to Sabine's. They had shared a bedroll since that first night, and Sabine welcomed his heat in more ways than one.

"You'll continue with us?" She hadn't dared hope.

"I will spend every hour I have by your side."

"How will we get there?" Rafi asked. "The mines are far to the north in the Tuneric Mountains. It could take weeks."

Sabine shot an anxious look at Brannon, knowing his deadline. For whatever reason, he had to return to Alioch by the winter solstice.

"There is another way," Brannon said after a long pause. "It would be quicker, but not without risk."

"What is it?"

"We go across Malgris Lake."

"Malgris Lake?" Sabine shuddered. "But it's poisonous. I've heard strange tales of the creatures who make their home there now."

"All true. It is now the domain of something ancient. But that is only a problem if we go by water, which I suggest we do not."

"Then how do we get across?"

"We fly." A boyish grin stretched across his face, and it did funny things to Sabine's heart.

Anora's smile was as wide as his. "I should very much like to fly." She hummed again, and the group of them relaxed.

Rafi nodded. "It's decided, then."

Sabine imagined herself flying, soaring over this forest into the wilds beyond. The thoughts filled her with longing as though she was remembering a forgotten dream. Brannon's arms drew her in as sleep stole over her. She glanced at Anora, whose face was serene, watching her.

"All will be well," she whispered. It seemed to come from far, far away. "Rest now." Her humming went deeper, rippling through the air.

As Sabine drifted off, the other words the Oracle had spoken, *you cannot save them all,* kept running through her mind. They felt truer than everything else.

Mageling Lessons

Soupy fog covered the ground the following day; shrieking and splashing rose from the Oracle pool. "Have they been at it all night?" Sabine grumbled. It was a miracle the Oracles didn't drown.

"They woke at dawn and emerged to greet the day."

Sabine raised an eyebrow at Brannon. "Is that all they do every day? How do they survive?"

"They are cared for by the Sabagh, who collect food from the forest and provide them with clothing. I can assure you, the Sabagh are excellent guardians of the young."

"You know a lot of these Oracles. Do you come to the grove often?"

To Sabine's surprise, Brannon blushed a deep shade of red, and Rafi, listening, burst out laughing. "You dally with the Oracles?"

His bronze skin reddened further, taking on a rusty cast. "There have been times, over the centuries, you understand, I might have found myself falling for a maiden."

"Did you compose songs for them?" Sabine's grin was wicked. "Poetry?"

"Well, now that you mention it, have you heard the ditty *Happy Nancy*?"

The other three burst into laughter. Rafi had regaled them with that lusty mining song on their journey into the forest.

"That was you?" Rafi's eyes were wide.

"Well, Nancy had a way of inspiring a man. It was a very long time ago," he said to Sabine.

She laughed so hard tears squeezed from her eyes. "I'm in awe, meeting the composer."

Anora clapped her hands to the beat as Rafi began to sing. When Rafi came to the part where the girls' skirts fly up and the men roar, he stopped in embarrassment. Sabine doubled over when Anora's voice continued on, her sweet voice taking up the chorus with relish. Rafi grabbed Anora by the elbow and swung her around in a jig.

"Are you sure it wasn't you who wrote the song?" Rafi asked her. "You seem to know it quite well."

Anora couldn't breathe for giggling. She had to pull away from Rafi to collect herself, her cheeks puffed out and red. "No, I didn't. Brannon wrote it. He just admitted it."

Rafi grinned. "Don't throw this back at him. I think you have a secret love of indecent songs."

"I do." Anora was still caught in fits of giggles. "I love them all."

"Where did you learn these songs? Not from the Helms?"

"I listened to you, of course."

Brannon burst out laughing. "The Oracle pool is affecting us."

Anora brushed at her streaming cheeks. "You're right. We need to get out of here before we become too far caught in euphoria."

"Where do we head? Do we veer to the west, through the forest that wants to kill us, or do we trek north to the dead lake?" Their choice seemed horribly funny to Sabine.

"Don't forget the option of certain death at the hands of the duke's men if we go through Aporos." Rafi grinned, and Anora giggled uncontrollably.

"Well, since a terrible death lies at the end of every path, let us go quickly. I say we fly." Sabine, still full of mirth, didn't notice the gloom of the forest. "Will we fly on carpets like in the tales of old? Should Anora start weaving now?"

Brannon shook his head. "We will ask my sister for help."

"You have a sister?" Rafi asked.

"I have four," Brannon said. "But Meri is my favorite. There is a way we used to travel, back in ancient days. It's time to stir some of the Old Ways too long forgotten."

"On the wind," Sabine whispered. "You said your sisters were the winds. We'll really fly?"

"We'll really fly."

That night, when Anora began her nightly routine of humming and weaving, Sabine watched intently.

As though feeling the scrutiny, Anora looked up. "Yes?"

"How are you doing it? Your magic?"

"I want it to happen, and I shove my intention into the act of weaving."

Sabine let out a frustrated sigh. "It doesn't work that way for me." She'd tried throughout the day to make glowing lights appear, and nothing worked. The harder she concentrated, the more her head ached.

Anora stopped pacing. "What if you made yourself invisible? You know you can do that."

Horror flooded through Sabine. "I don't want to disappear."

Anora shook her head. "Not disappear; you exist, as you always have. You only shape an illusion around yourself."

"What if it brings on the blight again?"

"That will happen if you don't use your magic. Here in the forest, you can access it without it consuming you, because magic is still free here."

Sabine stared at Anora. She had never become invisible on

purpose before; the goal had always been to become visible again, to thrust her magic away from her. But the goddess had told her Anora would help her control her powers. Sabine took a calming breath, concentrating on the steady measure of her paces, thinking of cool things like a gentle stream of water trickling over her.

Don't see me; don't see me. Let the light pass through. She reached out for the magic that spooled inside of her. She could feel it creeping over her, like a veil of sorrow, and then she was gone.

Acid terror washed over her.

"I cannot see you, Sabine, but I know you are there," Anora said.

Sabine brought a hand to her stomach, feeling herself, reminding herself she was there.

Novi let out a cry and came to land on her invisible shoulder. Sabine stroked its neck. "And you, Novi? How do you always know where I am?"

Your illusions do not fool me. I see who you really are.

"Who am I, really?"

"A powerful enchantress." Anora's white eyes shone in the gloaming. "Sabine, try something for me. Take Novi in your hands."

Sabine did so, the Ielzrie seemingly floating midair.

"Now, make Novi invisible." Sabine wanted to argue, but Anora put up her hand. "Not to make it disappear. You've confused the two. Just because you cannot see it does not mean it is not. Think about hiding it; protecting it."

Sabine gazed into Novi's glittering eyes, staring unerringly right back. *Invisible, invisible*, she thought with all her might, but Novi remained visible. "I can't do this."

"You can." Anora's voice was soothing. "You have cast your power further than yourself before; you hid me in the Ofhellen. Think about your connection with Novi."

Do not worry, Novi chirped. *I see to your heart. It is a heart worth knowing.*

A blanket of love settled over her as she thought of this creature. She nudged a bit of what she thought of as her spirit into Novi. It was easily accepted because the Ielzrie had been born of her soul.

Novi rippled out of sight, still warm in Sabine's hands. She gasped as Anora clapped her hands in delight. "I knew you could do it."

Brannon and Rafi, setting up camp, came over at the noise.

"What is it?"

"Sabine made Novi invisible."

"Sab?" Rafi called.

"I'm here." Worried Novi would become trapped in invisibility, she let the illusion go, ripping it away from Novi, who came back into view. She let out a sigh of relief.

Novi chirped again and crawled to her shoulder. *Now you.*

Panic seized her. "What if I cannot?"

It's your insecurity keeping you invisible. You are no longer the girl who hides from her power, imprisoned by fear. You are a great sorceress in your own right. You do not need anyone's permission, be it man or goddess, to be seen.

Novi spoke directly to Sabine's spirit. The feeling of power, of pride, rippled down to her essence, and she thrust it through her whole body, allowing it to spark to the very tips of her fingers.

Everyone stepped back as Sabine blazed into sight. She laughed in delight, holding up a hand in front of her. Her golden skin glowed like embers. "I did it."

Brannon went to one knee, awe spreading over his face. "My lady. As your belief in your power grows, so will your control over it."

The glow of her skin faded, and the rush of success ebbed. "Aurich told me only an object of great power would be able to bring me back. That only he could do it."

Anora took her hand. "He wanted you to believe that, to keep you under his influence. He made you feel worthless, as though you were nothing without him. It is your understanding of yourself that shaped the illusion. He made you want to hide, and so you became invisible. He was inflicting more damage than helping you."

"He treated you like that so you would do what he wanted." Rafi's eyes snapped furiously. "That bastard."

"He wanted you under his control," Anora said. "But he underestimated how powerful you are."

"How are you so wise?" Sabine asked

Her face brightened. "I study the past and peer into the future. It's confusing sometimes to put all the pieces together, but great truths can be revealed from the whole."

"Is it difficult to see into the future and still not know what's going to happen?"

Anora gave a lonesome sigh. "You have no idea. I just want to keep everyone safe."

Sabine clasped her hand firmly. "I am with you to the end. You know that, right?"

"That is so obvious, even I can see."

Monotonous days were punctuated by occasional terror when the Vargas prowled near enough for them to hear their growls. But for the most part, the journey was dull and tiring. They cycled through every song in their memories as they marched through the endless forest.

When a heavy silence descended, Anora called to Sabine. "Make yourself invisible."

"Right. Mageling lessons." Sabine reached for the cool feeling of invisibility. It washed over her, easier now, without the fear it once brought. Novi, dozing on Sabine's staff, peeped open an eye and gave a cheep of encouragement. Feeling the connection between them, Sabine let the invisibility wash over the Ielzrie. Novi and her staff disappeared from view.

Novi squawked and took flight. Sabine laughed as Novi flicked back into view. "Sorry."

"Do me now," Anora said.

"Turn you invisible?"

"You've done it before. Cloak me with your power."

The magical essence lapped inside of her. She was not connected to Anora as with Novi, but there was a bond between them. She thought of the guileless spirit who saw beauty without seeing. It was easy to nudge the power in her direction, and Anora rippled out of sight.

Rafi let out a whoop, and Sabine grinned. She thought of her little brother, of stealing fruit at the market to keep him fed when he was young, and holding his hand tight as they cried over their father's grave. Her illusion pushed further out, and Rafi disappeared.

He yelped. "Sab!" A pause. "This is incredible."

Brannon wheeled around to find the path empty behind him and gave a rumble of laughter. "Well done, enchantress. Can you hide me as well?"

Sabine eyed him. He was not a brother or spirit sister to her. And a god besides. But the connection between them was strong, all longing and heat. She focused on that. It hooked her to him like a cord, and she followed the thread with her mind's eye to his center.

His spirit was vast and all-encompassing, a well of darkness she could not comprehend. Looking into him was like looking past all the stars in the sky to see what lay beyond. How deep did he go?

She also found a spark of light and joy, his curiosity toward humans and how they lived and loved. She focused on what tied them together, desire and darkness both, and thrust her power into him, willing him to disappear. He vanished.

"You did it." Anora's invisible hand took hers.

Rafi stumbled into them. "Ouch. Can you bring us back?"

She didn't panic because she knew she could. "You were always there." With a thought, they were all visible again.

"You're gaining impressive control over your powers," Brannon said.

"I think I've unlocked how to work it." Sabine shrugged. "But at the end of the day, it's just a parlor trick. What can silly illusions *really* do?"

Alarm showed in his eyes. "Don't underestimate your power. The ability to create illusions means the ability to manipulate reality. You can make men see what they want so they become lost in desire. You can show people ghosts of loved ones or shape their reality into their nightmares."

"You could drive them mad." Anora's whisper was haunted. "I trust you to never abuse this great power you have been given."

Shaken by their intensity, Sabine shook her head. "No, I won't."

"I believe you, sister."

For the rest of their hike to the lake, they amused themselves by getting Sabine to make things invisible. She could make others invisible while remaining visible herself, and soon she made trees disappear, too.

That was harder, and it took focus. She concentrated on the earth under her feet and the roots that grew there, finding she could make swaths of the forest invisible.

"Excellent. Now, can you make a tree appear in the middle of the path?" Anora asked.

"I...that's different." Sabine chewed her lip. "That's creating something."

"You already have all you need. For me, I would look at it like weaving, only with light. Ask the light to twist into what it is you want us to see."

Sabine halted, concentrating. In her mind's eye, she imagined a wide Rukha reaching toward the clouds. A tickle of her spirit leaked out of her, then she got excited and lost it.

Sabine let her hands drop. What was she doing? She wasn't a great mage like Aurich; she would never figure this out. If she were cleverer, she would have already done so. "I don't think I can do this."

"You can and you will. You only need to trust in yourself more. Think of your connection with the world."

"It will have to wait," Brannon said. "We've arrived. The lake is over this ridge."

Malgris Lake

They stumbled to a stop at the ridge over the beaches. Malgris Lake *looked* dead. The water was metal gray and still as glass. Nothing stirred within; no birds flew overhead, and an unnatural stillness settled over the vast expanse.

The far shore was visible as a hazy smear of brown, the northern mountains rising beyond. The vegetation surrounding the beach rotted as though poison leached out of the water.

"Blazing hell." Sabine gaped at the decay. "I heard the lake died, but I thought it was an exaggeration."

"All living creatures were driven out by the magical blight, and the water itself lost its essence," Brannon said. "My brother is the element of water, and yet I sense nothing of him here."

"So you can't ask him for help?"

"No, but we won't need him today. I will call on my sister Meri."

She remembered the story he told in the glade. "What must we give for safe passage?"

Brannon gave a thin smile. "My sisters never demand payment from me. But they are less constant." He squinted into the overcast sky. "It's hard to trust the wind."

"They must have strange family reunions," Rafi whispered to Sabine, who shushed him.

"First, we need to find the right sails." Brannon frowned as he scoured the water's edge. "Everything is dead here. I must go further in." He retreated into the dark forest.

A howl sounded nearby. Sabine huddled close to Rafi and Anora, unnerved by the grim place.

"I found some." Brannon strode back to the beach, beaming. "They're spindly, but they'll serve." He held out his hand to show her his prize.

Four grains of dandelion fluff were dwarfed in his palm.

"I don't understand."

"They're pappi. Everyone, take one."

Sabine took one between her fingertips, biting back a giggle. "If you say so."

"Trust me," he whispered before offering one to Rafi. Brannon placed the last grain in Anora's fingers with great tenderness, then held up his seed. "Hold it like this." As they did so, he closed his eyes and reached out for the earth.

The grain in Sabine's fingers twitched as the pappi swelled. It grew to ten times its size, then twenty, but remained extraordinarily light. Soon she held in her hands something like an oversized parasol, as delicate as a cloud. She hooked her staff over one of the arms.

"Incredible."

"We played at this a long time ago." Brannon frowned at his sail. "We did this in the summer, though, when Meri was at her strongest. This close to winter, we must beware of Eskazi."

"Who is Eskazi?"

"Another of my sisters, the north wind. She can be cruel." A hollow look on his face leached away the pleasure. Sabine wanted to capture it and put it back. Within his russet hair was a hint of gray, which became a silver leaf. Sabine blinked, and it was gone.

"And Meri?"

"Meri is the south wind, and the best, although I shouldn't play favorites." Brannon lifted his arms wide. "Meri, I need you. Lend me your lungs and blow us away!"

For a moment, nothing happened. Then a gust of wind curled over the Dikisi Forest and descended on them. It was warm and jubilant, tinged with spices, like desert nights under the stars. Sabine closed her eyes to immerse herself in it when the wind caught the enormous fluff, nearly tugging it from her hands.

"Hold on to your seeds," Brannon said. "Here she comes."

Sabine's boots dragged along the beach, fighting the wind. "Wait, I'm not ready."

"Jump when you get to the edge of the water." Brannon took three great strides and leaped. The wind caught the seed and shot him into the air.

Allowing themselves to hurtle across the lake on the wind suddenly seemed like a terrible idea. What if she fell?

"Sabine, you must go with the flow. Stop fighting it, stop trying to control it. Just allow yourself to let go." And with that, Anora stepped off the lakeshore and was pulled up into the air.

Sabine's feet slipped over the rocks as she was pulled. She screamed as Rafi ran up behind her. "Might as well go with it." His bellowing laugh echoed across the lake as he too was caught in the air current.

She was about to be pulled into the dead waters, so Sabine squeezed her eyes shut and jumped.

And soared.

Heart hammering, she opened her eyes with a gasp. The lake swirled by under her feet. It was easy to hold onto her sail, as though she was weightless as well. She unclenched one hand to feel the air flowing around her; her black hair flapping behind her like glossy crow's wings. Novi soared next to her, letting out a great caw of joy.

For a few seconds, Sabine never felt so free. She reached out for Novi as the Ielzrie swooped around her, her heart soaring.

Rafi laughed like when he was a carefree boy. Sabine leaned toward him, setting her fluff spinning. Anora's face was alight with amazement, framed by snapping copper hair. Rafi spun close to her, his fingers brushing her outstretched hand.

Brannon swayed toward them, his frown bringing Sabine's joy to a jolting stop. "We don't have much time. Aim for the shore. Eskazi is waking."

"What could Eskazi do?"

An icy gust cut toward them on a slant, sending their seeds tumbling through the air. Sabine latched onto the sail as the sky spun.

Caught in the updraft between two battling winds, they shot high above the water. Sabine shrieked. The world spread out beneath her like a tapestry, everything very small from up here.

Then, the winds stopped altogether. For an endless second, they suspended in midair, the silence deafening after the howling in her ears. Her heart thudded once, and then she fell.

Faster and faster, they plunged toward the lake.

"Hold on!" Brannon shouted. "Anora, stay with us."

Anora's face was white as death, but she grasped the stem with her arms and legs.

Brannon met Sabine's eyes. "Just hold on." Somehow over the roar of the wind, she heard him and anchored herself to her staff and sail, bracing for impact. A million thoughts flitted through her mind like wildfire as tears were ripped from her eyes.

A hairsbreadth away from the water's surface, a hot gust of air whipped underneath them and sent them spinning up again. They hung on a cushion of warmth before their grains sank to the surface of the lake.

The shock of the cold stole her breath. Sabine's cloak soaked with water and pulled her down. She ripped at the clasp before it dragged her into the depths.

Beneath their feet, a shadow moved.

She broke the surface, sputtering with the others. The seeds were buoyant, and they clung to them.

Sabine spat out the foul water. "What happened?"

Brannon glowered into the sky, where clouds whipped by on an icy wind. "Eskazi happened. Miserable old girl, she never appreciated the joys of summer." He sighed. "Meri's strength is waning, and Eskazi's ascending. Meri saved one last breath to keep us from being crushed on impact, but she's used up. We're on our own."

"Are we?" Rafi peered nervously into the dark water. "The creature of Malgris Lake is just a legend, right?"

Novi circled above them, neck craning as though searching the waters.

"Natural things cannot live here," Anora said. "But with the deadness came something uncanny."

"What is it?"

"A Seeloq," Brannon said. "A creature of darkness. They drag their victims down to their underwater nests, where they feast on the drowned flesh."

Novi shrieked. Something clamped on Sabine's boot and yanked her under.

She was frozen with terror as an amorphous shape dragged her through the churning water. She made out a flash of blue-green scales before it released her. She struggled toward the murky light above, flailing for the surface.

As she took a gasping breath, Rafi went under.

Sabine screamed. She plunged under to see him pulled straight down, his eyes wide open and pleading.

The creature's front quarters were that of a horse, coated with fish scale and shadow, tendrils of seaweed streaming behind as a mane. But its lower half was that of a large water animal with a muscular tail as black as tar.

Rafi's boot was caught in its wicked curved teeth. Sabine reached for him, and the Seeloq's glittering black eyes went to her.

Rafi kicked, hitting a sensitive spot on its muzzle. It gnashed its teeth, dropping him, and disappeared in a swirl of smoky water.

Sabine grasped Rafi's hand and tugged toward the light. Rafi floundered against her, thrashing, but she forced them toward the surface.

Brannon hauled Rafi out and onto the pappi. Rafi grasped it with his arms and legs, shuddering.

"It's playing with us," Sabine said, before ducking underwater, the liquid stinging her eyes. The creature stalked them from beneath; its black lips pulled back in a hunter's sneer. This time it aimed for Anora.

Sabine thrust out her hand and Anora disappeared. The Seeloq pulled up short. It was cunning, though, and not entirely fooled.

Circling underneath the spot where its prey had suddenly vanished, it watched the swirling eddies with interest. It snapped its teeth, missing Anora by a hairsbreadth.

Sabine surfaced. "Stop moving. It can see the water churning around you."

"Then make it see something else," Anora said, her breath coming out in shudders.

The Seeloq's predatory gaze locked on the water thrashing around their dangling legs. Sabine reached out with her mind. *All is calm. All is still.*

She convinced herself this was truth. When she opened her eyes, Malgris Lake was once again motionless, and her friends had disappeared.

"You did it," Rafi said. The Seeloq cocked its head and lunged, barely missing.

"It can still hear you." Sabine clung to her dandelion seed, teeth chattering. They could not stay like this forever. She stared into the lake.

From the shadowy depths, a string of bubbles emerged, tiny like champagne trails. More joined them, becoming larger and larger as they rose to the surface. The Seeloq followed their path, descending several lengths before pausing.

Then larger bubbles began to swarm towards the surface, as though something massive stirred in the deep. Every living creature held its breath.

A black tentacle twisted out of the shadows, tipped in dark green spines. The Seeloq retreated near the surface, still circling. The tentacle wavered, then reached for the Seeloq. The drifting bubbles were giant now as something down below shifted, waves disturbing the surface of the lake.

Other tentacles rose, stretching toward them.

"What is it?" Rafi's voice was a terrorized whisper.

More tentacles darted toward the Seeloq, and the monster finally broke in fear. Its powerful tail thrust through the water, disappearing from view as several tentacles breached the surface. They fell on top of the travelers.

Rafi screamed, and Brannon let out a shout. The tentacle dropped without a splash and disappeared.

Brannon reached for where it had been. "An illusion."

"Anora told me to show it something else, so I did." Exhausted and freezing, Sabine tried to smile. "It worked. I can't believe I did that."

"Holy blazing hell, Sab."

"You saved us." Even through Anora's trembling, Sabine could hear the affection in her voice. "I knew you could do it. Your instinct was to save us. Your powers come from your desire to protect; you are a guardian, as I have always said."

"We're not out of it yet. Let's get to shore before we freeze to death."

Novi guided them to a sheltered clearing just off a beach. They crawled from the water, trembling with cold. The forest on this side of the lake was dead—miles of grey branches marching upwards toward the Tuneric Mountains, which stretched up jagged and forbidding above them.

Rafi shook his hair out like a dog. "Where do we go from here?"

"I know the way," Anora said. Her face was gaunt, her eyes limned with unshed tears. "I have dreamed of this path all my life. These mines call to me as though every footstep I take toward them has been foretold. I fear very much what lies at the end of that path."

"What is it?" Sabine asked.

"I cannot see what will be; it is all a black void. I have never been so blind."

Sabine shared a worried look with her brother. "Anora, you don't have to do this."

Anora gave a strained smile. "I do not know how to explain it, but something tells me I must."

Rafi reached out to her, rubbing her shoulders to warm them up. "Whatever happens, I will stay by your side."

"We all will." Brannon's voice was a distant rumble.

Novi flapped to Anora's shoulder. It let out a soft melodic sound, a single note of music that broke the heaviness of the air.

Anora graced them with a blinding smile. "With all of you to keep me brave, my fear does not stand a chance. You will lend me the courage I need." She turned toward the forest, and unerringly found a path between the trees. She began to climb, Rafi at her side, their faces lined with weariness.

The path was unnaturally straight and smooth, devoid of any sign of life. Sabine's skin crawled; it seemed as though the way should be more difficult than this. Why did it feel too easy, like they were being invited into the monster's lair?

Still, she would not let Anora down. Sabine straightened her shoulders and set her staff into the ground, carrying her forward.

"Sabine, a moment." When she turned to Brannon, her throat closed over in shock. There were more silver leaves in his hair, and he appeared physically diminished. When he looked up, his eyes shone gray in the light, as though all his color was fading.

"Brannon, what's happened? Did the lake poison you? Or did the north wind do something to you?" None of the others were as affected.

A flicker of despair flashed through his silvered eyes. "Do not care too deeply for me, beloved. I am not like you, and ever-changing. I feel myself weakening here."

"But you're a warrior and…a *god*. You're all-powerful."

He tugged her toward him so her body fit neatly against his, his cheek resting against hers. His skin was clammy, retaining none of his sunshine warmth. "Aye, a warrior god and all-powerful at that," he murmured. "You think too highly of me. I'm only a pretend man trapped in time, and from that, there is no release."

"I don't know what's happening, but we'll face it together." She brushed her lips against his. He placed a hand to cup her face, gently. Sabine wanted more and wrapped her arms around him, deepening their kiss. He groaned deeply and lifted her up, pressing her back until she came up against a tree.

She let out a gasp as his mouth met hers, ravenous, as though she was his lifeline. Caught between the roughness of the bark behind her and his steely grip, she pulled him even closer, matching his desperation with her own. Waves of want crashed over her as they lost themselves in each other.

He broke away, gasping for air, and cursed. "I am thoroughly undone by you. I must tell you—"

"Is this really the time, you two?" Rafi's voice found them, rife with irritation. "We have a mountain to climb."

Brannon tore himself away, a glimmer of warmth returning to his eyes. "Onward, then. But we must speak soon." His hair was its usual autumn russet, and he hiked with renewed vigor.

The terrain sloped upward, and they climbed relentlessly over the rocky ground. A rift of mountains hovered over them, sending them further into shadow. The mists swirled tightly around them as though to push them back, and they trudged along in their exhaustion as though fighting through a mud pit.

Rafi and Anora crested a hill and faltered.

"Blazing hell gods." Rafi reached for Anora's hand.

Sabine dragged herself up the hill with her staff as Novi swooped down to hide under her hair. They had reached a wide clearing in front of a craggy rock face, just as it had been in the vision. The black rock was smoother than it should have been, absorbing the light like it was made of shadows. The ground near the opening held only lifeless dirt, as though poison seeped from the rock. An opening creased the rock wall, wide enough for one person to enter at a time.

The vision hadn't prepared her for the hopelessness that permeated the place.

"Slag." Rafi's face twisted in disgust. "I've seen enough of this for three lifetimes."

"Is this where you work?" Sabine asked.

He shook his head. "No, the Awhye work in the mines closer to Aporos, to the west. But I know scoria, and it looks like there's a massive vein here."

"This is where we are meant to be." Anora's voice held quiet certainty.

Brannon sneered at the rock. "This stone is unnatural." He moved as though to put his hand on it but didn't touch it. "I sense it...it is magic. Held down for too long, it has become twisted, an abomination."

"Scoria is *magic*?" Sabine asked. There was something so profoundly wrong about the rock, as though it chafed against her skin. She rubbed her arms. "Anora, this is a terrible idea. Why do you have to go into this horrible place?"

Anora placed a thin hand on Sabine's cheek. "My darling sister. This is my quest; I am certain of it. All will be restored if I only have faith. I must enter the mines. You have come far, but it is not for you to risk your lives for me now."

"None of us is leaving you." Rafi took a step toward her as

though to shield her. "I will protect you with my body and soul. You will not face these dangers alone."

Anora linked her hands through his. "That is noble of you, Rafi Gillesella, and I pray with all my heart it is unnecessary." Rafi bowed his head to hers.

A tremor rippled through Sabine. The scene in front of her was so familiar, like a memory come to life. An immutable promise made between young lovers.

"We see this quest through to the end." Brannon faced the cave.

"Sabine?" Anora reached for her. "Will you stay by my side?"

"To the ends of the earth, sister."

Anora smiled and was both wise woman and maiden at once. "I have a gift for you." She pulled something out of the folds of her cloak, holding out a bundle of cloth to Sabine. It was her embroidery, the edges neatly woven. "I thought you might need it in these days to come."

"I lost it in the fire." Sabine ran her fingers over the thread.

"I found it and repaired it for you."

In the weaving, her portrait was in profile now on a background of shadows. In one hand was her staff; the other pointed forward. Novi curled around her shoulder. The Sabine in the embroidery was fierce, and courage filled her.

She bowed her head. "Thank you, Anora."

Anora grabbed her hand and squeezed tight. "I have seen so much. Remember this; more than one wrong can be righted before the night has passed."

A shudder passed over Sabine with the weight of Anora's words.

Novi cawed from Sabine's shoulder. *Let us face our destiny.*

Scoria Mines

"Follow me." Anora's whisper echoed into the tunnel. "I know the way."

"My lady," Brannon said to Sabine, gesturing her in front of him. His long knife was unsheathed, every inch the warrior. "Allow me to watch your back."

"With pleasure." Sabine couldn't help her instinct to sway her hips as she moved in front of him, gratified by his muted chuckle.

Rafi took Anora's arm, and they entered the cleft, stumbling into each other in the darkness. The shadows swallowed them whole as they descended deep into the earth, as blind as the woman they followed. Fumes drifted from the depths, smelling of sulfur.

"Sab," Rafi said. His voice seemed to come from far away, though he couldn't be more than a few paces in front of her. "Could you make some of those pretty lights you did before in the forest?"

"Create light, right. I can do that." Sabine had an idea of how to do it again, reaching deep within for her magical source she'd begun to cultivate. Only, there was barely any spark of power to find. Reaching hard, she brought forth weak lights, causing their shadows to stretch over uneven rock walls, thin and guttering.

"Something's wrong," she said, panting. The effort left a thin sheen of sweat on her forehead. "It's like my magic is dampened."

"There are forces here interfering with our powers," Brannon said.

Sabine glanced back and startled. His aspect was changing. One moment, a young man barely out of adolescence; the next, an old man, withered and broken by the ages. She blinked, and he was back to himself.

"Whatever it is, it's strong," she said, wary.

The tunnel rounded a corner and descended at a steep pitch. The air warmed, at first soothing to their chilled bones. Soon, though, Sabine's hair was damp and curling from humidity, sweat trickling down her back. Only Novi trilled in the heat, stretching out its wings.

At the base of the descent, the path opened, with many tunnels branching off.

"What way do we go?" Sabine asked. The enclosed darkness brought a fluttery feeling to her chest, like a trapped bird.

Anora stood still for a long moment before her body juddered, and she pointed to a hole at the base of the wall descending into more darkness. "There."

Sabine's throat closed over at the thought of stuffing herself into that crack, not knowing where it would end.

Rafi sighed. "Of course it is. I'll go first."

Novi cawed. *Let me. I am better suited to the task than your brother.*

"Wait, Rafi, Novi will go ahead," Sabine said. She stroked the Ielzrie's neck. "Be safe, my friend." The thought of losing her companion felt like losing part of her soul.

Novi cuddled its beak against her cheek, then swooped to the hole, creeping into the darkness.

Crouching, Sabine held her breath, imagining being trapped in the rock walls forever.

It is not far, Novi chirped from below. *Come and see. Feet first.*

"I'm going in." With a deep breath, Sabine slipped into the hole, dragging her staff behind her. Her shoulders caught, and panic flared. Twisting, she was able to find more room to slide through.

Nothing stopped her slide on the other end, and she fell with a sharp cry. It was a short drop, though, and she found her footing. Novi flew to her, and she hugged the dragonlet close to her chest as she surveyed the cavern she had fallen into. A red glow lit the black stone walls.

"Sabine?" Anora called, voice wavering. "Are you all right?"

"Yes, there's a short drop on the other side. Rafi, come first. You can catch Anora."

With much whispered cursing, Rafi entered the tunnel and lowered himself down. Sabine watched his legs lower through the hole, but he halted.

"It's a tiny drop. You'll be fine."

Her brother didn't budge. "I'm trying." His limbs flailed like an animal caught in a snare. Sabine grabbed one of the windmilling legs and gave a sharp tug, scrambling out of the way as he slid through, landing in a crouch.

He turned a circle, horror etched on his face. "What is this place?"

"I don't know."

Anora and Brannon's voices drifted to them. "Trust her," Anora said to the god. "She will accept you as you are." And she slipped through the hole on a whisper of fabric against stone.

Rafi caught her in his arms. Her hair tumbled over her shoulders in a riotous halo of fire and light. "Forgive me the liberties," he said, his hands sliding down her body as he placed her on her feet with a bow.

Something shifted between them, and Anora stayed in the circle of his arms for a moment longer. Electricity crackled around them.

Pebbles trickled down from the hole. “I’m coming,” Brannon said.

Novi let out a sharp cry of alarm. *He will be trapped if he attempts it.*

“Brannon, stop.” Sabine cried. “It’s too narrow. Rafi could barely make it through, and you are twice his size. You won’t make it.” Her voice ended with a sob.

“Wait for me. I will widen the hole.” A clang of metal hitting stone sounded, followed by a shower of dust. “I can protect you.” His voice was rough.

“There isn’t time,” Anora said. “It calls to me; I must go.” Her eyes stretched wide and frantic, seeing something the rest of them couldn’t. Something horrifying.

“Brannon, I must follow Anora.” Sabine’s heart broke at having to leave him, her chest weighted as if with lead.

There was a tense silence on the other side, and then he growled in anger. “I will come to you,” he said. The clanging continued, hard and sharp, as though Brannon was taking out all his frustration on the rock. If anyone could tunnel through rock with a blade, it would be him. In his fury, Sabine suspected he could bring down the entire cursed mountain.

“Farewell, Green Knight,” Anora said to him. “That we may meet again.”

His roar echoed down the tunnel as they turned away.

Anora stood at the threshold of the cave, silhouetted by red light. “We must move. It’s time to restore the world.” Her chin lifted as she marched down the path. She didn’t see the rock in front of her, though, and Rafi hurried to catch her as she tripped.

“Are you okay?”

Anora steadied herself on his arm. “Of course.” She gave a caustic laugh. “I descend into the mouth of hell to face my worst nightmares. Why wouldn’t I be fine?” Her face softened, and she held out a hand for Sabine. “And yet, I have you with me. It is strange that life has given me wondrous friends, right when things become infuriatingly hard." Her lip trembled. "It means everything that fate brought you to me."

They continued forward together as the cavern opened, ceiling stretching far above so it was lost in shadows. Steam wafted through the air, and a squeal like the release of pressure sounded from the wall. Sabine's clothing clung to her body, and she brushed a trickle of sweat from her hairline.

They staggered to a stop as the path ended abruptly at the edge of a black rock crevasse, where the earth yawned open. From below, a red-orange glow flickered.

The eerie light cast ghoulish shadows across Rafi's face. "This place is wicked."

"It's the magic." Anora's voice was steadier, her white eyes gazing at something neither of them could see. "It has been trapped here for too long. It has become something different. Perverse." Her mouth twisted as though she tasted something bitter. "But it has memories from before it was tainted. It was wild. It wants to be free again."

"Is that what we must do?" Sabine asked. "Free the magic?"

Anora's brow furrowed as she concentrated. "I...do not know. I only know we must go there." She pointed into the crevasse.

A surge of terror seized Sabine. "No."

Rafi stepped to the edge and grimaced. "There's a path. It's narrow and there are no handholds." He let out a long breath. "I am used to keeping my feet under me in the mines. Do you trust me, Anora?"

"With my life."

"Then I will carry you."

Anora held out her arms, and Rafi wrapped her up in his. She tucked her face against his neck. Without faltering, Rafi carried Anora down the gouges chiseled into the side of the crevasse, disappearing around a bend.

With her sweating hands slipping on her staff, Sabine took a shaky step over the edge, her heart beating like bellows. Novi trilled, and she took a deep breath. Focusing only on the next step in front of her, ignoring the fact she was inches from plummeting to her death, she balanced over hell. It seemed to take hours, yet it was still a surprise when there were no more steps to come, and a platform stretched out in front of her. She fell to her knees, trembles shivering over her body.

Anora and Rafi were still wrapped in each other. Rafi set her on the ground, but her arms stayed around his neck.

"Forgive me the liberties," Anora whispered and brushed her lips against his. Her eyes closed in the kiss, and Rafi embraced her, pressing her close. They stayed that way for an endless moment before Anora let out a sigh and rocked back. "All of this was worthwhile to have met you."

Rafi took one of her hands and pressed a kiss to her palm. They both closed their eyes, lost in each other for a moment. Then Rafi cleared his throat. "Now, I believe we have things that need to be done. World saving is in order."

Anora's smile was dizzying. "In this very moment, I do believe I could save the world."

Where Dreams Go to Die

On the other side of the platform, a fissure split the scoria wall. Every ounce of Sabine's self-preservation demanded she not enter.

Anora squared her shoulders. "Let us face this together, my loved ones, so the nightmares may end." She disappeared into the inky black of the fissure.

Even a glancing brush of the rock against her skin caused Sabine a stab of nausea. Contorting her body to avoid touching the scoria, she followed Anora. Novi trembled against her skin. *The rock is bad.*

"Yes," Sabine whispered. "Stay close to me, Novi, whatever happens." The dragonlet hid under her hair.

The fissure widened into a small chamber. In the faint reddish glow, she could make out vague shapes. Above them, stalactites dangled like tentacles. They pointed to a slab of stone on the ground of obsidian black. A bitter smell drifted in the air, clouding Sabine's mind.

"This is where everything is restored?" Rafi had drawn his knife. "*This* is where the land will begin to heal again? Because it looks like the place where dreams go to die."

"Not only dreams." The voice came from the walls. They spun, searching for the source in the darkness. "Hope and magic, innocence and faith, they'll die here as well." Torches along the walls throbbed with fire, lighting the cavern.

Anora screamed and Sabine's thoughts stuttered, disjointed. The walls had eyes, staring at her, and rock creatures lunged forward, grabbing them.

As her arms were wrenched behind her, Sabine's head cleared with the pain. They weren't monsters hewn of stone but guards hidden inside the folds of the rock walls. They wore the duke's colors.

"It's a trap."

"It was delightfully easy, sweetness." One moment, there was nothing; then, in a haze of flame, the duke stood in front of her. "The Oracles played their part so well."

Sabine blinked at Duke Aurich's face, the cruel lines so familiar to her. She shied away as he approached. "The Oracles betrayed us?"

A smile twisted his face. "Sabine, you've always been so easy to manipulate. It would have been better for you if you had only done what you were told and stayed with me."

Her pulse pounded in her temples, making it hard to bring any sense to this. "But why bring us here? If you knew where we were, why not just grab us in the forest?"

"It had to be here, and you had to enter willingly. The ritual demands it."

"What ritual?"

Aurich grabbed her chin, forcing her to face him. Sabine tried to jerk away, but the guards held her fast, yanking her hair until tears sprang to her eyes.

"I had hoped to spare you this, but you just never listen. Never knew your place."

He sneered as his hand trailed down to her neck: his fingers dug into the soft skin of her throat, and his power scorched her.

Sabine gritted her teeth as her skin sizzled. Waves of pain threatened to overwhelm her, and tears dripped down her cheeks, but something else blazed inside her. Fury. Rebellion. She held his gaze, refusing to look away. Never again would she be cowed by him.

"I'll deal with you later." He shoved her away, and she sagged with the pain, propped up by her guards.

Aurich turned his attention to Anora, lifting her face up to inspect it. "You, my child, are the reason we are all here, the daughter of the goddess. With your help, I will ascend to the greatest level of power ever known."

At the words, *my child,* everything fixated to a razor point. The duke and Anora stood face to face, their profiles mirroring each other. The fair skin, the fiery hair, the proud noses. There was no mistaking it.

Anora was the child of Duke Aurich, conceived with a goddess in an enchanted glade when he was a young man searching for glory.

"Don't hurt her." Sabine struggled against her captors. "Aurich, she's your daughter."

The duke snatched his hand away. "I would know if I had a child."

"Just look at her. You were lovers with The Lady of the Forest, weren't you?"

"How would you know that?" Eyes round with shock, Aurich tilted Anora's face one way then another. "It can't be true."

"I hope with all my heart it is not." Anora spat at his feet. "To be the daughter of a monster, a vampire who feasts on the souls of innocents. I pray it is not so."

A gust of air left him, and for a moment, Aurich slumped. His hand went to his mouth, and he gave a slow shake of the head. "Have I been a pawn in this too? Everything was set into motion years ago. She promised me so many things."

His face darkened. "And I intend to collect. It doesn't matter where you come from, only that you are the key to the ritual."

He grabbed Anora by the arms. Stifling pressure grew around them until Sabine could barely move against the crushing weight.

Rafi struggled as his captors shoved him back. Sabine fought to cast an illusion, but the unseen force smothered her magic.

The hands holding her loosened. She looked back at the guards; they were as affected as she, their eyes bulging and their hands at their throats, gasping for air that was not there.

Only Aurich and Anora were unaffected as he forced her to the stone altar. Anora fought him, struggling to get loose, but his grip was ironlike.

Novi stirred but slowly, as though bound by the same magical pressure holding them all in place.

Aurich dragged Anora onto the black stone as she beat her fists against his chest. "You are practiced at this, aren't you, *father*? Because I'm not the first, am I?"

Aurich didn't meet her unseeing gaze. "This will be over soon."

"You will *never* have what you desire." Her voice echoed through the cavern, strengthened by a power Sabine did not understand. It sounded like a declaration that could not be undone.

The duke's eyes bulged. "You little heathen, you think anything you say matters? *I* have the power. No more silly prophecies or you will first see your friends tortured."

The duke drew a jagged blade of scoria. The edge had been honed to a high shine, reflecting the hellish light around them.

Anora's head twitched. "Don't you dare hurt them. Or I swear you will be cursed to the last of your days, may they be short and miserable."

Sabine's head was fogged with pain and panic. She collapsed even as her captors let her go. Next to her, Rafi fell but crawled forward, fighting the spell with all his might. A tear trickled down his contorted face. "Anora," he gasped.

"They will not be harmed." Anora's white eyes glowed.

"Do not test me further, for I know how to make your beautiful companion scream."

Anora's face was rigid as carved stone as she faced her father. "Your soul is forfeit." The air around her crackled, and her hair lifted of its own accord, a snaky halo of fire.

For a moment, Aurich stared at his daughter, terror shining in his eyes. Then his mouth tensed. "Enough. You have lost." He grabbed her hair in a fist.

Sabine screamed, though it made no sound.

For a moment, time froze, and Anora's spirit expanded in an aura around her. A tendril of light connected to Sabine; she felt it in her chest. Anora reached out a hand to her with a flicker of a smile. "Sister," she whispered.

Aurich dragged the blade across Anora's exposed throat, a deep and ragged wound. Bright red blood bubbled, running down the pale column of her neck. She struggled feebly against his hold as her blood pumped from her body.

Aurich dropped her, and she crumpled on the altar as the gush slowed to a trickle. Her head lolled to the side, and she let out one final gurgling breath, blood staining her lips. Her white eyes stared, forever unseeing.

The halo light surrounding her swirled toward Aurich's outstretched hands as he absorbed her essence. He seemed to swell in stature, his eyes reflecting firelight as though he glowed with devil light.

The air shimmered, and from a ripple in space, The Lady emerged in the cavern.

She wore a gown of glimmering light as though made from the fabric of magic itself. Her hair shone, and her skin glowed; it hurt to look at her. Her eyes matched the great emerald dangling from her neck.

She stared at the body of her child, still bleeding out on the sacrificial stone, while the duke stood over her, bloody knife still in his hand.

And she laughed.

It began low in her chest, a deep rumble. It was like rocks tumbling over one another, thunder tearing across the prairies, flaying against Sabine's skin. She tried to cover her ears. The goddess's power pressed against them until there was no room for air.

"The ritual is complete." The goddess's voice boomed through the cavern. She held out a hand to Aurich as though blessing him. "You have done well to bring this to an end."

"What?" Sabine gasped. She still fought against the pressure.

The Lady glanced over her shoulder at Sabine, as though just noticing her. Her glowing eyes were rimmed hellfire red, and her smile stretched far too wide for her face.

"We have all come to where we needed to be. A crossroad of power and magic."

"*You* did this? You wanted Anora killed?"

The Lady sighed as though burdened by the weight of the world. "It was necessary. I would not expect you to understand."

She faced Aurich. "For your loyalty and in performing the ritual as promised, receive your payment." Reaching to unclasp the chain of her pendant, she let the emerald fall from her throat. The Chalice of Life, the stone that had given her power for millennia. The duke watched with blatant greed on his face, a splash of blood cutting across his pale face.

A ball of energy and light exploded from The Lady as the emerald lifted off her skin. The force of it struck Sabine, and she staggered back. An earthy smell filled the chamber, edged with rot; the dark, loamy scent found at the bottom of graves.

The Lady of the Forest transformed, her skin becoming dusty gray. She looked like a decrepit statue riddled with fissures of light. At that moment, her eyes met Sabine's and a complicated emotion flitted across her face.

"Forgive me," she croaked as the duke snatched the emerald from her outstretched hand.

With a crack, the Green Goddess crumbled into a pile of ash.

Sabine let out a sob of horror as she fell forward, suddenly able to breathe again. All the guards and Rafi slumped, too, as the pressure that held everyone back released suddenly.

"The Chalice of Life." Duke Aurich held it aloft. It glittered in the scarlet light of the cave. "All of her power, concentrated in this single vessel. All mine."

Sabine gazed at the scene before her: Her dead friend, the goddess in ashes at her feet. She whimpered, catching the duke's attention, his eyes lit with malevolence. "Now I have everything I want."

Novi, finally freed, let out a ringing shriek. The sound clarified Sabine's muddy thoughts. Her powers were no longer stifled, and she became invisible.

The men near her let out shouts of surprise, and Sabine took quick advantage, scrambling toward Rafi. She grabbed him and used her momentum to roll into a corner, dropping an illusion that the cave wall extended over them.

"Kill the boy but bring me the girl." Duke Aurich's eyes were wild, his neck corded with tension.

The men jostled in the crowded chamber, attempting to draw their swords and threatening no one but each other.

"Enough." The duke sneered at the inept display. "It doesn't matter. Are you listening, Sabine? *You don't matter*. Awhye scum, nothing more. I will live forever. If you will not come to me, then you will rot here."

One by one the torches went out as the men filed from the cavern. Soon, only the duke stood at the entrance. His smile was so familiar. "Enjoy your tomb."

He raised his hands above him, then brought them together. The scoria walls obeyed, dragging through the ground with a groaning squeal to knit together. Sabine let out one last raw scream of terror as the seam of the stone closed, leaving her in darkness.

A God's Bargain

Sabine stared into the black of their tomb, taking steadying breaths. Her body shook, but she forced herself to move. She crawled to where the wall had joined, trying to find a crack to slip through.

"Brannon," she said out loud, her voice cracking. All those guards, *Aurich,* would be heading straight for him. Would Brannon be able to fight them off? He said he was weakening, and Aurich was more powerful than ever. She collapsed forward, her face falling against the scoria. It was cold as ice, sticking to her face. The burn at her throat sent tearing pain through her with every gasping breath.

Rafi heaved on the floor next to her and let out a scream, the sound magnified in the cavern. He scrambled to where Anora's body had collapsed on the altar. He screamed again; the sound ripped from his throat.

Sabine crouched over herself, pressing her face into her knees. The pain of grief building inside of her was going to explode.

A vibration hummed against Sabine's throat. Novi began crooning in a way she'd never heard before. The sound was both soothing and grievous, and her heart shattered. It was a death song, ancient and eternal. It reverberated through her bones to the center of her soul.

Tears slipped down Sabine's cheeks as she began to hum. She didn't know the melody, and her voice was raw, but somehow it added to the song.

Novi leaped from her shoulder, circling the cavern in tight spirals. The Ielzrie's body glowed white-purple, and the cavern seemed no longer hellish, but rather holy.

Sabine raised her head as the song cascaded to the ceiling. She saw Rafi now, cradling Anora's still form, covered with her blood.

Novi came to rest next to Anora, singing its grief. When the song finished, a single note hovered like a tangible thing. Sabine took in a breath, finding it easier, and her hand flew to her throat. What should have been a painful oozing burn was clean, perfect skin. "Novi, how?"

Magic is surrounding us, growing more and more powerful by the minute, Novi said. *I asked it to heal you.*

Sabine stared at her Ielzrie, eyes filling with tears. "Magic and power. Is that what this was about? How could the goddess have done this?"

Novi warbled in grief.

Rafi roared. "Anora was brought here like a sacrificial lamb. *We* brought her here. The Oracles..."

"They were in on it. Or The Lady tricked them too. It's like she planned the whole thing. Only now she's dead. None of it makes sense."

"The only thing I know is that I will murder that man." His face was alight with pure hatred. He slammed his fist into the wall. "I'll kill him!" He stumbled back, tripping over Sabine's staff. He grabbed it and, with a scream of rage, struck the wall again and again. Chips of wood flew, but it made no difference to the uncaring rock face.

Sabine wanted to lie on the cool floor and close her eyes. She was so tired.

Novi cawed, sharp and commanding, clearing her head. *Enough of this. Now is not the time to wallow.*

"Right. No time to rest." Sabine groaned and knelt at Anora's side, brushing a tendril of hair away from her still face. With all possible care, she closed her eyelids.

"We won't let her murder go unpunished. We're not going to die here." Novi's eyes flamed purple. Its shriek rang through her, reflecting Sabine's rage, lighting a fire within. She shook out her arms as though to rid herself of clinging grief. "Brannon...he will be in the path of the guards. We need to help him."

"How? We're entombed in this hellhole."

Sabine inspected the seam of the rockface. "Anything made by magic can be unmade. But this is not my kind of magic." She slapped her hands against the solid rock wall in frustration.

The rock responded to her strike, reverberating under her palms. She held them against the stone, perplexed, as the earth rumbled and shook.

"Sab, what are you doing?"

"It's not me."

The stone groaned, shrieking as it shifted. Sabine grabbed her brother and dove to the center of the cave as Novi swooped to join them. They crouched over Anora's body, protecting it.

The thunder of moving rock engulfed them, earth crashing all around. Sabine didn't realize she was screaming until she choked on a mouthful of dust.

The quaking quieted to a residual judder, and she coughed in the settling dust. The air cleared to reveal one side of the cave wall ripped away.

"Blazing hell." Rafi gazed over her shoulder, face alight in awe.

Brannon stood at the entrance of the cavern. Cloaked in shadows, he was the god of death, with antlers and black eyes that swirled in a void.

Then he was Brannon again, although so dust-covered he could be a statue.

Sabine threw herself into his arms, relieved to feel him strong and secure under her weight. "What happened? Are you okay?" Her fingers grazed his face, set in stern lines like granite.

"I'm unhurt, beloved. I could not find a way through the rock, so I asked the rock to move for me."

"You asked it to move?"

"I asked my brother, the element of earth, although it cost me dearly. He warned me children of flesh were trapped in his belly. He lent me his strength, and together we opened this cursed cavern."

"What did it cost you?" Sabine ran her fingers through his hair, silty with dust.

Brannon's face twisted as though he struggled with something. Finally, he sighed. "I cannot say. I'm sorry, Sabine. I wish I could."

Releasing her gently, Brannon took in the scene for the first time and staggered. "What in the goddess's name?"

Rafi knelt on the altar, Anora's head cradled in his lap. Her fiery tresses stood out on the black stone, as did the angry red slash across her fair throat.

Brannon knelt next to Anora. "I have failed. I was supposed to protect her."

Fury blossomed in Sabine's chest, giving her strength. "The Lady betrayed us. She intended Anora to die here, Brannon. *She* led us here with a false prophecy from the Oracles, where the duke was waiting to perform an unholy ritual. We were never supposed to restore anything."

Grief and bewilderment made Brannon seem very old in the dim light. "The Lady of the Forest has always been a staunch protector of our ways."

"Not anymore. She was working with the duke. She gave him the Chalice of Life in payment for killing her daughter. It looks like he betrayed her too, though, because she turned into a pile of dust." Sabine pointed, numb to the horror of it all.

"No more than she deserved." Rafi's voice was vicious.

Brannon's face drained of color. "How can this be? She was an ally for millennia."

"She cracked, then, because she was a monster. She *laughed* when she saw Anora's body. And then she was gone. I think she set everything up from the start." Sabine paced a circle around the crumbled rock littering the floor. "She insisted we go on this quest, sent us to the Oracles, who guided us here. Like we were being funneled to this place. So she could have her daughter murdered." She trailed off as she blinked away tears, remembering the Oracle's prophecy that sounded different from the rest. *You cannot save them all.* The only true prophecy made.

"But *why*?" Rafi asked.

The wall shook as Brannon punched it, roaring. "She played me the fool."

"She played us all for fools." Sabine carefully took his hand in hers, bloody and streaked with dark dust. "It doesn't matter now. We need to leave."

"Where do we go?" Rafi's question echoed over the desolate stone.

Sabine gazed at Anora's body, marred only by the gash at her neck. "Alioch." A painful lump grew in her throat, and she swallowed. "It was the only place she was ever truly happy."

"But Alioch was The Lady's stronghold. Can we trust anyone there?"

Sabine lifted a shoulder. "It's a place to start. We'll discover who knew of The Lady's treachery."

"It'll take ages. With the winter setting in, we could freeze."

"We'll be cold, and tired, and full of despair." Brannon removed the dust-covered cloak from his back, brushed it out, then laid it alongside Anora on the altar. "But we must figure out who played a hand in her murder. Are you with me?"

Rafi's gaze was fierce, and he gripped Brannon's forearm. "I will never rest until she's been avenged."

Brannon nodded in cold determination. With a gentleness hard to imagine of a man his size, he lifted Anora as though she were a doll, setting her on his cloak. He wrapped the fabric until her face and head were covered, every strand of her copper hair hidden. Nothing of Anora was left but an insubstantial shrouded figure.

He cradled her in his arms. "We must leave these caverns. Something has happened; the scoria holding the Hunt has become unstable. Soon, it will gain enough power to release itself."

"The Hunt? You mean wild magic, like in the stories?" Sabine asked, picking her way over rocks as she followed her beloved. "Uncontrollable magic that ravages the earth—that's what scoria is?"

He nodded. "The Hunt is a predatory, destructive force. You understand why we don't want to find ourselves underground when the magic is released."

Outside the cavern, they were faced with the treacherous climb over the crevasse. Weary with exhaustion, Sabine closed her eyes and, for a moment, thought of simply crumpling to the ground and giving up. But Rafi's face showed his battle between tears and vicious anger. And Brannon looked as if he were about to break apart, holding Anora carefully in his arms. She took a deep breath and together they climbed.

As they came over the last step, Sabine peered into the crevasse and stifled a scream.

"What is that?"

A boiling substance glowed with heat, letting off hisses of steaming vapor. Sweat dripped down her neck from heat and fear.

Brannon looked into the crevasse and cursed. "It's molten scoria. My brother warned me of this. The mines are going to blow."

Thoroughly motivated now, Sabine sprinted up the twisting

tunnels. Curving around a bend, though, she came to the place where Brannon had been trapped. She froze, transfixed.

The walls had collapsed inward, leaving a wide sloping tunnel. Piled around the area were the duke's guards. They lay where they died, bearing the marks of swift death. The coppery smell of blood choked the cavern.

It was only then she realized under the dust that coated Brannon, he was drenched with blood. His eyes were black as he watched her.

"I never claimed to be a peaceful man," he said. "When the duke's men emerged from the caves, smelling of death, I feared the worst." He put a hand out as if to touch her, then snatched it away.

Sabine caught that hand, placing a kiss on the palm. "I worried they would ambush you. I should have known better." She glanced at the bodies. "But the duke?"

"He did not come this way. I would have gladly removed his head from his shoulders if he did."

"On that, we are in agreement," Rafi said, and the earth trembled under their feet. "But now is not the time to plot our revenge."

They fled the mountain tunnels as though hell was chasing them. Reaching the surface, they staggered into a winter storm. The wind howled, buffeting them with stinging lashes; the steely-gray sky difficult to see beyond the swirls of blowing snow.

The cavern groaned, and a gust of hot air rushed over them, sulfuric and stinging. The contrast of hot and cold caused Sabine to break into a terrible sweat. It felt as though the fabric of the earth would tear itself apart.

Sabine drew Novi away from her neck. The Ielzrie shivered, and Sabine grieved for what had to be done.

"There is something I must ask of you, and I fear it is too much."

Novi crawled forward and nuzzled Sabine's cheek. *Nothing in the world is too much for you.*

Sabine blinked back tears. "My people, the Awhye, are forced to toil in the mines near the city. They must be warned of what is happening to the Scoria. Is there any way you could get to them, to let them know the mines are unstable and they need to get out?"

Novi straightened its neck. *I will travel there, with the speed of the Ielzrie.*

"And my mother, her name is Hesta. She is a baker who lives in the Wilt, in Aporos. Could you find her?"

The Ielzrie considered this, tilting its head one way then another as it studied Sabine's face. *You are connected to her by a thread of love. I could find her anywhere.*

"Good. I need you to tell her everything. The Awhye must be warned. Terrible things are coming."

Novi let out a cry, then disappeared in a puff of black smoke.

"Stay safe," Sabine whispered.

They stumbled down the dead path away from the mountain, holding each other up. Weak with exhaustion, Sabine forced herself to put one foot in front of the other, the earth trembling as if it would shake itself apart.

They had reached the lake's edge when the ground bucked under their feet.

She caught a look of terror on Brannon's face just before it happened.

A colossal explosion convulsed the ground hard enough to send them sprawling on the ground. Trees throughout the forest crashed down, and a shower of rocks rained down around them. Brannon caught Sabine in his arms as she fell, holding himself above her as a shield as they rode out the destructive waves rippling through the earth.

As the shaking settled, Sabine blinked dirt out of her eyes, coughing to clear her lungs. A massive black cloud billowed into the sky, lit in fiery red. It seemed to go on forever, the shocks stretching out for miles.

"The mines." Rafi looked back the way they came, mouth set in a grim line.

"Hell gods," Sabine whispered in horror. "Our men."

Rafi shook his head, unable to speak. They had no idea whether the annihilating force inside the mountain went as far as the mines where the Awhye toiled.

"The Hunt has been released," Brannon said. "Raw magic has been unleashed into the world."

At his words, a wind blew around them. It wrapped around Sabine, her hair and clothes whipping up in the maelstrom. She was surrounded by voices and animal growls, all trying to be heard over the other.

Inside Sabine was a wild longing to lose control, to fly with the beasts that sang on the wind.

Then the whirlwind blew away, traveling up and over the Dikisi Forest, leaving her behind with a loss she didn't understand. Sabine drew in a shuddering breath. "Oh, gods, what do we do?"

"We keep on going." Rafi stalked toward Anora's shrouded figure, the lines of his body taut. "I will carry her."

Brannon reached out. "Are you sure?"

"Yes. No offense, old man, but you don't look up to it."

Rafi stooped and cradled Anora into his arms as though she weighed nothing. One step in front of the other, he carried her down the path.

Brannon was still braced on one knee on the forest floor. He did look like an old man. Under the filth and blood, his skin and hair were entirely gray, as though all color had leached away.

Sabine helped him to his feet, tears running down her cheeks in her terror. "Brannon, tell me what's happening to you!"

He shook his head like a bothersome ox. "I can't." His eyes were icy white. "I am sorry. You deserved better than this."

“Is your brother doing this? Tell me.” She shook his shoulders, as though she could make a god obey her command.

Brannon tried to speak, and again, no words came out. His shoulders drooped, defeated. “I must return to Alioch.”

“But why? What’s going to happen?”

He could only hang his head in sorrow. Gone was the proud warrior god. Brannon had become a broken old man.

Rituals

The journey to Alioch passed in a freezing fog of grief and snow, trudging around the shoreline of Malgris Lake. The wind blew without relent until Sabine thought she might go mad with the howling in her ears. The bitter cold stalked them during the day while at night, they piled together under a single cloak, curled dangerously close to the fire, and still Sabine never stopped shaking, wondering if she would wake in the morning.

But every day, she did wake, blinking frost from her face. No one dreamed of singing. It seemed sacrilege to the shrouded body Rafi brought up into his arms every day. He only set Anora down at night, near enough so no scavenger would take her. He had gone silent and barely ate, fueled only by rage.

Brannon suffered the most. He no longer burned with an inner heat, fading day by day. The cold racked his body, every shudder like an earned punishment. His hair was dusty white, and lines were engraved deep in his skin.

The further they went, the harder it was until Sabine supported him, his arm slung over her shoulder. It wasn't difficult to hold him up, shriveled as he was, as if a part of him had been left behind in the earth. No matter how many times she pleaded with him to tell her what his brother had done, he only shook his head.

Sabine hoped they would find respite in Alioch. But when she finally stumbled into the glade, she halted with a gasp. The Rukhas, the gardens, the very ground were blackened and dead. The well was no more than a cracked hole in the earth, slowly filling with drifting snow.

The Eyanrac people crept from crooked tree knots and holes in the ground. No joyous children scampered to meet them. Warriors came forward, led by Feamair and Kerrick; the look they shared was an old one, exhausted and despairing.

"What happened here?" Brannon asked, his voice a creak.

Kerrick stepped forward. His voice was raspy, unused to working.

"There was a great shaking of the earth. Many Rukhas were toppled. A jet of flame shot out from where the well once was."

Sabine stared at the haggard faces, aghast.

Feamair stepped forward, her glare fierce. "What happened on your quest? Did you find something that would help us? The reason why the land is dying?"

The trio exchanged laden glances, and Rafi carefully laid Anora's body at the feet of the Eyanrac, causing an outbreak of gasps from the gathered people. Brannon bowed his head and stepped forward. "The last daughter of The Lady of the Forest..." He choked on tears. His voice was weak and ragged like an old man's, his back crooked like a hook. It was Rafi who stepped forward.

"Anora was murdered by her mother." He unsheathed his knife with an anguished cry. "Who knew of this? Who knew of The Lady's treachery?"

The Eyanrac backed away, hesitantly putting their hands to their weapons, though unwilling to draw.

Sabine put her arms out, shielding Rafi from the others. "Wait. We don't know if they were involved."

"They could be lying, just like *her.*" Rafi's face twisted in anguish; he didn't see the forest people staring at the shrouded girl in horror.

"We were tricked; why not them?"

Feamair was the only one to not look confused. Instead, heavy horror settled over her features. "No, it cannot be..."

"Why are you speaking now?" Rafi pointed a knife at her.

Feamair exchanged a long look with Kerrick as though they communicated silently. "There is much to discuss, but this isn't the place. Follow us."

"What of Anora?" Rafi hovered at her side, but she was not left alone. Eyanrac people of all ages approached her body with hushed adulation. Some carried lengths of woven leaves. Sabine pulled away, repulsed, as spiders gathered near Anora's body but remembered they were weavers, too.

"She'll be cared for." Sabine put her hand on his shoulder as the shroud was unwrapped and a length of coppery hair spilled out. "Come on, Rafi. There is nothing more we can do for her." Tears choked her voice as she tugged her brother away.

Feamair led them to the gourd-like hut where her mother used to work. Inside the apothecary workshop, they gathered in uneasy silence. Brannon lowered himself into a chair, letting out a wheeze of pain. He'd aged decades over the past week. Sabine paced the ground behind him, unable to settle.

A fire crackled in the hearth, and Sabine approached, holding out fingertips blue with cold.

"Here." Kerrick brought her a steaming mug of sludgy brown liquid. It looked revolting, but she tilted it into her mouth anyway. She expected it to taste like earth, but it was full of stewed autumn fruits and fragrant spices, warming her to the core. She held the clay vessel against her frozen cheek.

"Thank you." The herbs imbued in the drink strengthened her voice.

"You're welcome."

Sabine stopped him with a touch on his arm. "How are you able speak?"

"The spell our mother cast over us ended with her death."

"We don't have time for this." Feamair bristled, uneasy. "What happened to the goddess child?"

"The Lady betrayed us," Sabine said. "The Oracles guided us to the mines, but it was a trap. The duke was waiting for us and slaughtered Anora." Brannon's shoulders slumped at Sabine's straightforward explanation. "The Lady appeared and gave the duke her emerald in thanks."

The Eyanrac siblings drew back, staring at each other as though reading minds. "Where is The Lady now?" Kerrick asked.

"She's a pile of ash."

Kerrick gaped at Rafi, who glared defiantly, while Feamair looked away, toying with some of her mother's potions. Sabine pinpointed her with a glare.

"You know something, and I've had enough of secrets."

"Many years ago, my brother and I witnessed something. In the middle of the night, our mother drugged The Lady of the Forest and her guards. She took the goddess child from her mother's arms and brought her to a place where she hoped the goddess would never find her. The Ofhellen of the Halwardians is surrounded by destructive fire magic, one that shielded Anora's essence. She was never supposed to be found."

"Idona is the reason Anora grew up in such misery?" Brannon broke off with a harsh cough and took a moment to recover.

"Perhaps Brannon could have another cup of that brew," Sabine suggested, not wanting to offend him even as she forced back her panic. He sounded like he was dying.

Feamair slammed her mug on the wooden table. "I don't have time to nurse an old man. Will you listen to me or not?"

Brannon cleared his throat, humor returning to his voice. "She's right. I'm becoming a nuisance in my old age." He accepted a mug from Kerrick, trembling as he brought it to withered lips.

"Let us listen." He squeezed Sabine's hand, his skin dry like old leaves.

"Long ago, The Lady confided in my mother that she was weary. My mother wondered if that was so, why not lie down and rest? In this, she meant to die, to follow the natural course of things. But the goddess couldn't die, for her essence was so wrapped up in the life force of the earth itself. To cut herself off from this life force, a sacrifice needed to be made."

"Her own child?"

Feamair nodded. "She did not disclose this, but my mother did her own research, revealing the truth. The goddess planned to bear a child of great power and sacrifice her for the ritual."

"Blazing hell," Rafi whispered.

"Several years ago, a young man of fire and passion came to her seeking wisdom, and she seized her opportunity, taking him for a lover and begetting a child by him."

"Aurich," Sabine said.

"My mother discovered the goddess's plan and ensured Anora would not be found. She cast a spell over us that we may never speak a word to reveal the location to The Lady." Feamair grimaced. "She tried many different ways to make us speak, but the goddess was unsuccessful."

"Did she know it was Idona who stole Anora?"

They both shook their heads. "She suspected, but our mother had powers of her own, and The Lady could not condemn the wise woman of the Eyanrac without proof. For many years they circled each other in suspicion, neither able to move against the other."

"Until the firestorm," Sabine said. They turned to her, puzzled, and she clarified. "The goddess was working with Aurich this whole time. She was probably the one who called him here. It ended when your mother was killed. Perhaps once she had Anora, she had no need of Idona anymore."

Feamair glared. "And whose fault is that? You two led the goddess child straight into the arms of her murderess mother."

"How dare you!" Rafi jumped to his feet.

Sabine held her arm up for silence. "Anora was desperate to get back to her mother. She knew the path to Alioch through visions." She stumbled to a halt. "Blazes, The Lady hoped to lure her back of her own accord. And we merrily helped her along."

Blinking back tears, she relived once more the last moment of Anora's life when she called her sister. And Sabine had been complicit, too, in her murder.

Brannon sat back, eyes fluttering shut. "In all my long years, I've never known such cruelty. That girl was all things good in the world." He coughed again, and this time did not stop. A wheeze rattled through his chest, and he tensed around every breath as though in pain.

"He needs help." Sabine rushed to his side. "I don't care if you don't have time for this. You *will* do something. He made some kind of deal with his brother, and now his life force is fading."

Feamair eyed her in dislike, then glanced outside at the darkening sky. "We must follow the Old Ways, though I have no idea what good they will do us now." She stood and didn't speak again, leading the way out of the workshop.

Kerrick came to Brannon's side, hoisting him to his feet. Brannon was helpless, like a rag doll.

"What are you doing?" Sabine rushed to them frantically. "You're hurting him."

"The rituals must be followed," Kerrick said.

"I've had enough of rituals."

"Sabine, it is my time," Brannon said between racking coughs. "I wish things were different. Time was never on our side." He broke off as the warriors half-carried him outside.

The wind blew harder than ever as the sun set behind gray clouds. The air stung her cheeks as Sabine followed behind

Brannon and the Eyanrac. She halted in the winter winds when she saw what was prepared in the clearing.

A plank was set on the bare earth, surrounded by bonfires. A crowd of Eyanrac gathered there, and more joined, forming a silent procession behind the faded god, a dim echo of the festival of the dead. They chanted; the sound was hollow in the bleak air.

As they passed the bonfires, they dropped herbs, sending billows of fragrant smoke into the cold winter air. Children darted forward to place dried flowers on the plank before returning to their parents.

The Eyanrac settled Brannon on the plank, shuddering with cold. There he sighed and lay back, hands crossed over his chest. He looked a corpse, although tremors still shook his body.

Seized with horror, Sabine knelt, taking a gnarled hand in hers. "Please, I don't understand." Tears fell freely onto his gray skin. "You're a god."

With great effort, Brannon raised her hand to his lips, pressing a cool kiss there. "Even gods have limits," he whispered, and she leaned to hear him. "My beloved, I am sorry I cannot stay by your side. You must do this on your own. You have the strength."

He drew in one more rattling breath, then his body went slack. The bonfires went out in a gust of cold air. The north wind, of course.

"No." Sabine plucked at his hand helplessly. "I can't..."

To lose Brannon, to lose Anora. The hope she had found in Alioch; a second chance already spent.

She shuddered with sobs as Brannon's hand fell heavy when she dropped it, and Rafi dragged her away as his body collapsed to ash.

"No," she howled, struggling away from Rafi as he tried to hold her still.

"Sabine, where are you going?"

The pain was so great it squeezed the breath from her lungs.

She couldn't face it; she needed to move. She wished to be consumed into ash like Brannon, to never feel this again.

She stumbled through the crowd of Eyanrac, who watched over the spectacle with stoic eyes. Though they had different ideas about death, she could not believe them to be so heartless.

Sabine wrapped her grief around herself and became invisible.

"Sabine!" Rafi dashed after her, searching the crowd in vain. The last thing she saw before plunging into the forest was her brother's tear-lined face.

She barreled through the trees without a thought as to where she went. The darkness of the winter night enveloped her, and she ran until she was dizzy with grief and exhaustion.

The biting wind had grown into a menacing storm. With her last reserve of self-preservation, Sabine crawled toward an oak tree with roots snarled around its base. She tucked herself in the hollow beneath, protected from the worst of the freezing wind. The snow piled up quickly, making an efficient cave.

Wrath and grief built inside of her until she could no longer stand it. Sabine screamed, a cry of ancient loneliness. An answering howl went up somewhere in the forest. The wolves might find her, and she wished them to come, to rip out her heart so she wouldn't feel it anymore.

All is Not Lost

Sabine's first drowsy thought was that everything was white. She had been buried overnight in a snow cocoon, which had prevented her from freezing.

A scratching at the edge of her cave had woken her. She wondered if it was an animal seeking a meal.

The snow to the side of one root shifted and collapsed in on itself. Through the hole poked Novi's scaled head, lavender eyes sparkling with annoyance.

Of all the ridiculous things to do, burying yourself alive has got to be one of them. Novi's slim body slipped through the hole. Behind it came a trickle of fresh air. As Sabine breathed it in, her head cleared.

"How did you find me?" Sabine reached out to cup the shivering Ielzrie. Novi's skin was cool to touch, so Sabine pressed the dragonlet against her chest, letting her hair fall in a curtain around it. Novi closed its eyes in appreciation and shoved its muzzle under Sabine's arm, surprising a yelp out of her.

The cold shock brought her back. Reaching deep inside herself, she found her a reserve of magic that had refilled itself as she slept, and she became visible.

Novi peeked out again. *I would find you anywhere. I delivered your message to your people before the mines blew. Then I found your mother. You are very similar; did you know that? But I heard your call through the darkest night and knew you needed me.*

"Brannon's dead," Sabine whispered to her companion. Novi wound around Sabine's neck and rested cheek to cheek. Waves of love and comfort flowed over her. She cried soft, soothing tears, her heartache finding respite.

All is not lost.

Sabine sniffled. "Except everything is lost. Anora is dead, and The Lady. The duke has the power to become a god now. He will live forever, and everyone will suffer."

You will allow him to win?

"What can I do? He has the Chalice of Life."

What does that matter?

"He's immortal now." Sabine tried to find her footing in the argument. "What difference could I make?"

Novi dug in Sabine's pocket, pulling out the tapestry.

Frowning, Sabine spread out the portrait on her lap. Her embroidered self stared straight out from the tapestry. In her outstretched hands was the shimmering emerald.

"Is this true?"

It can be. He is not immortal yet.

"How do you know?"

Novi clacked its beak. *I heard many things while in the city. The duke has enclosed himself in his tower and has not been seen in many days. Great plumes of fire and screaming can be heard from within.* Novi chittered angrily. *He has demanded that the Awhye children be brought to him. They are rounding them up in the Wilt.*

Sabine reared back. "What? All the children? Not just the magelings?"

The children are being held in the Ofhellen.

"He's going to kill them." Sabine's voice was a horrified whisper.

We have no time to lose.

Sabine struggled up, cursing as the smothering snow collapsed around her. Blinking in the sunlight, she peered at the cobalt blue sky above the treetops. Since the mines erupted, the sky had been overcast with sooty black clouds, but now all was clear.

Her heart pounding with urgency, Sabine slipped over the snowbanks until she reached the edge of Alioch. Anora lay on an altar draped in spider silk and adorned with winter foliage.

Someone shouted her name. As she turned, Rafi grabbed her, pressing his forehead to hers. "Sabine, where did you go?"

"I'm sorry, Rafi. I needed to...bury myself in a pile of snow. But we must leave for Aporos at once."

"What are you talking about?" Rafi was wild-eyed, and Sabine's heart panged to have caused his distress. But despite all her grief and her burning drive to get to the city, her heart felt strangely light. Her brother was still with her; she wasn't alone.

"Look." She held out the tapestry. It showed her with the emerald.

Rafi sucked in a breath. "What does this mean?"

"It means, brother, that all is not lost. Everyone else may be gone, but you and I are still here, and there are still things that need to be done. We're going to stop Aurich." She took a deep breath. "He hasn't become immortal yet. I don't think he has enough power, so he's rounding up the Awhye children. I think he's planning to kill them; try to eke out every last scrap of magic he can find."

Rafi stumbled back in horror. "Blazing hell gods. But how can we stop him?"

She raised an eyebrow. "Rafi, don't you know that I'm the best thief in all Aporos?"

He gaped. "You're going to steal the emerald from the duke."

"Yes. Aurich needs to be stopped."

"And you figured now, *now* that he has a gemstone of unknowable power, we should make this move?"

"Exactly. The last thing he's going to expect is that we break into his stronghold and steal his most precious possession." Rafi continued to stare at her, and she felt a tremor of uncertainty. "Are you with me?"

The sunlight caught a glint in his eye, and his face hardened. "I've got nowhere else to be."

Feamair and Kerrick approached. They nodded at each other in silent agreement. Novi let out a soft caw.

"We would help you kill the monster who slaughtered the goddess child," Feamair said. "We were tasked with keeping her safe, and we failed."

"Why did you allow her to leave Alioch to go to the Oracles in the first place?" Sabine asked.

Feamair's glare was ferocious. "We didn't know what the goddess planned. I had thought getting her away from here would be safest."

Kerrick put a comforting hand on his sister's shoulder, and they both looked to Sabine. She bowed her head. "It would be an honor. But we must leave today."

Feamair nodded, satisfied by Sabine's reaction. "We'll prepare now." The siblings strode away.

Rafi twisted her staff, holding it out. The carvings had become more intricate and so life-like she swore they moved. She could see her depiction holding up a stone. Anora was there, too, eyes closed and hair floating around her face. "Are you ready to face him?"

"Yes, I think I finally am. No more hiding; no more running away." Sabine gripped his shoulders. "Having you by my side means the world to me. Wherever this journey takes us, we'll see it through to the end."

Rafi blinked hard as though fighting his tears. "It's been a long time coming."

He returned her hug and then went to prepare their bags. His movements were brusque, determined, as though he would do anything to escape the grief that consumed him. She hoped his anger would sustain him through their journey.

Novi yawned, beak clacking shut, and curled around Sabine's neck. She stroked its head.

Some of us have traveled far to be here.

Sabine stroked the Ielzrie's throat. "Rest now. I'll watch over you." Novi gave a sleepy, contented purr, and Sabine's mouth curled into a smile. "And I am nothing like my mother."

The dragonlet let out an un-dragon-like snort.

The Hunt

The warriors gathered around Anora's woodland shrine before they left. The low-riding sun cast a red hue over the ashy snow covering Alioch. Sabine carried her staff, where Novi perched like an ancient god.

The Eyanracs each carried a spear, with a bow and arrows slung over their shoulders. Rafi tied several knives around his waist and wrists.

As she contemplated her friend's altar, Sabine's certainty built. The atmosphere crackled, energy prickling over her skin.

"We are going to the heart of the enemy's stronghold," she said. "We will take back the Chalice of Life. We will avenge the death of our sweet friend and sister, and we will never allow the duke to murder the people of Illyamor ever again. I will lay down my life to make this so."

The words were binding and rang with power, echoing through the grove.

"I will lay down my life to make this so." Rafi knelt at Anora's side, raising a hand as though to take hers but did not disturb her body. A fierce light glowed in his eyes, and they turned to the forest.

Sabine entered the shade of the snow-bound trees, conjuring fire globes to light the way. Draughts of magic whipped by them, but she no longer feared the darkness of Dikisi Forest.

"The forest has changed," she murmured to Novi. "Or is it me who's changed?"

Novi's tongue flicked out, purple eyes closing. *Both. You now understand how powerful you are. But the very world has shifted. Ancient magics are stirring and you are a part of it.*

Sabine ran her hand over the current of power passing her by. Despite her grief and the magnitude of their task, her spirit spiraled out to dance with the flow. She lifted her chin, daring the ancient magics to come. She would pay whatever price; she was ready to see how far she could go.

In response, the clouds darkened and boiled in the sky. The power in the air roiled, sparking over Sabine's skin, and her hair twisted and curled of its own volition.

The black clouds bounced with purple light, full of malevolent energy. The trees shifted and groaned, under siege by magic. The wind gusted with such force the group braced against the violence.

Then, all went still. Nobody moved, and a heavy, pregnant silence settled over the forest. It smelled of ozone the moment before lightning struck, and Sabine's hair stood on end.

A shrieking howl pierced the air, and she resisted the urge to run.

A wave of black wind crested the tops of the trees and slammed into them. Swirling magic eddied around Sabine, shadows building and taking the shapes of predatory animals. Dark wolves raced through the trees with the currents, along with other giant creatures. The hulky form of a bear groaned at her side, then the tearing growl of a leopard. Here was the Hunt, wild magic that roamed the land.

Giant creatures paced at her side in misty shadows, and her blood thrilled. Above their heads, the ominous flap of eagles' and owls' wings filled the sky before being consumed again by the rippling clouds.

Rafi jerked. Sabine gasped as a warm furry body pressed against her leg before racing away, baying into the din.

"They're real," she whispered.

As real as magic, purred a voice inside her head. The frenzied flow of magical beasts traveled on, but dark forms remained on the path with them. In the eerie stillness that followed, they were left staring at the vengeance wolves, the Vargas.

The chief Vargas licked her chops, eyes lit by the flickering lights of the skies. *Curious weather, is it not?* She spoke into Sabine's mind.

The pack surrounded the group, snarling, stalking closer with every circle. *That which was bound has been released. Somebody has removed the cork and unleashed an onslaught.*

"What released it?"

The answer hissed through the trees. *Sacrifice.*

"Sacrifice? You mean Anora's death. Now wild magic is free to destroy everything?"

Nature is both destructive and nurturing, but there must be a balance. The unleashing of the Hunt is the first step in righting wrongs long ago wrought. Magic is not to be cultivated; its nature is wild, savage. Ancient forces have been denied for too long. The wolf sniffed. *You smell of deep magic. It takes great power to attract the forces of chaos. Who are you?*

"I am Sabine." She bowed her head. "And you?"

I am Louvras, the first and oldest of the Vargas. Her companions howled.

The haunting sound echoed through the bare trees. Other howls answered, and the air rippled. Soon, the Hunt would descend on them again.

Louvras paced, her hackles standing on end. *You call to it.*

"I don't mean to."

Louvras snorted. *Of course you do. Your anger, your demands; it is all connected. You will join us.*

"If I do not wish to?"

You already have. Can you deny the thrill of the Hunt that surges through the veins, even now?

"Why do you help me?"

Our interests are aligned. Many cry out for vengeance so powerfully the tide cannot be held back. We go where you go.

"Aporos," Sabine whispered as she realized. "The Awhye want their children back."

Louvras snapped her jaws. *We will take you there. But know this: there is always a price.*

"I will not be the same?"

You are never the same, only ever-changing. Come with us.

The Vargas' howl sang in her blood, and Sabine responded, trembling with desire to join in the faceless chaos. Her hair drifted around her as though she floated underwater. It took all her strength to turn back to her companions.

"I go with the Hunt. You can join, but there's a price to pay if you do."

"Why would I do it, then?" Rafi stared at the wolves in dismay.

"If you don't, your anger is going to consume you. Come with me and let it out."

Feamair and Kerrick put away their weapons and joined hands, taking Sabine's outstretched one. They looked to Rafi. He hesitated. "It's not natural."

"It is." Sabine's voice rolled with power strengthened by magic. "Nature is wild. And we have to get there before it's too late."

Grimly, Rafi placed his hand over hers.

A flash of purple lightning lit their faces as the chaos descended.

This time, as the Hunt swarmed them, Sabine did not flinch away. The predators of the forests whirled around them, and she stepped forward to join them. She was surrounded by howls, and snarls, and growls and snaps, and gloried in it. She poured her spirit into the wildness, and they were swept away.

On a thrust of wind, they soared into the air. Sabine was only vaguely aware of possessing a body as it shifted and transformed under her. The Hunt filled her, turning her into a predator as well. One moment she seemed to be covered in feathers, the next moment fur.

She roared and cawed; she stalked and pounced. Never had she felt such freedom, such release. She screamed in wild joy, and the sound rang out across the kingdom.

A shrieking caw responded, and at her side flew Novi, eyes narrowed to slits. Lightning flashes flickered along its lithe body as the Ielzrie swooped and plunged through the air, a dance of pure ecstasy.

Sabine had a sense she was herself but more, flying through the air of her own volition. Her hair whipped around her, and she was powerful, like a witch from the stories of old.

Beneath them, the forest dwindled, the plains of Illyamor stretching beneath them. The slopes of Aporos loomed in front of them, and they descended.

In a whirlwind, the Hunt released them, swirling away into the clouds, which boomed threateningly. Sabine, Rafi, Feamair and Kerrick tumbled into a pile on the earth in front of the scoria gates.

Wild magic still flooded through her, and Sabine gurgled with laughter. She held up her hand and was startled out of her euphoria. Her nails were long and sharpened like claws.

Feamair and Kerrick remained eerily quiet. Feamair's eyes glowed in the light, and as she tilted her head, the lengthened pupils of her iris were evident. The color had changed to a golden green, like a cat. She narrowed her eyes against the light and turned to her brother, who felt his ears. They now had a pronounced point.

"What in blazes?" Rafi's voice was muffled. His hands flew to his mouth, feeling his teeth. His lengthened incisors curved over his bottom lip. "What happened?"

Sabine dragged one of her nails along the tender underside of her arm, hissing as she drew blood. "We've taken on aspects of predatory creatures. A gift from the Hunt."

Rafi stared in horror. "Is it going to last?"

Sabine stretched out her claws, spreading them, and sliced through the air. "I hope it lasts long enough." She stood and held out her hand to her brother, careful of her claws. "How do you feel otherwise?"

"I feel...strong." Rafi stood in a graceful movement. "I feel hungry." A deep growl ripped out of his throat.

"And you?" The Eyanrac warriors nodded and stood, twisting one way then the other, taking in a world of new senses.

As one, they faced the city.

"The Hunt travels quickly," Sabine said.

The Hunt travels on the winds before a storm, on the rumble of thunder. Louvras stalked toward them, followed by her pack. *You have opened the gates to wild magic, and they cannot be closed. I hope it was worth it.*

"It was worth...everything." Sabine flexed her claws.

The Vargas sat in front of her as if waiting instructions.

We stay with you. We seek vengeance, and you will bring more than enough.

"I cannot unleash you on the city. It is full of innocent people."

And yet you seek to destroy.

"The duke. And his supporters."

Then use us as weapons. The Vargas were once protectors of the innocent. We wish to right wrongs.

The pack snarled and yipped, jumping over each other in their excitement.

Sabine looked to Novi, perched on her staff again. "Can I trust them? Are they able to hold themselves back as they say, or is it madness to even consider?"

Novi's eyes glowed. *They speak the truth.* The Ielzrie tilted its head. *A Vargas has never harmed a child.*

The Vargas growled, stalking to the city's edge, licking their chops. Rafi did the same.

"Are you okay?" Sabine asked.

Rafi shook his head, then nodded. "I feel new." He gave a wolfish grin. "I feel like I want to rip someone's throat out."

"Can you control that urge?" she asked, alarmed at his ferocity.

"There is only one throat I want to rip out." Rafi threw back his head and howled. The Vargas joined him, and the gates of the city shivered.

Revolution

Rafi glared at the gates barring their way. "I suppose it would have been too much for the Hunt to drop us *inside* the walls?"

The foul stretch of the scoria was all the more horrendous now that Sabine understood it was magic, bound and twisted. It would not be contained forever. She could feel its desire to be released, to join in the destruction.

"It won't be a problem." Wild magic still coursed through her veins. She placed a clawed hand against the stone. It was cold and sucked at her, siphoning her magic.

Instead of shying away, she forced her power into the gate.

The pressure binding the magic exploded outward. With a boom, the gate expanded at the speed of lightning, transforming into black mist. The clouds above thundered, and the mist swirled into them, becoming one with the Hunt.

"Blazing hell, Sab." Rafi's arms covered his face. "A little warning next time."

She smiled and entered Aporos. The Vargas slipped into the darkened streets like shadows, stark against the piles of snow gathering in the corners. Sabine followed, as much a huntress as the rest of them. She flexed her claws.

"To the Keep."

Wait, Novi cried. The Ielzrie tilted its head as though listening to something beyond Sabine's hearing. *She waits for you.*

"Who?"

Your mother.

"Mama?" Sabine's voice sounded very young. "What do you mean? We're here for the gemstone."

And to rip out the throats of our enemies, Louvras said. Rafi gave a growl of approval.

"Yes," Sabine said, eyeing them. "I don't want my mother involved."

Not just your mother. All of them.

"What do you mean, all of them?"

"All of who?" Rafi's feral look disappeared for a moment. "The...Awhye? All of our people?"

I smell revolution. Louvras snapped her teeth in satisfaction. *It ferments in the very air. Blood will be spilled tonight.* The Vargas paced, restless, back and forth on the streets, eager to join in.

Sabine's panic tamed the rush of magic, bringing her back to herself. "If blood is spilled, it will be Awhye."

"Maybe not," Rafi said, his eyes lit with anticipation. The sky rumbled. "Maybe the balance has tilted in our favor, Sab. Much can happen before this night has passed."

Sabine was brought up short as her brother's words crashed against her, so like Anora's prophecy at the mine: *More than one wrong can be righted before the night has passed.* Gooseflesh rose up over her skin. Had Anora foreseen this?

"Take us to them," she said. Novi cawed and took off down the road. The streets of Aporos were littered with garbage and refuse. After weeks in the fresh air, the smell was almost more than she could bear. They headed through scoria smoke toward the Wilt.

Sabine recognized the buildings, the street corners, the homes of people she once considered friends, and yet it was as if seeing it with new eyes.

And then they arrived at a place she knew by heart. Hesta's Hearth was alive with people. The Vargas howled, and people streamed out, brandishing weapons.

"Stop." Sabine gasped for air as she ran in front of the wolves, putting herself between the mob and the monsters. They wouldn't recognize them as allies. She created an illusion so that her fingernails appeared normal and Rafi's teeth no longer curled in a snarl.

She screamed to be heard. "We've come to help."

"Sabine?" The familiar voice made her want to weep, and her mother stepped forward.

"Mama." Sabine forgot all of their arguments and rushed forward. Hesta promptly wrapped her daughter into a tight embrace.

"Oh, my daughter. The night bird told me you would come."

Novi perched on Hesta's shoulder, cuddling the prickly baker. To Sabine's disconcertion, Hesta cuddled the creature back, letting it rub against her cheek one last time before it returned to Sabine's staff.

"You're just in time. Tonight, we march against the Halwardians. We listened to the night bird."

Many familiar faces were set in grim lines. So many men and women bearing pickaxes, torches, makeshift clubs. Her mother lofted a wicked knife, one Sabine recognized from her kitchen.

"Novi, what did you tell her?"

That change was coming.

"The night bird did its job." Hesta's voice was a rasp. "Most of our men escaped the mines in time. But by the time they got back, it was too late. The duke's men had already come, blades out."

The crowd rustled with grief and fury.

"The children," Sabine whispered. "They took the children."

"They slaughtered any who tried to stop them." A man stepped forward. Boldo, the man who tried to organize the miners all those weeks ago. "By the time we returned from the mines, starving and injured, they were already rounded up."

"My babies, taken from me." One woman's voice was hoarse with grief. Her face bore the marks of a nasty beating.

"The guards now descend daily into the Wilt, taking more of us to their dungeons," Boldo said.

"Not tonight, though." Hesta stretched her face up to the boiling clouds. "Tonight, the soldiers cower in their stone towers. The night calls to us; we feel it in our skin."

Rafi whistled, a feat with his new teeth. "The Awhye people congregate together on a night when wild magic roams the streets."

Hesta eyed the Vargas, who paced and growled. "Something has been unleashed, hasn't it? You've come to change things."

"Yes, I have a mission, but it wasn't supposed to be this. I must take back something the duke stole."

"Let us help you," Hesta said. Cries of assent went up behind her. The crowd shifted, and Gregoria, the *Vadovis,* pushed her way to the front.

"Sabine," she said. "We stand with you."

"What would you have us do?" Boldo asked.

Sabine stared at the people lining up before her. "You'd be risking your lives."

"They've taken our children," Boldo said over the shouts. "What more must we suffer?"

"But if we take the Keep..."

"She wants us to take the Keep!" Boldo roared, and the crowd roared back. The Vargas joined in with vicious growls. People pushed forward, and Sabine stumbled back.

"That's not what I meant."

"Sabine, listen." Her mother's voice was raised to be heard over the riot. "I haven't always been the mother I should have been. I cannot change what was done in the past but let me be here for you now. Let us fight alongside you."

Sabine wavered, and her mother pressed her advantage. "You need to get something done. What better way to create a distraction?"

Rafi nodded. "She has a point, Sab. No one will be paying attention to you if you start a revolution somewhere else."

Sabine studied her mother, thoughts jostling together. There was another player in this. Someone who was overlooked for so long, made to feel invisible too. It was risky, but if it played out right, it might actually work.

It was then that it struck her. If she led the Awhye...they could win.

"I have an idea. Gregoria?"

She faced the *Vadovis* who had guided her so much when she was younger, now ready at her command. "Take a group with you to the Ofhellen. That's where the children are being held. You go and take back all of them, including the novices they've stolen from us for years. I want those Awhye children back where they belong, in the arms of their parents."

A cheer went up from the crowd.

Gregoria's eyes glistened. "It would be a pleasure."

"Louvras, can you spare some of your pack to help Gregoria? She will go to rescue imprisoned children. Kill anyone who stands in your way or threatens a child."

Louvras growled, and three dark Vargas stalked forward.

Stunned, Gregoria nodded, her eyes enormous.

"Once the children have been released, come to the Keep. That is where the rest of us go."

Rafi crowed into the night sky. "Tonight, we'll have our freedom!"

The crowd thrust forward, hunger glinting in their eyes. Things were spiraling out of control.

Sabine slammed her staff on the dirt road.

A bolt of violet lightning shot straight into the sky. It was only an illusion, but it stopped the mob in their tracks.

"Listen to me, now." She glowed, and the crowd around her drew back. "We march on Asael Keep. We will be heard, and we will make change."

Another bolt of lightning shot from her staff. The darkened sky, lit with purple light, cast them in ghoulish shadows. Novi cawed, its eyes glowing to match the magic. Sabine's hair lifted, caught in a magical vector. This wasn't an illusion: She could feel the shiver of the Hunt rippling through the air. The night would be a wild one.

Subterfuge

In the Halwardian districts of the city, the streets were empty. The citizens had barred their doors, anxious faces peering through windows at the torch-lit mob that moved on the Keep, inevitable like the tide.

Next to Sabine, Rafi's eyes gleamed with predatory intent. And Hesta's face twisted into an eager sneer, as though the Hunt ran in her veins as well.

Chaos was alive in the air as they ascended the steep streets of Aporos toward Asael Keep, the Vargas stalking along next to torch-wielding Awhye.

"We'll storm the Keep?" Boldo asked, eyeing Louvras, who snapped at anyone who came too close.

Sabine kept her eyes ahead of her, making sure they were out of sight of the Keep as they came to a stop. "No storming. We're doing this my way. We are simply going to walk in."

"And how do we do that?" Boldo was rife with skepticism.

Sabine raised an eyebrow at him and smiled. "Things aren't always as they seem."

She turned to the crowd and allowed the illusion over her and Rafi to fall. Lit in a flicker of lightning, Kerrick and Feamair stood behind them: silent, otherworldly warriors. The mob came to a stop, recoiling.

"Tonight, we seek the equality long denied us," Sabine cried. "But first, we must enter their stronghold. We will not beg at their gates, so listen carefully to what we must do." She explained her plan to the crowd, who listened in disbelief.

"I don't like it, Sab," Rafi said once she had spoken. "Why should we hide?"

"Look around you." She gestured to the ill-armed crowd. "They are not fighters. If you put them up against the duke's men, what do you think will happen? We have to even out this battle. My way will give us a chance. Or would you prefer we are all cut down at the gates?"

The siblings faced off, but Rafi looked away first and flashed his fangs.

"There will be fighting tonight, Rafi. Let's make sure we're on the winning side."

He gave a short nod.

"Wait for my signal, then you will lead our people. Feamair and Kerrick, stay here and control the crowd; they must remain silent. Louvras, you're with me. And Mama?"

Hesta came forward when Sabine held a hand out for her. "Come, this is important. We're going to meet the queen."

Hesta sneered. "That insipid foreigner? She's a bowl of oatmeal."

"That bowl of oatmeal will become our greatest ally tonight. She's been a pawn for many years, but she'll hear us out. She cares about her son more than anything in the world."

"So we threaten him, and she'll do what we want," Hesta said craftily.

"No. Mama! Definitely not. He'll be vulnerable if the duke dies. The council will seek to take power for themselves and try to dispatch the king. She is threatened on all sides."

Hesta shrugged. "My heart is hardly bleeding. What do you intend to do?"

"I intend to offer her another option. One she cannot refuse."

Sabine turned to the Awhye. Her connection to her people was so strong she was linked to each of their spirits—they shared a fury and a hope that things could be changed and made better. Her heart swelled. They might succeed on the power of their conviction alone.

Lowering her hands, she shielded them all in invisibility. The crowd hushed until all that could be heard was the rustle of clothing and crackling torches as they moved forward. At the gates of the Keep, the Halwardian guards were lined three deep, swords in hand. On the ramparts, a contingent of archers stood at the ready. They cringed at the clouds boiling overhead, but they did not turn toward the unseen armed mob.

Sabine changed her illusion as she approached the gates, appearing alone, resplendent in the red armor of the duke's guard. She swaggered forward, the picture of arrogance. She had fashioned herself into Kosoch, the duke's captain of guard. "I have information for the duke."

A guard blocked her way with a spear. "Nobody is to enter."

She crowded into his space, staring haughtily down a long nose at him. Everything about her features was Kosoch's, down to the carefully trimmed mustache.

"Do you honestly wish to take this up with the duke? He requested information on the Awhye scum. They march through the streets tonight."

When the soldier didn't budge, Sabine sighed. "Very well, fetch His Grace if you feel it necessary. I doubt he'll be happy to be interrupted, but do so with all haste." She smirked as though relishing what would happen to the men.

They stirred and quivered.

"Blazing hell, just let him pass," one of them muttered. Finally, the guard barring their way relented and stepped aside.

Sabine stepped forward, confident the men would move out of her way. At the gate, she waited, chin high, for it to be opened. The men scrambled to get it done. Once the way was cleared, Sabine paused long enough for the invisible Vargas to slip past the gate, then strode forward again.

Hesta remained unseen at her side.

"Secure the gate," Sabine whispered. She sensed Hesta's uneasiness.

"But the men?"

Sabine watched as the guards made to close the doors behind her. "They will be dealt with." She hesitated only a moment, knowing what had to be done. "Louvras?"

On a snarl, the Vargas attacked the nearest guard. With no warning, his throat was ripped out by invisible teeth. He gargled and flailed as blood gushed down his chest. All men froze in horror.

Sabine lifted the illusion from the Vargas, which set everyone in motion. The guards stumbled and shrieked to find themselves surrounded by giant wolves, fangs bared.

Any man who raised an arm against them was slaughtered. Most fled, and the Vargas chased them deeper into the Keep. Alarms sounded from deep within the walls, as well as the chilling sound of strangled cries.

"We must move quickly," Sabine said. She and Hesta struggled to push the heavy gates open, jamming the doors to remain that way. "Novi, give the signal."

Novi flew to the invisible crowd waiting outside the gate and let out a cry that sent gooseflesh crawling over Sabine's arms.

She could feel rather than see her people as they entered, protected by her power. The deep connection linking her to each of them allowed her to keep them cloaked even as they spread out through the Keep.

"Don't engage with the guards yet," she said as Rafi passed.

He grumbled. "You ask a lot, Sab."

"And Louvras, protect our people. Kill any Halwardian that attacks, but no other."

Louvras's muzzle was slick with red, and her tongue lolled out of her mouth. *I hope they all attack, then.*

"Let's try to keep the attacking to a minimum. Boldo?"

"I am here."

"Take some Vargas and head to the dungeons. Release our people and arm yourselves as well as you can."

"Yes, chief." She sensed his salute, and two Vargas followed as he lumbered to the dungeons.

"Now Mama, with me. We have an audience with the queen."

Allies

They made their way invisibly through the vast Great Hall, with the sweeping grand staircase and walls of smooth white stone. They swept to the side as a group of Halwardian guards passed, chased by nobility demanding to know what was going on. A scream echoed down the corridors.

Hesta chuckled under her breath. "This is very satisfying."

"This way," Sabine took her mother's hand and guided her to the royal chambers.

Two men guarded the queen's rooms. Sabine recognized them, young men loyal to Liesl. Sweat beaded on their brows, and their swords were raised.

Sneaking behind them, Sabine tried the door and winced to find it barred. She blew out her breath in frustration, then took a thin knife from her belt to fiddle with the lock. The door was ancient and the mechanism simple, so it took less than a minute before it clicked. The clamor of the panicking Halwardians muffled the sound.

Sabine let herself and her mother into the queen's chambers. The guards saw nothing of this.

"That's a sneak-thief skill," her mother hissed.

"Then you're lucky your daughter's a sneak thief," Sabine hissed back.

The outer chambers of the queen's rooms were darkened, and Sabine created a globe of light as they became visible again. As was her habit, she looked to the wall tapestry, the one she had always loved, and stopped short.

The intricate embroidery had been woven by the finest hand in the kingdom. No doubt it was Anora's work, the realism extraordinary. A knight, his hair tied back Awhye-style, stood before a red-haired lady, their hands entwined. Though she'd admired it before, she finally recognized them. She had witnessed this scene, the tragic princess and her knight, before Rafi and Anora had entered the mines.

She drew in a rasping breath. Anora had foreseen it all.

"What is it?" Hesta hissed. Sabine startled, forgetting her mother was there.

"Nothing."

"Let's get on with it."

Sabine shook her head, refocusing, and tapped at the inner chamber. She made herself appear respectable, a diminutive maid. Somebody no one would be frightened of.

"I don't want to be disturbed tonight." Queen Liesl's voice shook.

"Apologies, Your Majesty. But tonight of all nights, you must rouse yourself, or all will be lost."

A silky rustling sounded behind the door, which opened a crack. A sliver of the queen's pale face appeared. "I...I know you, don't I?"

"I once served as a maid, Your Majesty. But tonight, I come as a representative of the Awhye people."

Queen Liesl examined her, recognition lighting her face. "You were kind to Leopold. You left him a gift once, a rag doll he loves. But you disappeared. I heard such terrible tales...my brother..." Liesl made way for her, wringing her hands. Her copper hair fell lankly into her face, and long shadows stretched under her eyes.

The king slept, sprawled across the sumptuous bedding, his hair matted and his mouth hanging open. He was like any other small boy. A chair was placed next to his sleeping form, where the queen worried over him.

Hesta entered the room.

"Who are you?" The queen flew in front of her son to block him from the strange woman.

Hesta cackled in response. Leopold shifted uneasily, and Sabine held out her hand to still her mother. The king rolled over, cuddling something to his chest. The Awhye ragdoll she had given him, she realized with a pang.

"Mama, stop it," Sabine said. "Queen Liesl, this is Hesta. She also represents the Awhye people. And we come to unify this kingdom before evil tears everything apart."

"What do you mean?" Terror lined the queen's face.

"I mean, tonight is the end of the Halwardian oppression of the Awhye people. Tonight, everything changes, and it's up to us that those changes head in the right direction. It's up to you."

Liesl's mouth flapped open and shut. "But I have no power."

"You could have power. You are Queen Regent. You speak as representative of your husband and former king, and for your son, his heir and king."

"The council..."

"The council will have to change," Hesta interjected. "To include an equal delegation of Awhye people, among other things."

"You can no longer count on Aurich's control over the kingdom and the safety he provided you," Sabine said. "Although I wonder how safe you've ever been." The flash of fear on Liesl's face told Sabine everything she needed to know, and she continued. "The important thing is you must act now before someone else does. The Awhye are in the Keep. You must meet with our leaders.

Support us tonight and we will support your reign. It's his only chance." She nodded to Leopold.

"He could be killed." Liesl reached out as if to shield him from the very thought.

"His life is at risk, as it has been since he was born. Your only choice is to take the power for yourself. If you truly wish to protect him, don't cower in your rooms. Don't be a pawn anymore."

A tear slipped over Liesl's cheek. "My brother..."

"Will no longer torment you."

Sabine dropped her illusion. She grew in power and space, her curves flowing, her nails lengthening. Her hair unfurled into snaky tresses floating on currents of magic. Novi unraveled from her neck, letting out a croak. "Leave Aurich to me. He will never hurt anyone ever again."

Queen Liesl gasped. "Sorceress." She didn't sound frightened but rather impressed.

Sabine stepped forward. "Your Majesty, an immense responsibility has been placed on your shoulders. But you have the courage and strength to step forward and take the mantle of power. Do this for yourself and for the innocent lives that may be saved tonight. Do it for him."

A light sparked in the queen's eyes, her posture straightening. She settled her shoulders back.

"What must I do?"

"If you would rule, it must be in justice and equality. The Awhye and all the people of the kingdom must be treated fairly. We will support you if you meet us halfway."

Liesl held her throat, gazing at the king in slumber. She bent over her son's tousled hair and pressed a kiss to his forehead. She straightened and nodded. "I agree to your terms."

"Then we are allies."

The queen called the guards standing outside the door to enter. Sabine kept herself and her mother hidden as Liesl asked them to protect the king.

"Like your lives depend on it, you understand? Call the other guards, those still loyal to me and the king. Have them meet us in the Great Hall and wait for my order."

Liesl was known to be fragile, cringing away from conflict. But she stood with her feet firmly planted, head lifted high, meeting each guard's eyes. They straightened, as though sensing her power. Perhaps Sabine made her appear taller, her skin glowing as if with an inner fire. But this only added to the queen's confidence.

The guards bowed low to her with great deference. "Yes, Your Majesty. With our very lives."

They left Leopold where he slept, and Sabine sent up a prayer that when he woke, it would be to a kinder world.

As they strode down the hallway, guards lining the halls bowed to Queen Liesl. Wide-eyed, the queen whispered out the corner of her mouth. "Are you doing this, sorceress?"

"No, Your Majesty. They are responding to your power."

Liesl's chin lifted higher. She strode past the frantic crowd of nobles, and many stopped as though seeing her with new eyes.

In the Great Hall, Sabine reached out with her mind's eye. Her people were near, buzzing with anticipation. Using the currents of wild magic that pulled at her, she found Louvras. *We need you,* she pleaded silently.

A howl echoed from down the stone corridors. Answering howls came from every corner of the Keep. The Halwardians milling in the Great Hall took flight as the massive shapes converged on the figure of the queen. Surrounded by wolves, she shook, but held her ground.

Sabine appeared at her side, nodding to calm her. "They are Vargas."

Louvras stood facing Liesl, eye to eye, her fur bristling. The queen licked her lips. "You are creatures from nightmares."

Louvras huffed out a breath. *You know of us?*

Liesl straightened. "I've heard of you at my mother's knee. You are creatures of vengeance and seek to right wrongs. It is said you protect the innocent."

Yes.

Liesl and Louvras stared at each other in hushed silence. Finally, Liesl reached her hands out, palms up. "An innocent needs protection. He is a child who will one day be in a position to right great wrongs."

What of it?

"In the stories, you are ferocious, but you are just. Join me. Protect the king and become the justice we need."

The surrounding Vargas snarled, but Liesl didn't break eye contact with Louvras.

What's in it for us?

"You bring justice to the kingdom and enact vengeance when necessary."

Louvras growled and snapped, then bowed her head. *We accept your offer. We will protect the little king this wild night.*

Liesl let out a pent-up sigh. "Thank you."

"It is time," Sabine said. She lifted the illusion covering the Awhye in the Keep. "Come forward, my people, and be seen. Be heard." The moment they appeared, Feamair and Kerrick strode to Sabine's sides, weapons out. The Awhye came forward into the Great Hall, some tentatively, watching the queen through lowered lids.

Rafi strode to face her. He held Queen Liesl's gaze, not bowing in deference as was expected. He looked as though he was trying to hold back a snarl, even as his eyes ran over the queen's face. Anora's aunt: now that Sabine knew, the resemblance was obvious.

Liesl blinked at his fangs but recovered. "I am Queen Liesl, ruling monarch of Illyamor."

"We are the Awhye, who would no longer be ruled by you."

Liesl nodded at Rafi's pronouncement, casting her gaze over the crowd of Awhye, armed with the weapons of the poor. Behind her, there was a clatter as her guards appeared, dressed in the king's colors. They advanced on the Awhye, swords drawn, as the mob huddled back. Sabine feared all would be lost and there would be bloodshed right there.

But Liesl held up a hand to hold off her men. "The Awhye are not to be harmed." She held out her hand to Rafi. "If you do not wish to be ruled by me, then rule *with* me. I want my son to be safe and to bring in a new era for this kingdom."

Rafi raised an eyebrow at the queen. "Pretty words, but how can we trust you?"

"We will show you by fighting for you."

An edge of defiance remained in her brother's eyes as he considered the queen. Then he reached out and grasped her forearm.

"Enough of this." A cry came from the balcony above.

The duke's chief in command, Kosoch, stood glaring down at them. Behind him was the duke's elite guard. His gaze pinpointed Sabine. "Kill them all, by order of the duke. Take the queen."

Liesl stepped in front of the Awhye to shield them. Her guards turned, facing the duke's men in red and gold. "Duke Aurich bears no power here." A great plume of fire spouted from her hand. Her voice rang out to be heard in every corner of the hall. "I am Queen Liesl, Monarch of Illyamor, Princess of Lunengren. I control the fires here. You will stand down." Her eyes glowed molten gold.

A booming crack of thunder sounded. The Hunt responded to the queen's ire.

Kosoch sneered. "You are nothing at all. Men, attack."

The queen's men and the Awhye prepared for the rush as the red-and-gold-adorned men clattered down the stairs.

Sabine thrust out her hands, and before the army rose a wall of fire. The duke's men stumbled back, their momentum broken.

"It will only be a moment before they realize it's not real," Sabine said as she turned to her family. Her throat tightened at the thought of losing them.

"Distraction in full effect, I'd say." Rafi gave her a grin, canines on display. "Do what you came to do."

Sabine pulled him in for a fierce hug. "Be careful. I love you."

Hesta watched her quietly. "I'm proud of you, daughter." She blinked back tears and embraced Sabine.

"Let's go," Feamair said, blinking in an animalistic way.

"Give me a minute, please." Sabine's lip trembled, not ready to leave, knowing it could be the last moment she ever shared with her family. The Eyanrac's eyes, odd though they were, held a level of sympathy.

"Help them by doing what you came here to do. Kill Duke Aurich and save them all."

Sabine gave one last look to her mother, who went to stand with a group of poorly armed women, and Rafi, who unsheathed his knives and ran into the thick of the fighters. She sent up a prayer to the only god she could think of. "Brannon, please watch over them."

Holding back a sob, Sabine broke away and set her shoulders. As though sensing her thirst for blood, two Vargas came to her sides, growling.

Sabine gestured for Kerrick and Feamair to join her. "Let's kill us a duke, then."

The Chalice of Life

The Pyre jutted into the night sky. Overhead, clouds swirled by unnaturally fast, lit by hungry lightning. As Sabine watched, the grinning face of a wolf appeared and swirled away, then the graceful form of a pouncing wildcat. Their appearance was followed by the bellowing and baying of hounds.

The Hunt is with us, Novi croaked.

At the base of the Pyre were two guards. They trembled in fear as the Vargas stalked forward, stopping a few feet away and snapping vicious teeth. Sabine cloaked herself and her companions in illusion as they snuck around the guards.

"Can you take them out without killing them?" she whispered to Kerrick.

In response, he lunged. He rapped each guard smartly over the head with the butt end of his spear. They collapsed into a heap.

"Nicely done," Sabine said.

The door of the tower opened with a creak that echoed up the winding stone stairwell. The guardroom was empty, and they entered easily. The Vargas stalked next to them, a low growl the only betrayal of their presence.

Two guards stood at the first landing, their attention held by the tumult outside, unaware they weren't alone, until Kerrick sidled up behind them, knocking them out.

This continued on for two more landings. They were halfway there when a man ran upward. He slammed into an invisible Sabine, and she tumbled forward.

"Alarm!" It was Kosoch, come to warn the duke. He drew his scimitar. Sabine jerked back, barely avoiding his blind swing. The space was too close. Even unseeing, he could make a hit.

The clatter of guards sounded above them on the stairs.

"Go," she whispered frantically to the Vargas. "Take care of them."

With eager growls, the Vargas bounded up the steps, brushing by Kosoch's leg. He jumped, slashing at nothing. "Who's there?"

A bone-chilling scream rang out as the Vargas did their work. More screams followed, but it was over in moments, and an uncanny silence descended.

All sound was stifled but that of Kosoch's panting breath. "What witchery is this?" he whispered. Sweat beaded on his forehead, and his eyes darted around the empty space.

Kerrick crept behind Kosoch, preparing to strike. Sensing his movement, Kosoch whirled and struck out in the emptiness.

His sword slashed deep into Kerrick's belly.

The Eyanrac let out a groan, and the guard reared back to finish him off.

Feamair grabbed Kosoch from behind and brought her dagger up under his breastbone. The guard whirled, reaching out, searching in vain for his killer. He gurgled, struggling for breath before collapsing, blood flowing over his chest as he died.

Above them, the Vargas let loose an eerie howl. The Hunt howled back, and cries of alarm echoed through the courtyard. Then, all was silent in the Pyre.

Kerrick stumbled to the side, and Sabine lifted the illusion on them immediately. Feamair was there to catch her brother, horror flashing in her eyes even as she shivered from her kill.

"This is deep." Her trembling hands hovered over the sickening wound at his belly. She looked up, pain etched on her face. "I must tend to him. He will not survive otherwise."

"What do you need?" Panic welled inside Sabine.

"I have the essentials." Feamair whipped her satchel over her head, kneeling next to her brother. She ripped off pieces of her tunic, her movements jerky with desperation. She noticed Sabine hovering over her. "Go! Stop the duke."

The urgency in Feamair's voice hauled Sabine to her feet. The Vargas returned, muzzles spattered with red.

"Stay here and protect the Eyanrac," Sabine yelled at them as she mounted the stairs. "Kill anyone who attacks."

The yips of assent followed her as she wound her way up the remaining stairwell. At each landing, she passed the grisly remains of guards, each with his throat torn out and a look of terror in his dead-staring eyes.

The duke's circular receiving room was empty, the desk layered with dust. Sabine's claws splayed out as she approached the stairs to the upper levels, murder in her heart.

At the highest level, a ladder led to a trapdoor, open as if inviting her. Sabine wrapped herself in invisibility as she entered a place she had never seen before—the duke's study.

Sabine assumed it would be full of texts and potions, like Idona's apothecary in the glade. But the stone room was bare of furnishings or decorations, save for lanterns set on pedestals around the edge of the open space and one giant brazier set at the center. It glowed with the heat of a small star.

On a dais in front of the brazier sat the emerald, pulsing with green light like a heartbeat. The surrounding floor was splattered with blood.

The duke stood to one side of the room, hunched over as he stared at the gemstone.

Longing was blatant on his face. Red stubble spread along his jaw and his hair was long and unkempt. Dark shadows smeared under his eyes. Sabine had never seen Aurich look so unwell.

Sabine palmed her knife. One swift slash would do it. She crept up on the duke, keeping her movements slow and steady. He could not know she was there.

In passing the brazier, she heard a hiss, and the fire exploded in a mushroom cloud. A flicker of light passed over her, like a waver in the air, messing with her illusion.

Duke Aurich was upright in an instant, shooting fire from his palm. Sabine dropped, rolling to avoid being hit. Her knife clattered across the floor.

"Who's there?" he called, his voice weak and hoarse. "I'll kill anyone who enters, spirit or otherwise."

Sabine cursed. She would not be able to sneak up on him; he was too well protected by his own magic. She stood, dusting herself off, and dropped her shield of invisibility. Novi perched on her staff, hissing, wings out. The Ielzrie looked like a gargoyle come to life.

Sabine kept her appearance unimposing, as the pretty young maid Aurich had manipulated. He started when she appeared, and fire erupted out of his palms. As he recognized her, he slumped back, shaking his hands to put out the flames, grimacing. His skin was charred and gray.

"I should have guessed you'd be behind that rabble outside." He blinked at Novi. "An Ielzrie. It's been centuries since one has been seen in our world. You have been busy, sweetness. Burying friends, I expect?"

His look was of mild interest, and Sabine had to control the stab of wrath that pulsed through her. Instead, she focused on the duke's pasty skin, the stains on his clothes, his thinly veiled desperation. She glanced into the white-hot brazier next to her. Under the waves of heat, a gruesome sight met her: bones, charring and falling to ash under the extreme heat.

"You were *actually* killing children. Even at the end, I had hoped Anora was exaggerating, but she was right about everything."

Sabine couldn't look away. So many Awhye children had disappeared, and this is where they had ended up. Not to a school of magic to be saved. They were sacrificed to the duke's desire for power. To think she had worked for him, just under this chamber of horrors.

His nostrils flared. "I *did* try to help them. It was always what I wanted. I thought with proper control, they would be able to beat back the blight. But nothing I did worked. Every time I thought I made a breakthrough, they would still go up in flames or scream themselves into nothingness. Every time." His eyes bulged. "But I discovered at the time of death, there was an outburst of power I could siphon."

"You're a ghoul, Aurich."

He shook his head, hair falling into his eyes. "If I can get enough power, I can control anything, including the land. It all starts with the blight on the magic in the land. If I am a god, I can change that. Everything will be better."

"And the Awhye children you've taken now, the ones who aren't even magical? You thought you'd eat them, just in case?"

His glare was sulky, resentful. "You Awhye have always had more magic. What right does a group of ignorant fleabags have to all that power?"

Sabine snorted. "You don't know how to use the emerald, do you? The goddess gave it to you but never shared her secrets. Have you even slept since you murdered your daughter and stole a trinket you can't use? Is having all that power just out of your grasp driving you insane?"

Aurich wrapped his arms around himself, his fingers tapping out an incessant tattoo. "I just need a little more."

Sabine pressed closer, her voice soft. "It's eating you up. It would be so easy to put a stop to this. Let the children go. Let go of the dream of becoming a god. The world can be righted again, but not like this."

He stopped pacing and gazed at her. "You have always been so very beautiful, Sabine. I did love you, you know. There was a time I would have done anything for you. I wished with all my heart I could cure you."

Sabine's heart beat like a wild thing against her chest. "Then help me now."

He circled around her, a mad light in his eyes. "But you would never give yourself to me. You were so worried about your people, not seeing how attaching yourself to them brought you down. You insisted on debasing yourself."

Sabine circled the dais as well, ensuring the duke was always on the opposite side of the room. "Who are you to speak of debasement? You became powerful by stealing magic. It must be maddening to have to rely on others, like some vampire." She looked down her nose at him. "You'll never have access to the kind of power I have. Nor the power of your child. How you must stew in your little lair and hate us."

Aurich glared. "None of that matters now," he said. "Once I unlock the emerald, I will hold all the power, and all will bow to me. And you have power enough inside of you to make that happen." Arcs of flames bolted from his palms.

Sabine leaped back in time to miss the blast. Novi let out a shriek and soared over their heads, making tight circles in the rafters of the tower.

Sabine spread out an illusion. The duke appeared alone in the chamber, breathing heavily, hands aflame. He spun, shooting out blindly.

"That's not fair," he growled. "Hiding in the shadows. Don't you even have the courage to face me?"

"What do you know of fairness?" Sabine's sibilant hiss surrounded him, stretching out unnaturally long before fading into the shadows. He spun again, seeking her. "You steal children from their beds and eat them."

Unheard and unseen, she struck him hard in the back of his head with her staff.

He fell to the ground and Sabine swooped in, claws ready to slice, but Aurich whipped around and blasted a fireball. She was forced back, and he scrambled to his feet, panting.

On the dais, the emerald had disappeared. Instead, there splayed Anora's body, bleeding out as after he had murdered her, her white eyes wide and staring. Her head followed his movements as though still alive.

"No." Aurich pressed his hands to his eyes.

"You killed your own daughter. Tell me about courage." Tears streamed down Sabine's face as she struck out at him again, and he scrambled out of the way. She advanced, ready for the killing blow. But as she swiped, the duke lunged for the center dais as if to strike at Anora's form. Overbalanced, Sabine fell back and scrambled to catch her footing. Aurich heard her stumble and struck out with his fire magic again, tearing across her arm.

With a scream, she fell back, flickering into sight.

The duke laughed and raised his hands above his head. He drew fire from the lanterns and the brazier, amplifying his powers. A ball of flame gathered in his hands, and he sent it hurtling toward her.

It was too late; she couldn't move in time. Sabine raised her head to meet her death.

A dark shape whipped in front of Aurich. Novi flew directly into the fireball in an explosion of purple light. Both Aurich and Sabine were thrown back.

Novi skittered across the floor.

"No." Sabine's shriek resonated through the tower and into the night sky. Thunder boomed in commiseration.

She dragged herself to the limp black body and carefully gathered Novi in her arms. The Ielzrie was still warm.

On a sob, Sabine pulled shadows around them as she cradled Novi. Her Ielzrie cracked open an eye, showing a sliver of purple light.

I will not leave you, dear one. Sabine could tell the effort it took for Novi to communicate. *I will never leave you. We are bound as one, and I will always be in you. But now you must do this on your own. You will fight, and for all our sakes, you must win. Inside the emerald is the answer.* Purple eyes fluttered closed.

Sabine carefully set her faithful friend on the floor and stood. The room spun in a dizzying circle, then righted itself. The emerald was visible again, glowing dully in firelight.

On the other side of the dais, the duke stirred. As he rose, Sabine let him see her in full glory. Her hair twisted out from her head; nails sharpened to claws. Lightning outside flickered constantly, calling to her.

Aurich straightened, wary. He sent out a burst of flame and she ducked out of the way, then drew closer. He shot out again and again, missing every time, until she was only a few paces away from the dais. Her eyes flicked to the emerald.

Aurich saw and clapped his hands together, fire bursting toward her. Sabine fell back and with a cry of triumph, Aurich dove for the emerald.

Only to stumble when he found nothing there. Everything in the room had been shifted by illusion. It melted away as the real Sabine reached out to take the real emerald.

"Don't touch it," Aurich said. "It will drive you mad, cause you unbelievable pain."

Sabine plucked the emerald from the dais. Waves of power rolled through her, smelling of earth and greenery. Every cell in her body lit up with it, like when she drank from the spirit water. It was all connected, all the same force.

"It wants to be let out," she whispered.

Aurich grabbed at her. "You will ruin everything."

Sabine's eyes glowed, and she caught the duke's outstretched hand, claws digging into skin so he could not escape even as he screamed.

"See for yourself the power you sought."

Her voice boomed into the night, echoing into the sky, as she raised the emerald and called down the Hunt. As the destructive power hit the Chalice of Life, it cracked open.

The power trapped in the gemstone met the destructive forces of wild magic, and they crashed together in Sabine, shaking the entire kingdom.

Her arms splayed out as she allowed it to take her. A rush of pure energy enveloped her.

All the power of the living joined with the dark forces of the night. There was light and green, and trees and vines and growing things; cries of joy and shrieks of pain and grief; the first wailing cry of a newborn and the last rattling breath of a dying man. Sabine flung the power out even further.

She saw without eyes and heard without ears and felt...everything. Every emotion, every growing root, every desire, every earthworm, every living thing flowed through her. Light didn't exist, nor darkness, only energy.

The moment was eternal and instantaneous. Sabine let out one last great breath, and green light poured from her mouth. It dispersed over the land, sinking into the earth. A wisp licked over Novi's still form.

The duke slumped to the ground when she released him. The power surge had destroyed the roof and walls around her. The crumbling tower swayed in the swirling winds. The baying of hounds swept past, then the Hunt headed to parts unknown, life magic unbound and wild and free.

Sabine came back to herself as if waking from a dream and looked to her feet.

The duke stretched out beneath her. His body was old and wizened; his eyes stretched open wide as he stared at some unknowable horror. His fingers twitched.

She crouched. "See what your evil has brought you."

His hands spasmed, and he drew in one last hideous wheeze. The look of horror remained, but he was gone. His body erupted in fire, burning a bright, cleansing white.

"May the souls of your victims find the peace they deserve."

Glowing ashes floated up into the night sky, which now showed a brilliant display of stars. The sparks swirled in an eddy, and in them, Sabine made out the shape of an antlered man, carrying souls on to their next life. He was no longer of this world, but she felt that Brannon stood at her side then. Tears streamed down her cheeks, and she pressed her fingers to her lips, then out to the night sky. "Go in peace."

The embers disappeared. Spent, Sabine moved like a creaking old lady. As delicately as her claws would allow, she picked up Novi, a bundle of black leather, and cradled it against her chest.

You did it. Novi's voice sounded tired, but its eyes glowed with love. *You unlocked all the magic imprisoned for so long. Once more it is free to roam the world and bring life and death and everything in between.*

Sabine looked to the emerald, which had fallen to the ground. It was blackened and hollow, nothing more than a stone husk. "Life magic was trapped inside the gem like death magic was trapped within the scoria."

Yes, the life magic of the land has been released, creating balance. In doing so, the cycle of the world will begin again.

"And you?"

The life force that passed through you passed through me as well. I will heal and be strong once more, as will you. The duke did not allow the power to flow but sought to capture it. It consumed him instead.

Sabine felt as hollowed out as the emerald. Novi crawled up and nuzzled against her cheek, wet with her tears. She sniffled, wiping at her face. "I am happy you're still with me."

You and I are bound. I've told you this.

"So you have."

Sabine brought Novi to her throat, where the Ielzrie curled around her neck, tucking its head underneath a wing. Within moments, Sabine felt the rhythmic vibrations of the dragonlet's snores and let out a sobbing laugh.

Voices sounded beneath her. A guard poked his head through the trapdoor, peering at the ruins in bewilderment.

Sabine held up a hand to ward him off, too depleted to do more.

He crawled onto the open platform and knelt at her side. She recognized him now, one of the queen's guards. "My lady, I have been given orders by Her Majesty, Queen Liesl, to offer you the aid and support you need."

Sabine slumped further, wondering if she would have to be carried down the tower.

More soldiers came onto the platform, weapons out, searching for attackers. The guard at her side looked up.

"The duke?"

"Nothing remains of him but ashes."

"That's for the best. He was declared an enemy of the kingdom, and his private guard is imprisoned for the time being." The guard met her gaze, then flinched away.

"Two warriors were with me; one of them was wounded. Can you tell me if he's alive?"

"He lives and is in the courtyard with the other. We should join them. The tower is no longer sound. I'm surprised it's standing at all."

The guard stood, dusting his pants, and held out his hand for Sabine. She could do nothing but accept it and follow.

The Queen's Justice

Sabine limped out of the Pyre. Feamair and Kerrick waited for her outside, Kerrick leaning on his sister. Sabine bowed deeply to them, filled with relief and sorrow. They returned the gesture.

"Kerrick, you're upright! Your sister works miracles."

"It wasn't me," Feamair said stiffly. Grief still haunted her face. She knew how close it had been. "A green light filled him, and he was healed. I cannot understand it."

Sabine sent up a murmur of thanks to the wash of healing magic that had been released. "All that matters is you're alive."

"My lady," the guard said. "I fear for our safety. Please, come into the Keep before the Pyre collapses."

The tower gave an ominous creak, and stones crashed to the ground from above. Sabine faced the Pyre one last time. It leaned precariously to its side; the black stone darker than the night sky. It was obscene, a growth to be removed.

"Is anyone in the tower?"

The guard shook his head. "All living guards have been taken away."

Sabine closed her eyes, sensing the lingering magic. It

surrounded them, swirling through the air. It felt satiated, but she hoped it had room for one more meal.

She raised her hand to the sky, envisioning what she wished and made the request of the Hunt. She brought her staff onto the courtyard stones with a sharp crack. Wild magic descended like a cloud of roiling smoke, enveloping the Pyre.

With a thundering groan, the tower was ripped out of the courtyard, disappearing into a whirlwind of magic. Lightning flickered and the clouds dissipated, leaving no trace of the tower behind. A patch of loamy earth was left in its place, and the lingering smell of woodsmoke.

Sabine lifted her clawed hand and opened it, releasing the magic back into the world, to the earth and the sky. With a last rumble of thunder, the electricity in the air faded.

"Great goddess," the guard said, falling to his knees at Sabine's feet.

"Please stand." Wild magic rippled over her, her hair floating. Some of the strands had become violet. "I am no goddess. No one should have that power."

She offered her hand to the soldier, who hesitated before allowing her to touch him. He gazed open-mouthed at her. "The queen wishes to see you in the throne room," he managed. "She has called the first council meeting of her regime. She wishes for them to be public, where all may watch and hold the leaders accountable."

Sabine gave a tired chuckle. "Of course she does. Please lead us there."

With Kerrick and Feamair at her sides, they limped through the Keep. A massive crowd spilled out of the throne room. Tension charged the air, but there was nothing magical about it. It was the shouts and cries of people deciding their future.

The Awhye and the Halwardians faced off against each other, though the actual fighting had stopped. For the moment.

The Awhye side was full of shouts of joy as families were

reunited. Several filthy men wove through the crowds to find their loved ones. They carried an arsenal, and Sabine suspected they had emptied the dungeon armory. Some held their wives or were fussed over by their mothers.

Sabine passed by a woman sobbing uncontrollably, holding a tiny girl with shorn hair. The girl clung tight to her mother. Gregoria stood at the center of the room, surrounded by a gaggle of children, looking both pleased and harassed. More and more parents flowed toward them, desperate to find their stolen children.

At the end of the long room sat a raised platform, holding two thrones. Queen Liesl sat in one; the other was empty. Her son, King Leopold, was curled on her lap, blinking at the crowds around him and clutching an Awhye doll tight.

One Halwardian noble hovered near and whispered in Liesl's ear, gesturing from the child to the throne. She stumbled back at Liesl's icy glare, putting an end to suggestions it was improper for the queen to hold her son while on her throne.

The Vargas spaced themselves along the platform, seated or lounging on the ground like oversized dogs. No one could doubt they placed themselves at the hand of the queen. Louvras sat upright next to Liesl's throne, ears pricked forward and piercing black eyes roaming the crowd.

From the Halwardian nobles came anger. At the foot of the platform stood the lords of the former council. They frothed in indignation, yelling at Liesl from the base of the platform. Liesl paid them no mind, but when one lord approached too closely, finger jabbing in outrage, the nearest Vargas popped open an eye and growled. The man fell back, apoplectic with rage.

Sabine sighed, feeling ancient as the world. She limped through the crowd, and it split down the middle, a hush following her procession. When they caught sight of her, several Halwardians yelped in fright. She imagined she looked a faerie-tale monster herself. When the queen saw her approach, she held up her hand. As if she had cast a spell, the nobles fell silent.

At the queen's side, Sabine sought the only thing she needed to see: her mother and brother alive. Both bore marks of a struggle, clothing torn and hair mussed, but they were whole.

And they weren't alone. Around Rafi's shoulder slung a new Ielzrie, curled against his neck and fast asleep.

"What's this?" Sabine smiled through tears as he helped her onto the platform.

"I got a dragon," he said.

"I can see that."

"And I'm not the only one. Look."

Sabine turned to the crowd, and that's when she noticed more and more Ielzries perched on shoulders of Awhye warriors, who seemed stunned by their magical companions. Other clouds of black smoke were appearing even as she watched.

"Novi," she whispered in awe. "Are you seeing this?"

Her sleepy Ielzrie peeked its head over her shoulder and trilled. The newborn Ielzries raised their heads, calling in response.

Sabine watched the Ielzrie fondly, then faced her brother. His face was filthy, but he glowed with an inner fire.

"You survived," she said and then burst into tears. Rafi pulled her into a hug, and Hesta joined them.

"The duke?"

"Ashes."

Rafi growled in approval. "We've succeeded. We took down the duke's men and made a way forward for change. There were losses, though. Brave warriors, all of them."

That's when Sabine saw them, laid out behind the queen on the platform. Awhye, men and women, stretched out in rows, all died for their freedom. Boldo lay among them, and Rafi's friend Jaime. Sabine fell to her knees looking at them, every lost soul a sharp pain. There were men in the king's colors and behind them, more bearing the duke's.

"So many," Sabine whispered. "It's too much."

"We'll ensure their sacrifice was worth it." Rafi knelt at Sabine's side. Hesta came to her other. Taking Sabine's hand, she let forth a piercing wail of lament.

Behind her, the Awhye knelt to honor the dead. A gasp went up as the queen knelt as well.

The Vargas arose and howled, joining in the cries. The Awhye wailed or cried in sorrow, a wave of grief crashing over them.

Gregoria began to sing a mournful death chant, and something inside of Sabine's chest broke open. She cast an illusion over her fallen people as though they lay resting peacefully. Above them, she cast thousands of stars in a nighttime sky until the whole crowd seemed to spin in a galaxy, away from this place and time.

The death chant ended, and the illusion faded. In the hush, Sabine braced herself on Rafi's arm to stand.

"What of the wounded?" she said.

Rafi shook his head. "There are no wounded. After the earth shook, there was a wave of green light that passed over us. I had a sword wound, here." Rafi pointed to his shoulder, where his tunic had been sliced open. "It was deep, but it healed over in an instant."

"Thank the gods," Sabine breathed out. Many ugly deaths had likely been avoided thanks to the life force magic that was released.

Queen Liesl stood, Louvras stalking forward at her side. She held out her hands to the two groups of people standing before her. "These are the last victims of Aurich's evil rule," Liesl said. "They sacrificed themselves for a better world and will be remembered long after we have left this world.

"Our land suffers and needs to heal. The people of Illyamor, too, need to heal from the wounds of grave injustice. The time to begin is now. We have formed a new council, with members from the Halwardian and the Awhye peoples, although in the future, I would like to expand the council to include members from all Illyamor. The nobles, the merchants, the farmers, the miners, and those who have not had a voice before shall be given a chance to speak. With a council of equals advising me, I feel confident that I —and my son when the time comes—will find solutions to the longstanding divisions in our land."

Sabine, tears still streaming, had to bite back a smile at how deftly Liesl grabbed the reins of power.

"Louvras has agreed to stay by my side as the queen's justice. The Vargas will remain as protectors of the kingdom. They will enact vengeance in my name against those who seek to destroy the kingdom we would build."

Excited chatter resumed at this development. Sabine cocked her head at the Vargas sitting next to the queen. Louvras returned the gesture.

Liesl turned to Sabine. "Sorceress, I would ask you to join our council. You speak for your people and have connections with our cousins in the forest." Liesl nodded to the Eyanrac, who slumped against each other behind Sabine. "You have gained great powers, you have befriended creatures of ancient legends, and you have brought down the evil blighting our land. Surely you will stay to help rule the kingdom."

Sabine bowed her head in acknowledgment. "I am honored, Your Majesty. I would like to help as I can to rebuild the kingdom, but I believe that means something other than staying in Aporos. I trust my brother Rafi to speak for the Awhye, as well as Hesta, Gregoria and any other representatives the people choose. But as I grow in power, there is still so much more to learn, and I wish to deepen my knowledge. If you would accept me as a traveling advisor, then I would happily join your council."

Liesl lowered her voice so few could overhear. "I had counted on your power to support me."

"It is not my power but your own they listen to, Your Majesty. You do not need me, but I will be here if you ever do."

"Very well. The sorceress will be my advisor, venturing into all corners of Illyamor and beyond. She may speak for those who cannot. We are lucky to have her on our side."

The Halwardian crowd muttered in dissent, and Liesl smiled slyly, clearly understanding what they were thinking.

"The next few months will be a tumultuous time as we set in place these changes. But everyone will do their share to help even the inequalities that ravage our kingdom. I look to you, my Halwardian nobles, to provide the example." Greater rumbling sounded from the crowd.

"Many nobles have fled the Keep this night, which is understandable in light of the terrifying circumstances. However, I expect their full cooperation. *All* nobles will present themselves to the throne room within the week to pledge their full support to my son's regime, with me as regent until such time he has reached the age of majority."

The Vargas rose at the underlying menace in her voice and stalked forward to the edge of the platform. "Those who refuse to pledge allegiance will find their lands, titles and other properties forfeit."

The nobles' cry of outrage was swallowed by the Vargas' growls.

Sabine didn't even try to hide her smile. No, Liesl did not need her help. She almost felt sorry for the Halwardians.

Liesl clapped her hands above her head, and a spark of fire burst forth. "Now, we make a better world."

Rebuilding

Sabine rested on a chill stone, staring blankly into the forest. Her breath hung in the air in front of her, and she huddled into the fur of her cloak. The winter was colder in the forest, the wind sharp and lingering.

Not that she'd had much time to contemplate the cold since she'd returned to Alioch a month ago. She had left Aporos soon after the Great Change, as they were calling it, to rebuild with the Eyanrac. She'd come with Kerrick and Feamair, needing time to heal and grieve, craving the quiet of the natural world. She communicated with Rafi when needed, sending messages through their Ielzries. Hesta had been made Head of Awhye Affairs in Illyamor, a sign that change was truly in the making.

From morning to night, she bustled through the glade, building shelters, healing the wounded, learning about roots and potions with Feamair. It was satisfying and numbing at the same time. She rolled into a sleep sack in a makeshift cottage at night, cuddling close to the fire and Novi to keep warm, falling into dreamless sleep.

It was a rare moment like this when she roused before dawn to contemplate all she'd lost. She'd come to Anora's vigil. Her friend lay on a woodland altar, her shrouded figure decorated with woven twigs and winter berries. When the ground softened, they would inter her.

Novi called out from the sky. Sabine smiled to see her Ielzrie swooping in new sunlight. It was no small comfort to have her faithful friend at her shoulder. Novi always knew when Sabine was falling into self-pity and snapped her out of it.

The aspects of the Hunt had not faded. Feamair's eyes glowed in the dark, giving her exceptional night vision. Occasionally, Kerrick cocked his head, and Sabine knew he heard something far in the distance. Rafi remained in the city, playing up his fangs to terrify the Halwardians. He had become a constant advisor at Queen Liesl's side.

Sabine inspected her own hands. A week ago, she had discovered the trick to retracting her claws. If she flexed her hands just right, the claws would slip out, but she could relax them as well, hiding them so they were less cumbersome. A few accidents occurred before she got the hang of the retraction. She felt terrible about the mishap with the ropes during a build, and Feamair had laughed until she cried at her one attempt to suture a patient. In hindsight, it had been a mistake to try.

Now she splayed her claws for the pleasure of it. They made her feel powerful.

Novi shrieked again, this time in warning, and plummeted out of the sky onto her shoulder. Sabine cloaked them in invisibility and waited.

"What is it?" she whispered. The Ielzrie stared intently over her shoulder.

Sabine spun and gasped. A glowing light in the forest grew and took form. Over the space of a few breaths, the Lady of the Forest emerged. She gained color and form, though not fully corporeal.

She gazed at Anora's shrouded figure, ghostly tears swimming in her eyes. "Such a bright young spirit." Her voice was ethereal and echoed as though coming from very far away.

Sabine stumbled to her feet, anger warming her to her toes. "You did this."

The Lady of the Forest hung her head. Her silvery hair fell around her face. For all she was a ghost, she never seemed so human. Her face bore the lines of time, and while Sabine recognized her, she did not possess the breathtaking beauty she once did. She appeared a middle-aged woman.

"I am at fault for so, so much."

Sabine, who had been steaming into a rant, deflated. Confusion and anger warred within her. She was so tired, and grief stole her righteous indignation. "What?"

The Lady drew in a long breath. "I was so foolish for such a very long time. This is me before all of my many mistakes." She gestured to her face with a sad smile. "My name was Lucina Victoria, and I lived near here thousands of years ago. I was arrogant and full of magic, and I wanted so much of the world. The more magic I possessed, the more powerful I became, and the more I devoured."

"But you were the Lady of the Forest, a force for good."

"I wish with all my heart that was true, but when I was young, I was not interested in the greater good. I had influence and the ears of emperors. I traveled the world, visiting kingdoms that have since fallen to ash. I had lovers and children and lived very much in the physical world. I collected objects that resonated with magic, and I found if I stored power inside, I could hold back the hands of time. I lived many lifetimes over, untouched as generations rose to power and fell to ruin."

"The emerald."

"It became my favored object of power. At the time, I was blind to the harm it would cause. But very gradually, some wisdom seeped in. The land was failing, the magic of the earth stretched taut. Here in Alioch, the spirit water diminished, and I wondered why. It took me so long to understand...it was me.

"I was a thief, siphoning the power of the earth to fuel my

immortal life. But it is not the natural way of the world, and unnatural things happened. The flow of magic was impeded. The earth needed both the forces of life and death to thrive. To balance the dearth of life magic, the destructive forces of death magic, the Hunt, were similarly trapped, deep underground, warping with pressure."

"Scoria," Sabine whispered.

"The black rock should never be. Without the magic I had selfishly taken for myself, the land starved and could not grow. Small meanness grew in the hearts of humans, and the people suffered for it. And those children born marked with magic were unable to control it, as you well know. How many children died because of my arrogance?

"Once I realized, I wanted to release the magics and was prepared to give my life for the sake of the earth. But it is not so easy to end the life of an immortal."

"There had to be a sacrifice."

Ghostly tears welled in her eyes as she nodded. "A ritual sacrifice of my own blood. It was hideous, but perhaps fitting. Shortly after I discovered this, I met Aurich, a firebrand full of magic. I knew we could create a child powerful enough to end the suffering."

Lucina let out a bitter laugh. "I never imagined how good she would be. My brilliant, beautiful child. I loved her, you know." She nodded her head slowly at Sabine's snort. "It's hard to believe, but from the very moment I held her in my arms, I was besotted with that sweet child. She had aspects of the divine. They all did, my children. But even in her blindness, she was joyful and curious. Perhaps it was for the best Idona took her from me. If she had grown in my arms, perhaps I would not be able to do what must be done. I thought I had risen above my human emotions, but I was mistaken. I had no idea how painful it would be."

"You are despicable," Sabine said through gritted teeth.

"The world was going to die, with her in it. Would you sacrifice a child for the whole world?"

"No," Sabine said stubbornly.

"I did what I thought I had to. My selfishness endangered everyone, so if I had to cut out my own heart, I would do it." Lucina dropped her head into her hands as heaving sobs racked her transparent body. "It will shame me forever, knowing the suffering I caused that girl."

A long quiet stretched out between them. The sunlight glinted off the frost in the clear air, but Sabine didn't feel cold anymore.

"It was you all this time. The great Lady of the Forest was killing the earth." After a beat, she let out a huff. "I thought it was Aurich."

Lucina sniffed. "He didn't help," she said in a surprisingly dry tone.

"So why support him?"

"I had been leading him to find Anora this whole time and conveyed to him the secrets of the ritual. I needed him to play his part, to kill Anora at the right time and the right place. She had to go into the chamber willingly and be old enough to understand what it meant. He played perfectly into my hands, though I know that won't appease you. I'm happy you killed him, for what it's worth. He was nearly as evil as I, blinded by power."

"How did you find her?"

"Idona let it slip accidentally. It was a small thing, but she mentioned the fire gods and their ability to hide nature's magic. It wasn't so much her words but the panic in her eyes after she realized what she said that allowed me to understand, finally."

"Once you knew she was there, you created a disturbance in the forces around the Ofhellen. You expected the duke to find Anora and lead her to the mines."

"Only you found her first. I am happy how things turned out, that she was given friends who loved her."

Sabine blinked hard, trying to remain composed as rage and disgust swam over her. "Why are you here?"

Lucina gave a small smile. "I am always here, although on a different plane. I will do penance for centuries to come, providing guidance to those in need."

"What guidance could you offer me?"

"I do not come to guide you." At these words, Lucina grew in height and substance. She glimmered in the light, a goddess once again. "A pure soul has earned her peace, and it is time for her to move on."

Sabine wheeled around to the shrine.

Anora stood next to it, shining and ghostly like The Lady. Her smile was radiant.

"Sister," she said in a joyful voice. "You were with me until the very end. I will never forget that."

"Anora." Sabine's sobs came fast as she fell to her knees. "This shouldn't have happened. You should have lived."

Anora looked back at her still form on the shrine, giving it a fond smile. "Life is a precious thing. Mine was short, but I was loved. I know that much is true." She reached out as if to stroke Sabine's cheek. "It was worth it to find you, my sister, and your brother, my beloved. You gave me grace not all receive, no matter how long they live, knowing that I was not alone." She looked up. "But now it is time I move on. Do not think on what I lost because there is so much more to come. This is only the beginning." Her eyes glowed as she gazed into the distance at something Sabine couldn't see.

"But how can you accept what your mother did?"

Anora turned to Lucina, who bowed her head. "I know what she did and why. It is hard to understand, I know, but my suffering has passed, and she is forgiven."

Lucina looked up, startled, and Anora nodded. "Yes, Mother. I forgive you."

Lucina began to sob, holding a hand to her twisting mouth. "Though I don't deserve it. My wondrous child."

Sabine stood, her claws out, her outrage overwhelming. Anora pressed a kiss to her forehead. A spark spread there, soothing, radiating peace through her.

"I know what she was, and I love her still, Sabine. As I love you. Trust me in this. Forgiveness is the only way forward." She approached Lucina. "I am ready."

"Then come with me." She held her hand out to her daughter. Where they joined, a white light shone.

"No, wait." Tears streamed down Sabine's face.

Anora turned back once, her smile blinding. "Do not grieve, for it is time for the world to begin anew." She spoke with such surety that even Sabine's tears stopped flowing.

Sabine fought to stay near the blinding light. "What do I do?"

"Have patience and watch the seasons turn." The goddess's voice sounded in her head as the white light flared.

When she blinked away the spots in her vision, Sabine was alone in the glade. Anora's body was laid out on her shrine as before, but there had been a change. The air was warm, and the snow around the shrine had melted.

"What now?"

Novi let out a chirrup, nuzzling her cheek. *Now, it is time to rest and rebuild.*

Hope Springs Eternal

Sabine dug into the ground, satisfied as it turned over. The winter had passed, and the earth was now softening.

She had just returned to Alioch from Aporos, taking part in the Awhye celebration of *Chanam Ing*, the festival for the coming of spring. She had missed it last year, toiling in the Keep as a maid. This year, she led her people through the ceremony as a leader and sorceress.

For weeks, the city had been in a state of utter confusion. Some of the Halwardian nobles had accepted the changes and became allies to Queen Liesl. Other nobles fled, grabbing what they could on their way. They were hunted down by the Vargas and brought back for justice.

Liesl wished to honor the warriors of the final battle. A garden was planted in the spot where the Pyre once stood, full of fruit trees and vegetables that would be available to people in need. Although her name didn't appear anywhere, Sabine thought of it as Anora's Garden.

She worked hard rebuilding Alioch, planting seeds to get ready for the new season. As she worked next to the steadfast Eyanrac, her spirit was soothed. Much of the anger she carried inside of her dissipated, and Feamair told her she was healing from the inside.

A crowd of Eyanrac gathered, distracting Sabine from her work. She joined where they clustered, standing at the well where the spirit water once gurgled. It had been buried with snow for months, and sometimes she forgot about it. But now, water seeped through the snow, melting all in its path.

"Is it just the spring melt?" Sabine didn't dare hope.

Watch, Novi said at her shoulder. The water began to bubble out of the earth, gaining in strength with every breath.

Clear water crashed over the lip into a fountain. The liquid now geysered up into a plume many times taller than Sabine. She reached out; it was warm. Snow and ice melted in ever-growing circles. Crowns of snowdrops unfurled from the earth, the first flower of the season. The bright green popped against the wintery gray and brown.

An echoing laugh resounded through the clearing. Sabine's head shot up, but she couldn't tell who had made the sound. Still, her heart squeezed with such hope it hurt. Something tugged at her spirit, demanding she move.

She stumbled away from the fountain, her hands tingling from the warmth of the water. Novi took off from her shoulder and gave a caw of joy as she soared through the air. Sabine dashed through the forest to follow the Ielzrie. Surrounded by the dark trees, she stopped.

She no longer feared the forest, but she couldn't shake the feeling of someone watching her prickling at the nape of her neck.

She spun, claws out. The shadows swayed as though someone had just vanished.

Novi cawed from over the canopy and came to settle on her shoulder. It nuzzled her cheek before flying off into the branches again.

The Ielzrie didn't seem wary, so Sabine retracted her claws.

"Who's there?" Sabine called out. Her curiosity grew with every passing minute. "I won't hurt you."

Slowly, a shadow moved, and a tall young man emerged from the trees.

"Who are you?" The strange man was still shrouded in shadows. She approached, trying to get a better look at his face.

He wore a sleeveless tunic like the Eyanrac, and as he moved into the light, his bare skin showed palest green. His hair was in wild disarray, bright and vibrant in every shade of spring leaves. He glowed golden, heat rolling off him. Where he stepped, flowers and vines unrolled from the earth.

His eyes were sapling green and took her in with love.

Her head told her it couldn't be true, but her heart wanted so hard to believe. "Brannon?" she whispered.

He knelt in front of her. "Beautiful sorceress, mistress of illusion." She would recognize the twinkle in his eye anywhere.

"You're alive?"

"Very much so."

Her breath hitched. "How is this possible? I thought your brother took your life force."

"He certainly made those final days harder." Brannon scowled at the thought. "But I am the Green Knight and everlasting. I am the spirit of nature. I embody the seasons."

"The seasons? You are...spring?"

Brannon nodded, strands of pale green hair falling into his eyes. "For now. This is how it ever is. I live each year, growing in power, until I wither and die. I rest in the dark, and I am reborn."

Sabine let out a shaky breath. "Why on earth didn't you tell me?"

He hung his head. "I made a mistake. At first, I thought it might be too much for you. You were shaken to discover I was a god; I feared learning I would die over and over again would push you away from me entirely."

"It *is* a lot. But I had already accepted so much. You could have told me."

"I am sorry for underestimating you, more than you can know. When my brother helped me in the mines, the payment was silence. I could not speak of this to you, nor could you be told."

"But why?"

"It was cruel to us both. I suspect he was...curious. My brothers cannot live as I do and do not understand emotion."

Sabine pulled Brannon to his feet. Slim as he was, he still towered over her. "I grieved you."

"Sabine, I never wanted you to suffer, but I thank you for your grief. It nourishes and makes room for new life. Following the solstice rituals allows me to return as a man the next year. Throughout the winter season, I am nothing but a sprout, a seedling, cared for by Sabaghs in a secret place underground. Once the sun shifts, though, I can appear in the form of a man once more."

"Today is the spring equinox."

"Yes. And so I sought you out."

"Brannon, I..." Sabine threw her arms around him, finally believing it. He caught her up, spinning her around until the leaves were just a blur and there was nothing but him. He was sinewy and warm under her hands. "You're alive."

"And this pleases you?"

"Pleases me? Brannon, I love you. I thought I'd lost you forever. I'm..." Tears flowed down her cheeks, healing and full of joy.

"Let me see you, beloved." His strong hand reached to cradle her cheek with infinite gentleness. "You have been through so much."

Sabine turned her face to kiss his palm, tasting the salt of her tears. "I defeated the duke and released the trapped magic."

"I was with you, though you could not see me. You were glorious."

"The Awhye are rising up, freed from their chains. And Rafi is in Aporos, remaking the world."

"I suspected great things of him. But what about you?"

"Me? I'm helping the Eyanrac rebuild. They are resilient people. Despite everything they come up against, they will survive." She cut herself off, hesitant to voice her thoughts.

"And?"

"And, I have been thinking...what if I did what the duke promised to do?"

He raised a green eyebrow. "Take over the world? Become immortal?"

She shoved at him, and he caught her in his arms. "Not that part. He told me he gathered the magelings in a school to help them control their magic. He lied, but what if it were true? With the release of life magic, they no longer carry a blight that will consume them, but still, there is no one to guide them. Now that wild magic roams the earth again, I suspect there's going to be even more."

"The wild magic is potent. I have returned to life with many times my strength from before."

"Those children, they're going to need so much help. I hardly know what I'm doing, but I..." She trailed off, wondering if she presumed too much.

"They would be lucky to have you."

His tone warmed her, giving her the confidence she might be able to figure this out. "I thought a place in the forest where others wouldn't be hurt while they practice their powers. Perhaps Gregoria could help, and Feamair with her knowledge as an apothecary. Even the queen might be able to provide guidance. Did you know she was a fire mage?"

He chuckled. "It sounds like you have a new quest."

"Yes." She nodded, then met his green gaze. "That's what I'd like to do."

"Is it possible there would be room in your life for one more?"

His smile remained, but she saw the uncertainty in his eyes, the otherness, too, that would always set them apart.

"Brannon," she whispered. Her fingers entwined with his.

He bowed his head solemnly. "I would like to be your knight, Sabine, if you would have me. I would be your protector and a guide to your students in the Old Ways if that would please you. I would like"—he broke off on a rasp—"I would like to be your partner. In all things."

She put a hand to his chest, halting him. "I'm not the girl I was." She stepped out of his reach and unsheathed her claws. Her eyes blazed purple and her hair drifted on a stray current of magic, as it often did. "I descended so far into the Hunt, I'm not sure I'm entirely human anymore. I'm a sorceress, and I look it. I won't hide that from you. I don't want there to be any illusions between us."

"I hadn't thought it was possible, Sabine, but I want you even more like this. You are powerful, and you should never hide that. You should be worshipped instead." Hands at her hips, he gave a slow smile as he reeled her toward him, letting her know exactly what he had in mind.

"Most men would run from me in fright," she whispered.

"In case you hadn't noticed, I am not most men." That lazy smile was causing her insides to pull in funny ways. His arms were hard as steel as he drew her toward him. "Does that bother you?"

"Every year you will age and die, and every year I will grieve you." She couldn't take her eyes from his, a kaleidoscope of green, shifting like leaves in the wind.

"Yes."

"And every year, you will come back to me?"

"Without fail."

Sabine pulled him toward her, her lips hovering over his as they curved into a smile. "This is going to be very interesting."

Glossary of Terms

Alioch: (AL-ee-ock) the enchanted glade at the heart of the Dikisi Forest; it is the haven of the Eyanrac people and The Lady of the Forest's sanctuary

Amaranthians: a conquering people who took over Illyamor thousands of years ago; they settled the kingdom into farmland at the expense of the lifestyle of the original nomadic people, the Eyanrac

Aporos: the capital city of the kingdom of Illyamor; Sabine and Rafi's home

The apothecary: small Rukha growing outside the boundaries of Alioch in the Dikisi Forest; the home of Idona, the Eyanrac healer, and her children Kerrick and Feamair

Asael Keep: the stronghold of the Halwardians; the fortified castle sits at the top of Aporos

Awhye: (ah-WHY-ee) people who have lived in Illyamor for many centuries, the peaceful people worshipped the Old Ways; enslaved by the Halwardians for over a century, they have been forced to relinquish their religion and most men are forced to work in the mines

Blazes/blazing hellgods: curse words in Illyamor

The Chalice of Life: a massive emerald stone, said to contain the power of the Lady of the Forest

***Chanam Ing*:** The Awhye festival for the coming of the spring

Dikisi Forest: massive woods that still harbors pockets of wild magic; rife with magical creatures and monsters, it is considered close to a death sentence to enter the forest

Eerie: soul-sucking plant demons that feed off despair

Eyanrac: (EH-yen-rack) original peoples of Illyamor, they had been enslaved and killed by a conquering nation, the Amaranthians; thought to have died out millennia ago, they fled to the Dikisi Forest where they lived symbiotically within the magical glade of Alioch

Eskazi: (es-KA-zee) the north wind

Firewalk: the ability for a fire mage to enter flame and travel by spirit into fires in other places

Hakas truffles: highly valuable mushrooms, thought to have healing powers; found in the Dikisi Forest

Halwardians: an invading people who took over Illyamor from the peaceful Awhye; they rule from Aporos and follow the Order of Fire, worshipping fire gods, while oppressing other peoples on the land, most notably the Awhye

Helms: women devoted to the gods of fire; they live in the Ofhellen and tend to the novices

Hesta's Hearth: a bakery and gathering place within the Wilt slum; run by Sabine and Rafi's mother, Hesta

The Hunt: the embodiment of wild magic; a dark, destructive force

Ielzrie: (YELS-ree) small dragon-like creatures, born of defiance and rebellion, they remain bonded to their creators; they keep ancient wisdom and are excellent messengers

Illyamor: a kingdom where magic was once plentiful but

many years before became corrupted; now the land is dying of drought and those bearing magic die horribly

The Lady of the Forest: also known as the Emerald Lady, the Great Mother or the Green Goddess; a mythological figure of great power, known for her healing abilities

Lunengren: an island kingdom far to the north of Illyamor; populated mainly by Halwardians; Duke Aurich and Queen Liesl's home

Magelings: children, mainly Awhye, who are born with magical abilities which tend to show themselves in childhood; since the magical blight cursed Illyamor, they are doomed to die horribly in their magic

Malgris Lake: large lake in the northeast of Illyamor; it suffered under the magical blight that left it dead of natural life, and became the home of monsters

Meri: the south wind

Morasu grain: high-quality grain to make breads and pasties

The Ofhellen: (off-HELL-en) the seat of worship for the Order of Fire in Aporos; a fort-like structure of stone where Halwardians worship

The Old Ones: a pantheon of nature gods and goddesses; worshipped by many cultures but most recently the Awhye

The Old Ways: the religious practice of those who worship nature gods and goddesses

Olini bitters: weeds grown in the foothills of the Tuneric Mountains

Oracles: a group of three girls who practice the Old Ways; they live in the Oracle Grove and tell prophecies to passersby

Oracle Grove: a magical clearing in the Dikisi Forest outside of time; where the Oracles live and tell prophecies

Order of Fire: the religious practice of the Halwardians; they worship fire gods within the Ofhellen

Puka: (POO-ka) a bog goblin who confuses and tricks travelers with lights and voices to enter the waters, where they are drowned

The Pyre: the tower where lives Duke Aurich; rumors are that fires shoot from the upper windows

Royal Scoria Mines: mines set up by Duke Aurich to the north of Aporos; Awhye men are forced to work in the mines upon their sixteenth birthday

Rukhas: trees sacred to Alioch; the first grew when the surviving Eyanrac fled into the forest, created from their will and desperation; they respond to the needs of the people

Sabagh: (SAH-bah) fantastical creatures with skin like metallic gold; they are excellent guardians of the young

Seeloq: (SEE-lock) a creature of darkness that lives in Malgris lake; half-horse, half-sea mammal, they drag their victims to their underwater nest to feed on the drowned flesh

Scoria rock: a black rock found in the Tuneric Mountains; mining the rock has proved lucrative for the Halwardians of Illyamor and burning it produces energy, along with a foul-smelling black smoke

Slag: a slang word for scoria rock; also used as a curse word

Spirit water: water from a magical fountain found in Alioch; it is connected to the life magic of the world and has healing powers

***Toamna* festival:** (toe-AHM-nah) the Awhye harvest celebration

Tuneric Mountains: a forbidding mountain range to the north of Illyamor; scoria rock is found plentifully within the mountains and there are many scoria mines here

Vadovis: the spiritual leader of the Awhye; practices the Old Ways and specializes in herbalism and midwifery

Vargas: ancient magical wolves connected to wild magic and The Hunt; they are born of righteous indignation; they live to enact vengeance and justice, and serve as protectors of the innocent

The Wilt: a slum found around the bottom of Aporos; Sabine and Rafi's home

Yumil: Element of earth

Acknowledgments

I could not have completed this novel without the help of many people throughout the years that I have spent working on this, truly a labor of love.

Thank you to Marilyn Smith, Nika Teran and Heather Grab for your early reads of this manuscript; you helped me find the heart of the story. Behind every book is a team of editors. Thank you to Jennifer Rees for her insight and ideas that helped bring the true story forward, and to Marilyn Boake for the editing support and attention to detail she provided.

Thank you to Marilyn Smith and Annette Rivard for their help with the proofreading. And always, thank you to Zach Magnan, along with Alexandre and Élodie for the constant support and love that gives me everything I need to continue on this incredible journey.

I came up with the concept idea for The Sibyl and the Thief when I was walking in *le bois de verier* in Switzerland. It is said the Duke of Savoie used to hunt the land and only a fraction of its size now, it is an inherently enchanted place, full of liminal spaces and ancient wisdom.

I was also great inspired by the album *The Visit* by Loreena McKennit, which is magical to the core. I suggest you listen to it on a lonely autumnal evening in front of a fire. It evokes exactly the atmosphere I wish to capture with this story.

About the Author

Cordelia Kelly has been a lawyer and a journalist in past lives, but finally settled on writing stories and drawing illustrations after all that. She writes mainly horror and fantasy for young adult and middle grade audiences. The Well of Souls is her debut novel. All of her work can be found at cordeliakelly.com

Her anthology of horror stories, Then She Said Hush is also available. Several of her short stories have been published, and she was the 2019 winner of the Geneva Writers Literary Prize in Fiction.

To get all the giveaways and news for all Cordelia Kelly books, follow the monthly newsletter. Click here to sign up.

Please Leave a Review

Reviews are one of the best ways you can support indie authors. I would appreciate it if you could take a few minutes to share an honest review of *The Well of Souls*. Thank you from the bottom of my heart!

Amazon review

Want more?

Check out Cordelia Kelly's *The Well of Souls*, first of the *Port of Lost Souls* series. Available at Amazon, Barnes&Noble, Kobo, and Indigo.

THE WELL OF SOULS

Chapter 1

Every hour, Lola became increasingly hungry. Being cooped up inside this boat with the fishermen – or *edibles*, as Beau liked to call humans – was torture.

The deck of the ship rolled under Lola's feet and male voices cried out on the deck above her. She tilted her head to listen. The crew she had caught a ride with exclaimed over the unseasonal squall. A few cursed the last-minute passenger they had picked up on their way to Nova Scotia.

That would be Lola. She could tell from their resentful stares that her presence made the men uncomfortable. They wouldn't know why, of course, but they blamed her for the odd behaviour of the Atlantic.

Men of the sea had remained superstitious long after the age of rationality took over, especially when it came to women passengers. In this case, they had every right to be. Since Lola had boarded, they had been plagued by terrible weather, storms blowing up and half-submerging them in waves.

But she had good money to pay, and the fishing industry not

being what it used to be, the captain wasn't in a position to turn her down. They were on track to arrive early at their destination, even with this detour. Every storm they encountered pushed them unerringly in the right direction. *Unnatural*, the men muttered when they thought Lola was out of earshot. They glared if she came too close and refused to speak in her presence.

The sooner she was off this boat, the better for everyone. She needed to keep a low profile, and a boat of dead fishermen wouldn't go unnoticed.

She paced her cabin, barely two steps from one side to the other. It was not that she minded small spaces. How could she, given her line of work? But her hunger beat steadily against her, in the ever-slowing thumps of her sluggish heartbeat. It wouldn't pick up again until she fed. And the longer she was trapped on this boat, the more tempting the feast surrounding her.

She dug sharp nails into her palms, pins of pain distracting her from her suffering. Focus on the goal. She smoothed the ancient scrap of parchment laid across the worn desk. The stolen blood in her veins thrummed as she studied the map, pried from the bowels of a Spanish galleon.

The Well of Souls. This map was centuries lost; the treasure it promised lost for far longer than that. And Lola was going to find it, or die trying. She hadn't been given any other choice. Her immortal life had already been declared forfeit.

The parchment had been torn in half, but this half had the all-important map, faded over the centuries. A message in archaic Greek was barely legible: *Seek not for glory, nor for wealth. To only the worthy will the treasure be made great, and the power will be theirs.* Her fingertips played over the markings scrawled down the side, unlike any lettering she had encountered before. The dots and lines almost appeared to be constellations, but not of any stars she knew.

She had risked so much for this; she couldn't afford to lose focus now. What remained to be seen was whether the risk was worth it. They were close now, she could sense it. Land wasn't far off.

She rolled the parchment with every care, returning it to its container. It nestled at the bottom of her backpack. Everything else she had brought with her could fit around it. In some ways she packed like a typical sixteen-year-old girl: t-shirts, leggings and lip gloss. She was low-tech compared to the modern-day treasure hunter, relying instead on demonic instinct. But she doubted many humans carried with them a sack of ancient doubloons found scattered on the bottom of the Caribbean Sea. Loose change, in Lola's circle.

Still, she slipped her hand into the sack of coins, the weight heavy and pleasing. She had fenced what she could for cash in Havana, but she had been in a hurry. And transactions left a trail she couldn't afford.

She slipped on her raincoat and bag and climbed onto the deck. The spring storm this far north was fresh, like a slap in the face, one she relished. Though it was daytime, the thick cloud cover above them allowed her to be outside, shielding her from the harmful rays of the sun.

Land approached, barely visible in the veil of mist that curled around the island. The muffled flare of a lighthouse blinked, cautioning them to be wary. Anticipation tingled through her at the thought of setting foot on the fabled island.

Duchesne Island, haunted from one side to the other.

The boat lurched, and several men around her shouted in alarm as the boat veered too close to the jagged shoals.

Lola felt no fear. She was driving this boat, whether they knew it or not, and the heaving of it thrilled her. As she thought about it, the boat swung high into a wave, and everybody on deck but her was thrown off balance. If she wasn't careful, she'd bring the entire ship down with her. The pull of the sea always dragged at her.

All vampires shared an affinity with an element, and water was hers. Her demonic energy resonated and strengthened when she was near the ocean. It allowed her to nudge the currents in the right direction, taking them to their destination faster than naturally possible. But using her powers like this weakened her and made her crave even more the life-giving blood her body demanded.

She shook out her hands and calmed her thoughts, allowing the waves to settle around her. Several of the fishermen shot her dirty looks as they righted themselves, as though they knew she was responsible.

The captain of the vessel came to stand next to her, his eyes on the nearing island. Like his men, he was cautious around her. "Are ya sure you wanna be out in this weather, missy?" the captain called. She figured he meant he wanted her out of sight, so as not to antagonise his crew.

"It suits me fine, *capitaine*." She exaggerated her French accent, purring around the vowels. It usually buttered up tough old salts like him. She held back the snarl she wanted to unleash. She was always expected to play nice, to go along and keep her head down. It was maddening.

If Beau was in her place, he would have eaten them all and sailed into harbour on his own. But Lola needed to get to Duchesne Island under cover, without anyone finding out. Especially not Beau.

"It's a nasty one." He tugged at his hood. "Ya might be better off below deck."

The air smelled of ozone and held a weird quality as they pulled into the harbour, like the tingling before a lightning bolt strikes the Earth. The charge prickled over her skin and buzzed through her blood. The island they approached was magical to the core. "We'll be there soon," was all she said, ignoring the captain's sigh.

"We'll be putting in here at Port Despardoux for the rest of the night," he said. "We'll wait out the storm before heading to Halifax."

"It'll calm down by tomorrow."

He nodded, as though expecting this. "There's an inn near the docks, in case yer lookin' for some'er to stay."

She studied him from the corner of her eye. "Kind of you."

"Things're quiet here until the tourists come. And Sunday, besides. Most places'll be closed up. Pub on Saturdays, church on Sundays."

Lola snorted. "That's true in places all over the world. I'll figure it out."

The captain gave her a searching look, his cloudy grey eyes meeting hers for the first time. "Can't figure why a slip of a girl like you'd come here. She's a pretty enough place, but there're rumours, you know. Some say she's haunted, if you believe in that kind of nonsense."

She barely held back the wild laughter that threatened to erupt from her. "I believe in all that nonsense."

The boat juddered to a stop as it pulled in. As the men shouted to those on the wharf and threw out lines to the dock, they went out of their way to avoid Lola, falling over ropes and crates to keep their distance. The captain kept his gaze on her, probably wondering how she had convinced him to come to this curious place. "Some kind of ghost hunter, then?"

"Actually, I'm hunting something else."

He clicked his tongue. "Seeking out the legends, then, of buried pirate treasure? Yer not the first or the last, and yer joining a flock of fools if you ask me." He paused, then pointed. "The old treasure pit's over that ridge there, deep in the oak forest. Uncanny, that; oaks aren't supposed to grow here. It's a mystery." He scratched his beard. "But all the legends about hidden treasure and pirates' curses are only stories. The treasure of Duchesne Island was found long ago and spent. There's no gold left on the island, just fishermen like us doing their best to fill their bellies."

"You would be astounded what you can find if you scratch the surface." With a curving half-smile, she held up a coin with two fingers. "For your troubles, *capitaine*."

She placed it into his callused palm and pulled the hood of her coat over her tangled hair. As he gaped, she cocked an eyebrow at him. "And for your silence. I was never here, and neither were you."

He eyed her shrewdly, as though wondering whether there were more gold coins to come. "Men'll talk. Sailors can't keep secrets."

Fury boiled inside of her, her patience at a breaking point. She pretended she was Jacquotte, her former boss. Nobody ever talked back to Jacquotte. A small amount of her power shone through her eyes, just a hint at what she was, and what she could do if pressed. "They can if they're dead."

She winked as the captain blanched and strode down the gangplank. The men straightened and watched her pass, silent in her wake.

She hesitated at the edge of the dock. If the tales were true, the moment she stepped foot on this island, she would be cursed. She didn't know the nature of the curse, but if she didn't find the treasure of the Well of Souls, she was doomed anyway.

She trod lightly onto the faded wooden boards. A buzz of energy rippled through her, and then it was gone. Her fate was decided, one way or another, and she was going to see this through to the end.

Few people were on the wharf. Only the men working the docks braved the elements today. All sensible humans sought shelter from the blistering wind. Under the howl of it, the hollow thunk of boats hitting the wooden docks sounded, rhythmic with each slapping wave. And above wheeled the gulls and their lonesome cries as they reeled overhead in the gusts.

Wooden lobster traps were piled along the edge of the dock, damp nets reeking of fish guts. Lola licked her mouth, tasting salt.

It made her think of blood, and how very hungry she was. Her fangs slipped out over her bottom lip.

She turned to raise a hand to the captain, who inspected what he held in his hand: gold, authentic, and possibly Spanish. Then a heavy mist rolled in from the hills, devouring her and the rest of the wharf, camouflaging her movements. The last thing Lola heard before marching toward the crest of the ridge was the rumblings of superstitious men caught in the jaws of a supernatural spell.

www.ingramcontent.com/pod-product-compliance
Lightning Source LLC
Chambersburg PA
CBHW060617310726
48982CB00003B/585

9781068940811